The Long Highway Home is a compelling and convicting novel that brings the refugee crisis that's in today's news vividly to life. Elizabeth Musser weaves the individual characters' stories together with great skill and insight, creating a novel that touched my heart and made me ask God how He wants me to help. Every Christian who looks at the refugee crisis with fear needs to read this book. Unforgettable!

Lynn Austin
Author of *Waves of Mercy*

As the leader of a global non-profit that works with refugees all over the world, I am profoundly grateful for the research and accuracy that is apparent in Elizabeth Musser's *The Long Highway Home*. Readers should know as they read this book that while it is written as fiction, it accurately portrays the perils and miracles that are experienced along the refugee highway. Not only will this book keep you on the edge of your seat as you watch each character develop, but it will drive you to your knees to pray for those who need to know the love, grace, and compassion of Jesus and the dedicated people who work with them.

Scott Olson
President & CEO
International Teams

The Long Highway Home is Elizabeth Musser's best novel yet. With all the cloak-and-dagger thrills of refugee smuggling and dangerous border crossings, the story is also timely and important as it deals with the current highly-charged issue of Middle Eastern refugees fleeing to the West. Based on her own life experiences, Musser is able to bring authentic details and real human faces to those often impersonal issues. As with Musser's other books, she brings multiple viewpoints and exotic locations (including France, Austria and Iran) to converge in one exciting finale. In *The Long Highway Home*, American smugglers, missionaries, young students and seekers, persecuted Christians and refugees come together in a story of dashed dreams and second chances, faith and hope, and ultimately love and sacrifice. Highly recommended!

Robin Johns Grant
Author of *Summer's Winter* and *Jordan's Shadow*

D1453884

Figures on the growing numbers of refugees entering Europe are often cold and anonymous. Stories of people help us to relate. In *The Long Highway Home* Elizabeth Musser helps us to relate with people like Hamid and Alaleh. Musser has a wonderful way of connecting our souls with their lives. She allows us to put ourselves in their place and go through their life issues – the traumatic and the joyful ones. There are two aspects in this well-written novel that impressed me most. First of all, it is the hope that shines through the pages — hope that is based on Jesus Christ. Secondly, it is impressive to see how media, in this case radio, can become a powerful tool to broadcast this hope to people in need. This is an excellent, worthwhile read.

Dirk Müller
International Director – Europe
Trans World Radio (TWR)

Elizabeth Musser doesn't shy away from tough issues, but faces them head-on with intelligence and grace. As such, she has created a story that truly engaged my imagination. I felt as though I was not simply reading about but experiencing the lives of the characters—their fears, their joys, their triumphs. *The Long Highway Home* is truly a great book by a wonderfully talented author. I'm ready for Elizabeth's next book!

Ann Tatlock
Award-winning novelist and children's book author

Stories written from the heart are always my favorites, and Elizabeth Musser has, once again, given us her heart on pages of beautifully woven words. And, she begins her tale in Atlanta, so you know it has to be wonderful. But this is more than lovely. This is heart-gripping. This is the kind of book you'll think about long after you've put it down and, even more, this is one you'll hope everyone you know will read so you can discuss it time and again.

Eva Marie Everson
Author of *Five Brides, God Bless Us, Every One, The One True Love of Alice-Ann*

Musser expertly depicts the tragedy, peril, and utter despair that many refugees face. Despite delving into these difficult themes, the engaging narrative manages to present a unique vision of hope. It develops its refugee characters in an intimately human way, and readers are sure to find themselves drawn deeply into the lives of these characters. A heart-warming story, this is a must read for anyone who desires to better understand the struggles that refugees encounter on a daily basis.

Lucas da Silva
Refugee Ministry Coordinator
Trans World Radio (TWR)

BOOKS BY ELIZABETH MUSSER

The Secrets of the Cross Trilogy:
Two Crosses
Two Testaments
Two Destinies

The Swan House
The Dwelling Place
Searching for Eternity
Words Unspoken
The Sweetest Thing

Novellas:
Waiting for Peter
Love Beyond Limits
(Part of the Southern Love Stories Novella Collection:
Among the Fair Magnolias)

THE LONG HIGHWAY
Home

ELIZABETH MUSSER

Blessings!
Elizabeth Musser
Isaiah 58:6-12

MacGregor *Literary*

The Long Highway Home
Copyright © 2016
Elizabeth Musser

First English Printing 2016

Cover design by Ken Raney and Wil Immink Design

ISBN 978-1-5323-1259-5

Printed in the United States of America
Originally Published in Dutch
by Uitgeverij Voorhoeve

A highway will be there. It will be called the Way of Holiness.
~Isaiah 35: 8

CHAPTER 1

Atlanta, Georgia, October 2005
Bobbie

I rapped twice on the door of the seventh-floor apartment in the posh retirement home on Peachtree Street. "Peggy? You in there?"

I unlocked the door and found her, as I knew I would, sitting on her balcony looking out at the hubbub below. At ninety-two, Peggy Milner rarely strayed outside in the late afternoon. She reserved her errands for the morning, before her body pitched its daily fit, as she put it.

I knelt down by her wheelchair, and she slowly maneuvered it so that she was facing me. Her thin wrinkled face was surrounded by abundant white hair, cut in a bob. Her green eyes, still bright in spite of cataracts, met mine. "So?"

"The doctor says I have a year to live. And that's optimistic."

Her eyes misted. "I'm so sorry to hear it, Bobbie," she said, reaching out a feeble hand to stroke my face. "I wish it could be me."

I knew she meant it. Peggy had been ready to go meet Jesus for years. "Well, I'm thankful you're still here for me. What would I have become without you, Peggy?"

"You and the Lord would have done just fine, no need of me. What did the doctor say about treatment?"

"A pill for two months. After that, aggressive chemo, if the cancer hasn't spread."

"Then you know what you need to do. As I've been saying for nearly twelve years, Bobbie, go back."

Tears sprang to my eyes. "But I'm afraid. What if I can't make it right? What if I fail again?"

She sat back in her chair and said, almost sharply, "Dear child, what have you to lose now? Go back."

"Tracie wants to go with me."

A smile spread across Peggy's face, lifting the sagging skin. "So you have made plans."

"I didn't say yes yet."

"Say yes, Bobbie. Close the wound. Let it heal. Go back."

Still on my knees, I laid my head in Peggy's lap, let her hands rest softly on my back, heard her voice, the sound of age, the sound of wisdom, whisper a prayer for me. "Dear Jesus, take Bobbie back, so she can forgive herself. So she can remember what she knows. You make all things new."

Timisoara, Romania, a few weeks later

Slowly, deliberately I walked into Timisoara's Victory Square where back in December, 1989 thousands of protestors fighting to bring down Communism had stood with their candles lit. Where I had stood on that fateful night. I placed my cane carefully between the cobbled stones. I couldn't afford to stumble or fall. There was the statue of Romulus and Remus surrounded by students and businessmen, the fountain spraying water, a multitude of pigeons waiting their turns to splash beneath it. The gardens were planted with bright purple petunias, and roses were everywhere. Timisoara was called the city of roses. I'd forgotten.

With Tracie at my side, I hobbled along, trying to make the limp less visible, determined to blend into the scenery, heading purposefully in the direction of the Orthodox church at the end of the square. The wonder on my niece's face reminded me of the way I'd felt all those years ago, discovering a whole new world.

"Oh, this is beautiful!" She drew out the syllables as we stepped into the cathedral. She'd said the same thing at every single church we'd visited.

We watched as a line of several elderly Romanian women approached a painting of the Virgin and Child that stood on an easel in the center of the church. One by one the women moved forward, bowed, and kissed the icon.

"How weird," Tracie whispered. "They actually kiss the painting. That's not very hygienic."

I shrugged and gave her a wink.

"And why aren't there any pews in this church?"

"It's Orthodox," I whispered. "Everyone stands."

I actually wished a bench would magically appear before me. Pain throbbed in my left leg, and I leaned heavily on the cane.

"Aunt Bobbie, are you okay?" Tracie took my arm. "You're trembling!"

"No worries, dear. Just a little tired."

"Look, over there. Against the wall."

She took my arm and I didn't protest, just planted the cane in front of me and walked slowly toward a mahogany bench where two older women were seated. I settled beside them, and a wave of anger surged within me, taking me by surprise.

I'm thirty-nine, Lord. Isn't that a little young to die? I mean, don't get me wrong. I look forward to spending eternity with You, but there are so many other things I wanted to do here first . . .

Tracie

I watched Aunt Bobbie sitting beside two elderly women on a well-worn bench inside the Metropolitan Orthodox Church. The older women, with sagging, wrinkled skin, talked animatedly to each other while Bobbie leaned back, head against the wall, eyes closed, her right hand clutching a cane. Something was definitely wrong with this picture.

Bobbie was the young, cool aunt all my friends admired as we were growing up, and practically a second mother to me. She loved history, loved travel, loved to be spontaneous, loved people. And she was dying. When my mom called to tell me of Bobbie's diagnosis, I dropped my cell phone on the floor in disbelief. And the next week I called Bobbie to say it was time for that month-long trip to Europe we'd always talked about.

My aunt had lived in Europe for ten years as a young woman. She had a mysterious career there, and I'm sure I hadn't heard the half of it—she actually smuggled Bibles into Communist countries in the 1980s, and worked at an orphanage for deaf children in Romania. But then my father dropped dead of a heart attack at forty-two, leaving Mom to care for six children. Bobbie got the word and hopped the next plane to Atlanta, where she swooped into our lives in her flowing bright orange pantsuit, the "eternal rescuer." That's what Mom called her. To me, and to my five younger brothers, she was an exotic creature, all fun and adventure and generosity, taking our minds off the fact that our father had just died and placing them on the gifts she had brought to us from Europe. I'll never forget the look in Mom's eyes—extreme gratitude in the midst of her grief. There was nothing subtle about Aunt Bobbie, and yet she had an almost imperceptible quality of grace about her, something strong and yet comforting and cozy, something that made me want to be with her and hope and pray it would rub off on me. She never made me feel that whatever drama was going on in my life at the moment was ridiculous or unimportant.

Bobbie knew how to rough it. Once in a village in Bulgaria, when her contact didn't show up, she dug a hole in the ground to keep the wind from slicing through her and slept outside in the freezing cold. She said it was "an awesome experience." But another time, while I was in high school, a girlfriend invited her to take a cruise on the Mediterranean, and they stayed in the best suite on the ship. She loved that too.

"You just have to appreciate whatever comes," she used to say to us kids. "Each day is a twenty-four-hour adventure."

So Mom and I had decided that Bobbie needed a quaint luxury hotel in Venice, and she agreed—on the condition that she could plan our next stop, in Timisoara. The place we were staying here was definitely not luxurious. In fact, Bobbie called it a "Communist hotel."

"You know, it's all dark, heavy wood, oppressive, unimaginative."

I watched her remove her slip-on Keds—always before she'd worn high-heeled boots or sandals—pull herself into the low and sagging double bed we were sharing, set her cane down, and smile at me.

"Ah, that's better." She made light of her earlier moment of exhaustion at the church and said, "It's completely to be expected as a side effect of the meds."

It did not exactly placate my fears, but she dared me with those bright blue eyes to disagree. My throat constricted, and I blinked back tears. I hopped on the bed and flicked on the little side light.

"Do you ever think about what you used to do? All those

years living in Vienna and smuggling Bibles? Do you miss it?"

Bobbie loved to tell me stories of that life, but when I'd asked her this question in the past, she'd always said something like, "How could I miss that life when I have you and your brothers to fill my days and nights?"

But now she stared at me, and somehow her eyes dimmed. "I think of it every single day of my life." She quickly reached for my hand and squeezed it. "That doesn't mean I haven't been happy. Aching for one thing and enjoying something else aren't mutually exclusive."

"I suppose you're right." I made a face and focused my attention on a piece of peeling beige paint on the wall in front of me. I knew what she was referring to. My aunt was infamous for making a point from something in her life so that I could apply it to mine. "Yes, I'm loving every minute of this trip. But it still hurts so bad that Neil broke up with me. I don't know if there will ever be a single hour in any day when I don't think about him."

She sighed. "Love is painful sometimes, isn't it?"

"It sucks." Then, glancing at her, I dared to ask another question that I'd asked her loads of times before, a question to which she usually gave a silly reply. "Come on, Aunt Bobbie. Tell me for real—did you ever want to be married?"

She smiled. "Well, of course I've thought about it—still do at times. You know, people do marry even after forty!" She laughed. "Thought about it, but then I inherited a family, a large family with a lot of kids, and I didn't even have to bother with a husband."

"But you would have preferred to stay in Austria, do your work there?"

She cocked her head, rested it against the red-cushioned headboard, and closed her eyes. "Tracie, life has seasons. I entered a season of nurturing your family. It wasn't forced upon me. I chose it with gladness, and I have never regretted that choice. Another season might be coming now."

Another *season*? That's what she thought of dying? I didn't want her to enter that season. Ever.

CHAPTER 2

Somewhere in Iran
Hamid

*H*amid was so tired of running. For two months now he'd been constantly looking over his shoulder, afraid of who might show up with a gun and pull the trigger. He shuddered as he pulled the filthy blanket around his shoulders, thinking of the news he had heard the day before, coming through the radio in little patches of static. Four killed in a bombing in his Iranian village, massacred. Was Alaleh one of them? And seven-year-old Rasa? He could not allow himself to think of it.

And the baby . . . surely the little one would be born soon. Where would Alaleh go for the birth? Could the midwife be trusted? His stomach cramped with the questions. Did Alaleh show Rasa photos of her father, remind her how much she was loved? How Hamid longed for news. How he wished he could turn back the clock, had said "No thank you" to the neighbors when they invited Rasa to their daughter's birthday party.

Little Noyemi was Rasa's friend, and Hamid and Alaleh liked the neighbors, even though they were Armenian Christians. They were good people, kind people with strange convictions, brave people who held firm to their religion in spite of the pressure from others.

And Alaleh was so ill with the pregnancy. Twice she had miscarried, and the labor and delivery with Rasa had not gone well. But this time, the doctor said, with plenty of rest, Alaleh would carry this child to term. *Agar Khoda hast.* If God willed. Hamid himself was busy at the university and worried about rumors of the government's new plan to bring in the military against the intellectuals. Preoccupied with this and Alaleh's health, he had welcomed a place where Rasa could be with other children, even for an afternoon. How could he have foreseen . . .

But one afternoon turned into a week, as the neighbors explained that they had a guest from America who wanted to tell stories to the children each day. A special club for the children. How Rasa's eyes sparkled every time she returned from the children's club! She brought little crafts she had made and told stories of the nice woman. It was only on the last day, when Hamid came to pick her up, that Rasa had presented her father with the book.

"Baba, the nice lady gave this to me. It's a good book with wonderful stories. It is for me."

Hamid took the small colorful book with the Farsi title from his daughter.

"The nice lady said it was a good book, but"—and Rasa's eyes had grown wide as she leaned into him—"but it is a dangerous book. I must not show it to anyone. Only you and Maamaan."

He knew the book, and even holding it in his hand, he felt dirty. The *Ingil*, the New Testament. In their own language, Farsi. Blasphemy! He should never have let Rasa attend the club. It was brainwashing! He sat with the other parents, most of them Armenian, on the last day of the club, and heard the young American woman speaking in English and the translator beside her telling of the Christ, the prophet. Calling him God. Blasphemy!

He took Rasa's hand and led her away amidst her tears and protests. Why had he not left the book there? Instead, he had hurried out of the neighbors' house with Rasa clutching the book to her chest. It was a short walk to their home, a minute, less. But that day the religious police were on the corner of the street. Did they know of the American woman, of the children's club? Were they watching to see if any Muslims attended? Hamid saw them too late. They approached, as they always did, with authority, brandishing guns. His arm tightened around his daughter. He quietly took the book from her hands, then, feigning a cough, he bent over and slid the book onto the sidewalk behind him, near the Armenians' house where it belonged. The police searched them both, found nothing, and Hamid and Rasa fled inside their home.

Of course the police found the book eventually, and of course they came the next day to question him. He'd known they would be back. He knew the stories. Men who had disagreed politically were thrown into prison for months, years. But what would they do to a Muslim carrying a Christian book? The punishment for blasphemy was death.

There was no time to do anything but flee. Alaleh, heavy with child, her face streaked with tears, begged him, "Go now, Hamid. I will find you, no matter what happens. I'll come with our children."

Little Rasa hugged his legs, crying, "Don't leave, Baba! Don't leave! Take me with you, Baba!"

His mother cried and said, "You must leave now. Leave, Hamid, or they will kill us all."

The last kiss, passionate, terrible, the wrenching away,

then hugging Alaleh to him, feeling the tightness of her belly against his . . .

He had fled on a night like this one, with the moon cupping its hand as if to catch a falling star and the sky a cobalt blue fading to black. He closed his eyes to shut out the piercing memories of their good-bye, the frenzied packing of documents, the money hidden in every piece of his clothing.

Only twice since he left had he heard Alaleh's voice, whispering, fearful, full of love. "Rasa is growing strong, beautiful, she loves her father. The baby is kicking so often at night I don't sleep!" She had said it with humor in her voice, so he wouldn't worry. But Hamid did worry. "I love you, Hamid . . ."

After two months of running, he was still far from safe. The mountain village where he now hid was barely sheltered from the perpetual gunfire down in the valley. His traveling companions, two brothers named Ashar and Merif, were intellectuals chased from their home by the government. They thought he was the same. They had all walked from Tehran to the northwestern most part of Iran. It was there they met the smuggler, Zemar, who had led them into a Kurdish village where they stayed with a family. There had been food and blankets—for a price, of course. Then they were put onto a flatbed truck, zigzagging through the mountains. When they reached a police checkpoint in the mountainous area, the truck stopped and the smuggler took them into a house, told them to dress in warm clothes, and put them on horseback. They rode through the night to the next Iranian village, always with the hope of getting a little closer to Turkey.

They left the horses then, and together they had scaled mountains and hidden in caves, scavenged for food and huddled around campfires. Sometimes they traveled with Zemar, sometimes, as was now the case, they were left to follow a crude map on their own, trusting that Zemar would indeed meet up with them at the next agreed-upon location. Together with Ashar and Merif, Hamid had killed wild rabbits and drunk from streams in the middle of the night. And always they listened, they waited, ears trained for the sound of the enemy.

Last week Hamid had been shot in the arm as they raced through the mountainous terrain, following the silent smuggler. He had escaped only by sheer determination, forcing his feet to run, ignoring the exploding pain near his shoulder. The bullet had gone straight through his arm, and the wound showed signs of infection. Now his arm throbbed with pain underneath the makeshift bandage.

Soon they would cross the mountains of northwest Iran into Turkey and travel to Van, the city near the border where refugees arrived, terrified but alive. Another smuggler was to meet them there. From Turkey Hamid would travel to Bulgaria and then on to Austria! Austria, where his cousin Jalil now lived, having gained asylum. Where there was a possibility to start a new life. And then, oh then, God be praised, yes, Khoda be praised, then he could bring Alaleh and Rasa and the baby to join him. *Agar Khoda hast.*

The three men huddled around the fire, warming their hands, gathering the thick blankets around them as the November sky blinked down a thousand stars. The outline of the snowcapped Mount Ararat far in the distance, with the stars above shining like thousands of exclamation points, should have caused him to burst into song. He was a philosopher, and this night the perfect canvas for him to paint his words. Instead he felt a hollow aching and cold, cold fear.

What if Alaleh and Rasa were dead? Then what hope was left? Why keep running and hiding, why cling to a dream of building a better life of freedom and peace? If they had been murdered, there was no hope.

As the static on the radio grew worse, Merif reached forward and turned the dial, searching for another station with a stronger signal. Suddenly a voice came through, loud and clear.

". . . from every nation, it is there. The cry for freedom, for hope . . ."

More static. More fiddling with the dial, the three men glancing at each other, glancing up at the stars as if they might betray them, then back to the dwindling fire and the radio.

". . . and so there is hope in spite of the fear, in spite of the pain, in spite of the bloodshed. The words of the Savior call out 'Come to Me, all you who are weary and burdened, and I will give you rest. Take . . ."

The static increased, the words faded into nothingness, the men grumbled. With the fire dying away and the cold rushing in to steal their breath, they huddled together for warmth and listened for some other word of their village, of their home, something to give hope.

Hamid stretched out on the hard ground, pulling the blanket over him, cupping his hands under his head for a pillow, and thought of beautiful Alaleh, of bright-eyed Rasa, of his unborn child, of the fuzzy voice from the radio saying, "Come to me, all you who are weary and burdened, and I will give you rest."

Strange words. But oh, how he longed for rest.

The next two nights Hamid happened on the same radio program, broadcast from The Netherlands but in his own tongue. The voice in the box spoke of the Bible, of Christ—*Isa al Masi*—of hope, of a Savior. Hamid's heart swelled to hear the words, foreign words, dangerous words! Why was he drawn to them so? These were the words that had forced him to flee in the first place.

"Listen to the words! They seem to me to speak truth!" Hamid said to Ashar and Merif.

Ashar leaned in to hear the program. "Hamid! You listen to blasphemy! We are running for our lives because we are devout men who worship Khoda and believe in the power of mind and spirit. Our country sought to kill us for using our minds—what would they do if they find we not only use our minds but listen to blasphemy! They will make us die a slow and painful death. They will find our families."

Merif produced a knife, grabbing Hamid's left arm and jerking the radio out of his grasp. "We did not come this far to escape our enemies and incur Khoda's wrath!" He held the knife at Hamid's neck. "We are prepared to fight for our lives. Never listen to this again!" He let Hamid go with a hard shove to the ground.

Hamid said no more to the others as they traveled on together. Let them think he had taken their warning to heart. But in spite of their threats, in spite of his own fears, he could not get the words out of his mind.

The very next night Hamid was awakened out of his sleep by a voice. Was he dreaming? Ashar and Merif slept by the dying fire. Had the radio come on? Such a dream! Or was it a vision? The words burned in his soul. *Tonight! Tonight! Go now! Now!* He had heard the voice so clearly.

He got to his feet and, heart pumping, rushed away in the dark, stumbling on brush and roots, the radio tucked tight beneath his arm. He climbed through rough brush and shrubs, his shoes pushing the sand and dirt, climbing a little higher where there was better reception. Away from Ashar and Merif. He climbed higher and prayed to find this truth proclaimed in the middle of the night.

Finally, out of breath, he stopped and looked down from his perch high above the campsite. He was far out of hearing of his companions, even if they awoke. As he stooped down to set the radio on the ground, he saw a flicker of light by the campsite. He scrambled still higher, squinting in the darkness. Another spot of light, a sound. A gunshot. Another. Then stillness.

For a moment Hamid was too shocked to move. Gunshots! Had Ashar and Merif just been murdered? His hands trembled and perspiration broke out on his face. *You must regain composure! Breathe!* he admonished himself.

He waited all the next day, hidden in a cave with nothing but the radio as company. At last, when his canteen of water lay empty, knowing he must leave or die there, he had ventured quietly back to their campsite. The fire was still smoldering beside the two bodies. One gunshot in the head of each. Hamid turned and vomited.

He closed his eyes, backing away from the bodies, tears running down his face. He gathered up the few belongings and provisions the murderers had not taken. Did they suspect a third person in the escape party? Would they bring back dogs and find his trail? He took the hand-drawn map from his pocket. Painstakingly they had drawn it, had watched Zemar fill in the details for the next part of the journey. A two-day hike to the next village; then four days hiking to the border with the smuggler and others—would there be others who had survived?

Not freedom, not that yet, but hope. Two days. West. With a silent sob still in his throat, Hamid clutched the radio to his heart and began to walk. It was only early November, but as he made his way around the side of the mountain the air grew colder and it began to rain. He climbed and slipped on a slick rock. Two more steps and he saw that a cave opened up in the mountain. He bent down and crawled inside the small enclosure. Several bats flew out to greet him. His heart was still thumping hard as he collapsed in the back of the cave, listening.

He marveled at his escape. What strange vision had awakened him and told him to leave? He shivered now as he thought of it. The brightness, the urgency, the assurance that he must flee alone. The voice. *Tonight! Tonight! Go now!* What was this vision that had saved his life? And whose voice had given him the warning?

The answer came, barely a whisper into his soul. *Isa.* Jesus. The prophet. How he had hated that name. Isa al Masi. The very reason for his flight was Isa's book—the Ingil.

A prayer came to his lips. "Isa al Masi, I am running because of your book. My life is at risk because of you. And now I have nothing and nowhere to go. Help me, Isa, if you are God. Please."

Somewhere around dawn, he fell asleep.

Alaleh

The ricochet of bullets woke Alaleh with a start. She cradled her bulging stomach protectively with one hand. She listened in the stillness and shivered. "Rasa?" she whispered to her daughter, who was sleeping on the mattress beside her.

The little girl stirred and gave a yawn. "Yes, Maamaan?"

"It's time to go. Now. Come quickly."

She struggled to sit up in bed, and the baby gave a sharp kick. He was ready to leave the warmth of her womb, this little one. "Not yet. Please, little child, not yet." Alaleh closed her eyes against the pain of a contraction. *Please, little one, not tonight when all of hell has broken loose!*

She met her mother-in-law, Myriam, in the hall. "Hurry!" the older woman whispered, her face drawn with fear. Together Myriam and Alaleh held onto little Rasa's hands, propelling her through the hall. Once again there was a ricochet of gunfire. It sounded as if it were right outside the window.

Alaleh knelt down with a groan. Straining, Myriam pushed an old armoire aside to reveal an opening in the wall that led into a crawl space, the size of a small bedroom. "You first, Alaleh, then Rasa. It will be okay." But both women knew nothing would ever be okay again. It had started on a night two months ago when Hamid had fled to protect his family from the religious police. Alaleh had known that sometime they would come back for the rest of the family. They would not believe that only Hamid was responsible for the book, no matter how her mother-in-law argued and protested.

She struggled on her back to pull herself through, her rounded stomach grazing the top of the opening. Once inside, she shifted to her knees and held out one hand for Rasa. Then Myriam climbed through, and together they reached out and pulled the old armoire in front of the crawl space. Weeks ago, after Hamid's disappearance in the night, Myriam had nailed two makeshift wooden handles to the back of the armoire, precisely for this very reason. She had also insisted on stocking this crawl space with food and other supplies, in case there were a need to hide. Now, with the storm of military outside, Alaleh and Myriam held each other in silence behind the hidden door.

The shouting grew louder. They could hear the sounds of shattering china, splintering wood. Alaleh covered her daughter's ears even as Myriam held her in a tight embrace. How long must they stay hidden? Her contractions were coming steadily, with increasing force, and twice she cried out softly.

Myriam looked at her. "No one must hear," she whispered.

"Give me something to hold between my teeth," Alaleh begged, her face taut with pain. She remembered Rasa's birth, with the midwife there, the women of the village crowded around, the feeling of community in the midst of her pain. Her daughter's squeal after thirteen grueling hours of labor.

The joy.

But tonight she had only her daughter and mother-in-law there to help. They had planned for the possibility. The tiny heater was there, the bottles of water, the fresh sheets, the clothes. The food. But could she do it? And without making a sound? Most Iranian women were giving birth by Caesarian now. Her doctor had ordered it months ago, insisting it was imperative in case there were complications, as there had been with Rasa.

Myriam squeezed her hand hard. "You can do it. We will do it."

A guttural scream came from deep within her and burst through her throat, dying in a harsh whimper as Alaleh clamped her teeth on the wooden handle of the knife. How much longer could she endure?

Outside the door everything was quiet. Had the soldiers left? Did they leave one behind, standing guard, watching for the women to return? Alaleh turned her head toward the door and raised her eyes in a silent question.

"You must not think about what is happening out there," Myriam whispered. "You must concentrate." She wiped Alaleh's forehead again, dipped the rag into the bottle of water. "The baby is near. You can do it, my daughter. Wait . . . Wait . . . Now push!"

Alaleh clenched her teeth and once again pushed with all her might.

"Again, again! I see the head! It is almost over. Again, Alaleh!"

The urgency persisted, the contraction cut her in sharp pain. She groaned, waited, and pushed again. She felt the release of pressure, the mind-numbing pain give way to freedom, heard Myriam softly murmuring, "Thank you, Khoda, thank you for this beautiful boy."

From somewhere Alaleh heard the cry of her newborn son, and then she fainted.

Rasa

Rasa watched her grandmother working frantically to stop the bleeding. The newborn baby lay swaddled by Maamaan's side, sleeping, but her mother lay awake, eyes glazed, her breathing shallow.

Rasa knew her mother was dying. She saw the blood, she followed every whispered instruction of Maamaan-Bozorg, and still the blood flowed.

She thought back to the club she had attended at Noyemi's house and the big white woman—Miss Beverly—with the shining face and the strange, wonderful stories. She talked about a God who healed bodies and hearts.

And the book! Miss Beverly had given her the book that had forced Baba away.

"It is a good book, but it is dangerous," the shining woman had told her, looking straight into Rasa's eyes. "It is truth, but many do not like it. You must be careful with this book."

Rasa had not been afraid. She loved to read—she had learned at four and now could interpret all the swirls of the Persian alphabet for herself. She remembered the story Miss Beverly had told on the third day, a story from the Ingil about a woman who had been bleeding for years with no way to stop it. And then she had touched the Master, the one Miss Beverly called *Isa al Masi*, and the bleeding had stopped.

"God wants to heal our hearts and our bodies. Cry out to God, to Jesus, for healing. He loves you and forgives you," Miss Beverly had said.

Rasa went to her mother's side and placed her hands on Maamaan's limp arm. "Please God, please Isa al Masi, I believe you can stop the bleeding. We cannot do it, not even Maamaan-Bozorg, who is wise and has delivered many babies. Please, please stop the bleeding, Isa al Masi."

Her grandmother was watching her, her face haggard and mournful.

Rasa ended her prayer as Miss Beverly had. "In Jesus' name. Amen."

CHAPTER 3

Bobbie

*L*ittle pills can pack a punch. The doctor had assured me that side effects like the limp and the tremors were not a problem, I shouldn't stress over them. I just wished that Tracie wouldn't. And that I didn't have such trouble with steps. Europe *is* steps. Ancient, worn-smooth steps.

"What's our itinerary for tomorrow?" This was Tracie's question every night. I had reserved the right to plan the whole trip and tell her nothing. I pretended it was because I wanted to surprise her, but in reality, it was because I was putting off our main destination—a place outside Vienna called The Oasis. But Tracie wasn't fooled.

"So when are we getting to Vienna, Aunt Bobbie? You think about it every day. I don't want us to run out of time." Then her eyes grew wide and she started to stammer an apology.

"No worries, Tracie. I know what you meant, and you're right. It's about time we headed to Vienna."

We were standing in an open tree-lined square in Innsbruck, with the Inn River scurrying behind us and a group of little old men in front of us, casquettes on their heads, arms behind their backs, leaning forward intently as they contemplated the moves of two men playing chess on a board that was painted on the pavement. The chess pieces were life-size.

"Look at that," Tracie said. "It's the fulfillment of every European stereotype I've ever heard. Little old men in wool hats wasting away their days in tree-canopied parks playing chess with people-sized pawns! So much more romantic than playing a mindless video game." She sighed. "And young lovers strolling hand in hand and stealing kisses behind ancient statues of sylvan nymphs."

I glanced at my only niece. She had grown into a lovely young woman, had held her own in a lively household with five younger brothers, whom I had dubbed the T-tribe: Timmy, Travis, Teddy, Trey, and Thomas. Life hadn't been a piece of pecan pie for Tracie. I loved her as fiercely as if she were my own daughter, and I was thankful to give her this reprieve from the heartbreak she was going through.

She let out another long sigh. "If only life could be truly this romantic. If only guys told the truth and had the courage to stick around even when life is a little difficult. If only they didn't look you in the eye and say, 'You know, Trace, you're an amazing girl, but I'm just not ready for commitment!'"

She turned from staring at the young lovers and gave a bitter chuckle. "Neil was supposed to be giving me an engagement ring that night. Instead he broke my heart and didn't even have the guts to explain why." Tears filled her eyes, not for the first time on this trip.

I put an arm around her shoulders and pulled her in close. "Tracie, you're heartbroken. You're also young and alive and bursting with talent, and on the threshold of a wonderful new adventure. I promise." I stared at her, appraised her doubtful expression, and took a deep breath. "I've never talked about it, but I was in love once. Desperately in love." The words were barely out of my mouth before I wished I could take them back.

She wiggled out of my embrace, faced me with her arms drawn tight across her chest. "Well, go on, Aunt Bobbie. You've been holding out on me a long time."

I hesitated. With all we had shared over the years, she had to wonder why I had kept back something so important.

"He was a refugee."

"A what?"

"Tracie, you know what a refugee is."

"Of course I know what a refugee is! What I'm asking is what were you doing falling in love with one? I thought you were busy dodging the authorities and smuggling contraband behind the Iron Curtain."

I laughed. "You make it sound like a James Bond movie."

"It does sound like that, in all of your stories. Except instead of escaping with 007's ingenious tools, you were always rescued by God."

"Exactly."

"Or angels," she added. "As I recall."

"Yes, well, I'd give God the credit for that too. Who do you think the angels report to?"

Tracie stuck out her tongue, grinned, then leaned against a statue of two lovers—nude, of course—embracing. She sighed. "So go on—how'd you meet the refugee?"

"Well, we weren't smuggling Bibles 24/7, you know. There were days and weeks and even months when we were stuck at the little compound outside of Vienna, waiting for the next trip to be planned. And then there was Fred."

"Fred was the refugee?"

"No, of course not. Fred was part of the The Barracks team—I've told you about them."

Tracie nodded. "Yes, the Bible smugglers. And you all had fake names, right?" and she winked at me.

"Exactly. So Fred trained with us in the US and planned on smuggling, like the rest of us, but when the rubber hit the road, he just couldn't do it. He found he couldn't lie, couldn't keep a straight face and swear that he wasn't carrying anything illegal into the East. So here he was—stuck in Vienna for a two-year term of service, with a huge amount of guilt because his religious convictions wouldn't let him smuggle Bibles." I chuckled, as I always did when I considered the irony of Fred's situation.

"He was a wonderful guy, and nobody blamed him. Some people are made for that type of work and some aren't. Anyway, Fred started visiting the refugee camp in our village, and before long he was teaching the women and children to read and write in English, and playing chess with the men, and then he started some Bible studies. And pretty soon the refugees, many who came from Communist countries, were learning about Jesus and wanting to be Christians."

"Wow. Um, that's cool."

"It was very cool. And the rest of us, The Barracks crew, well, when we weren't traveling or planning trips, we went with Fred to visit the refugees."

"And you met *him* there?" She lifted her eyebrows, interlocked her arm with mine, and we began to slowly circle the park.

"Yes." It came out as barely a whisper. "Yes, I did."

"And . . . ?" She drew the word out.

But I could not do it. Could not bear even to say his name, because if I did that, all the other memories, the truly horrible ones, would fly into my face in living color. "Let's just say I got another calling and so did he, and it just didn't work out."

She made a face. "Bobbie, you can be absolutely maddening sometimes."

"I know," I acquiesced.

"And the refugee camp is still outside of Vienna?"

"Sure is. It's called the Government Refugee Housing Center."

"So come on! What are we waiting for?"

It was my turn for tears, real tears, and one slid down my cheek. I brushed it away.

"Oh, Bobbie, I keep saying the wrong thing. I'm sorry."

I turned to her. "You said a perfectly beautiful thing."

"Even if I made you cry?"

"You didn't make me cry, Trace. It's just that I didn't quite think I'd ever get there again, in this lifetime at least."

Tracie narrowed her eyes. "I hate it when you talk that way!"

I cleared my throat and faced her. "I would love to take you to see 'the camps' as well as the ministry center that Fred started—the one that's called The Oasis. Both are located in an adorable little village on the outskirts of Vienna," I explained. "Nowadays the refugees are by and large from Middle Eastern countries and often are Muslims. Back then they were from Eastern Europe and fleeing Communism. They were intellectuals—professors, doctors, lawyers . . . poets."

I got a little catch in my throat and covered by stopping to inspect a statue of a nude little boy with his arms interlaced around the neck of a fawn. But when I glanced over at Tracie, I saw that she wasn't listening.

"How odd to find this statue here," she whispered. She ran her hands over the fawn's head, across the child's cheeks.

"You know it?"

Tracie shook her head. "No, no, it just reminds me of something . . ."

Her voice trailed off, and we stood there in silence. I didn't know what Tracie was remembering, but I was thinking about Amir, the refugee I'd met in the camp outside Vienna. The man I'd fallen in love with all those years ago.

Tracie

Maybe I shouldn't have come on this trip. I loved my aunt, but it was impossible to spend much time with her without getting back to the topic of God. And God and I had not been on speaking terms for a long, long time. Bobbie didn't know why, had never understood how I simply refused to consider "making God a priority in my life," as she put it.

Well, maybe on this trip I would tell her. Maybe she could understand now. After all, wasn't God betraying Aunt Bobbie? Turning His back on her and looking away, just as He'd done to me so long ago?

I was ten years old and at church camp. Five days, the longest I'd ever been away from home. Away from the T-tribe. Away from their stupid boy-jokes and endless energy. Time to be alone and time to race around with other kids.

On that last morning I was out in the woods having devotions. That's what they called it. Every morning the camp director gave us a sheet of paper with a few Bible verses and some questions. The verse on the last day was "As a deer pants for water, so my soul pants for you, O God." I had just finished reading it when I heard the brush of something in the woods. I looked up and not ten feet from me stood a mama deer and her fawn.

They were frozen, fearful; they smelled me. I held my breath and didn't even blink. Then they turned and loped off together.

A breeze blew slightly, warm, inviting, and I felt a presence. Like something still standing beside me. Or Someone.

I looked back at the paper and read *Have you ever felt close to God or felt God close to you?*

A chill ran through me, and then I felt a deep-down happiness, something so real that I wanted to break into song.

I hummed a chorus that we'd learned that week and just sat there with my eyes closed and felt the joy of the moment.

From somewhere far off I heard a voice over the camp PA. "Tracie! Tracie Hopkins, can you please come back to the meeting hall?"

I had no idea why I was being called, but I jumped up and ran through the woods, imagining myself loping like the deer. When I got to the hall I found my counselor and the camp director there waiting for me.

I rushed up to Lisa, my counselor, and blurted, "Wait till you hear what just happened to me!" But then I realized that both of them looked really serious, and I stopped my story. "What's the matter? Did I do something wrong?"

"Oh, no, Tracie. No, of course not." Lisa put her arms around me and hugged me tight.

The director said, "Tracie, we have some hard news. Your father . . . your father had a heart attack."

By the look on her face, I knew my father was dead.

I pulled away from her and threw my hands over my ears and backed away. I kept backing up until I bumped into a tree. Then I turned and ran back into the woods to the exact spot where I had seen the deer. I stood stiff and quiet, but nothing came. God had come to me when I was just a child and then, on the very same day, He ripped my father out of my life. I never wanted to have much to do with God after that.

The sight of the stone deer had brought the day back so vividly. I straightened up, dried my eyes with my sleeve, and looked around to see that Bobbie had gone to sit on a bench nearby. As I walked toward her I saw that her hands were shaking, almost violently.

"It's nothing, Tracie."

But I was already so emotional, it was all I could do to keep a sob down.

Bobbie took my hands in hers. "It's simply a side effect of the treatment. Just what the doctor predicted." She treated it so lightly I wanted to scream. Then she peered into my eyes. "Listen, Tracie. I'm okay. You don't need to worry about me, you hear? I would never have come on this trip if there was any danger of my dying on you!"

I flinched.

"That's what you're worried about, isn't it?"

I nodded. Aunt Bobbie was being slowly eaten to death by a vengeful God who betrayed those who loved Him. The tears spilled down my cheeks, and I said, "Look at you! You're shriveling up! What kind of cruel God would do that to you, after all you've done for Him?"

She looked at me with that peaceful determination, then her forehead wrinkled slightly, and she leaned back on the bench. She took a sip of bottled water, smiled, and nodded toward the sun glistening on mountains in the distance.

"Do you think it's fair to accept only the good and not the bad in life?" She didn't wait for an answer. "I'm doing okay, Tracie. I consider every day a gift—this life."

"I don't see how you can say that," I snapped. "Not with what's happening, with the way your life has turned out."

"You used to think my life was cool. You liked to hear my stories."

"Yeah, well, your God was a lot nicer back then—He showed up in good ways."

"And yet, He's still the same God." She said this under her breath, as if simply talking to herself, maybe even convincing herself that her faith was real and worth it.

"Look. I have a month of pills left to take before starting the next treatment, and the doctor gave me his approval, and I'm just fine. Please don't worry."

"But you said it's aggressive and no treatment is really effective. How can I not worry?"

Aunt Bobbie closed her eyes again and turned her head up to catch the fading sun. "It's called trust, Tracie. If you can't trust God, can you trust me?"

I didn't budge, didn't nod or acquiesce in any way.

"Will it help if I promise you that I will call my doctor tomorrow and tell him about the tremors?"

I gave a sigh of relief. "Yes, oh yes."

"Consider it done. And no more of this talk!"

But later that night, I kept thinking about her question long after she'd gone to bed. *Do you think it's fair to accept only the good and not the bad in life?*

Amir
Traiskirchen, Austria

A new batch of refugees had arrived two days ago. Amir could imagine them stumbling into the Government Refugee Housing Center in Traiskirchen, tired, confused, and cold, with fear and despair in their eyes. He remembered his own arrival sixteen years earlier.

Traiskirchen meant "three churches." Amir had never researched the history of the village; all he knew was that here he had found Church with a capital C. The hands and feet of his Lord Jesus, before he had even known His name. In the dark hallways, huddled with the other refugees, the whisper had begun. "There is a place in the village with kind people who offer clothes and food. It's called The Oasis."

No one dared to whisper the other thing the kind people offered: hope.

Now Amir was a pastor in an Iranian church in the little town of Mauthausen—who could have imagined it? And once a month, he helped the multinational team of Christians who ran The Oasis. And even after all these years, the memory would suddenly come over him again.

The bombing started at midnight. Amir woke with dread

in his throat, threw on his clothes, and ran to the other room in the tiny apartment. "Maamaan! Baba! Get dressed right now! We have to leave." He rushed them out of the building, down the stairs, across the street, and through the alleyways of the town. Every few minutes the sky lit up with bright orange light. The troops were approaching. They would slaughter anyone in their way.

It shouldn't surprise him to be reliving the memory tonight, with The Oasis's main room jampacked with young men from Iran and Afghanistan and Iraq. Young men who looked a lot like him. They swarmed the bar area, where two volunteers from a church in Vienna quickly, almost frantically, filled cups with coffee or chai tea. One cup per person, they said, over and over. Amir stood guard at the door. The men looked hungry, desperate, confused. Just as he had, as a broken young man of twenty-three, a man who had climbed the mountains of Iran, Turkey, and Albania to save his parents.

A happy outburst sounded behind him, and he looked around to see a group of five young men, Iranian no doubt, laughing, arms around each other's shoulders, posing for a photo. JoAnn, a full-time worker at The Oasis, counted to three in Farsi and snapped the photo. Tomorrow she would print it off so that next week when they returned, she could hand them the photo. JoAnn was always coming up with some way to show love and concern for these young men.

Amir looked away. She reminded him too much of someone else he'd once known—her dark hair, her blue eyes, her enthusiasm. Her Southern accent, all the way from somewhere in Georgia—Georgia the state in America, not Georgia the country next to Russia. All those years ago. A beautiful young American girl bringing him coffee, comforting his mother after his father's death, finding a coat for him on that freezing first night in Austria when snow covered the streets, convincing him to attend Bible study . . .

Amir snapped back to the present. The rooms in the back of the building were darkened with newspapers across the windows, the back entrance locked. Later, much later, after the coffee and tea ran out and the hoards left, several men would sneak to that entrance, protected from their compatriots' scrupulous gaze, and knock three times on the door. Would wait. Would knock again. Would sneak in to hear truth.

Amir welcomed another young man, patting him on the back. "Sami, good to see you tonight."

Sami motioned with his eyes to the hallway.

"Later," Amir said. "Nine p.m. Not now."

Sami nodded. He was thin, almost feeble-looking, curious, disillusioned, asking questions.

Yes, later Amir would teach him from the Bible, would hold the Ingil up and proclaim Jesus as Lord, just as Jill had done to him all those years ago.

CHAPTER 4

Hamid

*H*amid stumbled into the little village, half frozen and completely exhausted. For two days he had walked up the mountain and down again and through the snow and then through the forest of trees. At every turn he would stop, his heart pounding, and listen for the crack of a twig, the echo of a dog's bark. The crude map seemed pointless, and yet he was here. Another dusty mountain village, another pitiful stranger looking for food and lodging. And somewhere Zemar waited. Would the smuggler risk his life for Hamid? Perhaps he had already heard of the fate of his companions. So now, would he show himself?

Hamid could not recall what day it was. Exhaustion permeated every inch of his body. His lips were parched and his stomach growled continuously. He had perspired so heavily climbing up and down the mountain that his clothes were soaked through, no matter that it was near freezing outside.

From out of nowhere in the waning light, a small veiled woman appeared, motioning with her eyes for Hamid to follow. She led him along a narrow street that twisted and turned, revealing stone houses built directly into the mountain. She disappeared inside one of the buildings, with Hamid behind. The ceiling was low, the single room dark. A thin trail of smoke came from the corner.

Hamid squinted and saw, with relief, the face of Zemar turn to him. A face as stony as the walls of this little house, with its dark, expressionless eyes and thick black beard.

"Alone?" he said.

Hamid nodded. In a whisper he recounted the fate of his companions and his long, perilous journey.

Zemar's expression never changed. "We must leave immediately. The police will be here soon."

Hamid groaned. He had no strength left; he was shivering with cold and so hungry.

As if reading his thoughts, the small woman produced a plate of rice and beans. "Sit," she said, offering it to him.

Hamid sank to the ground and ate the food like a ravenous wolf . . . like one of the wolves he had heard sometimes came through the mountains and attacked wandering refugees, leaving only tattered clothes behind.

"One hour, you sleep. We will leave as soon as it is completely dark." Zemar tossed his cigarette on the dirt floor and crushed it out with his boot.

The sky was pitch black now, and Hamid had regained a little strength. He had slept soundly, so soundly that he had awakened only after Zemar slapped him forcefully on the side of the face.

"I thought you were dead! I have been trying to awaken you for ten minutes! You're frozen." Zemar instructed the little woman to bring Hamid dry clothes.

Perhaps he *had* died, Hamid reflected. For a few moments he had dreamed. He was warm and dry, and home with Alaleh and Rasa, beautiful little Rasa who was smiling at him and cradling something in her arms. A baby. His child.

It took him awhile to shake the sleep and change into the clothes the woman brought. Now he followed Zemar through the street along with five other men, Iranian and Afghan, who had appeared from different corners of the village as he and Zemar had stepped out into moonlight.

Zemar spoke the warning, his face always hard, his eyes cold. "No conversation. If we are lucky we will cross the border into Turkey tonight."

Silently the six men followed the smuggler, staring ahead as if each were completely alone.

To escape the first police checkpoint, Zemar led them on a three-hour detour, trudging along slowly in the snow, the black sky screaming down their whereabouts, the clouds momentarily hiding the moon. At last the voice of Zemar broke the silence. He turned to them and whispered fiercely, "Now! Run. We must run."

Heads down, clutching their few belongings, they crashed through the forest, the snow crunching beneath their worn shoes, the limbs of bare trees scraping their faces. Still they ran.

At last Zemar slowed to a walk, held his finger to his lips, and said, "We are in Turkey."

The men smiled, lifted their eyes to thank the heavens.

"We will cross through this village. I will go first. It's still very dangerous. Police are everywhere. You follow two by two, keeping a distance between each group. Complete silence!"

Hamid watched as Zemar went first and then motioned for Hamid and another young man to follow. Hamid felt his heart pounding in his ears as he watched the ground, careful not to trip on the mass of roots and rocks hidden under the snow. They had walked no more than two or three minutes when they heard a commotion behind him.

Another sound, angry voices.

"They got them. Run! Run!" his companion whispered, panicked.

They bent down low, fleeing on tiptoe lest their footsteps betray them, then crouched behind a thick expanse of trees as flashlights lit up the forest. Heart racing, Hamid watched three Turkish policeman fan the woods with light. At last they turned their flashlights away from the woods and back towards the four refugees who had been caught. Hamid heard the sound of beating and muffled screams and then the booming voice of one of the policeman as he pointed his flashlight back toward the border of Iran, across the mountains.

"Here's the way to go," he yelled. "If you're lucky, you'll make it. Maybe the police will catch you and send you back to Afghanistan, or you will freeze to death and be eaten by wolves!"

As soon as the woods went black, Hamid and the other refugee tore through the dark, arms stretched in front, pushing away the limbs. Suddenly, they stumbled out of the trees onto a dirt road. Still jogging, they had only gone a few hundred feet when they heard the sound of a car pulling up beside them. Hamid veered back toward the woods, hoping to outrun it, knowing he could not.

Someone grabbed the back of his shirt and yanked him around. "Get in!" the voice commanded.

Hamid wept with relief—Zemar's voice. They climbed into the backseat as Zemar joined the driver in the front, the car never fully coming to a stop. When both doors were slammed shut, Zemar turned and smiled at them from across the seat. "The car is part of the escape plan."

Hamid could not tell how long the car sped through the night—an hour, maybe two—for he dozed off and on. At one point he awoke with his head on his companion's shoulder. Embarrassed, he pulled back. The other man was fast asleep too.

Then, as suddenly as it had appeared, the car stopped on another dirt road, depositing the three passengers and then speeding off through the night. Once again the two refugees tagged along behind Zemar.

He led them to a small path that curved along the side of a mountain. Below was a gaping ravine. "Stay here," Zemar said. Two words, that was all.

They stood for hours, backs flattened against the frozen rock, sheltering themselves from gusts of wind that whipped up from the valley. Hamid fished in his backpack for a few pieces of stale bread and handed one to the young man, who nodded with relief. They had no water, so they bent down and ate some snow. When complete exhaustion enveloped them, they sat back to back, their heads resting against the side of the mountain.

When they could not sleep, the other man began to talk in a whisper, as if the mountain and the ravine were the secret police. "My name is Rasheed. I fled Iran because of my political convictions. The government knew of the group I belonged to and came looking for us. My friends were not so lucky. Taken to prison, tortured."

Hamid could hear the grief in his younger companion's voice as he turned his head down, his curly black hair falling in his face.

"If I fail, I have failed for all of us."

"I'm Hamid. And we will not fail. We are almost there." Hamid pronounced the words through chattering teeth, but in his mind he was crying, *Isa, this is too hard. Will we never find freedom?*

They waited for hours and hours for Zemar to return, the night wind blasting through their thin coats, their hands and feet chapped and bleeding. *So close and we will freeze to death right here,* Hamid thought. Rasheed began to nod off.

"Tell me about your family," Hamid said, loudly, above the rush of wind. "Talk to me so we will stay awake."

And so for hours the two men related stories of their families, urging each other when one fell into silence. "Don't sleep. We mustn't sleep."

When at last Zemar returned, he held out his hands as if in apology. "We cannot make it to Van tonight. I'm sorry."

Hamid wondered if they would make it anywhere or if they would simply die on the mountain. Van, the city where safety awaited. One more day!

"But I have a place for us to stay. Follow me." Once again they stumbled through the mountain paths, forcing their frozen feet to move, one step in front of the other.

At last Zemar turned and said, "Come inside."

Hamid and Rasheed settled on the dirt floor of a little house, where they slept next to the oven. Rasheed gave the faintest of smiles. Hamid felt warm for the first time in many days.

Rasa

Ever since the bleeding had stopped, Maamaan-Bozorg had treated Rasa with alarm mixed with respect. "How did you do that?" She'd asked it again and again.

And Rasa's only answer was, "I prayed."

"I was praying too," Maamaan-Bozorg insisted. "Your prayers were different. You have a power in you, child. You can heal."

The way Maamaan-Bozorg said it scared Rasa. Almost as if this power were something to be sold and used like money. But Rasa didn't believe she had a special power, only that she knew a special God. The American woman's God, Noyemi's God. She had wanted to whisper the name *Isa al Masi*, and yet it stayed stuck in her throat. She was too afraid, especially after the trouble Baba had had with the book.

She sat beside her mother, who was huddled in the corner of their hiding place, watching. Baby Omid was snuggled tight against Rasa's chest. Soon he would awake and be hungry, but for now Rasa watched her mother watching her baby. Maamaan was still so very weak. And there was no more food, no more water.

Omid let out a soft cry, and Rasa cradled him in her arms. She could not stop smiling at him, his dark solemn eyes turned so intensely on hers. He was perfect in every way, her little brother. She whispered down to him, "You will be a strong brother, a good brother. Maamaan has lived. You will see. Isa al Masi has protected us."

Yes, Maamaan was still very weak, but she was alive. And now she lay, weak but with a smile on her face, as Rasa placed little Omid in her arms. "Thank you, precious child," her mother whispered, eyes filled with gratitude.

They were still in their house, still living in the windowless room, and now the supplies were gone. Maamaan-Bozorg bent down beside Rasa, held her hand. Her eyes were sad, her voice broken. "You must crawl out, Rasa, crawl out and see what has happened."

Together she and her grandmother pushed and pushed on the armoire that blocked the crawl space until at last it groaned and budged enough for her to slither out. With only one bottle of water left in their hideout, there was no choice. Maamaan-Bozorg held her tight, recited a passage from the Koran, then sent her out with Maamaan watching from where she lay on the mattress with tiny Omid. Rasa escaped through the opening, trembling.

The house was empty. Nothing but broken glass and furniture scattered everywhere. The soldiers had forced their way in and overturned the chairs and tables, had taken everything from the kitchen, from the refrigerator. Rasa went back to the hideout to report the news. She stopped before the armoire. Its doors stood wide open, the china plates broken, smashed on the floor. She reached inside the armoire to remove the broken shards and saw it, a dark green little vase, a vase that she had never seen there before. But she had seen it somewhere else. At Noyemi's house the day of the birthday party.

"Oh, it is so beautiful! It's too bad it's broken," she had said to her friend. The little vase had been glued back together, but with pieces missing. "Are you going to throw it away?"

"No, of course not!" came her friend's indignant reply.

"Why not? It will never hold water again. My grandmother would say it is useless."

"It is chipped and broken, but it's still useful. Look." And Noyemi had put a lovely silk poppy inside.

"We are like this vase," Miss Beverly had said then, in her broken Farsi. Then she had motioned to the interpreter and explained, "I brought that vase to show you what Isa says. We are jars of clay and He is the potter. He can choose to use us in any way He wants, even the one who seems broken beyond repair . . ."

But what was the vase doing here, in her armoire? Had Noyemi come to her house after the soldiers left? As Rasa removed the vase, she saw that there was something inside. She reached her small hand down deep and pulled out a thin piece of paper. Quickly she climbed back into the crawl space.

"Look what I found," Rasa said, and she read aloud the words written in her friend's childish script.

I am sorry. We saw the soldiers come. We saw them take many things, but not you. Where are you and your mother and grandmother? We are hiding in our house. Mother says we will escape when the full moon has passed. Come find us, Rasa, if you are here. If you are alive.

Maamaan-Bozorg and Maamaan wept as they read the letter. What should they do? Rasa did not know.

But she knew one thing. Miss Beverly had told the story of Isa al Masi. He too was born on a violent night; he too was sought by evil men; he too was forced to flee when only a baby to a foreign land. And the lady had said it—He always protects His own. He was not a prophet, as Rasa had always heard. He was God! God come as man. God of the impossible.

She watched little Omid sucking at her mother's breast. Omid would live. Isa al Masi would protect them all. They would flee with Noyemi and her family into another land. Alone, but not alone. Isa was with them. Rasa knew this. She was sure.

Hamid

Hamid and Rasheed huddled by the little stove, drinking the hot tea, eating the bread and cheese. It was not much, and Hamid still felt ravenous. They stayed in the room all day. Nothing else was offered to eat, but surely they were nearing freedom! Hamid felt it, tasted it, prayed for it . . . to Isa, though he would never dare admit it to his companion. He clutched his small backpack close to him, with his papers, a few stale pieces of bread, and his radio.

As night fell they once again got into a car, which drove them to the next police checkpoint. Three times during the long night they repeated the same process. The car would let them out, they would follow Zemar on foot as he took them on a detour. Then a car would appear out of nowhere and pick them up and drive to the next checkpoint. Fatigue and dizziness were their constant companions, as well as that terrible gnawing hunger. Hamid shared his last crumbs of stale bread with Rasheed, and they ate snow as they trudged along. Rasheed's eyes held a look of numbness combined with sheer panic. Would they survive? They slept outside in the day, exhausted, again their clothes drenched with sweat so that they froze on them. Surely they would not die so close to freedom?

"This is the very last leg of the trip," Zemar said as night fell.

They walked again for hours and hours, around yet another checkpoint and over several small hills. Rasheed stumbled once, caught himself, and moved forward. He stumbled again and fell headfirst to the ground, where he lay still.

"We're so close, Rasheed. Get up! Get up," Hamid urged.

"Go on," Rasheed whispered to Hamid. "I can't continue. I can no longer walk."

"Leave him there!" Zemar said. "He will be eaten by wolves, just like the others."

But Hamid could not leave his traveling companion, who after these days of journeying together felt more like a younger brother now. He turned back, leaned down, and slowly hefted Rasheed to a standing position. Then, with Rasheed's arms around his shoulders, Hamid slowly, painfully pulled him along.

Ten minutes passed, fifteen. Hamid could no longer feel his feet, his vision blurred. It would end like this—both of them dead and Zemar walking on, seemingly oblivious.

But then Zemar turned around, arms crossed over his chest. "You are stubborn," he said to Hamid as he came on the other side of Rasheed, and together they helped the young man continue.

"We are very close now," their guide said at last.

Hamid felt a stirring of hope; Rasheed had finally regained enough strength to walk along without help. At Zemar's words he turned to Hamid, grinned and mouthed, "Thank you."

It was then that Hamid heard the police dogs. The search-lights came on, and terror enveloped every part of Hamid's body. Now it was Rasheed who grabbed his hand, who whispered frantically, "Crouch down! Come on, Hamid. You can do it! Come!"

The temptation to lie down and die was so strong. Hamid could not be sure he was even awake, for the dogs' barking seemed at times far off and at times right in his ears. The searchlights swept across the frozen fields. *Isa. Help.* It was all he could manage.

Then he felt a supernatural strength surge through him, and he began running, and ducking and running again. The sound of the dogs' baying came closer and closer. Hamid felt his lungs burning as he pushed forward, faster and faster. Surely they could not outrun police dogs! Rasheed pushed Hamid to the ground and fell beside him as the searchlight scanned the countryside. When the beam moved on, leaving them in darkness, they popped up and ran again as if they were in some action film. The dogs barking, the searchlights, the whistles blaring. And then suddenly silence.

What had happened? Had Isa picked their pursuers up and carried them away? Hamid did not know. He only knew that at last he and Rasheed stumbled behind Zemar into the city of Van, cold, starving, and completely exhausted.

Rasa

Maamaan-Bozorg and Maamaan made the decision: they must escape. While Rasa held baby Omid, jostled him and patted him and whispered songs to him so he would not cry, they searched throughout the house for the papers, the clothes, the few belongings they would take with them. There was not much left of their belongings anyway after the police had pillaged it. Rasa had gathered two small dolls and her favorite dress.

Then it was time to walk out into the deep of night. They were leaving their home, perhaps forever. Her mother held Omid, swaddled in blankets, close to her chest, and Rasa held Maamaan-Bozorg's hand tightly as they slipped out into the dark. The blast of cold air made Rasa smile momentarily. She smelled the richness of the jasmine, the crisp sting of the frosty wind. She relished it, turned her face upward and saw stars, dozens of them, blinking down on her. Maybe they were God's angels. Maybe one of these stars would lead them to a safe place, to Isa's home, just as the Morning Star had done in the Ingil. *Isa. Isa.* She said the word again and again in her mind.

The first part of their journey was very short, just down the street to Noyemi's house, but it felt like hours and hours. Now they were huddled on the cushions in the main room of their neighbors' home, every light extinguished. Maamaan-Bozorg held Rasa in a tight embrace, a heavy blanket pulled over them both. She moaned softly in her sleep. Beside them, Maamaan and baby Omid slept. But Rasa was wide awake. She dug one small hand down into the pocket of her skirt and closed her fist around a smooth wooden object, remembering what Miss Beverly had said to her all those weeks ago at the club.

The large American woman had knelt down and looked her right in the eyes. In her broken Farsi she said, "Rasa, I want you to have this little wooden cross." She had handed her a very simple ornament, two pieces of wood glued together. Rasa knew about the cross! The cross Jesus died on was very important. She frowned a little. Isa al Masi had died. But He had come back to life, as only God can do, and now Rasa could know Him, and He lived in her.

Through the interpreter, Miss Beverly had continued to explain, "In many countries, Christians wear a cross around their necks to show they are followers of Isa. But here in Iran, some people do not want you to be a Christian. So you will not wear this cross around your neck. You will put it in your pocket, and every time you touch it you will remember that Isa al Masi is with you. Jesus will never leave you."

Now Rasa removed the cross from her pocket and brought it to her lips. She kissed it softly and whispered, "Isa, we are going to leave on a long journey. I don't know where we are going, but you do. Be with us. Make us brave. Keep Maamaan strong and Maamaan-Bozorg and Omid too. And Baba. Protect him, wherever he is, and may he find you too." Her eyes grew heavy as she whispered that one little word again. "Isa."

Alaleh

Alaleh would have given just about anything to hear from Hamid. Just a word—one word: *alive!* It could come by phone or e-mail or text or smoke signal. All she wanted was the assurance that he was somewhere on his path from Iran to Austria, alive. Sometimes her stomach was in knots with fear, as she nursed baby Omid and watched her mother-in-law and daughter. Sometimes she shivered with it. At times when they were asleep and she was nursing Omid in the middle of the night, she let the tears fall.

What would this crazy hiding and flight mean if there was no Hamid in the end? For as long as she could remember, Hamid had been her life, from the first time she saw him when she was sixteen and he was twenty-two. One of the brightest students at his university, Hamid had taught philosophy at her high school for several months when the teacher was ill. One stolen glance his way, as he stood at the front of the class room pondering his notes, and she felt her heart jump. He met her eyes, and she saw in them kindness. A deep well of caring, something beyond explanation, beyond his boyish face, his quick smile, his rugged beauty.

Yes, Hamid was beautiful in the way of men. She had said it to her mother only days after first seeing him. "The men do not wear makeup, do not paint their fingernails and toenails. And yet they are beautiful." Her mother had scoffed at her, but Alaleh did not care. Some men *were* indeed so perfect in their manliness that it shone like beauty. This young man was one of them.

Even now Alaleh blushed with the thought. How he had wooed her, in spite of every restriction, every taboo. Now, ten years later, she was his wife, and they had a little daughter and a baby son. Their children. They must be her life now. But the deep longing for Hamid kept her awake even after Omid had taken his final suck and lay peacefully against her breast, the hint of a smile resting on his sleeping lips. She ached for Hamid.

Little Rasa promised her mother that Baba was fine. Lately Alaleh just did not understand her daughter. Rasa had always been a bit different. Precocious. Serious. Wise beyond her very few years. Alaleh remembered when Rasa at three had said, "Maamaan, look, I can write my name. Isn't it beautiful?" Sure enough, she had written her name in the flowing Farsi script.

But lately, the things Rasa said made her sound more like a prophet than a child. "Baba is fine, Maamaan. Isa al Masi has told me that Baba will make it safely to Austria. He will bring us, too. You will see."

At first Alaleh had felt only anger and bitterness at this prophet, Isa al Masi. Jesus! Oh, she'd heard of him plenty in the Koran. And she knew the Armenian neighbors worshiped him as God. But when Rasa began talking about him as if she knew him—really *knew* him, like a friend—Alaleh had been afraid. And then the Ingil, that book! That book was why Hamid had fled.

She had cursed the Ingil and Isa al Masi and her Armenian neighbors.

But then little Rasa had saved her life and the life of Omid. There was no other explanation for it. And her little daughter had not shown any fear as they gathered their belongings and slipped down the street to their neighbors' house. Last night, with a perfectly calm countenance, she had announced, "Maamaan, don't worry so. Isa has ordained it all, so that we can be free! For how many years have you and Baba talked about freedom? And now Isa has pushed us along so it can happen. Do not be mad or worry. It is written that Isa will take care of his own. He will not leave us."

It did not seem to matter to Rasa that her mother had no belief in Isa. Evidently since Rasa believed, Isa would protect the whole family. This was Rasa's conviction. What a strange daughter she had. And yet, Alaleh could not deny the little girl's inner strength, her calm, her happiness. "Not happiness, Maamaan. Joy. Joy that Isa gives."

Alaleh closed her eyes and thought of Hamid, hiding somewhere in a mountain cave, cold and terrified. She thought of the dogs, the guns, the police and soldiers. Oh, she knew the stories. Let Rasa believe her father was fine. All Alaleh wanted was a word. One word. That was all.

She shuddered, thinking again of their dash through the night, she clasping baby Omid so tightly against her chest, little Rasa holding Myriam's hand. The silence, the fear, the darkness. The relief when they stumbled into their new hiding place, their Armenian neighbors' home, just a few minutes down the street. Here in this little house, tucked in a corner of Tehran, they would be safe for a few days. She let out a long sigh and stared down into baby Omid's lovely sleeping face. She was sure she saw the trace of a smile on his lips. She wished Hamid could see his son, could at least know he had a son.

How she worried for him! Hamid the philosopher, the

linguist, the one who stood back and observed. Always ideas! So many ideas. And languages! He spoke not only Farsi, but Turkish, English, and Arabic. And such exhaustion when he came home. He needed his space, and that was not understood in their culture. He was so often preoccupied. But she understood. He was brilliant, her husband, but he needed routine, he needed structure, he needed silence and principles.

"He is so complicated, my Hamid! Why must he think through everything?" That was his mother's constant rant, and sometimes, when the two women were alone together, they would laugh about it. Hamid the philosophical, Hamid the passionate—passionate, that is, about his books.

Alaleh blushed in the darkness. He could be passionate about her too. He loved her; his devotion was so very strong. But he was weary of the system in which they lived, weary of rules that did not make sense. "There is no logic in the way we are forced to practice our faith!" He had said it a hundred times. Then he would laugh bitterly and quote a well-known Persian proverb. "Injustice all around is justice."

His job at the university suited him perfectly, and the students loved him, the wise man who quoted Rumi. How he worked hard to reach out and listen to his students. But Alaleh had always had a silent fear. Would he someday speak out against the government? Would he say what he felt in his heart?

For years they had talked of fleeing. He called it that. *Fleeing*. Going to Austria, where Hamid's cousin Jalil had found residence. Jalil had sought asylum and was now a legal alien.

Alaleh closed her eyes. Legal. Nothing in her life was legal right now. Would Hamid even make it to Austria? Would he survive the mountains? Oh, dear Hamid was not made for risk and adventure. And yet for her, for Rasa, for his family, he had left, had run into hell to escape an even greater hell at home.

Omid let out a soft cry, and Alaleh bent over and kissed his forehead. A tear slipped down her cheek. Rasa must not see the tears. Myriam could not know how she trembled for her husband. Better she keep at the task at hand. She would manage this group of people, she would help them move to freedom, and only the night would hear her fears for Hamid. The night and a god who perhaps was not listening anyway.

Hamid

Hamid jerked his head around in one of the crowded squares in Van's downtown, strained to see who could have said it. A word. One word, but he had heard it, as if it had sailed on the wind to his ears. Only for his ears. *Isa!* Yes, he was sure of it. Someone had pronounced it. Jesus.

The market was jammed with bodies bobbing and moving slowly, methodically, picking up fruit, smelling, touching and checking for ripeness. The meat stands were covered with pig heads and cow torsos and flies, flies in this cold weather! He swatted as he passed the stall and leaned into the wind, hoping to hear it, the word, one word again.

He turned the corner and almost ran straight into a vendor. Perhaps in his early thirties, like Hamid, he was a tall, thin man with a black beard. He wore a turban, but Hamid could see he was not Turkish, not Middle Eastern or North African. The man met Hamid's stare, smiled, motioned with his eyes to the table sitting before him.

Hamid turned his head down, averted his eyes. This must be the man who had spoken the word, because there on the table were books! Books in Turkish, books in Farsi, the beautiful curves falling across the covers, the words there for anyone in the market to read: *The New Testament, The Holy Bible, The Children's Bible, The Life of Christ.*

He looked again, and before he could stop himself he had reached out and touched the same book that Rasa had held on that fateful day. The Ingil. His heart pinched, the deep ache came over him. Rasa. Little Rasa with her eyes shining, and clutching the New Testament as if it were life itself.

The man was busying himself with a carton at his feet, as if he knew too much attention would frighten Hamid away. Slowly Hamid held out the Ingil toward the man, his hands trembling. Could this be a trap?

"Greetings in the name of Christ," the man whispered in Farsi. "You know this book?"

Hamid tried to speak, the weariness of the trip overwhelming him, his throat parched. "I fled," he scratched out. "I had to flee because of this book." He felt his knees buckle. "To save my family, I fled."

Now the horror and fatigue of these months came over him, and he felt the sky swirling around him. He reached out to balance himself on the table stand, but missed. The book fell from his hand, landing with a soft pat in the sand, and then he was falling and the turbaned man had risen, thrusting out his arms as he leaned across the table to catch Hamid in his arms.

"Do not be afraid. I will help you," Hamid heard him whisper as he closed his eyes and the swirling sped up, and then . . . nothing.

CHAPTER 5

Tracie

I waited outside the little hotel office in Innsbruck while Aunt Bobbie spoke with the doctor in Atlanta, waited with my fingers crossed and a lump in my throat. I peeked through the little window in the door twice, saw Bobbie talking animatedly with her hands, saw her wrinkled brow, her nodding head, and the way she collapsed on the sofa. That's when my heart really flitted. But at last she emerged from the office and announced, "We can go!"

"He said it's okay?"

"Not exactly. He gave me a piece of his mind and then I gave him a piece of mine, and in the end we came to an understanding."

"Which was?"

"'All right, Miss Blake. There is nothing I can do from here other than warn you. Please promise you will have a biweekly check of blood pressure, follow the diet restrictions, use the cane, et cetera, et cetera.'" Bobbie rolled her eyes and laughed her confident-sounding Bobbie laugh, and she looked as fresh and strong and robust as always. She climbed into the passenger's seat of the rental car and concluded, "What could he say, after all? It's my life, and I'm a grown woman."

I wished she hadn't said that. It carried a hint of fatalism.

The drive from Innsbruck to Vienna was like a revisiting of my high school days. Bobbie and I sang all the silly songs we both knew, we shared gossip, we gasped at the beauty of the Austrian Alps. I'd needed a distraction from being dumped by Neil and from questions about my dreams of a future in musical theatre. Austria might be home of *The Sound of Music,* but it was far enough away from the sounds of my former life to let me put that other world out of my mind for the time being.

"So tell me about these refugees we'll be meeting," I said. "You said they're coming from the Middle East. Where exactly, and why?"

"From Iran and Iraq and Afghanistan and Chechnya. Like all refugees, they're pursuing a dream for something better. They're fleeing an oppressive government that has threatened their lives. Some bring their whole families, but many men, husbands or sons, come alone and hope to someday bring the rest of their families to freedom."

"And what happens to them when they get to Europe?"

"Ah, that depends upon which country they land in. In Athens they're on the streets, no government aid, no housing. Here in Austria they become part of the complicated bureaucracy—red tape that can take years and sometimes ends in deportation or prison or even death." She gave a little shrug. "But there are happy endings too—many are eventually granted asylum.

"The team that works at The Oasis now is made up of two single women from America, two American families, and one Australian family." Bobbie proceeded to name them all. "And there are many volunteers from the Austrian churches who help out."

"So you have kept up!" I accused. "You know all about this place."

"Of course I've kept up. I receive every team member's prayer letter. I haven't been back, but I've stayed a part of the team through prayer. As are many other ladies at New Dawn Church. The Prayer Band prays weekly for them all."

I rolled my eyes, but Bobbie didn't see. *Prayer letters*, a missionary term if ever there was one. When I was little—before my father died—I looked forward to Aunt Bobbie's quarterly reports about what was going on in Austria. I read them over and over again, almost like a serial novel.

I also knew about the women who called themselves the Prayer Band. They met every Monday morning to pray for different missionaries around the world. Some of those women were probably praying for Bobbie before I was even born, back when she first left for Austria. Like Peggy Milner, a classy lady in spite of being over ninety. She was a missionary herself once, in China, of all places, and had to leave when all the missionaries were kicked out a long time ago. Bobbie had her over to our house a lot of times when I was little, and I hung on her stories, too.

Those women had prayed for Bobbie as she smuggled Bibles—that I knew for sure—and I imagined they prayed for her and the rest of the team when they started meeting with the refugees. So when Bobbie moved back to Atlanta, I suppose it was only natural for her to join the Prayer Band.

I had no interest in that group of ladies anymore, but as I drove along the highways in the little Peugeot we'd rented in Innsbruck, with the mountains in the distance, I suddenly felt very interested once again in the life Bobbie had lived in Vienna so long ago.

I'd been imagining the Spanish Riding School and Lipizzaner stallions leaping and pirouetting in the air . . . music of Mozart and Bach and Beethoven playing at the Opera House . . . sitting in a sidewalk café eating a Sacher Torte.

But here we were in a small village on the outskirts of Vienna, and looming before us was a massive building surrounded by vineyards on every side.

"That's it," Bobbie said, as I slowed the car. "The Government Refugee Housing Center."

"It's huge. And, I don't know, imposing. It's got a certain beauty about it."

"Don't be fooled by the appearance. Inside is squalor." Bobbie squished up her nose.

We twisted along the little side road beside a high red brick wall that surrounded the refugee compound, and at the second intersection, Bobbie closed her eyes for a half a second. "Turn here!" she said. "Right! Now left! Ah, we're heading in the right direction, yes, I remember."

A few minutes later I pulled the car in front of a two-story cream-colored building with a long storefront window and two glass doors. Above the doorway was a large Plexiglas sign that held a simple green palm tree and two words in bright blue: *The Oasis.*

We rang the bell, and after a short wait a slender woman in a blue sweatshirt and jeans appeared at the door. She took one look, let out a stifled scream, and opened the door to envelop Bobbie in her arms. "We heard you were coming, but we didn't quite believe it!" she said, laughing and crying at once. "Oh, Bobbie!"

Bobbie was crying too, and watching the two women embrace, I think I felt a tiny stab of jealousy. As if I finally realized that long ago, my aunt had lived a completely different life and her stories were true. She had another family in

Vienna.

Bobbie introduced us, and Carol gave me a warm welcome and encouraged us to come back at seven for a "coffee house" that evening. We got back in the car, and after a ten-minute drive arrived at a little hotel called Gasthaus Müller. Bobbie let out a contented sigh. "It looks the same," and she explained it was, in fact, run by Christians who were also involved in ministry at The Oasis.

To me, it looked like a cozy bed-and-breakfast, clean and inviting, with light green stuccoed walls and window boxes filled with pansies and primroses. A young woman that Bobbie didn't seem to know checked us in and gave us our key. Then we followed her up the polished wooden stairs and unpacked our belongings in our little room with its two single beds, each covered with a fresh white duvet. The walls were painted a soft yellow, the windows open to let in the fresh air, and the view was of vineyards and hills in the distance.

I left Bobbie in the room to take a short nap and went downstairs to a spacious room filled with a ping-pong table, bookshelves, an oversized couch in the corner, and a big-screen TV. I looked through the books and DVDs on the shelves, but what I wanted to know was how these people— these missionaries from all over the world—had come here and why. Why leave the comforts of America or Australia to come here—a beautiful land, sure, but one that was swamped with refugees?

Of course Aunt Bobbie wanted to go back to The Oasis that evening for the coffee house Carol had mentioned. When we pulled up, the street in front was crowded with Middle-Eastern-looking men waiting to get inside. Bobbie slithered right through the crowd and into the main room, with me holding on to her hand for dear life. More men were jammed inside, dozens of them, of every race and age, and a few women and children as well. Some sat at tables with cups of coffee and tea and little cookies. Some played cards or chess. In one corner a group of young men huddled together for a photo, all smiles. A cacophony of languages bombarded our ears; the only one I recognized was German. I half expected a bomb to go off, or someone to produce a knife and start slitting throats. And then maybe an angel would show up, like the ones in Bobbie's smuggling stories.

I glanced at my aunt to see how she was responding to the bedlam around us, and I couldn't believe the expression on her face: sheer happiness. She headed to the main room and immediately squatted down next to a little girl and began talking to her in what I supposed was her native tongue. The little girl giggled at first at Bobbie's rusty attempts, then happily took Bobbie's hand and led her to a table where they both sat down.

And Aunt Bobbie was glowing, her eyes lit up like an angel's, lost in the wonder of her former life.

I was still staring at this scene, when I heard Bobbie call out, "Oh, there's Julie!"

The woman she pointed out was a small bundle of energy. As I looked, I saw her spot Bobbie, and her face brightened. I prepared for another teary reunion, but Julie held up a finger. She paused her conversation with several young Iranian men just long enough to flit toward us and say, "Bobbie, welcome! Can you pray?"

That was her greeting after not seeing each other for how many years? *Can you pray?* I'm sure my jaw dropped.

Bobbie didn't seem to think anything was odd. She took my arm and led me around the mass confusion toward a bar where the coffee and tea were dispensed. Through a small pass-through window, we could see into the kitchen, where several older women were washing and drying mugs.

"Would you mind helping out in there?" she asked me, and what could I say?

"Oookaaay, if you think it'll be all right."

"You'll be great!" Then we introduced ourselves to the women. One was from Iran, another from Australia, another from North Carolina, and the fourth was a Brit. A little United Nations.

Bobbie said, "I'll be back in a little while. You'll be fine with these ladies," and disappeared. To *pray*, I guessed. *Really, Aunt Bobbie?*

Carol, the slender woman—around Bobbie's age—who had greeted my aunt with such emotion earlier in the day, gladly received me after Aunt Bobbie had volunteered me to help in the kitchen and serve coffee. "Coffeepot's here. We keep one brewing at all times. Soon as it's ready, fill the cups and start another. Strong. They like it very strong."

I set about my task, thankful to hide behind the counter—as if it would protect me in case one of the men stood up in the midst of a chess game and declared, "Jihad!"

The men were dirty. Some smoked. Very few smiled. But my imagination notwithstanding, they didn't look violent. At one point, three young men left the coffee bar area and followed one of the missionary workers, a jovial blond-haired man named Tom, through a door that led into the back part of The Oasis.

"Where are they going?" I whispered to Carol, afraid of some grisly punishment.

"They're going to watch a movie about the life of Jesus in their own language."

What a strange place this is, was all I could think.

Later, Bobbie appeared beside me with the woman she had called Julie, who looked to be in her late sixties at least. She had a matter-of-fact way about her, reminding me of a lieutenant managing his troops. After all, she'd whispered *Pray* to Bobbie, and my strong-willed aunt had immediately melted into submission.

Now Julie announced to us, "You've got to see this. Unbelievable!" She led us through a hall behind the kitchen area, up some stairs and into a small room filled with at least twenty men, sitting close together on a mishmash of old chairs. Julie nodded to a middle-aged man who was standing in the front of the room, speaking eloquently in a language I did not know.

"He's an Iranian evangelist," Julie said. "He's explaining the Gospel to them, but they are afraid—afraid of what the others will say. Afraid of being accused. Yet some listen with hungry hearts."

Evidently Julie thought I was as fervent as Bobbie about this faith stuff because she kept looking back and forth at both of us, her countenance fairly glowing.

I watched a young man with dyed yellow hair, his jeans too big on him, his T-shirt so tight, his eyes straying to mine, meeting mine, looking down, looking up. A thousand questions in those eyes. I felt my face get beet-red.

"The one in the white coat with the scarf is Kameel," Julie whispered. "He and his wife met Isa in Iran, and they had such a strong witness for Him there. When she was diagnosed with cancer, they came to Austria for help. She died a few months ago, but he lives on here to share . . . "

Bobbie turned away quickly, the delight on her face momentarily overshadowed by something . . . Ah, that one word. *Cancer.* Seeking to change the subject, I whispered, "Aunt Bobbie, who in the world is Isa?"

That caused her to smile, blue eyes twinkling. "Isa is the name Muslims use for Jesus. Isa al Masi."

The smile faded and the tremors began.

"Thanks, Julie, for showing us this . . . this interesting meeting," I said, too quickly. I took Bobbie by the elbow, led her down the stairs, and seated her in an overstuffed chair in a little room off the back of the kitchen.

"You're tired. Worn out. It's time to go home." I tried to make my voice as authoritative as Julie's.

Bobbie was rubbing one hand over the other. "It's just so many memories." She paused, took a deep breath. The tremors subsided. "Hard memories and good memories, Trace. Every space on these three floors, these rooms, every possible inch is crowded with people straining to hear truth. They hear it through the Jesus film, through that evangelist upstairs, but also as two of the volunteers play Uno with a group of teenaged boys."

I saw tears glisten in Bobbie's eyes.

"Did you notice that table in the far corner of the main room? Grown men are coloring, Tracie. Grown men. Coloring with crayons and pencils and writing words of hope in beautiful Farsi script."

I perched on the side of her oversized chair and gave her hand a soft squeeze. "Yeah. I saw them. I've gotta admit that this place is very, very . . . different. And good grief! All the languages. Do you recognize some of them?"

She nodded. "Most of them. Someone is speaking Urdo in the hallway, and I heard several ladies babbling in Chechen in a back room, and upstairs you heard the evangelist talking in Farsi. And Serbian and Kosovo gypsies, Kurds, Iraqis, North Africans, and Iranian families are all playing games in the main room and drinking coffee and tea."

"A real melting pot!" was all I could think to say.

"Yes, where everyone seems so needy, so helpless, yet strong. Suspicious, and yet hopeful."

Bobbie stood up and pronounced, "I feel great now," and launched out into the crowded main room, laughing with a fellow missionary named JoAnn and then moving to a corner of the room where several burka-clad women were huddled. She began talking with her hands, leaning in to listen to these women and then every once in a while nodding enthusiastically and reaching and signing.

If I had not known the extent of the disease and what it had already done to my aunt's body, I would have sworn that Bobbie Blake was the picture of perfect health. At any rate, despite the disease, she radiated a joy I hadn't seen on her face for a while, as if this place in the midst of the vineyards in a village outside Vienna was the one place she wanted to be. Yes, it looked to me like Bobbie Blake had indeed come home.

I left Aunt Bobbie in the large room and went back into the kitchen to help when a young man came over to me with a tray of dirty dishes.

"Hello," he said in English, his accent thick. He definitely looked Middle Eastern with copper skin and thick black hair. "My name is Naseef."

I nodded, my throat dry, suddenly aware that the other women were all out in the main room doing other things.

"Your name?"

I cleared my throat. "Tracie," I barely got out.

"You are new here? New missionary to Oasis?"

I knit my brow, deciphering his words. "Oh, no. No, not at all. I mean, yes, yes, I'm new here, just visiting. I'm not a missionary."

"Ah. But you are from America?"

"Ye-es," I said, afraid he would begin begging me to help him find a way to get to the land of the free and the home of the brave.

"Where in America?"

I liked the way he pronounced it a-mer-EEE-ca. "The southeast. Atlanta."

He nodded and smiled. "Atlanta, Coca-Cola!"

I laughed. "Yes. Where are you from?"

"Iran. You know Iran?"

The knot in my throat again. Oh, yes, I knew Iran. The

country of the crazed Ayatollah, the country that beheaded women who didn't wear the veil. I nodded.

"I had to leave my country." He now stood beside me with a whole tray of dirty dishes and was putting them into the soapy water.

He seemed so completely at ease that I asked, "Do you work here?"

"I volunteer. I cook." He smiled again, and I felt something melting in my heart. "I wash and you dry, okay?" He pointed to a stack of dishtowels on a drying rack beside the sink.

"Okay."

So we washed and dried the cups and saucers together, and while his arms were stuck in the soapy water, he told me his story. He had grown up in a good Muslim family. "I was doing all the things that were expected of me as a Muslim. I had a job as a chef at a hotel in the center of Tehran."

"You cooked!" I said and laughed, and he laughed too.

One day, as he was walking home he got caught up in the midst of a student protest at Tehran University. Forced off the campus for striking, hundreds of students had spilled out into the streets where the police could arrest them. Over five hundred students were arrested that day, along with Naseef, who had simply been at the wrong place at the wrong time.

"We were put into a prison—the men separated from the women—left in a dark room with only bread to eat. We had no idea where we were." He flicked soapy water on the counter and wiped it with a rag, then plunged his hands back into the sink. "The policeman who came to our cell laughed at us and asked which we preferred—to be beaten in the head or have our fingernails pulled off."

"No!" I said so loudly that I surprised Naseef.

"Yes. The religious police are very cruel. It is against the law in my country to believe other than how the government believes. These students were protesting. It is against the law.

"Day after day they took students to be interrogated. Some died, others ended up in the hospital for months, from severe trauma. I will not say the details. Too terrible." He shook his head, eyes down, shoulders slumped. "As I waited in that putrid prison, I asked God, 'Why? I've been a good Muslim and was just in the wrong place. It wasn't my fault. What have I done wrong?'"

The way Naseef talked, I could tell he had told his story many times before.

"Perhaps you do not want to hear more. I am sorry. It is not nice. You are a visitor."

"No, don't stop. I want to hear, Naseef."

I got a pinching in my chest as I imagined the terrifying wait before he was taken in for interrogation, and then my eyes stung with tears as he described the seven hours of torture, the cruelty, the way the sun had been shining through the window when he arrived in that room and by the time they were through it was dark. Because Naseef had nothing valuable to share, the interrogator turned on him at last in rage and beat him in the head with a board. He lost consciousness, and when he woke up he was in a hospital.

"Days passed at the hospital with me coming in and out of consciousness. They would let me contact no one. But finally I found a way to get a hold of my parents." He set the last clean cup in the rack and dried his hands. "My parents were allowed in the prison because I wasn't part of the uprising. They paid a great deal of money to lawyers, but I didn't receive justice. In the end, the safest thing for me to do was to flee the country. Through it all, I prayed to God to help me.

"The night before I left, I had a dream. A dream of light, a dream of a voice telling me that he was the way. 'The way to what?' I asked again and again. "I left Iran for Turkey. A long, hard trip."

He diverted his eyes as if it was too difficult to remember. I couldn't imagine anything being worse than the torture he had already endured. He turned and opened cabinets on the far side of the kitchen and began to stack the cups methodically. When he turned back around, he was staring at me with a huge grin on his face. "That is when I first heard of Jesus!"

His eyes were sparkling and he had an expectant look, as if he thought I was going to smile and shout hallelujah. I simply listened.

"I met an Iranian who invited me to a church. I had of course never been to a church. It is forbidden in Iran for a Muslim to enter a Christian church. It would cost your life. But in Turkey I went to this church. I wanted to see it, and there I met Christians for the first time. Even Iranian Christians! And to see them worship—they were so nice, so happy. They worshiped out of love and with joy. This was so different from the Muslim way of worshiping—out of fear and duty. I went back to this church many times. I found a job as a cook in Istanbul, and I went to the church.

"But my Muslim roommates had become suspicious of where I was going on Sundays, and one week they followed me. When I returned from the church, they mocked me and beat me. I knew they would kill me if I went back to that church, but I was so eager to hear the truth about Jesus."

There was such passion in Naseef's voice. He talked about Jesus as if he were a superstar or a star quarterback.

"So I left my life in Turkey. I traveled hard time and got to Bulgaria. You know?"

I blushed, admitting to myself that I was not quite sure where Iran was, even, or how exactly it was connected to Turkey or Turkey to Bulgaria.

Just then Carol came back into the kitchen. "Oh, Naseef. Thank you for helping. I see you've met Bobbie's niece, Tracie. Thank you both for cleaning up." She smiled at me. "Bobbie is looking for you. We'll be closing The Oasis in just a few minutes."

"Thanks, Carol. Tell her I'll be right out." Naseef started to follow Carol out into the main room, but I caught up with him. "And then what?" I asked, surprising myself with how eager I was to hear the rest of his story.

He turned back. "I had heard that there were ways to get to England from Bulgaria, and that there were jobs in England. But by the time I arrived in Bulgaria, it was just after 9-11, and the laws had changed. No refugees allowed into England." He shrugged, hands out to his side, then began stacking chairs against the walls. I copied him. "And so I walked. I walked and walked and walked, for seven months, through five countries, until I arrived here."

"Tracie! There you are! Carol said you've been washing all the dishes. Good for you. Are you ready to leave?" Bobbie's face was shining.

"Almost. Just one minute." I grabbed another chair and added it to Naseef's stack.

"At the Refugee Housing Center I heard about this place, The Oasis, and that there were kind people who gave clothes and drinks and showed movies. They were Christians. And so I came here." He nodded to the crowded room, toward Bobbie, who was now deep in discussion with Julie, the woman who had asked her to pray. "I came here and received an Ingil in my language, in Farsi."

"Ingil?"

"New Testament. I read it; I watched the movie of Jesus's life; I studied the Bible. Then I knew why I had left my country. To find Him here."

Naseef was smiling a wide smile, showing his teeth in the midst of his olive skin. He looked as if he were telling me that he'd won the lottery.

"I was baptized, and now I help out here. I cook, I serve the drinks, I translate for my people, for I have learned English. I attend the Iranian church in town. And I await asylum. I have not seen my parents for three years. I cannot go home. But I have a new country. I am a citizen of heaven, and I have found peace."

That night I couldn't sleep. I replayed scenes at the coffee house in my mind, but it was Naseef's story that kept me wide awake. After everyone else left, Carol had said to Bobbie and me, "He's a real sweetie, Naseef. He has a hole in his head from where he was beaten in the Iranian prison and he suffers from horrible headaches. But he is faithful. He shows up. Sometimes he fixes us specialties from his region."

"How does he live?" I asked. "Does he have an income?"

"The Austrian government provides him with a very small stipend and a room in a private residence."

I had heard one refugee's story, but I was pretty sure that the other stories of all those people in that crowded room were equally as difficult. And the thing that kept ringing in my ears was the joy that Naseef expressed at finding faith in Christ.

On one hand, I believed him—I mean, he certainly looked radiant—but on the other, I just couldn't buy it. His life was really pretty pitiful. Was he serious when he said that Christ was everything to him? Did he truly have peace in spite of his circumstances?

I did not want to feel a stirring in my spirit now. I did not want to let myself care about any of these people, the refugees, or the missionaries, or the volunteers. I didn't regret coming, because everything on this trip was for my Aunt Bobbie. And clearly, she was overjoyed to be here.

Just don't go rubbing off on me, I challenged the night. I didn't want God to speak to me, either through a dream or through a smiling refugee. Certainly not through a vision. He had done that once and it had ruined my life. I just wanted Him to leave me alone.

CHAPTER 6

Hamid

"Second-degree frostbite and severe malnutrition."

Hamid heard the English words floating somewhere in the fog. Where was he? Who were the people crowded around this bed where he lay? He struggled to open his eyes, but everything swirled around him.

The voice spoke again. "They show up here in this condition, half dead, starving, frozen. They think they have found freedom, but they don't know it is not safe here."

Not safe here! Visions of the last weeks of flight, of dogs and police and cold. Of Rasheed . . . Rasheed! He must let Rasheed know where he was.

"Can you keep him for a day or two? No doubt he is housed in the worst room in a squalid hotel. I've seen these, believe me. They call on me when it is too late."

Hamid wanted to stay awake, to hear this man, to ask questions, but he was slipping, slipping . . .

He awoke later and struggled again to open his eyes. This time the room did not move in his vision. He was lying on a single bed in a small room with white walls. He squinted and focused on two bright paintings on the opposite wall. White buildings, some with flat roofs, others with rounded roofs, the sea, turquoise blue. Then he remembered. He was in Turkey! No more terror in his soul as he crept behind the smuggler. They had crossed the border into Turkey, outrun the dogs and the police. More walking until he thought his feet would literally fall off. And then the hotel. The suspicious look from the hotel manager, the smuggler explaining in his coded language. Hamid handing over the money. He and Rasheed being led to a room in the basement with peeling paint and a broken window. Filthy. But safe.

They don't know it is not safe here.

Hamid struggled to sit up in bed, and as he did so, a young woman appeared in the opened doorway. "Ah, you're awake! I was worried you would never wake up!" She spoke in English, with an American accent. "Do you understand me?"

Hamid nodded.

She was pretty, with long wavy brown hair; she wore Western dress and was cradling a baby in her arms.

She came into the room and stood a respectful distance away from his bed. "I've made you some soup. Do you think you can eat a little now?"

"Thank you, yes. Eat," he murmured. Then, "Where am I?"

She placed the baby over her shoulder, patting its back. "You're in Van, Turkey. You fainted at the Medina. My husband brought you to our house. The doctor came and gave us medicine. If you rest, you will get better."

She smiled. He expected to see suspicion and fear in her eyes, but she radiated peace. "My husband—Jim—is gone for now. He'll be back soon. I'm Anna. What is your name?"

"Hamid. Hamid." He reached for his coat, but he was wearing someone else's clothes. Panic surged through him. His backpack, his papers, his money!

"The doctor changed you to clean warm clothes. Yours are over there." She motioned with her eyes to where his ragged clothes hung over a chair in the corner of the room. "I'll wash them if you wish. I have done nothing yet."

The way she looked at him he knew they had found the money and left it there. His heartbeat calmed. He felt the dizziness returning.

"Let me get you the soup. I just need to put the baby down, and I'll be back in a moment."

"Thank you," Hamid murmured as the room spun round and round. He sank back down into the bed and slept.

Hamid sat up in bed, his back resting against the wall. Slowly he spooned the soup into his mouth. It tasted like paradise! He took a bite of bread, chewed, so slowly, swallowed. The young woman, Anna, had moved the chair with his clothes on it beside the bed. Before he took the first bite of soup, he inspected the pockets, found the money that was sewn in different places. His papers were safe. The little radio was tucked into the backpack with the papers. He ate in silence.

Anna came back into the room. "There you go, Hamid! Good, you're eating. You'll get your strength back soon, I'm sure."

He tried to smile, but his lips felt chapped on his face. Even the way he held the spoon in his hands seemed so unfamiliar.

"You have frostbite. The doctor said it may take a while to get the feeling back in your hands and feet, but he said it will come."

Hamid finished the soup and set the bowl back on the

little tray table. "Very good. Thank you."

"I'll get you some more."

He could not understand this woman. She didn't ask for money, didn't talk gruffly. Then he remembered . . . the Medina. He had left Rasheed asleep in the hotel room and ventured out to the market to buy some food. And then he had heard the word. *Isa!* The bearded man at the market. Yes, he was in the home of Christians. He should be afraid, as he had been when he'd stepped inside his neighbors' home in Iran, but he was too weak and tired to feel afraid.

"Children?" he asked softly, and Anna smiled.

"Yes. We have three. William is eight. Jacob is six. And you've seen baby Lilly. She's almost six months."

"Baby," he repeated. "Baby."

"Do you have a family, Hamid?"

He nodded, then reached for his coat. He fumbled in the pockets and brought out the crumpled photo. "Alaleh, my wife. Daughter—Rasa." He pointed to their smiling faces.

"They are beautiful."

"And baby. Maybe baby now."

"Your wife was expecting a baby when you . . . left?"

Hamid nodded.

"And could be here now?"

He nodded again.

"You must call her then. Call and see if she is well."

He shook his head slowly. "No phone."

"You will call on our phone."

What a strange woman! "No, thank you." He would not put her family at risk, no matter how he longed to hear Alaleh's voice, to be assured she and Rasa were safe, that the baby had come. Or perhaps he was simply terrified to call. If the secret police had come, had found them, had done the unthinkable?

Anna came to his bedside, reached down and took the

empty bowl. "Rest now, Hamid. When Jim gets back, he will explain it all to you. You are not the first sick man who has come here and needed to call home. It will be okay." She left the room and closed the door softly behind her.

Hamid sank again into sleep, hearing Anna's kind words. *It will be okay.*

Hamid waited, hardly daring to breathe, listening to the ring on the other end. Jim had put the phone in his trembling hands, reassured him, waited while the call went through and then slipped quietly through the door.

A sound of crackling, then a quavering "Hello?"

"Alaleh!"

His wife began to weep. "You are alive. Oh, my Hamid. Where are you?" She spoke in a whisper, as if she feared the very walls would betray them.

"I've made it to Turkey. I am safe." He didn't try to explain further. "And you, my Alaleh, how are you? Where are you?"

"We are hiding with Noyemi's family. The police came for us on the night of your son's birth."

"A son?"

More crackling. He feared the connection would be cut off.

"Yes. Your son was born in the secret room with the police searching for us. His name is Omid and he is perfect. Your mother delivered him and your daughter saved my life."

She whispered the story in a rush, and then for a moment there were only the sounds of both Alaleh and Hamid weeping softly.

"I will get to Austria," he said. "And I will get everything you need so you can join me. Can you keep hiding for now? Is it safe?"

"Yes, for now. These Christians are good people. They will help us get away. Pray for us, Hamid."

"I pray every day. All day. I love you, Alaleh. I love you.

Give my love to Rasa and my mother and my son. Omid."

Hamid could not explain his feelings. Relief, delight, urgency, and fear. All wrapped into one confused package. He had a son. A healthy baby boy. But there was danger for all of them. His family could not flee Iran as he had, on the back of horses and running from dogs. But they must flee.

He relived the joy of hearing Alaleh's voice. He would like to stay in this warm place a little longer, but surely Rasheed was worried, perhaps convinced that after all the secret police had found him and sent him back into the Iranian mountains.

The stabbing in his toes caused great pain. His fingers were moving more nimbly. He needed to leave.

A rap sounded on the door, and the tall, thin man named Jim came into the room. "Hello, Hamid. It's good to see you awake again."

"Thank you for bringing me here. For food, for the phone call. Now I must go. My friend will be worried."

"You were not traveling alone?"

"I came with a friend, Rasheed. We are staying together." How much could he reveal to this stranger?

"Where can I find Rasheed? I'll let him know that you are well."

"It is best I go. He will be afraid if he sees you."

Jim pulled up a chair and sat down next to Hamid. "When I saw you at the Medina, you said you were fleeing your country because of the Ingil. Do you know Isa al Masi?"

Hamid considered the question. Did he know Jesus? He knew that every time he heard the stories on the radio, his heart burned with hope. He knew his daughter believed. He knew that he had been warned in a dream to flee, and he thought that warning came from Isa. But did he know him? Man could not know God. He shook his head.

"Would you like to tell me your story, Hamid?" Jim asked, and the kindness in his voice melted Hamid's heart. "The God we trust and serve is interested in every individual. Your story is an important part of our God's bigger story. It fits in, no matter how hard and difficult it has been."

His story? What could he say? Was it safe to talk? Instead, Hamid asked, "Where are you from? Why are you here?"

"We're Americans, originally from the South. I work as an engineer in Van. Anna and I came here three years ago after living in Austria for five years."

He was staring so intently at Hamid that Hamid looked away. Austria! The country where Hamid hoped to find asylum.

"We worked there among refugees in a camp outside of Vienna. We heard many, many stories of the refugees who were escaping from Iran and Afghanistan, and the difficulty they had even after they reached Turkey. So we came here to help. Where we can. When we can. On Saturdays I have a little stand at the marketplace—you know, the Medina. I was very happy to meet you there."

"How do you help refugees?"

"We offer a free meal at the community center once a week. We teach English lessons; we help with official papers. And for those who are interested, we read the Ingil together. I answer questions."

Hamid felt it again, a burning in his soul, a hopefulness. He decided to trust this strange man.

"You lived in Austria. That is where I am headed, to find asylum for my wife and children. I hope." Then he whispered, "I had to leave Iran because my little daughter had been given an Ingil. I hated the book, but I fled to protect my family. But on the radio I heard a program about Isa. For all the weeks I have traveled I have heard about Isa on my radio, and I wonder if it is true."

Before Jim could reply, Hamid hurried on. "I would like to read the Ingil with you, but I'm afraid. And my friend Rasheed will be worried for me."

"Let me assure Rasheed that you are safe and will be back soon. Tomorrow evening. Then we can look at the Ingil together tonight, if you wish."

Hamid hesitated, then he shrugged. "You will find him at the New Moon Hotel. Do you know it?"

"I'll find it. No worries."

When Jim returned later that evening, he reported simply, "I have communicated to Rasheed that you are very weak, but getting stronger. I took him some food. He was very relieved to know you are alive. I told you you will come back tomorrow."

Hamid talked with Jim until deep in the night, until his fatigue overtook his curiosity and sleep forced itself on him. They talked of the Ingil, of Isa, of Austria and asylum. So many words. And Jim explained how to get papers in Van. He was kind and serious. And realistic. He knew the refugee stories, knew where help could be found, but also knew that Hamid's difficult journey was not over yet.

"And what of my wife and children and mother? How long until I receive asylum in Austria?"

For this the American had no answer. "It is different every time. First you must get stronger. Then you and Rasheed can travel through Bulgaria towards Austria."

Hamid dreamed that night of Austria with its pure white mountains and fresh, pristine air and the flowers tumbling over the wooden balconies. He had seen photos on the Internet and from Jalil. He had heard of the beauty and peace in this country.

He dreamed of it and then, in his dreams, there was Jim. His face was not soft and kind. His face was terrified. *Run,*

Hamid! Run! It is not safe here!

Hamid woke in a sweat, felt the hammering of his heart, and reached for a glass of water. He could not interpret dreams, but one thing he knew. His journey was far from over, and it would be a long, long time before he met his infant son.

CHAPTER 7

Amir

*I*n the ancient little church in Linz, Amir sat on the front row and listened as a young refugee gave his testimony. Leaving family, leaving everything. The escape in the night, the flight through the mountains, the cold, the fear, the unknown, the police checks, the long, long journey . . . Amir listened, and wiped tears away with the corner of his sleeve. He knew this young man, Josef, very well. It was Amir who had met him on the first night he came to The Oasis in Traiskirchen. Amir who had contacted the church here in Linz, when Josef had received word that he was to be transferred to this city. Amir had begged, practically on his knees, that the little church of fifty-three faithful worshipers allow an Iranian refugee, fresh on Austrian soil, to live in the parsonage apartment of the hundred-year-old church.

"For three months. Just three months. Please. I will watch out for him," Amir had assured the congregation.

Three months had turned into three years, and these dear faithful people, many old and withered, had welcomed Josef into the apartment, welcomed him into their homes, and eventually, welcomed him into their faith. Faith in the mighty God, in Isa al Masi.

No one in the church spoke Farsi, so for weeks it had been simply communication in sign language until Amir came for a visit and brought a Bible in Farsi. Then Gustav, one of the elders in the church, had taken to studying the Bible with Josef. Gustav read in German, Josef followed in Farsi, and somehow they communicated.

Josef's testimony was so familiar, Amir could have recited it by heart, for his escape all those years ago was through the same route. The Refugee Highway, some called it. The Highway from Hell, said others who had traveled its tortuous path.

Josef finished talking, and Gustav stood beside him. Dear Gustav, dressed in his Sunday best, his white hair abundant, his face weathered by eighty years of life in the Austrian Alps. He cleared his throat. His blue eyes, watery with age, turned up to the ceiling, turned up to his God. "We praise you, our heavenly Father, for who you are, God of the Alps, God of snow and ice, of the winter wind and the spring wildflowers. God of the earth. God of Josef."

Gustav was a poet in his heart, as was Amir. The prayer continued, beautiful and melodic, but completely heartfelt. No show in old Gustav's words. Just what flowed from his heart. Jesus said it was from the heart that proceeded the evil—or the good. And good had been coming out of this old man's heart for many decades, beaten and flattened and nurtured and molded by years and years of hard work, hard hits, and deep faith.

Now three other men, all elders, gathered around Josef, whose face was beaming. This was his send-off. Just like in the Book of Acts. The elders were praying, laying hands on him and sending him on a mission.

Josef had a heart for the Afghani people. His desire for the past years had never waned, as he lived in that little apartment beside the church, as he swept and cleaned the church until it shone, as he lifted heavy boxes of groceries at the Skop store for nine hours a day, six days a week. Burning in his soul was the truth, and that truth he must share with his Afghani brothers and sisters, no matter the danger. No matter that he, an Iranian, would be suspect from the moment he stepped on Afghan soil. It burned there! He would go.

Gustav called Amir up to the front. "Amir, you have walked the path to freedom like Josef. Come and pray for him in his language."

Amir stood beside Josef and looked out at the people. Where three years ago there had been fifty-three parishioners, mostly elderly, all Austrian, now the room was crowded with over a hundred people of different colors, races, and ages. Four or five little children played in the aisles beside their mothers, women clad in long shawls and bright Iranian dresses.

One by one, other immigrants had found refuge at the church, had found kindness, had found Christ. Now there was an Iranian church that met on Sunday afternoons and, at times like this, on Sunday morning with the Austrian fellowship to worship, to celebrate, to pray. Such different cultures, such different lifestyles, but the same God. He had changed all of them—the Austrians who had learned to open their hearts to refugees, and the refugees who had learned to trust again, in people and in this new God, this God of compassion, mercy, and love.

"Josef." Now it was Werner, another elder, who spoke. "You have been called to go to a dangerous land. You will be leaving everything, all your material goods, everything you have to go into this land. Are you ready?"

Josef, young, diminutive, strong, serious, face still beaming, nodded vigorously. "Yes, I am ready." He removed his jacket and held it out to the congregation. "This jacket is my only possession. You may have it, if you would like. I am ready."

Amir left Linz late in the evening, driving back to his village of Mauthausen an hour south. His heart was full tonight as the moon lit the roadway, beaming down its light in the stark cold night. It had begun all those years ago, in 1989, when Amir, at twenty-three, had been sent away from Traiskirchen like Josef, with only the shirt on his back, a Bible in his hands, and hope in his heart. For the five previous months he had known something strong and good and pure. A fledgling ministry, a little coffee bar, serving up hot drinks and hope. An oasis. And he had known Jill. He thought of her now as he drove through the night. Jill with the black hair and the brightest blue eyes, filled with fun, adventure, life! She was a smuggler of Bibles when he met her, but soon thereafter the Iron Curtain began to be torn down in many Eastern European countries. As he left for Mauthausen, she settled into ministry at The Oasis in Traiskirchen. Sometimes her work brought her to his village.

"Jill! You came! So good to see you." He'd spoken in broken English or the German he was quickly learning. "I have missed you."

And Jill, eyes twinkling, glove-clad hand reaching to shake his, would answer in a very broken Farsi, "I'm so glad to see you too." And they would laugh at their garbled mix of languages. "You can call me Bobbie now," she would remind him. "The walls are down. No more smuggling."

But in his heart she was always Jill.

And so it continued. He got his asylum, became Austrian, found a job. By God's grace he helped to start the first Austrian-Iranian church, made up of the refugees who continued to stream in. And when he rode the little train to Traiskirchen and walked the short distance to The Oasis, Jill was always there, waiting, smiling, welcoming him.

He had been living in Mauthausen for five years when she told him about her plans for the upcoming summer, to go work at an orphanage in Romania as she had the two previous years. Amir didn't want to dwell on what had happened next. Their declared love, the trips with the orphans, their plans. And then the accident . . .

Afterwards Jill left, so suddenly. Fled, he thought in retrospect. That the death of her brother-in-law had coincided with the other horrible tragedy was strange, disturbing. How could a person live through two such life-altering events within the space of a few weeks? She had declared it was God's will for her to go back. He begged her to reconsider. But by that time she could hardly even look at him with her beautiful blue eyes.

She left, and in the twelve years since he had only received one letter from her. He had respected her silence, respected her last words to him in person and then repeated in the letter: *Please, Amir, if you love me, don't ever contact me again.*

He had died a hundred deaths by respecting her wish.

But he caught snippets of news about her from the others at The Oasis. He knew all about her life in Atlanta, caring for her older sister and her tribe of children. And he was pretty sure she knew all about him; she read the newsletters on the Internet, and she wrote to Julie and Carol.

And now she was back. Carol had called him last night with this news.

"Amir, I don't know how to say this, so I'll just blurt it out. Bobbie is here with her niece, for a week, maybe two. I . . . I thought you'd want to know."

What she didn't say, he also knew. Bobbie was very ill. She had inoperable cancer. This news had come through The Oasis grapevine to the church in Linz and into his village. Bobbie Blake was dying. He had literally felt intense physical pain wrench through him when he heard the news. And how he had argued with the Lord.

So Bobbie had come back for one last look at her life. Maybe, thought Amir as he drove through the night, maybe he could see her.

Lord, I promise I won't tell her I still love her. I won't try to be her poet again. Just let me see her.

And maybe, if he could see her, he could make that one wrong thing, that horrible hurt—maybe he could make it right again.

Bobbie

On our second day at Gasthaus Müller, I woke Tracie and announced my plans for the morning.

"Carol's got a group of young American exchange students coming to help out at the center. I told her we'd be at The Oasis bright and early to get lunch ready for them."

Tracie gave me a questioning look. "Surely Carol had all that planned out before you got here. She seems like a very organized sort of person."

I smiled sheepishly. "You're right, of course. I suppose the truth is I just can't wait to go back." I tossed a pillow at her. "But you can stay here in your pjs and watch DVDs all morning if you prefer."

She stretched and yawned. "No worries. Just give me thirty minutes to get a cup of coffee and some cereal. They do eat cereal in this country, don't they?"

When we arrived at The Oasis, Carol welcomed us inside where the group of college girls were sitting in chairs that last night had been occupied by refugees.

"The girls are on a study abroad program in France, but for the next two weeks they'll be helping out at The Oasis," Carol explained. "I'll let them introduce themselves."

In addition to the twelve young women, who were from a Christian university in Ohio and were studying in Lyon, France, there was a woman named Connie. She was a fifty-something American, petite, fashionable, and timid, and had joined the team at the last moment.

"Is Connie the team leader?" Tracie asked over lunch. Connie had disappeared from the room with another staff member to find the rest room.

"No, not at all. She's just an American who lives in Lyon," said a blonde named Dee. "We met her at an event at the church we've been attending in Lyon, and she seemed lonely."

"I think her husband travels all the time," added Alice, a skinny brunette.

"When she heard about our trip, she begged to come with us. Apparently she used to live in Vienna. So Carol gave her permission to come along, even though she's not officially a part of the team," Dee finished.

"I guess she needed to do something to feel good about herself, just like the rest of you," Tracie said. She gave a little chuckle, as though she was making a lighthearted remark.

Her comment was met with dead silence.

Tracie had always been a moody child. She was bright and talented and pretty—and responsible. And with five younger brothers, she knew better than to play the drama queen growing up. But when she left for college, I could see all the pent-up anger tumbling out. There were plenty of misunderstandings with girlfriends and tumultuous relationships with guys. It seemed to me that she was scrambling hard to find her place in the world, away from her family, but her family's baggage kept tripping her up. And though I'd tried to help her work through her stuff, Tracie was as stubborn as I was, and I knew she wasn't telling me everything.

I was embarrassed by her comment at the table, but I could hardly reprimand her. She wasn't a child. And while I knew that "ministry" was uncomfortable territory for her, I had never expected her to be rude. I could see on Carol's face that she was upset, and I wasn't surprised when she pulled me aside after lunch.

"You know all the hoops the short-termers have to jump through, Bobbie. I'm sure Tracie has reasons for her anger, but you have to admit they seem a bit 'light' compared to the refugees' stories." Her voice dropped. "Tracie is your niece, and I like her. We can bend the rules a little. But you'll have to help me figure this out."

I was thankful that Carol had planned a sightseeing trip for the whole team the following day, and I mentioned it to Tracie that night, when we were in our little room at Gasthaus Müller.

"Tracie, I thought we'd join the team for the day in Vienna tomorrow. A visit to the opera house, St. Stephen's Cathedral, and the Kunsthistorisches Museum. Then we'll eat dinner in a little town right outside Vienna to the north, about thirty minutes away. What do you say?"

"Sounds fine," she said, her legs drawn up under her.

I was planning to join the college girls—who were also staying at the guest house—downstairs for games, but Tracie had already changed into her pajamas. "Wouldn't you like to hang out with the others downstairs tonight? I saw Pictionary and Boggle on the shelf."

"No, dear Auntie, I do not want to 'hang out' with the other girls tonight." She winked at me. "I'm the introvert, remember? I need a little alone time." She brushed her hair back over her shoulders. "You go on down, Bobbie. I'm fine here reading my novel. Honest."

"Mad at me?" I asked.

"Nope."

"Mad at someone?"

"Maybe. Maybe mad that we Americans just think we can sweep in and make things better for anybody in the whole wide world."

I sat down beside her on the bed. "You're right, Trace. We do tend to act that way. We're born American, born wealthy, born elite. Whatever it is, we tend to feel entitled. That this life is due to us. It can be almost impossible to imagine the abject poverty and horror of other lives. When I first went to Austria I was filled with lofty ideas and a heart to serve, but I'd been raised in privilege. And then I got to the field. I saw the suffering of my Christian brothers and sisters behind the Iron Curtain, and later the suffering of the refugees, and it pierced me. I cried for days at my hard, entitled heart."

Tracie had put down her book. She leaned her head back against her pillow. "Yeah, we feel entitled, then we feel guilty, so we go on little trips to help out and make ourselves feel less entitled. I don't know, it just feels like a huge quantity of hypocrisy." She was staring at the ceiling. "And I've done it right along with everyone else."

"Good things to think about, Trace. But maybe it's not a black-or-white issue. Let's just say that I don't think The Oasis would have ever come into existence without the help of American money and short-term teams. They gutted the building and built it back little by little."

"Whatever," she said, still staring at the ceiling.

I got the message. "I think I'll head on down and see what the gang's up to." I gave her hand a squeeze. "Good night, Trace."

"Night, Aunt Bobbie." But she didn't look at me.

We played games in the lounge, and as I got to know the girls, I couldn't help but recall similar experiences I'd had with so many other short-term teams when I lived in Trai-skirchen. First they had come to transform an old apartment building into this guest house. Then they came and stayed here while they rehabbed the empty building that would eventually become The Oasis.

I understood Tracie's struggle—her comments weren't all misplaced—but that evening, as we laughed and played board games, I felt a deep thankfulness for this team and so many others who had given up a vacation to serve a ministry outside Vienna.

Around nine thirty Carol peeped her head in the door. "Just checking up on everyone before I head home."

"I thought you were already at your apartment and tucked in bed! Go home. I'll make sure these kids behave."

She smiled, and I noticed for the first time just how weary she looked. I got up and walked her to the front door. "You okay?"

She nodded. "You know—it's just jet lag."

"Jet lag? Where've you been?" I had been with her for two days and she'd never mentioned that she had just returned to Austria.

"I was back in the States for two weeks. My grandmother's funeral. I got back three days ago."

"My goodness, of course you're exhausted. Seriously, go home and get to bed."

She flashed me a smile. "You're a jewel. Oh, why can't you be here all the time, Bobs?"

She said what I'd been thinking for the past two days. Why couldn't I?

That night I lay awake for a while. I prayed for Carol, knowing without her saying it, some of what she was proba-bly experiencing. It was always wonderful to see friends and family, of course, but it was exhausting too, both physically from the jet lag and emotionally from the "reverse culture shock."

I remembered my first visit home to my church in Atlanta.

"Bobbie! Great to see you! How was Austria?" asked a friend of my parents. He'd known me practically since I was born.

"Oh, it was really amazing," I began.

"Yeah, the snow-covered Alps, the quaint villages, the music." A chuckle. "Tough life, but somebody has to do it." A smile. A pat on the back. "Great to see you again."

I stood planted in that hallway of the church I had grown up in and felt like a complete foreigner. People greeted me with smiles, sometimes a wrinkle of the brow. "Germany? No, France?"

"Austria."

"That's right. *The Sound of Music.* Rough life as a missionary! Anyway, we're glad you're back."

I couldn't say I hadn't been warned. *You'll feel as if all they want to hear is "Fine." No details, no explaining that you weren't touring Europe and singing Julie Andrews songs. They'd be happy for you to pick back up and join in their lives, but don't expect them to care too much about all you've been through.*

I was hiding in the bathroom sniffing and dabbing my eyes when Peggy Milner found me. I knew who she was—a "pillar of the church," a "prayer warrior," a widow. She was tall and thin, with her white hair pinned neatly in a bun. She wore a colorful skirt and a green silk blouse. In all the years that followed, I don't think I ever saw Peggy in pants.

"Bobbie! Bobbie Blake! I heard you'd returned from Austria." She gave me a quick hug, then stood back, held me by the shoulders, and surveyed me. "Oh, my dear child. When did you get in?"

"Friday, late afternoon."

"And this is your first time back at church."

I nodded.

"And you feel like you're on another planet."

I must have looked surprised.

She chuckled. "Coming back home, honey, can be harder than all the hard things you've been through overseas. People forget you've been gone, expect you to slip back into life as usual."

I began crying again. "They don't even care! They act as if I've been on a two-year vacation!"

She took me in her arms and held me tight. "They can't understand, honey. And many don't really have the time to care. But there are some who *do* care, and who *have been* praying for you."

Peggy invited me to attend the Monday morning Prayer Band and to share about my work in Austria.

So I went, every Monday for three months, and I told many of my stories. I survived that first furlough home because of the Prayer Band, and more specifically, because of Peggy Milner. She became my mentor, long before the word was in vogue. I learned that she had spent ten years as a missionary in China. We shared our stories, and I soaked up her wisdom.

When it was time for me to go back to Austria, after furlough, I listened again.

"Bobbie, give yourself three days of doing nothing. *Nothing*, you hear me? Remember how hard it was coming over? Jet lag is worse the other way. You're going to wish you were still here, now that you've finally found your place. You're going to feel the oppression—it's real. You're fighting in enemy territory and Satan isn't pleased. Expect it to be harsh; expect conflict with others. Give it time." Then she offered me a lifeline. "I promise to call you once a month, and we'll talk for thirty minutes. You understand?"

"But that will cost a fortune," I whispered.

Peggy smiled brightly. "I have connections! My son just started a phone card business—very reasonable."

And that was that.

Peggy was right, the fog of jet lag was much worse returning to Europe. It took me a full week before I could sleep through the night, and when I did, my sleep was filled with nightmares. During the day I literally felt a weight pressing down on me. I found myself getting into conflicts with teammates, and I listened with dread to scary stories of other missionaries being caught by the authorities in one Eastern European country.

My phone calls with Peggy kept me afloat.

Now, as Tracie slept in the bed beside mine in our little room in Gasthaus Müller, I tossed and turned for a while. I thought about Peggy, my dear, dear mentor, who at ninety-two was still my lifeline.

I fell asleep with a simple "Thanks, Lord," on my lips.

"Thanks for Austria, for The Oasis, for short-term teams, and the faithfulness of Carol and so many other long-term workers. Thanks for Tracie and all her doubts and questions. Thanks for another chance to experience this life that I loved and left."

And thank you for Amir. I let that thought slip into my mind as I drifted off to sleep.

CHAPTER 8

Keith

$\mathcal{T}$he sun was just coming up as Keith McDaniel climbed on his bike and began the thirty-minute ride to his office, bumping along the cobbled roads that twisted beside the canals, watching the little city of Amersfoort come to life. He loved the centuries-old brick homes, all connected, a stream of never-ending flats, each with its large bay windows with drapes opened for all the world to see. He loved the cheeses, the *pannenkoeken*, the canals, the art. He loved living in Holland.

He parked his bike outside the radio station where he worked as an engineer for World Wide Radio, went into his office, and settled into his morning routine. Coffee first, then e-mail. He opened a message from Jim Harris in Turkey.

Met a refugee, Hamid, just escaped from Iran, interested in Ingil, on his way to Austria. Advised route. Contact Oasis. Jim. PS Carries transistor and listens at 20h30.

He typed a one-word response: *Received.*

Their Internet connection was secure, hypersecure, but they still used few words and a few codes. Keith smiled to himself. Talk about networking. Jim in Van writing to Keith in Amersfoort, who would write to Julie in Traiskirchen, who would contact the Iranian pastor in Mauthausen who would get this Hamid in touch with other Iranian believers.

Keith had never aspired to write Bible studies or preach—those weren't his gifts. But to sit in an office and work with a bunch of frequencies? Now that he could do! He and his wife, Lindsey, had left Houston for Amersfoort seven years ago. The job was demanding, and exactly right for his skill set and introverted personality.

Apparently this Hamid had been listening to the messages of hope from an Iranian believer, living in America now, who spoke in Farsi every night at eight thirty Dutch time. Hope. A beautiful word in every language: *espoir, hoop, Hoffnung, amal, omid, esperanza.*

Keith had been raised in the Middle East, the child of missionaries, and in addition to English he knew Farsi, Dutch, German, and French. Lindsey was fluent in Spanish and Arabic. "You pretty well have the bases covered," Jim had said all those years ago, when they studied engineering together in college. "Except Mandarin. Mandarin would be helpful."

Three times a week Keith lent his voice, his "made-for-radio voice," as his boss, Koen, put it, to insert a live update at the end of the prerecorded Farsi program. He had never planned on this part of his job. Typically, WWR engineers in Holland only organized the schedule; the actual programs were made by people who lived in or came from the countries they broadcast for—often at great risk to the individual.

But six months ago an emergency had arisen and Koen asked Keith to do it, since his Farsi was flawless and the need was immediate. And it was so well received that he'd asked

Keith to continue these live updates regularly. Reluctantly Keith had acquiesced . . . he was only a voice, hidden between the airwaves. But to his own surprise, he found he was actually enjoying this new role, offering a slice of hope to the listeners.

Last night he had read in perfect Farsi, from the book of Hebrews. *Now faith is the assurance of things hoped for, the conviction of things not seen . . .*

He wondered if this Hamid had heard him. Sitting at his desk, he said a prayer for this refugee, that he would have courage and stamina, that he would reach Austria in safety, and most importantly, that he would put his trust in Isa al Masi. Keith traced the route in his mind. Papers at the embassy in Van, the long trek across Turkey into Bulgaria, then what? Romania, Hungary, Austria? Walking, buses, trains, cars, planes, boats. Somehow they made it. Some of them.

He typed the e-mail to Julie at The Oasis and opened the next.

The day passed quickly, and Keith was just packing up to go home when Koen called.

"Keith, the frequency is all wrong for the mountain regions in Afghanistan. Word is that the programs have been all but unintelligible the last few nights. Even in Iran and Turkey, often the signal is lost. Can you get the frequency right before you leave tonight?"

If he were a cursing man, Keith would have cursed. He was tired, Lindsey was expecting him home twenty minutes ago, and their Bible study group was coming to the house tonight. But he went back to the computer and began to check the settings for the program.

Lindsey would understand. They were encouraged over and over again by stories of men in Muslim countries huddled around transistor radios, hearing words from the Bible for the first time. Women hiding behind closed doors, their heads veiled, their hearts open to the Gospel. People hearing the words of the Bible in their own language, listening to the message in secret, many writing to say *I am now a Christ follower. I love Isa al Masi.*

Keith thought of the revival being sparked in the Kabyle region of Algeria, of the Iranian churches started in Austria, of the scattered letters from the Middle East. *I have heard the Gospel on your radio station. Thank you. I believe.*

He thought of his colleagues, spread throughout the world, working in offices behind desks in nondescript buildings so that people in countries hostile to the Gospel could hear. Sometimes he wondered what it would be like to be part of the "real" action, to actually meet the refugees in person and help them along the highway to freedom.

He stretched. Never mind. His was an important job, and one he was good at. Maybe someday he and Lindsey could take a trip to Vienna—a little vacation—and they could visit The Oasis in person.

Thirty minutes later he left the office, wished the night crew a good evening, and headed out to the bike rack. He unlocked his bike and backed it out from among the tangle of cycles and headed home.

Hamid

Hamid had held baby Lilly and thought of his own Omid. He'd played with the little boys, William and Jacob, the same games that only months ago he had played with Rasa. For two short days, this family had been his, and Hamid had gained hope from them. He smiled. Was it perhaps the God of the Ingil who had inspired Alaleh to name their son Omid? *Hope.*

Last night Jim showed him the path he must take from Van to Istanbul, tracing it carefully on the computer screen. "If you follow this route, you will not have to pay a smuggler.

Not until you get to Istanbul . . ." Jim pressed several hundred Turkish lira into his palm and said, "God be with you and protect you. We will be praying for you and will ask others at our church to pray."

Hamid wished he could to go to this place called church. It was forbidden to Muslims, of course, but Jim and Anna had said there were other Iranians, refugees like him, who attended. But he had to get back to the hotel, and Rasheed. And no matter how long it took him to get papers so he could leave Van, he knew it would be too dangerous for him to attend the church. What if Rasheed found out?

The two men had exchanged their stories of fleeing Iran as they traveled. When Hamid told his fellow refugee about Rasa and the Ingil that the secret police found, Rasheed had expressed deep concern. "Oh, that is very bad. The Ingil is very dangerous. You must be careful, Hamid. Your child must never read it. You either!"

After that Hamid had taken care not to share anything about his growing interest in Isa al Masi or the radio messages in Farsi he longed to hear. Nor would he tell Rasheed the truth about the kind Americans who had taken him in and cared for him for two days.

Back in the hotel room, he found Rasheed pacing nervously, his curly black hair falling into his face.

"Hamid, I am glad you are back, and you are well. We must leave soon. Yesterday I saw the police come and beat three men and drag them away while they were standing in line to receive their papers at the United Nations."

Hamid looked at Rasheed in surprise. "But you are not going to Austria, are you? I thought you wished to stay here."

It was what the other man had said from the beginning. His goal was to get to Van, gain asylum here, find work, and then bring his family to Turkey to be with him.

Rasheed continued his anxious pacing. "I don't trust the

people here. I see betrayal in their eyes. You have good information. Please, will you let me go with you to Austria?"

Rasheed looked desperate.

"Yes, of course, of course you may come if you can get the
papers. That I cannot do for you," Hamid said. He had come
to care for Rasheed. Care for, yes. But not trust. Not after
his experience with Ashar and Merif, his companions on the
first leg of the journey.

Rasheed had made friends with two other Iranian refugees who were staying upstairs in the dingy hotel. Hamid
waited patiently for him to go out with them, and then, alone
except for the roaches, he turned the dial on the little radio.
Jim had written down the frequency and told him the times
of the programs.

*We will be praying for you, Hamid. God will go with you.
Isa is your Master and Guide.* With tears in her eyes, Anna
had hugged him good-bye. Jim had placed a worn copy of the
Ingil and the Psalms in Farsi in Hamid's backpack, hidden
inside the covers of another book—and filled the rest of the
space with fruit and rolls and candy from America. "Read the
book every day, Hamid. A psalm and a chapter from Jesus's
life in the Gospels. You will see. He will lead you."

Yesterday he had read the first psalm. *How blessed is the
man who does not walk in the counsel of the wicked nor stand
in the path of sinners nor sit in the seat of scoffers, but his delight is in the law of the Lord and in His law he meditates day
and night.*

Day and night. Day and night.

He fiddled with the dial again, and at last the radio came
to life. The sound was so low he had to put his ear to it to
hear. For thirty minutes he listened, drinking in the words of
hope, of power, but all the while with his eyes trained on the
door, fingers ready to turn the dial to a local station in case

Rasheed should return.

At the end of the program, a voice that had become familiar to Hamid came across the airwaves. He liked hearing this deep voice; it was filled with strength and compassion. Somehow it calmed him, comforted him.

After the Scripture there was an interlude of music, "praise songs" they were called, a joyful type of music with words in Farsi. But in the middle of the second song, the signal was lost and there was only static. For five minutes Hamid played with the dials, walking around the basement room, hoping for a better signal, but there was none. He sighed and turned the dial to the local news. A moment later Rasheed burst into the room with his new friends.

"Hamid! You must meet my friends!" Rasheed patted the young men on the back and introduced them to Hamid. Two other Iranian students who had fled just like Rasheed.

But Hamid did not want to make more friends here. He only wanted to move on. He listened to their banter for an hour, but in his mind he was thanking Isa that the radio signal had disappeared at the right moment.

Hamid looked at the tattered map for the dozenth time and wanted to cry. Hope had seemed reasonable last night, as he listened to the comforting voice on the radio speak of it . . . but it was such a long way to Austria, hundreds and hundreds of miles across four different countries. And he had to do it all without being caught.

Jim had explained to him that the first country he entered in the European Union as a refugee would legally be the one where he must seek asylum. So he had to get through Bulgaria and Romania and Hungary without being stopped and fingerprinted. Hamid traced the line from Van, six hundred miles across Turkey to Istanbul, then north into Bulgaria. Then where?

What route had his cousin Jalil taken to get to Austria? That was what he needed to know.

With his small pocketknife Hamid had cut open the lining to his jacket and carefully removed another wad of the bills Alaleh had so quickly but carefully hidden. The next day, taking Jim's advice, he exchanged his rials for euros in the busy downtown area of Van and purchased a cell phone. Then he found a bench to sit on and dug out the paper with his cousin's phone number and address. Linz, Austria. With trembling fingers he pushed the numbers. His escape had been so quick, he had left with no chance to tell Jalil he was coming. What would his cousin say?

He thought of Jalil's letters, filled with photos of the mountains and the clean, clean streets. He thought of Jalil, who had found a job and a wife in Austria. Surely he would offer help.

He listened as the phone rang on and on. At last the answering machine flipped on, and Hamid listened to a computer-generated voice instructing him to leave a message.

And if this was the wrong number? No, Hamid could not take that chance. He would wait; he would call back later.

Rasa

Rasa held little Omid and sang to him over and over, the songs that she had learned from Miss Beverly, the songs that she also sang with Noyemi as they hid in the dark basement of the house. Three days ago Maamaan had heard from Baba, and that made everything better. Hope! Maamaan had hope now. Rasa saw it glistening in her eyes.

Baba was alive and in a place called Turkey! He had escaped and soon he would arrive in the other country—she could not remember its name—the country where a cousin lived, a cousin who had left Iran many, many years ago. Rasa closed her eyes and tried to imagine this other country.

Maamaan said it had beautiful mountains, mountains covered with snow and pretty lakes and fine, sturdy people.

"People who will not be mad if we read the Ingil?"

That had made her mother frown for a moment, but then she nodded. "Yes, people who will let us read whatever we wish. A free country . . ."

Rasa could not imagine this part of it. She thought of her class in first grade. She remembered the terrible day last fall, her second day in school, when their beautiful young teacher spoke to the class.

"Children, this morning we are going to play a game. This will help us get to know each other better. It is a game called 'what I have at my house.' I will hold up an object, and if you have this at your house, you raise your hand."

Eagerly the children nodded. The first object was a stuffed animal. Every hand in the room shot up, and the children chattered excitedly about their favorite stuffed animals. The next object was a pot for cooking. Again, every hand shot into the air. Then a radio. Several children looked around; some raised their hands, others did not. Rasa kept her hands folded in her lap.

Next a children's book. Every hand flew in the air. Next a newspaper. Hands everywhere, but not Rasa's. Many of the children could not read Farsi yet. But she could. She read the title on that newspaper, the one in the teacher's hand. It was the paper Baba read at the table every morning, the paper about which he had said, "Rasa, this is our home and we read this in our home, but you must never tell anyone that we read this paper, you understand?" And she had nodded, although she did not understand at all.

Then the teacher reached under her desk and brought up a beautiful shining bottle. A dark brown bottle with a bright red label. "Do your mothers and fathers have this pretty bottle at their house?" she asked, smiling.

Some children shrugged, others stared and shook their heads, but three children raised their hands. "Yes, Baba likes this bottle very much!" one child volunteered.

Rasa knew that was a bad thing to say. It was not a bottle that the government allowed people to have in their homes. It contained a forbidden substance: alcohol.

Rasa had gone home and told her parents about the game the teacher had played. Baba loved to explain things to Rasa.

"You're a smart child, precocious, my dear. So you will understand. We love our beautiful country, but we do not agree with everything the leaders tell us. They tell us which books and newspapers we can read and which ones are forbidden. They tell us what we can eat and drink and what we cannot. They tell us what we can listen to on the radio, on the TV, on the computer, and what we cannot.

"What we read and watch and do at home, with Maamaan and Baba and Maamaan-Bozorg, we never talk of outside our house."

"I understand, Baba. I will never tell."

On the third day of school, the children who had raised their hands about the bottle and the newspaper were no longer there.

Waiting in hiding at Noyemi's house, Rasa remembered all this, and she wondered again. She had kept the secret of the bottles and newspapers and books, but she had not been able to keep the secret of the Ingil. It was the worst book of all, so bad the teacher had not even dared to hold it up, Rasa reasoned.

But no! The Ingil was a very *good* book and held words of hope and life. That was what Miss Beverly had said. That was what Noyemi's family believed. So which was true?

Every night Noyemi's mother, Dina, bowed her head and prayed for Alaleh and Rasa and Myriam and Omid. She often had tears in her eyes. "I'm sorry that the Ingil has brought you such trouble," she said. "Beverly was too naïve; she didn't realize how often the religious police patrol the area, nor how well informed they are about our doings." She twisted her hands together.

"You don't need to be sorry. We are happy to have found the Ingil, to have heard about Isa!" Rasa told her.

"Yes, it is of course wonderful that you have discovered Isa, little Rasa, wonderful."

But Rasa didn't think her mother agreed.

Three more days passed, and then Noyemi's mother told them it was too dangerous for them to stay there any longer. "We will send you by bus to the west, closer to freedom, to another family we know who will help you." She looked down. "But after that, it may be a difficult journey. Especially for Myriam and for the children."

Maamaan-Bozorg shook her head. "I will not leave. I have lived here for seventy-nine years. The government has taken my husband and my first son. Now the second son is running. I have nothing else they can take. You have told me about a Savior who gives eternal life. I believe this. I will stay here; I am not afraid of what they will do to an old woman."

Then she looked at Maamaan with an urgency in her eyes. "But you and the children, Alaleh, you must be brave. You must go as Dina says, and you must hide. Hamid will find a way to bring you to Austria. I know he will."

So it was decided. Maamaan-Bozorg would stay with Noyemi's family, and the others would go on. Dina hugged them tightly when she said good-bye.

"Go in courage, go in peace. We are praying. And remember, little Rasa, never speak of Isa out loud. Never! Keep Him close in your heart and prayers, but do not speak of Him to others."

Rasa understood. And she had hope. She was sad to leave Maamaan-Bozorg, but Baba was alive, and she and Maamaan and Omid were alive and soon they would join Baba in the land with snow-covered mountains and fairy-tale music and freedom. A land where she could read any book in the whole wide world.

Rasa stared out the window as their bus bumped along the road to another town. West, Maamaan had said. They were going west. Rasa remembered that her teacher did not like The West. That was how she put it.

"Very bad things happen in The West," she had said. "Many people do not believe in Khoda. They dress inappropriately. The women do not cover their heads."

"Are we going to that bad place—The West—that my teacher told us about?" Rasa had asked her mother.

Maamaan had smiled. "No, dear. We are simply going to another town in Iran. A good place, and we will stay with kind people, and Baba will perhaps send for us soon."

The bus pulled to a stop, and two policemen stepped inside. One policeman was frowning at them, looking carefully at Rasa. She turned her eyes down and reached for little Omid's tiny fingers. The policeman stood over the three of them, and she could feel his hot breath on her neck. *Help us, Isa,* she prayed, fingering the wooden cross in her pocket with her other hand. *Make the mean man go away. Please don't let him ask us any questions.*

He moved down the aisle and motioned to a couple sitting three rows back. "Show me your papers!" he growled.

Rasa didn't look behind her, and she tried not to shiver. Maamaan's arm was tight around her; they were huddled so close together that baby Omid shared their laps. Rasa's fingers traced the smooth wood of the cross and she prayed again, *Isa. Save us! All of us.*

At last the two policemen stepped off the bus. The rattley bus roared to life again, jostling along the gutted road. Rasa stared out at the rugged mountains in the distance, covered with snow. Did the mountains in that other country look like these mountains?

Rasa did not think so. These mountains looked frightening. They seemed to wrap themselves around the old bus, as if trying to prevent it from going further west. She breathed in and out slowly and whispered in her heart, never out loud, *Thank you, Isa, for keeping us safe so far. Please take us to the other mountains soon. Please, Isa. Soon.*

CHAPTER 9

Atlanta, Georgia
Stephen

When I got to the office—late, thanks to a fender bender on I-75 South that brought traffic to a halt for twenty minutes—everyone in the newsroom was huddled around the television.

Dale Sims was already making jokes at eight thirty in the morning. "I propose a toast!" he cried. "To our dear friends in Gaul! Good job dealing with the Arabs!"

The large-screen TV showed burning cars, angry youth, and police looking more than a little bit out of control. In short, chaos.

"Hey, come take a look, Stephen," Frank Dodge called to me. "France is lit up like a Christmas tree! The Arabs are rioting everywhere! How many cars did they say were burned last night, Dale?"

"Nearly a thousand. Serves them right, those lousy frogs. Didn't want to join with us to fight terrorism in Iraq. Well, now they can see what's going to happen to their country."

I rolled my eyes inwardly. *Here we go again. Bring on the freedom fries.*

"Boss wants to see you, Stephen. He's been pacing around, waiting for you to show up." Frank nodded toward the office of Anderson Kimball, head editor of the *Peachtree Press*. The *Press* is a small trendy newspaper in south Atlanta with a growing constituency both online and hardcopy.

I walked into his office. He looked up, formidable in every way from his crop of white hair to his bulging physique. "Stephen, glad you could make it." He raised a bushy white eyebrow.

"Sorry, Mr. Kimball. Traffic."

"It happens. I need you to work on a story. It'll mean travel."

My position often took me to dinky towns all throughout Georgia. "Sure, boss. Where am I going?"

He thumped his hand on a stack of newspapers on his desk. "I need a story about the problems in France. Reported live. Take these—read 'em on the plane. Can you leave tonight? Plane takes off at seven from Hartsfield."

I'm sure my shock registered on my face. I'd been with the newspaper for eighteen months and, except for a story about Hurricane Katrina in September, my longest assignment was for college football.

I found my voice. "Um, sure, boss. I'd love to go."

"You're the logical choice. You have the language and familiarity with the culture."

My father was French, my mother American, and the only word to describe my sisters and me was multicultural. Papa had a big job with Peugeot that meant that my family moved every three years or so. We'd lived in Paris, then Brussels, Tunis, London, and Vienna, and now they were back in France. Everyone said it was a great advantage, growing up as I had. I was fluent in three languages and had a pretty high level in two others. I'd lived in five different countries, gone to school with diplomats' kids, gotten the prestigious International Baccalaureate. I went to the US for college, graduating summa cum laude from Emory with a degree in journalism.

And then I stopped. The glamour of being a "citizen of the world" had its downside: I didn't belong anywhere. The wanderlust imposed on my youth had run out and I decided to settle down in the good ole US of A and be a journalist. But even out of college I found myself the object of bemused laughter when I showed my ignorance of popular culture. Not that I cared about some vapid sitcom or teenage idol I'd missed growing up . . . but it seemed every day I'd have another reminder that I just didn't "fit."

Andy Kimball looked at me through the puffy slits that hid his black eyes and leaned over the desk so that his ample gut almost touched the desktop. It was not the moment to argue.

"Yessir. I'll do my best."

"You do that, Stephen. You know this is a powder keg. Three-fourths of our constituency thinks every Arab is a terrorist. They're mad as hell at France for wiggling out of Iraq."

"I know."

"Don't be afraid to be personal. You've lived there. You know the culture. Your first article is due tomorrow at noon our time. Check with Kate—she's scheduling your flight."

I nodded and walked out of his office in a daze. Leaving for France tonight? No doubt about it, I felt the adrenalin pumping. Then I thought of my girlfriend. *Blast. Pam is not going to be happy.* Things had been a little rocky between us lately, and I'd promised her we'd go out tonight. Surely she'd understand.

"Hey, Stevo, you okay? You look a little shaken up. Paler than your usual pale, freckled self," Frank teased. "Bad news from the boss?"

"Not bad. Just surprising." I settled into my cubicle, glancing again toward the TV screen.

". . . Angry youths from the poorest parts of Paris and other major French cities have burned cars for the tenth night in a row . . ." the reporter said.

I sat down with a strong cup of coffee and began reading through the angry diatribes Mr. Kimball had given me . . .

Paris

As the taxi turned down the rue du Rivoli, I said, "Pretty crazy stuff going on around here." I spoke in French, but the language felt thick on my tongue and my head throbbed. Though it was only midafternoon back in Atlanta, I was feeling the effects of a nine-hour flight, too little sleep the night before, and an anything-but-tender farewell with Pam, who hadn't shared my excitement about an unexpected, expenses-paid trip to France.

The driver, who looked North African, cursed and threw his cigarette out the window. A gust of wind swept through the taxi. *"T'as raison, mon pote."* He added several choice expletives that I hadn't heard since high school.

Youths from the *banlieues*, or ghettos, mostly North African and Arab, were rioting. On October 27 two young Arab men had been accidentally electrocuted as they tried to escape police interrogation. It was the straw to break the camel's back, and the furor and tension, pent up for years, was now exploding in France's poorest suburbs. And while I was flying across the Atlantic, Paris and the surrounding area had suffered the greatest unrest since the rioting and burning began. I'd read on my laptop that 247 towns had reported incidents.

We pulled up in front of the hotel, and as I reached for my wallet to pay, I hesitated. "Would you be willing to take me to the banlieues? Can you wait ten minutes? I'll make it worth your time."

The driver gave me a wary smile, pulled out another cigarette, and cut the engine.

I quickly checked in to the hotel, then hurried back to the waiting taxi. As we drove through the villages outside of Paris I saw dozens of carcasses of burnt cars littering the streets. Roads were barricaded. I caught site of a bus burning as firemen turned their hoses on it. My taxi driver didn't seem a bit concerned. In fact, he seemed pleased at my obvious discomfort. After an hour and a half touring the sites, clicking photos with the digital camera that my boss had sent with me, I was ready to head back to the hotel, get a strong cup of coffee, and start my story. I knew how I would frame it.

Just a few days after the deaths that had set off the cycle of violence, Minister of the Interior Nicolas Sarkozy imposed a strict law-and-order-like stance, calling for *tolérance zero* for the perpetrators of the violence. He called them *racaille*—a derogative little word that basically means "scum." He was referring to the French-born youth of North African descent, the ones largely responsible for the burnings. *Racaille.*

Tracie

There were twenty of us going out to dinner that night, so Carol asked if I would drive our rental and follow the two minibuses. Two girls around my age, Alice and Dee, plus the middle-aged woman named Connie, rode with Aunt Bobbie and me. We chatted about all we'd seen on our tour of Vienna that day.

"I loved Steffi, all 337 worn and winding steps of her," said Dee, referring to our climb up the tower of St. Stephen's Church. "My parents will be happy to hear I'm getting a little exercise."

From that high perch we had stared down at the church's astonishing roof, made up of a patchwork of green, black, yellow, and white tiles laid out in geometric forms. Further out, the city of Vienna beckoned.

"My favorite was eating the Sacher torte!" Alice laughed. "After our exertion at St. Stephen's, we deserved it!"

We had sat at the sidewalk café of the Hotel Sacher eating the dark chocolate cake made famous in this city.

"I climbed St. Stephen's for *my* Stephen," Connie confessed. "My son lives in Atlanta, but I just today got a voice mail saying he's in France now, covering the riots and the car burnings—he's a journalist. He's on his way to our house in Lyon today, and here I am in Austria. Bad timing." She gave a little shrug. "I miss him."

"I couldn't be a journalist," Dee said. "He comes to cover the riots that we were so relieved to get away from! You should invite him to come here and visit you while he's in Europe."

"Right!" Alice said. "Tell him about everything you're seeing, and maybe he'll want to write about snowcapped mountains and the hills being alive."

"I don't know. I doubt he could get off."

"Wouldn't hurt to try," I chimed in. Connie seemed like the kind of mother who desperately missed her kids. In the two days I'd known her, she'd mentioned them a bunch of times. "Anyway, you can truthfully tell him you've seen some amazing things today."

I had stood breathless in front of the works of art in the Kunsthistorisches Museum, amazed to see in real life the paintings I had studied in my art history classes in college. But my favorite moment by far was standing onstage in the ornate auditorium of the Vienna opera house, hearing our guide's explanation of how much work it took to change the scenes for the different operas performed there weekly. Although musical theater was my area, not opera, it was fun to look out past the thick red velvet curtains at the lavish red cushioned seats and imagine singing an aria from *La Traviata*. The sun was going down as we twisted our way through miles and miles of vineyards, startlingly beautiful with bright red and orange leaves, perfect rows of abundance. Alice started singing. "DO—a deer, a female deer, RE—a drop of golden sun, MI—a name I call myself, FA—a long, long way to run . . ."

Pretty soon we were all singing along at the top of our lungs, skipping along like the Von Trapp kids from one song to another. It was when I belted out "The hills are aliiiiiiiiiive . . ." that Alice leaned forward and said, "Wow, Tracie, you have a great voice."

I kept staring straight ahead. "Um, well, thanks."

"No, I mean, you have an amaaaazing voice—like professional quality."

"Yeah, you really do," chimed in Dee.

"Have you done much singing?" asked Connie.

I felt the heat rising in my cheeks. "Oh, you know. I was in a lot of musicals in high school and college. I've . . . studied voice some." I had, in fact, played in *The Sound of Music* so many times growing up that I'd been each of the Von Trapp girls and finally Maria.

"Well, you should really keep pursuing it, dear," Connie said.

Bobbie was the least subtle person on the planet, and she stepped in before it got more awkward. "Tracie's being humble. She has a degree in voice and music therapy—and a few months ago she was cast in an off-Broadway musical, but she had to back out because of family issues."

To my relief, she stopped before detailing what my "family issues" were. Aunt Bobbie was an athlete, a cook, a fierce leader, a pastor, but she could not sing. On key, that is. Maybe that was why she exaggerated my success.

I could hear the girls talking to each other in muted tones

in the backseat, and then Dee spoke. "Tracie, um, would you consider helping us with something we're planning for the refugees next week?"

Here it comes, I thought. *They're planning some sort of American evening and they want me to sing "The Star-spangled Banner" or "Amazing Grace."*

When I didn't answer, she continued, "Carol said they love to sing, so we're asking them to prepare their favorite songs from their countries. We'll try to learn a few of their songs and then teach them one or two of our favorites. Would you mind teaching a song or two?"

I felt a little rebuke in my soul, as if some unseen force had reached down and slapped my hands. Shame on me for mocking their good intentions. What was the matter with me?

"I'd be glad to help," I said. "But please don't ask me to emcee the evening. Aunt Bobbie would be great at that."

We met eyes across the front seat. Bobbie's were twinkling, and she winked at me. For some reason, I laughed and winked back.

It was almost dark when we reached the tiny town of Grinzing on the outskirts of Vienna, having driven through the vineyards for almost an hour. I felt like my soul was filling up for the first time in months, and I wanted to hop out of the car and perch myself on some distant mountain and sing at the top of my lungs, twirling in my dirndl dress just like Maria. The hills and vineyards and this little village did feel alive.

We parked and began walking along the cobbled road. Carol played tour guide, telling us that Grinzing dated back to the twelfth century, had survived the plague in the eighteenth century, and became annexed to Vienna in the nineteenth. "Now it's best known for its many *heurigen.*"

At our baffled expressions, she explained. "A *heuriger* is

the name given to many Austrian wine-drinking locales, specifically in this region of the country. *Heurig* literally means 'this year's,' and these little taverns serve the wine produced from a specific family's vineyards that year. The heurigen are different from other taverns or restaurants—there are legal restrictions. They can only serve their own wine, and then usually there is a buffet where the clients can choose from a variety of typically Austrian dishes. The wine is very affordable and the food is delicious."

The buildings were freshly painted in hues of yellow and beige and orange, and perfectly clean. Each heuriger had a big lantern out front or hanging from the building, often with wrought-iron ivy surrounding it, and a tasteful name painted on the wall.

"As you can see, there are dozens of heurigen in this town," Carol said. "But the government protects them by only allowing certain ones to be open on certain weeks, staggering the availability. The way to tell if a heuriger is open is if the lantern out front is lit."

We passed several establishments with extinguished lanterns before we came to the one Carol was looking for. The door opened into a foyer with wine bottles stacked attractively on old wooden tubs, and decorated with pumpkins and flowers.

We ordered glasses of the house wine and ate thick potato soup and Schnitzel and reminisced about our day of touring. I even joined in the conversation without making one condescending or cynical remark.

"You remind me of my Ashley," Connie said to me, as she sipped her wine. "Pretty, strong-willed, independent, bright."

"Well, thank you, I guess," I mumbled.

She laughed. "I meant it as a compliment. You seem to have a good head on your shoulders. What kind of job will you be looking for after this trip?"

"I honestly don't know. I was planning on looking into some sort of work in music therapy. And I want to keep singing. But, well, plans changed. I guess I'm in a holding pattern."

"My son, Stephen, the one I mentioned earlier? He was headed out to conquer the world after he got his degree in journalism, but his plans changed too, I guess." She said this with a sense of wistfulness.

"And where's your daughter now?" I asked. "Ashley, I think you said her name is?"

"Oh, Ashley." She sighed. "I have no idea."

"Traveling like me?"

"Oh, no. I'm sure she's settled somewhere. She just doesn't want me to know where."

I must have shown my surprise, because Connie added, "I'm used to it by now."

Which I could tell was a big fat lie. I couldn't imagine my mother ever getting "used to" not knowing where every member of her brood was at every second of the day.

I continued eating my *knodel*, soaking up the savory flavors of sausage and onions, and thinking about a daughter who didn't want her mother to know where she was.

We were just finishing up dinner when I noticed that Aunt Bobbie's tremors had begun again, at first very slight, then more pronounced and then coming with a vengeance. She tried to cover her shaking right hand and arm with the left one and said, "I'm just going to scoot to the ladies' room," but as she reached for her cane and tried to stand, her legs buckled and she caught herself on the table.

I leapt to my feet and took her arm and helped her sit again.

Carol looked startled. "Do you need to lie down, Bobbie?" she asked.

She gave a nod, and I said, "Carol, can you watch her

while I get the car?"

But before I could leave, Bobbie slumped forward with a thud, her head hitting the table and her arms falling to the side. "Aunt Bobbie!"

She didn't respond.

"What exactly is your aunt's condition?" Connie asked. In a flash she went from timid, middle-aged mother to professional nurse, leaning over Bobbie, taking her pulse.

"She's got an aggressive type of cancer. She's on some kind of experimental oral treatment for two months, and she says it's normal for her to have tremors."

"This is not a normal reaction!" Connie barked. "We've got to get her to a hospital quickly!"

To my surprise, she rushed to the back of the heuriger, found a waiter, and began speaking in rapid-fire German. I stayed beside Bobbie, who looked deathly white and was still shaking. I couldn't imagine finding any kind of hospital or care center in this ghost town, but no more than three minutes passed before we heard the sound of what I assumed to be an ambulance, its *pam-pon pam-pon* siren loud and jarring.

"You follow in the car, and Connie and I will ride in the ambulance," Carol said. She wiped a cool cloth over Bobbie's face, which had suddenly swollen horrifically.

Connie seemed perfectly in control, and I had no idea what to do except obey. Carol turned to Dee. "Call Julie and Tom at The Oasis and tell them what's happened. They'll arrange for someone to direct the rest of you home."

The winding roads dizzied me as I leaned forward over the steering wheel, peering into the black and thankful for the flashing red light of the ambulance to guide me.

A thought zipped through me, something Bobbie's doctor had told her. *Follow the diet restrictions.* As I drove through the night, a chill ran all the way from the top of my head to

the bottom of my toes and the memory shot through me—
my little brother, Timmy, at two, had almost died because of
a nasty allergy to nuts. He had started swelling horrifically
and only a mad dash to the ER and a fancy shot had saved
his life.

The vineyards on either side of the road looked like rows
and rows of camouflaged troops, and the wind made eerie
whishing sounds. I heard Mom's voice in my head. *Honey, I
think it's a lovely idea to go to Europe with Bobbie, but she is
very, very ill. You know your aunt. She'll make light of it. She'll
rise to the occasion, but I'm not sure it's wise.*

And me in tears, then angry, then determined, and Mom
as always succumbing to Bobbie's charm and coercion. *Oh,
Sally, it's a wonderful idea. Of course I can go.*

Suddenly, out of nowhere, a question occurred to me.
Had my mother wanted Aunt Bobbie to stay around and help
her for all those years? I had never even considered any other
scenario. Of course Mom had wanted Aunt Bobbie, needed
her help, been oh so thankful for it.

I remembered an evening when I was twelve. The boys
were sleeping and I was finishing up a Nancy Drew mystery,
curled in the little breakfast nook.

"Time for bed, punkin," Mom had said.

"Oh, can't I stay up a little longer? Just one more chapter?"

"Nope. School tomorrow." Mom's sweet, tired voice.

"Oh, Sally, for heaven's sake, let her finish her chapter.
Fifteen minutes won't matter."

The scene was crystal clear in my memory, and followed
by other instances of Aunt Bobbie usurping my mother's authority, albeit with humor and poise. Of course Mom was
grateful for her sister's help . . . but after a year or two, had she
maybe wished that Bobbie would leave, and let her manage
us kids in the way she thought was best? I had always seen
Aunt Bobbie as the one who had held our family together

and my mother as weak and tired. But was she? *You know your Aunt Bobbie, Tracie. She thinks she can control the world. She thinks she has a direct link to the Almighty and maybe she even expects Him to obey her orders.* Mom had said it with a smile, but now I knew she was speaking truth. That was how Bobbie operated.

As I followed the ambulance's strident red light, I thought about Bobbie's promise that she wouldn't die on this trip. Who could make a "promise" like that? Was it just one more instance of Aunt Bobbie thinking she could control the uncontrollable?

Then another question crowded in: When Bobbie came running to help us after Dad's death, was she also running *from* something? Afraid, filling her life with my family because . . . because what?

I had no idea why I was asking myself these questions as I sped through the Austrian night, but they came at me, one after another, so that before I knew it we were at the hospital, the ambulance's siren screaming its dire message again and again in front of the entrance to the emergency ward of a hospital whose name I could not pronounce in a town I did not know.

I dashed into the ER as the paramedics wheeled Bobbie's gurney down the hall, with Carol running beside it and Connie hurrying behind, carrying Bobbie's purse over her shoulder. I caught up to Connie, grabbed the purse, and fished through it, retrieving the little brown bottle that had come from a pharmacy in the US.

"Connie, can you translate for me?"

She nodded, speaking in German even as I spoke in English.

"This woman is on a treatment for cancer." I thrust the bottle into a doctor's hand. "The medication causes her to have tremors. Tonight it began with tremors—twenty minutes ago—and then she started having horrible swelling and then she blacked out. Could it be that something she ate combined with the treatment provoked a potentially lethal reaction?"

The doctor was leaning close to Connie, straining to understand her German. He nodded and they pushed Bobbie through the ER doors. I collapsed in Connie's arms.

An hour later the doctor stepped out of the ER and smiled at us with a weary nod. As tears of relief sprang to my eyes, the doctor confirmed my suspicion—Bobbie had suffered from a complicated reaction to her medication because of something she had eaten, something normally innocuous—the walnuts in a piece of bread.

"Danke, Danke," I kept murmuring to the doctor. He smiled again and put a friendly hand on my shoulder. In heavily accented English he said, "You must thank yourself and your friends, young lady. Your quick response helped to save your aunt's life."

It was the middle of the night by the time I got Aunt Bobbie tucked into bed at the guest house. I was too exhausted to even talk, too upset, but I needed to call my mom. Bobbie had promised she wouldn't die on me, but she was doing just that. We had to go home. At least we'd had these ten days of travel.

It was past midnight in Vienna, but only a little after six p.m. Atlanta time.

"Hello?"

I could tell by the squeaky voice that it was Thomas—on the verge of puberty.

"Hey, Thomas, it's me, Trace. How are you?"

"Oh, hi sis! Good. Just got in from football practice. Isn't it late over there?

"Yes it is. I just need to talk to Mom for a sec."

"What's the matter?"

"Nothing's the matter, Thomas. Is Mom there?"

"Yeah. Love you too."

I smiled to think of my youngest brother now taller than I was, all gangly and awkward.

A minute later Mom answered. "Trace? Hey sweetie. Everything okay?"

"Hey, Mom!" Just hearing her voice, I felt relieved. Then the tears came. "Um, Aunt Bobbie isn't doing very well. She's got these tremors—she said it was normal with the meds, but now it's worse." In a whisper I explained what had happened, our terrorized rush to the hospital and the result.

"Oh, honey. Oh no." She took a deep breath. "Where is Bobbie now?"

"She's in bed, in our room here at the guest house. The doctor said she could go home and rest. Mom, I was so scared."

"Of course you were, sweetie. Thank the Lord she's resting okay."

"Should we come back home? She seems okay now, and she definitely doesn't want to leave, Mom. Most of the time she is so happy—kind of as if she's forgetting the illness—and you should see her at The Oasis. She's amazing with the refugees. With everyone."

"Listen, Tracie. You go on and get some sleep. I'll try to get in touch with Bobbie's doctor right now. I'll call you back tomorrow around two your time with news."

"Thanks, Mom." I gave a sniff and made myself change the subject. "Are y'all okay?"

"Just fine. Trey broke his arm yesterday, but it's not too bad."

Broken bones were par for the course with the T-tribe. Mom didn't even flinch over them anymore.

"Thomas scored a touchdown in yesterday's game. Tim,

Teddy, and Travis are at basketball practice."

"Have I gotten any phone calls or messages?" I couldn't resist asking.

"No, sweetie," she answered, knowing full well what I meant. "Well, Lynn called. She wasn't sure when you were getting back. But no one else."

We chatted for a few more minutes and then I hung up.

For a brief time afterwards, I forgot about Bobbie and the scare we'd had and the bleak diagnosis. I was thinking of Neil and how he had broken up with me two days before I was to give my answer about performing in the off-Broadway musical.

I had purposely not brought a computer on the trip—to keep me from endlessly checking my e-mail. Still I hoped that he would write or call. I wanted him to say he was wrong, he was devastated, that he realized his mistake and was begging me to come back.

But it wasn't going to happen.

I had known from the beginning of our relationship three years ago that we had different interests. Neil's idea of a fun night was watching Sumo wrestling; mine was *Romeo and Juliet*. He liked fast food, I liked sushi. He'd never seen *West Side Story!* But those were trivial differences, weren't they? Don't they say opposites attract?

Aunt Bobbie had never thought he was right for me, and didn't mind telling me. But I hadn't listened. Nor had I listened to a little voice in my head that told me I shouldn't be constantly thinking *If only this and this and this and this could change about him, he'd be perfect* if I truly loved him. I told myself that in spite of our constant arguing, the life we were creating together was good enough.

Now I was heartbroken—and yet, somewhere deep down, relieved. I was too proud to admit it to anyone, but now, far away from him, I could admit that I didn't want to settle for "good enough."

So although my heart hurt and I longed for Neil to miss me, in some sort of twisted revenge, to have his heart hurting too, I was thankful that I was single, unattached, and able to watch out for my Aunt Bobbie in the midst of her struggle to survive.

CHAPTER 10

Hamid

*H*amid stood in the long line in front of the government building where others like himself waited to apply for refugee status. The UNHCR—United Nations High Commissioner for Refugees—supposedly represented hope, but the building with the light blue flags of the United Nations stood behind thick fences that were patrolled by policemen wearing blue suits and caps with the United Nations inscription. Impregnable. Perched on a hill overlooking the city of Van, the building seemed removed from the rest of life. Indeed, Hamid felt removed, in a parenthesis between what he had known and an unforeseeable future.

The line stretched out into the gray-stoned square where a few children played beside a stand offering drinks and kabobs. Forlorn-looking people of many nationalities waited in the early morning chill, blankets over their shoulders. Some, Hamid heard, had been waiting for weeks.

Next to him, Rasheed stamped his feet impatiently. "We must prove we were persecuted for our political ideas," he said, not for the first time. "Then they will listen; then we can get the exit papers necessary to leave for Austria."

Twice more Hamid had called the cell number of Jalil, only to hear the ringing, ringing, four times, five times, and then the computer-generated voice. What if he had the wrong number? He'd finally called Jim Harris, and the kind American had reassured him.

"Okay, Hamid. We have your cell number now. I'll send it on to the workers in Austria. Surely someone knows of your cousin. I'll call you if I have news. We're praying for you, Hamid."

Lost in his thoughts, Hamid jumped to hear the shrill cries of those standing in line in front of him.

"Stop him!" screamed a young woman who was cradling a baby in her arms.

He turned to see a middle-aged man, a refugee they had met the night before at the New Moon, running across the square holding a plastic container over his head. "I will ignite myself if you do not grant me the papers!" he cried.

Hamid broke out of line and ran toward the desperate man. "Please, please, Kalim," he shouted, suddenly remembering his name. "Don't do this. Surely there is still hope."

Kalim's eyes were glazed, perhaps with tears, perhaps with insanity. "No hope! No hope!" he shouted in Farsi. Dousing himself in kerosene, Kalim yelled his threat again and then, suddenly, he was in flames.

People screamed, and Hamid took off his coat and threw it over the burning man. The smell of burning flesh stung his nostrils as he knelt by Kalim, trembling with repulsion. The police were quickly at his side, helping to smother the flames, but when they were done, Kalim lay still on the ground.

Hamid tried to stand, but his legs buckled under him and

Rasheed caught him around the waist.

"He had no more money, and he was turned down for asylum three times," Hamid sobbed. "He lost hope. He told me last night he had lost hope, but I did not expect this."

Hamid could not rid his mind of the image of Kalim in flames. The next morning, the same line, the same refugees. There was tension in the air, among the refugees and the Turkish police. It was not good propaganda to have the evening news lit up with a burning refugee.

"The police fear an uprising," Rasheed said, rubbing his hands together in the frosty morning air.

Hamid nodded. But the people did not look violent. They looked exhausted, afraid, and despairing. Young and old stood in line, children clinging to their parents, young couples huddled together with worry written across their faces. An old man with a long scab on the side of his face leaned on a makeshift cane.

"I spoke with him yesterday," Rasheed whispered, motioning with his eyes to the elderly man. "He was tortured by the Turkish police last week. That was the story. Only it wasn't the police, it was the Iranian secret service. They are here too, Hamid, trying to denounce us. They buy their information from the hotel managers, from the other refugees. They come in the night and arrest people."

Hearing the panic in Rasheed's voice and seeing the anger gleaming in his eyes, Hamid wished he were traveling alone. Rasheed could explode.

For a moment Hamid felt trapped in this in-between country, terrified of secret police and of something even worse—the way hopelessness led to insanity. What could he do? What *should* he do?

He thought of his students in philosophy class. Strange how their faces floated into his mind at this time. "What should we do, professor? What hope do we have?"

He saw himself, months ago, or years and lifetimes ago, writing the ancient proverb on the whiteboard: *If one has to jump a stream and knows how wide it is, he will not jump. If he does not know how wide it is, he will jump, and six times out of ten he will make it.*

Hamid took a deep breath as he inched forward in line. He did not know how wide the stream was, and so he would jump.

That night, back in the New Moon Hotel, Hamid and Rasheed were awakened by fists banging on the door. "Open up!" voices demanded.

Hamid motioned with his eyes for Rasheed to stay in bed. Slowly he got up and pulled on his pants. "Yes?" he asked in Turkish through the closed door.

With a splintering sound, the door flew open and two policemen entered, grabbing him and yanking Rasheed out of bed.

"Come with us."

As they struggled behind these unknown men, Hamid cried silently to Isa, *I am afraid. I am jumping into this stream. I am jumping with only you there to help me across.*

The two policemen escorted Hamid and Rasheed at gunpoint to a dingy room in a forgotten building on the other side of Van. For hours Hamid hung from a bar, his hands tied together, his feet off the ground, his mouth taped shut. He could not see Rasheed. Every once in a while he heard a blood-curdling scream from the next room, and he prayed to Isa. *Help Rasheed. Help him.*

Hamid thought of Rasa and Alaleh and baby Omid. He tried to rid his mind of the terror that seeped in as he awaited his turn for questioning by these police who were not police but Iranian secret service. When they dragged him into another room with cement walls and floors, he saw the form of Rasheed huddled in a corner.

The beating began—to his face, his skull, his groin. The electrical shocks. The board slammed into his head. They would kill him before they asked one question! *Isa, let me die before I reveal something that would endanger my family.*

He felt the warm ooze of blood down his back and fainted.

He did not know how long he was unconscious, only that he was awakened with a burst of cold water to the face.

"You tell us who you work with!" one man screamed. More beating, more cursing. "You will tell us or we will have you expelled and you will be executed back in Iran."

Hamid remained silent, though his body trembled involuntarily. The pain was blinding. The blood now seeped into his eyes. He felt as if his skull had cracked open. Perhaps it had.

Throughout the night, they alternated between Rasheed and Hamid, the questions, the fury. The only sounds that the two refugees made were sharp piercing screams of pain and low moans.

Then, as light began to stream through the one small window in their prison, Hamid's phone started ringing, ringing, ringing, as one man raised his hand for another blow. Rasheed gave Hamid a terrified stare.

The bigger of the two men laughed gruffly. "Answer the phone, you idiot! Perhaps it is your family, and we will have the news we need."

Rasheed held the phone to Hamid's mouth, and he choked out a muffled "Hello?" in Farsi. *Dear Isa! It must not be Alaleh! Only yesterday he had called her from this phone, had heard her voice for just a few precious moments . . .*

"Hamid, this is your cousin Jalil."

"Jalil." The word came out thick on his swollen tongue. "Help, Jalil."

The taller of the two secret police grabbed the phone and screamed into it in Farsi. Through blurred eyes, Hamid watched the look on the torturers' faces when they realized that Hamid had family in Austria.

Through the phone line, Jalil repeated, "Are you all right? Hamid? Hamid?" in Farsi. "I will contact the embassy. Hamid . . ."

The phone went dead as Hamid grasped it in his hand. The secret police began cursing and yelling. Then, pulling Hamid and Rasheed up, they dragged them out of the dank room and through a hallway. The door opened to the blinding light of day, and suddenly Hamid and Rasheed were out on the street, alone.

Stephen

I stayed in Paris for three days covering the rioting and unrest, but the plan, understood and approved by Mr. Kimball, was that I'd attach a few days to the trip to visit my parents at their lovely French farmhouse on the outskirts of northern Lyon. And as it turned out, there was plenty of action to cover there as well.

Unfortunately, when I called to let my parents know when I'd be arriving, I found neither of them at home. I decided to take the rapid train—the TGV—down to Lyon anyway and report firsthand on the unrest that was going on there.

I'd been calling the paper twice a day, and so far the boss seemed satisfied with my reports. I dialed his number and waited for him to answer.

"Anderson Kimball, *Peachtree Press.*"

"Mr. Kimball, it's Stephen."

"Stephen! Great story from Lyon! People are getting into the French action. Gobbling up the news. Are things calming down any?"

"Parliament just approved a three-month state of emergency, and curfews are being strictly upheld. The violence has died down outside Paris, though there are still some problems in the *banlieues*. I guess a drop in car burnings from fourteen hundred to three hundred is good news."

"Okay. Well, take a couple days with your parents, and we'll see you back here on Monday."

He hung up the phone before I could say *Well, actually, Mr. Kimball, turns out my parents are nowhere to be found.*

I finally reached my father, who was somewhere in Hong Kong. Papa said that Mom was in Austria. On the spur of the moment she had hooked up with a group of religious college students who were heading to Vienna. What was that about?

My mother wasn't answering her cell. I got her voice mail: her strong Southern drawl seeping into her French. *"Bonjour, vous êtes bien sur le portable de Connie Lefort. Veuillez laissez un message, s'il vous plaît.»* Then in English: "Hi there! This is Connie's cell phone. Please leave a message."

I wandered around the house, looking at the photos of family that Mom had so lovingly hung on the wall in the *salon*. There we were, all four kids, posing in sports gear or sitting on the grass in front of an ancient chateau or crowded around a table laden with good food. It was an American room.

"Mais alors, Connie! You certainly are proud of your little family. Flaunting photos all over the wall. Ça ne se fait pas!"

My French grandmother was not above making condescending remarks, criticizing every aspect of Mom's cooking and decorating. I picked up a framed photo of Mom and me when I was about six. We were petting a lamb, and I had an expression of wide-eyed innocent wonder on my face. Mom was fairly glowing.

I tried her cell again and left a message.

"Hey, Mom. Just trying to reach you. I'm still here in Lyon. Papa said you're in Vienna. Give me a call when you get a chance."

She was going to be devastated when she learned that I was at their home in Lyon and she was doing who-knows-what in Vienna. I clicked my cell shut and sighed. All I really wanted to do was go home. But where in the world was that?

Mom hadn't picked up on my first call, or my second, but just past midnight I decided to try her one more time.

"Stephen! Darling! So nice to hear your voice. I got your message, but I haven't had a minute to call back. I can't believe you're in Lyon!"

My mother, who checked her voice mail and her e-mail manically, hoping for a word from her kids or Papa, "hadn't had a minute" to call me back?

"I can't believe you *aren't!*" I said. I filled her in on my time in Paris and then turned the conversation. "Are you doing okay, Mom?"

"Am I doing okay?" Mom sounded breathless. "Oh, Stephen, I've had some of the most marvelous days of my life. The girls I'm with drove with me from home through Switzerland and then through the Austrian Alps. So breathtakingly lovely, you remember. We spent the most amazing evening at this place that serves refugees from Iran and Iraq and Afghanistan—it's called The Oasis. I played cards with children, and a lot of the men watched a movie about the life of Christ and it was just—well, I'm at a loss for words. Amazing."

Alarms were going off in my mind, worse than when I'd been caught in the riot on Place Bellecour in Lyon yesterday. Mom sounded . . . how did she sound? Not drunk, thank goodness, no, but high? Yes, high on some drug. I knew my parents' marriage was not very strong these days, and I could well imagine her finally deciding to leave Papa. I also knew that she suffered from depression. In a vulnerable state, had she been duped by some religious cult?

"Mom, um, that's great. I'm glad you're enjoying it. Um,

who exactly did you say this group is?"

"Oh, honey, they're Christians, don't worry. You know, those really serious kinds of Christians that believe the Bible. And missionaries."

Missionaries in Europe? "Serious Christians" sounded like fanatics to me. I cursed under my breath, holding the cell phone away from me.

"Have you heard from your father?" she asked.

"No, not today. I think he's in Hong Kong now. Haven't you talked to him, Mom?"

"Not today—we were sightseeing. Oh, we've seen such lovely things. And then Bobbie—a woman who used to be a Bible smuggler—had an attack and suddenly all my nursing instincts came back, along with my German, so I was at the ER with her till late tonight. She's fine now. Anyway, I'm sorry, but it's been just nonstop."

"How long do you plan to stay there, Mom?"

"Oh, I don't know." Silence. Then, "Why, I might just stay my whole life, Stephen!" She laughed.

I rubbed my hands over my eyes. Oh. My. Word. Surely this wasn't happening. She'd already been sucked in. I took a breath and tried a different tactic. "Mom, I thought perhaps we could see each other in a day or two—here in Lyon."

"Oh, I don't think I can get back to Lyon, Stephen. Not for a while."

I could not believe my overpossessive mother was choosing a coffee bar for Muslim refugees run by a Christian cult over seeing her son.

"Stephen, I can hear you're worried. Don't be. I'm fine and really happy. But I would love to see you. Why don't you come *here* for a visit before you fly back to Atlanta?"

We talked for a few more minutes, but when I said bye and hung up, I thought to myself that I would do just what she'd suggested. I'd ask the boss for a few more days—and go rescue my mother.

When I called in the next day, I took a deep breath. "Mr. Kimball, I was wondering if I could cover another story over here once I'm done with the riots."

"Such as?"

I could picture Andy Kimball leaning across the desk, tiny slits for eyes, massive shoulders resting on his bulging arms, staring through the phone.

"The refugee crisis in Vienna. Um, I've had news about all the Iranians and Afghanis pouring into the refugee camps, and I have a lead about a religious group, made up of Americans, that is working with refugees outside Vienna."

I left it hanging. I didn't want to play the "family emergency card" unless I had to.

"Refugees. And why do you think it would be of interest here?"

"You know the refugee issue is a hot button with Americans. I think it would be a cool human interest story. My sources are pretty sound." That was a lie.

"Hmm. Well, since you're there, I'll give you three days in Vienna to see what you come up with. It better be good, young man."

"Thank you, Mr. Kimball. I'll make it good. And I'll fly cheap. You won't be wasting money on me."

I said good-bye to my boss and then took a deep breath and dialed Pam. That conversation didn't go quite so well.

"Stephen, do you know how long you've been gone?"

I rolled my eyes. *Yes, dear, I know exactly how many days I've been gone.* And I was surprised at how little I'd missed her, or even thought of her, during those days.

"I'm trying to redecorate the apartment, you know. As *you* asked me to. I guess I'll just have to move ahead without your input."

"That's fine, Pam. You're the interior designer. I'm sure I'll like whatever you do."

Pam was talented, and smart and savvy and sexy. She was also beautiful—blond, tanned, bewitching green eyes. We'd met at a party nine months ago. She was going places and so was I. We decided we just might like going together. Four months ago she'd moved in. When things were going well she was fun—but she also, I had learned, was very controlling.

"So now you're off to Vienna! It must be nice."

"Pam, it's for work." Another lie, kind of.

"Whatever. Have you seen your mother or father?"

"Nope. Papa is in Hong Kong and Mom's in Austria with some religious group. Very strange."

"I'll say. All of your family is strange."

"Look, I'll call you from Vienna when I have a better idea of my schedule. I'll make it up to you, I promise."

"I hope so! I'll have to find a date to the Decorators Ball, since it doesn't sound like you'll be back by Saturday. Maybe I'll ask Jeff. You think he'd mind accompanying a poor young woman who's been stood up by her boyfriend?"

I felt a tiny prick of jealousy, but I stuffed it down. "Look, Pam. It's work. What do you want me to say?"

"Say you miss me, that you think of me every time your head touches the pillow in your plush hotel room, that you can't wait to get home."

Loser, I told myself. Yes, I should have been saying these things. "All of the above," I said. "And you don't think I was in Paris for three days without picking out a little something for you, do you? Can't wait to see you in it."

"Really," she cooed. "Well, it's about time you told me something more interesting than how many cars the Arabs burned now. Well, I've got to get back to work. I've got a client who will burn *my* car if I don't get their house design to them by Friday."

I hung up a few minutes later, smiling to myself. I hadn't been lying about the gift anyway—a lovely little negligee. *You're not a total loser,* I told myself. If I played my cards right, Pam would get over it. She always did.

CHAPTER 11

Tracie

For once Aunt Bobbie obeyed me. I'd begged her to stay in bed, and she agreed. Of course, it helped that Carol had strictly forbidden her from coming to The Oasis. I read Bobbie's disappointment.

"I feel fine now," Bobbie insisted. "It was just an allergic reaction."

"You almost died last night!" I retorted, then felt my face fall. "Oh, Aunt Bobbie, I don't want to watch you die."

She pulled me close. "Trace, I'm sorry. You've been a rock star. I'll stay here and read like a good girl."

"I'll stay with you. We can watch DVDs all day."

Bobbie shrugged. "If you want. But if you'd like to hang out at The Oasis, I promise I'll be fine. And, yes, I know your mom's going to call and tell me what my oncologist said. I could have called him myself, you know."

"Sure—but you *wouldn't*. That's what I know."

"You're right. But I'll take your mom's call. I promise." She held up the cell phone and smiled.

A little self-consciously I admitted, "Well, if you're sure, Bobs, I think I will hang out down at The Oasis with the team. We're going to practice some songs for that little evening thingy they're planning next week."

Bobbie's eyes twinkled. "That's the best news I've heard all day."

I left her and went downstairs to find the others. Thirteen of us squeezed into the van, and we sang vigorously during the fifteen-minute drive from Gasthaus Müller to The Oasis. We moved from *Fiddler on the Roof* to *Mary Poppins* and on to *My Fair Lady*, and then Dee piped up, "Let's sing 'How Great Thou Art.'"

"I don't know the words to that one," I admitted.

"No prob. I'll start it. I'll bet you've heard it before."

Of course I had. I'd heard it at Aunt Bobbie's church. The girls sang it in beautiful harmony, and I don't know why, but I got chills, the good kind, running down my spine and my arms and legs. Oddly, I wanted to stay in that van, singing with these girls for a little while longer.

It was around nine o'clock when we got to The Oasis, and four of the full-time workers were already there: Carol, Julie, Tom, and his wife, JoAnn.

Connie, who was staying at Carol's apartment, was there too. She was talking excitedly to the others, and when she saw us, she cried, "Oh girls! The most wonderful thing has happened. My son is coming here to visit me tomorrow!"

"That's nice," Dee and Alice said politely.

"Stephen? The one you were telling us about yesterday?" I asked.

"Yes, and oh, it's more than nice. I haven't seen him in almost a year." Then she launched into the story which a few of us had already heard. "As you know, my husband and I live in

Lyon right now, but our son lives in Atlanta. He's a reporter. His boss has sent him over to France to cover the riots and car burnings. Stephen was in Paris for three days and then he went to Lyon."

"What's happening there now?" asked another girl, Janet. "We haven't heard much news since we left. My mom was really glad we were leaving for Austria. All those car burnings were pretty scary."

"Yes, it was scary. Crazy Arabs!" Connie slapped her hand over her mouth. "Sorry. I'm not prejudiced, but . . ."

I rolled my eyes.

"Stephen says things have calmed down," she continued. "I'm sure he'll fill you all in tomorrow."

"How old is your son?" Dee asked nonchalantly.

"He's twenty-five. A journalist. Good-looking and smart as a whip."

Dee raised her eyebrows. "Cool. It'll be nice to have a guy around. Short-term teams are notoriously lopsided, you know. Very few guys."

"Or in the case of our team, no guys," Alice added.

Connie laughed happily. "Well, he's adorable, if you can trust a mother's opinion." Then she made a face. "But girls, I should warn you that he's taken. He lives with his girlfriend. And he isn't very . . ." She searched for a word. "Very religious, if you know what I mean. But he's great. A fine young man."

We spent the morning planning the "musical evening" for the refugees. Carol taught us several songs in Farsi and Arabic, and then we added two in German to our growing repertoire.

Bobbie called me on my cell phone to report that her oncologist had not ordered her back home on the next plane. He was e-mailing her a long list of foods to avoid—a list he had apparently given her back home, but she had failed to bring.

After lunch the team put on a "kids' club" for a roomful of refugee children. I watched Dee and a strawberry blond named Neta and Connie patiently explaining, with ample use of sign language and laughter, how to make the craft they'd prepared—a little cardboard box, painted and decorated with bright colored pieces of construction paper—as a gift for their parents. The children's excitement was palpable, and they touched the scissors and crayons and paper almost reverently, as if these were precious objects.

I laughed along with them as I helped them cut out little squares and paste them on cardboard boxes, our fingers getting really sticky with the glue. Then the children taught me songs in their language. As I sang along with them, trying to mimic their Farsi, several little girls whispered something.

"They're saying that you are a beautiful American with a beautiful voice," Carol translated, and I felt my face go beet-red.

After the kids' club, Julie gathered the short-termers and the full-time workers together in the little room above the coffee house. We sat on comfortable old couches, the walls around us dotted with photos of refugees' smiling faces.

"We have an urgent prayer need," Julie explained. "Jim and Anna Harris live in Van, Turkey. Jim is an engineer, but he and Anna are very involved with helping refugees. They teach English lessons and help people with official paperwork and, if they are receptive, tell them about Jesus. They met an Iranian named Hamid who is trying to get to Austria. He has a cousin in Linz who may be able to help him gain asylum here, but so far the two men have not been able to get in touch. An Iranian pastor here in Austria knows Jalil and has contacted him. We must pray specifically for Hamid's protection and that Jalil will be able to reach him. And pray for Hamid's wife and daughter and little baby, who are in hiding somewhere in Iran. Hamid was very interested in hearing about Jesus. Jim shared the Gospel with him and gave him a New Testament and Psalms in Farsi."

As everyone bowed their heads and different ones began praying heartfelt prayers for this man they did not know, I felt chills again. I thought of Naseef's story, and I imagined Hamid's precarious journey. I did not pray out loud—or silently—but something in me warmed a little.

And when the refugees, again mostly young men, came to The Oasis that evening, I was overflowing with a strange feeling. *Goodwill*, I thought.

I did not want to turn into a superficial short-termer who served refugees to feel good about myself. Or maybe I did.

Maybe the way I had looked at so many things before was just a little bit off kilter.

Stephen

I flew to Austria on Thursday, after staying up half the night writing my latest story for the paper and sending it off to Mr. Kimball. The budget airline got me to Vienna in record time, and I hired a taxi to take me to what Mom had called "an adorable little Christian guest house" where she had reserved a room for me.

The place seemed normal enough. No incense or dark rooms with beads and crystals. No strange music or people milling about in a zombie-like trance.

An older African man was manning the reception desk, and his wife, also African, showed me to a small, tidy room. "Showers are down the hall. Facilities also."

There was a sink in my room, and I shaved quickly, in a hurry to get to the "refugee coffee house," as Mom called it. Evidently there was some activity planned there this evening, and I was welcome to participate.

No thanks, I thought to myself. *I'll be happy to observe.*

The taxi let me off in the midst of a small village, beside the train tracks. I paid my fare and walked across the street to a building with a Plexiglas sign above the door identifying it. Out front on a bench were several youth, definitely not Austrian. I nodded to them and one called out, "Amereecan?"

I was surprised I had given myself away without opening my mouth, so I decided to play my third-culture-kid card. *"Non, en faite, je suis français."*

I said it without a trace of an accent, and they smiled. One boy, he couldn't have been over sixteen, started babbling at me in French. He was from Algeria. I grinned, and to his question of where I lived in France, I answered—this time in Arabic.

Now the other two youth looked at me and started jabbering excitedly in Arabic. "You know our language? How do you know our language?"

I cannot say what happened in that moment as I watched these three boys' eyes light up, their faces transform into smiles. They shook my hand and introduced themselves.

"I'm Fareed," the tallest one said. "I'm from Iran. I speak Farsi, but I know Arabic too."

"I'm Rachad, from Algeria."

"Saquib, Tunisia."

I had not stepped inside The Oasis yet, and already my heart was lifted, just hearing the familiar languages of my youth. I grew up speaking French and English at home, no matter where my father's travels took us. When we landed in Tunisia for four years while I was in elementary school, I learned Arabic too. I loved languages, and the fact that I could speak five fairly fluently did not strike me as odd. It was simply a fringe benefit of my strange upbringing.

The youth began to tell me their stories as if I had asked for an interview, pouring out their journeys in a mixture of Farsi and Arabic. I listened intently, memorizing their faces, their stories, the lost look in their eyes, and the sudden delight to find someone white with whom they could talk. I wondered if the people inside The Oasis spoke German, or Farsi or Arabic.

"You are a Christian? You work here at the American church?" Rachad asked.

"No. No, I'm just visiting."

"You are American. But you are not Christian?" Fareed clarified. They seemed intrigued.

I was speaking in Arabic, trying to remember the words from so long ago. "Well, I'm not a Muslim or a Buddhist or a Hindu, if that's what you mean. Let's just say I don't go to a church."

"So you are not a *practicing* Christian," Fareed said. He elbowed Rachad. "Rachad is not a practicing Muslim. Only during Ramadan—when everybody must practice—or else." He hit the boy hard on the back and jolted the cigarette from his mouth. The three boys laughed. "We are glad Ramadan is over."

I nodded. "Yep. It ended on November 3, right?"

They looked at one another and grinned. Fareed said, "An American who does not practice Christianity but knows about Ramadan."

When I mentioned that I was looking for my mother, they stared at me as if they had misunderstood. "Your mother?" Saquib repeated.

"Yes, she came here from Lyon with some American students."

They broke into those smiles again, apparently at the thought of a grown man like me looking for his mother. They patted me on the back and opened the door to The Oasis. We stepped inside into a large and very crowded room. Boys and men were playing board games, especially chess, at tables set up toward the back. To my left there was a long counter, behind which stood two young women—probably Americans. I was just turning to see the other part of the room when my new friends began shouting "He's looking for his mother!" first in Arabic, then in Farsi, and then one of them made a stab of it in English. It came out as *mozair*, and other boys and men chuckled.

But within seconds I was rewarded by Mom's deep cry of "Stephen! You made it!" and she grabbed me in a tight hug, the kind she used to give me when I was a boy. The kind that was not holding on possessively or begging *Please please don't leave me.* The kind that did not make me shiver with fear that my mother had dropped into the depths of depression.

This hug was warm and affectionate, and then she released me and said, "Let me introduce you to some of my friends. That's Dee and Neta behind the counter."

The two college-aged girls smiled and waved. They both had long hair pulled back in a ponytail, looking innocent and fresh as white linen in the midst of a room predominantly filled with dark-skinned men.

"They're studying in Lyon—can you believe it? That's where I met them." Then Mom pointed towards a group of young guys who were animatedly talking with another girl. She wore a yellow sweatshirt and jeans and had her dark blond hair twisted back carelessly off her shoulders in a clip. "That's Tracie over there," Mom said.

Hearing her name, she glanced our way and looked at me a bit suspiciously.

Mom led me around and introduced me to more people, refugees and workers, until names and faces were a total blur. Eventually, though, the refugees all left, and I found myself surrounded by twelve college women who were pumping me for information about the events in Lyon, events they had witnessed firsthand just a week before.

This isn't so bad, I told myself, and then felt a pang of guilt thinking of what Pam would have to say if she could see me.

"The riot police were standing in groups of four or five interspersed along rue de la Republique," I told the girls, and I knew they could perfectly picture the scene. Exchange students loved to hang out on rue de la Republique, a cobbled pedestrian street next to the biggest open square in Lyon. "Other police were in cars and a few sat in the blue police buses, waiting for orders. Then all of a sudden they moved forward, blocking the entrance to the Place Bellecour where there were probably fifty guys gathered on the square, yelling insults. The kids started attacking the booths on the Place, as well as the cars."

"Booths? There aren't booths at Bellecour," Alice objected.

"Not usually, but there was some sort of fair going on, and artisans were selling their wares—until the Arab youth started attacking. All the shoppers got the heck out of there, running up the rue de la Republique, and the shop owners put down the metal bars on their entrance doors. Do you know the bookstore FNAC?"

The girls nodded. "Of course."

"Well, quite a few shoppers were locked *inside* the bookstore, behind the metal bars."

"Awesome," said Dee.

"It was actually pretty scary," I commented. "The entrance to the Metro was temporarily closed because of all the uproar. I could hear kids yelling at one another, encouraging each other in Arabic to torch cars and worse. The riot police began throwing tear gas into the crowd. As the gas sprayed out, the kids spread out and some of them fled. Others turned and began throwing whatever they could find at the riot police—bottles, rocks."

"Did you get hit with the tear gas?" asked one of the girls whose name I couldn't remember.

I nodded. "Yeah, and it hurt like hell. I finally got inside a store that hadn't been barred and found a bathroom to wash the stuff out of my eyes. When I went back outside, the Metro entrances were closed, the buses weren't running, the shops still had their doors locked behind bars. Very weird feeling. The whole city had shut down temporarily."

"Sounds terrifying," Alice stated, and the others nodded in agreement.

"The police set up a curfew for all minors, from ten p.m. till six a.m., but I seriously doubted it would do any good. I learned that Lyon was the first city whose center of town had been disturbed by the activities and also that it earned the record for the most car burnings so far in the month of November."

"And to think we missed all the excitement," said Dee dramatically.

"Oh, Stephen, darling! You could have been hurt!" That comment of course, came from my mother.

Only one girl—Tracie, the one in the yellow sweatshirt—didn't seem interested in my story. She was busy helping the older women—JoAnn, Carol, and Julie—clean the room. I figured she must be one of the full-time workers, as they called themselves.

"So are you a missionary too?' I asked her, when I found myself sweeping the floor a little later as she stacked clean cups in the cupboards.

"Nope, not me. I just came along for the ride with my Aunt Bobbie—who is actually not here tonight. She, um, she got sick." The girl looked uncomfortable.

"Sorry to hear it."

"Yeah, a bummer. Anyway, we're traveling around Europe, and she used to work here."

"Here? In this place?"

"Sort of—she started back in the eighties, smuggling Bibles behind the Iron Curtain."

"Whoa. Serious stuff." I jutted out my lower lip. I suddenly remembered Mom saying something about being at the emergency room with a Bible smuggler named Bobbie. "So, um, your aunt. She's part of this . . ." I searched for a polite, neutral word. "Organization?"

The girl laughed heartily, her face relaxing, and it changed her appearance dramatically. "You pronounce that word as if it's poison." She shrugged and said, "Yes, just say it. You wonder what missionaries are doing in Europe instead of Africa or India or maybe China, and you think maybe my aunt is part of some fanatical religious group."

"Wow. Is all that written on my face?"

She laughed again. "No, but it's what I thought." She dropped her voice. "I expected all the Middle Eastern refugee men in here to be terrorists—and I had no idea what to expect of the missionaries. But hey, the refugees are really pretty normal people who've had awful things happen to them. I've heard enough stories in the past five days to give me nightmares for the rest of my life."

Stories. Surely Andy Kimball would want stories.

"And the missionaries are just pretty ordinary people too—I mean, they come from regular lives. But they do have this really deep-down faith and a heartfelt desire to help these people. But it looks to me like the only thing they can offer is clothes and Bibles." She gave another shrug, then glanced over at the counter. "And tea. Lots of coffee and tea."

"Do you mind if we sit down, and I jot a few notes?"

"Oh, that's right. Your mom said you're a journalist."

"Let's just say I need a really good excuse to be here. I got my boss to let me come to Vienna to cover stories of refugees, but my real reason was to check up on Mom. I wanted to make sure she hadn't been kidnapped or something."

Tracie rolled her eyes. "Aha. You thought that she'd been brainwashed by a bunch of fanatics who grabbed her in Lyon and forced her here so she could join a cult. Is that it?"

I grinned. "I guess it does sound foolish, but Mom's a bit nutty at times."

Tracie frowned. "I don't think she's nutty at all. I think she's an amazingly gifted woman who isn't sure what to do with her life. And I think she's lonely."

I had never thought of my mother as amazingly gifted.

"She used her rusty German and her nursing skills to help my aunt last night, and you should see her with the kids. She can make a game up with nothing but a pebble or a few hazelnuts. She entertained them for an hour with this great game where you toss a nut into a pile of other nuts. The kids loved it."

I smiled. "Yeah, she learned that from the island children on one of her stints with Papa."

"You call your father 'Papa'?"

"Yep. He's French, and that's how the French say Dad." I flashed her my best smile.

"Aha. And what exactly does your father do?"

I hesitated. "It's not easy to explain. Let's just say he works for an international company that transfers him to some of the biggest cities in the world on a regular basis, about every two or three years."

"Or to a remote island?"

This girl didn't miss a thing.

"Right. Once it was to an island. La Reunion—it's not so remote—it's a French department."

"And you always moved with him?"

"Yep. My sisters and I always trailed along, until we each headed off to college. We lived in Brussels, Paris, Tunisia, London, and Vienna, and then back in France. I did high school in Lyon."

"Sounds exotic! Did you like it?"

I shrugged. "Sometimes, sure. But it was hard, changing

schools and having to make new friends every couple years. I learned flexibility, for what that's worth. I guess I liked it, until Papa's job started messing with the family."

"Your mom says your father travels a lot."

"Yeah, I didn't see him much when I was growing up. My sisters and I did okay, but Mom . . . well, understandably, it's been hard on their marriage."

"Well, at least you have a dad. My father keeled over from a heart attack when I was ten. Mom was left with six kids to raise. I'm the oldest. The rest are boys."

"Six kids. Are you Catholic or something?"

"Not exactly. Anyway, I think I'd prefer my father to be traveling lots and still alive."

"Of course you would. Sorry."

"No, I'm sorry. I didn't mean to diminish your story." She was looking at me intensely with her soft brown eyes. "Listen, I'd love to hear more about your family, really, but I need to finish stacking the dishes. I guess I'll see you later."

I guess you will, I thought to myself.

CHAPTER 12

Hamid

*R*asheed knelt down beside the bed where Hamid lay, back in the New Moon Hotel. Hamid groaned as his friend removed a blood-soaked bandage from around his head. He tried to forget the horror-filled night, the torture, the fear.

The phone ringing.

In spite of the pain, Hamid almost smiled as he remembered hearing Jalil's voice, the secret police's confusion, their release.

Now the phone rang again, and Rasheed held it up for Hamid to answer. Again he heard his cousin's voice.

"Hamid, Hamid, what have they done to you? Where are you?"

Hamid closed his eyes to shut out the light that made the blinding pain throbbing in his head worse. He whispered, "At the hotel. I'm okay."

"I went this morning to the embassy; I told them of the

torture. I will go back with more details." In a worried voice, his cousin explained exactly what Hamid must do, the office at the UNHCR where Jalil would arrange an appointment. "Sometimes the wait is much shorter when there is family on the other side," he said.

And when there is money. This Jalil did not say, but Hamid knew that money bought access to many things.

"Jalil. I thank you. I can never thank you enough." Then, as Rasheed stood close by, he added, "I must tell you that there are two of us. My friend has also endured so much . . ."

When the call ended, Hamid collapsed on the bed, his head spinning.

"I must get you to the hospital," Rasheed said.

"Too dangerous."

"Here it is dangerous too."

"I know where we can go."

It took some persuading, but eventually Hamid overcame Rasheed's resistance, and the two companions went to the home of the kind Americans.

Anna Harris clucked her tongue as she cleaned Hamid's head wound and spoke to him in English. "This really needs stitches, Hamid."

"I will not go to the hospital." Hamid trusted no one, no one except this American woman and her husband who had already rescued him one time in the past week.

Anna sighed. "I can understand your fear. I'm thankful you're both alive." Then to Rasheed she said, "You must keep the wound clean; make sure it doesn't get infected."

She helped Rasheed clean his cuts and bruises, clucking again. When she turned to leave the room, Hamid said, "We were afraid to stay at the hotel. But I'm sorry to put you in danger. We were careful coming here. We were not followed."

"Shh," Anna said. "You'll stay here until you are stronger. We're not worried."

But Hamid was worried. He hadn't had the chance to tell Anna that Rasheed was not interested in Isa; in fact, he was vehemently opposed to the Christ. But he supposed Anna did not need this information. She made no reference to Isa or the Ingil.

When Jim returned home that afternoon, he said, "I'll call Keith again. Perhaps something else can be done."

Keith

Sometimes it was wiser to mix things up a bit, no matter how secure the phone lines and Internet. So when Keith received an e-mail from Jim Harris in coded language, he understood perfectly well. Unfortunately. Two Iranian refugees had been taken by the secret Iranian police in the middle of the night, tortured, then miraculously released, and now were hidden at the Harrises' apartment.

He texted Julie at The Oasis. *More prayers for Hamid. Beaten by secret police. Awaiting papers. Hopeful because of torture. Travels with friend who does not like Papy. Staying with J and A in Van.*

Every time Keith used the coded word for God the Father, he smiled. Papy.

Keith's boss, Koen, called a meeting of the engineers that morning. Ten men sat around a table, sipping on coffee. Lindsey kidded that engineers didn't have a normal quota of words they needed to speak a day. "You've all got numbers and frequencies running around in your brains, but they don't make it out of your mouth."

He smiled as silence filled the room. At last Koen began to talk in his perfect English. He was a big man, over six foot four, with thick strawberry-blond hair cut in a crew. And he was typically Dutch—blunt, to the point. Engineers might have few words, but Koen had even fewer.

"Time to pray." That was it.

The men in the room came from as varied backgrounds as Keith's; their nationalities were Dutch, American, British, Brazilian, Afghani. They shared two things in common—an engineering mind and a Christian heart. In just a few minutes, they would be discussing frequencies and something called Facebook, which was suddenly exploding onto the social media scene. Koen believed this Facebook would eventually become a great boon for communicating with Muslims in closed countries who wanted to hear about Isa.

But before they discussed strategy, the eleven men bowed in prayer, and the engineers with their heads filled with numbers put names on their prayers for men and women who were hearing the Gospel through the radio, perhaps for the first time. Keith's prayer was for Hamid.

Bobbie

The tremors had once again disappeared, as had the fear that had lodged itself in my gut all the previous day. Now, surrounded by the short-termers, I relaxed and joined in the preparations for the musical evening. Tracie had suggested I emcee, and I was only too happy to do it.

I was headed upstairs to find an old guitar when Julie met me in the hall, her face downcast. "Bad news?" I asked.

"It's the refugee I told you about—Hamid. He's been tortured. Our contact in Van is housing him for a day or two, but it's precarious. I just got off the phone with Amir. He's met with Hamid's cousin, and they have gone to the embassy to state the case on this end. Evidently . . ."

Amir. I was no longer paying attention to Julie. I felt my face flush.

"Bobbie? Bobbie? Are you all right? Here, come sit down."

Then Julie's face softened as understanding came over her. Julie had been serving at The Oasis for almost fifteen years. She knew my story. She reached out and squeezed my hand. "Do you want to see him again, Bobbie?"

I closed my eyes and heard Peggy's voice on the phone from yesterday. "It is not too late, young lady! You *will* see that man, you hear me! You are not going to weasel your way out of it. No excuses. And no fear. I am absolutely convinced that our Lord wants you to deal with this. He will not let you go before it's done."

But to Julie I simply said, "I don't know. I just don't know if I'm ready."

Julie's eyes brightened. "No, I'm sure you will never feel ready. Thank the Lord that He respects our feelings, and yet He sees fit to push us forward in spite of them."

Dear Julie. At almost seventy, she had not slowed down a bit, still the same bundle of energy and faith that I remembered from years ago. I knew that the refugees regarded her as a mother figure, especially the young men who showed up in increasing numbers day by day.

"Amir usually drops by The Oasis once a month. He's due for a visit soon," she said and winked at me.

Rasa

Rasa knelt beside the little cot in the basement of the kind people's home. Maamaan and baby Omid were still upstairs with the family, but Rasa had hurried downstairs to their little secret room. She needed to pray to Isa. Baba had called today, but Maamaan's face had not lit up with joy like the previous times. Her forehead had creased, and she had gasped and then a lone tear had slid down her cheek.

When she got off the phone, Rasa had asked, "What is it? What is the matter with Baba?"

Her mother had wiped her hand across her face and forced a smile on her lips. Rasa always could tell when Maamaan was pretending to be happy. "Baba is very tired. That is all, my little Rasa."

But she saw it on Maamaan's face. Something very bad had happened to Baba. He was not tired. He was hurt. Now, on her knees, she began to pray as Miss Beverly had shown them. "Dear Jesus, You see everything and everyone, and You are much bigger than all the bad things in the world. Please take care of Baba. Help him get well, whatever is the matter. And take him to a safe place. I thought he was in a safe place, but Maamaan says he still has a very long way to go on his journey. But You are with him, Isa. Remind Baba that You are with him and You will never leave him. Never."

Hamid

Hamid's head throbbed continually as he and Rasheed made their way back to the UNHCR building the next day. At least he and Rasheed were strong enough to present themselves to the officials just as Jalil had instructed them. This time they avoided the long line of refugees and were ushered in a side entrance. They handed their papers to a government worker, who motioned for them to take a seat on the metal bench in the hall and then disappeared.

Long minutes passed. At last she returned and said, "Follow me."

One foot in front of the other, Hamid slowly climbed the flight of stairs. Rasheed kept his hand on Hamid's arm to steady him. The woman knocked on a door, opened it, and then motioned for them to go inside, where they were greeted by a thin, dark-haired man.

"Good afternoon," he said. He smiled and offered his hand to each. "My name is Polat. Please be seated."

He indicated two chairs in front of his desk, and Hamid sank into one gratefully while Rasheed took the other.

"Do you speak English?"

Hamid nodded. "A little. I am Hamid. And this is Rasheed."

"We've been expecting you." Polat directed his gaze at

Hamid. "We heard from your cousin in Austria."

Hamid breathed in deeply, relief washing through him.

"He has sent this to you." Polat handed him an envelope with a wad of Turkish bills in it.

Hamid squinted as the pain in his head intensified. At last he managed to ask, "How long until we receive papers and can join him in Austria?"

Polat kept the same friendly smile on his face. "That is hard to say. When it is a question of immediate family being separated—children from their parents or wives from husbands—the case falls in the category of family reunification regulations. Even then it can take weeks or even months before the exit visa is issued.

"But your relative is only a cousin. You and your friend will have to go through the same process as any other refugee—applying for refugee status in hopes that it will be granted and some countries will be prepared to accept you. The fact that you have a relative in Austria may indeed be helpful, but there is no guarantee that you will actually end up there."

Hamid felt his hope falling, falling. He didn't dare to look at Rasheed.

Then Polat continued. "But now there is this instance of abuse." He nodded to the bandage around Hamid's head. "This is a serious issue. We are thankful you were not killed." He stared down at the forms. "You have left Iran because of religious beliefs, and you have been persecuted."

Rasheed sat perfectly still as Hamid nodded again, the room suddenly spinning around him.

"Generally in these extreme cases, the process goes more quickly. Do you have a way we can contact you?"

His throat dry, Hamid simply nodded and jotted down the cell phone number on a piece of paper that Polat handed him.

"I wish you both well. I am sorry for this circumstance. You have perhaps been to the hospital to care for your wound?"

"No, no hospital," Hamid said.

"But it is cared for?"

"Yes, well cared for."

As the two companions made their way back to the house of Jim and Anna, Rasheed tugged Hamid to a stop and looked him in the eye. "I am thankful that 'religious persecution' is the reason we can leave Turkey," he said. "But remember, I am not interested in this foreign God."

CHAPTER 13

Tracie

I had sung in front of many a large audience in many a large auditorium, and yes, I loved the applause. But singing at The Oasis was more amazing than anything I had done before. Tonight I performed for people who were needy. And then, suddenly, I wasn't performing any more *for* them, but *with* them. The short-term team sang the songs we'd prepared, and we felt such a rush of joy when the refugees recognized the tunes from their different countries. Many joined in, their faces relaxing into smiles and laughter.

We sang a few songs in English, and I led the kids in "Head and Shoulders, Knees and Toes," complete with motions. Suddenly all the refugees, adults as well as children, were on their feet, shouting out the English words and touching their eyes and ears and mouth and nose, bending and laughing, as we sang the words more and more quickly. When we finished, collapsing into giggles, the children begged, "Again!

Again!" in their one-word English.

Then we opened up the evening for different refugees to teach a song or sing for the others, or play the piano or guitar. A young Afghani named Armagan broke down sobbing as he sat in front of the very old keyboard that Carol had dug up from somewhere. Tears ran down his face as he played Beethoven's *Für Elise* flawlessly, with deep feeling. In that moment, all those precious dark-skinned would-be-terrorists became their true selves to me—young boys so afraid and so homesick and so thankful to catch snatches of beauty in the midst of their broken lives.

Another teenaged boy, Fareed, had the most gorgeous tenor voice I had ever heard. While another young man was playing a guitar, I approached Fareed. "I want to sing with you," I said, using sign language and pointing between us and then to my mouth and his. "You have such a beautiful voice."

"Thanks!" he said, and his accent was pitch-perfect American.

I burst into laughter. "Oh, I'm so dumb. I didn't think you understood English."

"I watched a ton of American TV shows and movies when I was growing up. In my country"—where was his country? I suddenly couldn't remember—"nothing is dubbed. We hear the native tongue and then there are subtitles. It's a good way to learn English. American English."

"Sounds like it," I said, and then added, "But your voice is beautiful. You must have had training."

"Yes. Early on, I was rewarded for my beautiful voice. My town and then my country were proud of me." Then his face fell. "But I saw that I would never be free to sing what I really believed. To think for myself. So I left. My family is still there, but they told me to go. To run. To find another life."

"I'm sorry." It was all I could think to say. Fareed couldn't be over fifteen or sixteen. "I'm glad to have met you, though.

I'm Tracie."

"Yes, Tracie. You too have a lovely voice."

I repeated my question. "Will you sing with me, Fareed? Do you know any song we could sing together?"

"I would be honored, Tracie, to sing with you."

So we did. We sang "The Prayer," made famous by Josh Groban. When we finished, there were no dry eyes in the room, mine included.

Everyone was begging for more songs and clapping along with each performance, and really, the feeling in the room was just a burst-your-lungs type of joy. The refugees' faces were simply glowing.

Though I'd had lots of accolades for my singing over the years, the one person whose approval I never felt was Neil's. He was good-looking and athletic, and he liked to be noticed, and though it sounds crazy, I think he was always a little jealous of my voice and the attention it brought me. But here, in a room crowded with displaced people singing in a dozen different languages, I felt approval, a good kind of approval . . . as if this was what I was made for. As if our musical evening was somehow very important in an indefinable spiritual way. I felt a part of these people as we shared the joy of music.

I think I was falling in love, with the refugees like Naseef and Fareed, with Carol and Julie and Tom and JoAnn who worked so hard every day, and even with the short-termers, who seemed like amazing girls who came only to serve. I understood all of a sudden how Aunt Bobbie would miss this odd world, would long for it. It was intense, gratifying, heartbreaking, and sometimes awe-inspiring. It was about as far removed from life with the T-tribe as I could imagine, and I began to wonder again why in the world Aunt Bobbie hadn't come back. Sure, stay with us for a few years, until Mom got her feet on the ground, but why had Aunt Bobbie stayed in Atlanta for twelve long years—twelve—when there was tons

The Long Highway Home

of work to do here, and she was ever so ready to do it?

I was so wound up after the evening, I couldn't sleep. I changed into my sweats and brushed my teeth and then flopped onto the bed. "That was a really awesome evening, wasn't it, Aunt Bobbie?"

She was already in her bright orange pajamas. She nodded, but I thought she looked very tired.

The doc says she just needs to take it easier.

"I think I'll head downstairs for a sec. I'm too pent up to sleep." I stood up.

"You do that, Trace." She closed her eyes and breathed in deeply, almost as if she were praying. I was about to leave when she spoke again. "Thanks so much for insisting that I come back here, Tracie. Every day is a gift. My life has been one surprise after another."

I couldn't let that pass. "Maybe so, but it seems to me like your life came to a halt the day you flew back to America and moved in with us. After seeing you here, I think we kinda ruined your life."

Bobbie frowned. I'd made her mad. I'd done it on purpose, I guess. I needed to hear what I knew she'd say.

"Never, ever say that again, Tracie Hopkins! You hear me? My life has been one adventure after another, and I wouldn't trade it for anyone else's."

"How can you say that now? Your life sucks! At least the part about the cancer sucks!"

"That's because you're looking at it with your regular eyes. You need to look with eyes of faith."

I rolled my eyes in front of her, showing her the whites. "You mean like this?"

"Very funny. Eyes of faith see potential. They look behind and know that the past was just a stepping-stone for the future."

"Really."

"Really. Like with this trip. I wanted to come back to The Oasis, had planned to, and yet never quite could do it. And then God picked me up, and here I am."

"Wait a minute. Are you telling me you think God caused me to ask you to go to Europe to get you here at The Oasis for some crazy plan of His? That's nuts, Bobbie. It was *my* idea, and I haven't consulted God in a long, long time."

"I realize that, Trace. What I'm saying is that I don't think God gets surprised very often."

For some reason that made me laugh out loud, and I nodded. Then I tiptoed up to something else I needed to ask. "Did my mom always want you to stay?"

"What do you mean?"

"I know you were such a help in those first years. But afterwards. Did she really need you? She was handling us okay, wasn't she?"

"We were a team, Trace, you know that. Your mother and I."

"Yes, but did she really need you after a while? Why did you stay with us when you could have come back here? You said you thought about it every day. Surely Mom would have let you go. Lots of women raise their children on their own."

It was the first time in my life I had ever seen my aunt look defensive. "Why in the world would you say that, Tracie? I stayed for all of you."

My heart started beating a little faster. "I think you stayed because you needed us as much as we needed you. Maybe more. I think you stayed because you were *afraid* to come back here, for a reason I don't know. Maybe you were afraid, like I am, of letting yourself love someone again."

One large slow tear slid down my aunt's cheek, and immediately I regretted my words. I bent down and kissed Aunt Bobbie's cheek. "I'm so sorry. I don't know why I blurt out such stupid things. I'm sure it has to do with all the anger I've stored up inside."

"Perhaps," my aunt said, eyes closed. "But I think you're asking questions that I've been ignoring for a long time. I may have eyes of faith, but I think you may be seeing more clearly than I am right now. Or at least you're willing to admit what's inside."

I threw my arms around her as if I were a young girl again. Then I took her hands and said, "Whatever reason it was that you stayed with us, Aunt Bobbie, I'm so glad you did. I don't know what I would have done without you."

She squeezed my hands. "Thanks, Trace. You go on downstairs and hang out with the others. I better obey the doctor's orders and get some sleep."

"Good night, Bobs. I love you."

"Night, Trace. Same to you and more."

As I walked downstairs to the game room, I berated myself for hurting Aunt Bobbie. But she'd probably say that God had prompted me to ask my out-of-place questions.

I don't think God gets surprised very often. Yes, I agreed with her on that point.

And if the truth be told, I could agree with her on another. Aunt Bobbie and I had different perspectives on so many things because we looked at the circumstances with different eyes. Eyes of faith, she had said. And here came those chills again. Whether I liked it or not, something was happening in my heart, and it was affecting my eyes—the way I looked at life. I didn't have eyes of faith, not yet, but perhaps someday . . .

Bobbie

After Tracie left the room, I could not sleep. Her words, her questions, haunted me. Why, why, why hadn't I come back? Poor dear Sally. Did my intrusion in her family keep her from loving again? Had I scared men away from my sister? I had certainly done a good job of scaring them away from me. Tracie was right. I was afraid to love again.

But she was wrong too. I wanted to tell her that I *had* let myself love again. I had loved her. I had loved them, all six of my sister's kids. I had opened my heart after it was crushed, and I had loved. She was right, and she was wrong . . . I'd told her that I'd been in love with Amir . . . but I'd never even mentioned Vasilica . . .

When the walls of Eastern Europe tumbled down in 1989, our mission board scrambled to find new jobs for us. Bible smuggling was no longer necessary; we could go into the Eastern countries and hand out whatever we darn well pleased. Some of my teammates settled in Romania and Bulgaria and what was then called Czechoslovakia. But I had fallen in love with refugees—and one refugee in particular—so I stayed and worked at the burgeoning ministry in Traiskirchen.

The summer of 1992 I was invited to work in an orphanage in Criscior, a little village in Romania where few people had cars and everyone had chickens. In preparing for the summer, I planned many activities for the children, but the orphanage had neglected to tell me one small detail: all the children were deaf and mute. They could not hear me, and most could not read lips.

So I improvised. Channeling Marcel Marceau, I brought mime to the broken-tiled-floor "stage" of the refectory in Emmanuel Orphanage. On my first day, I acted out the story of Zacchaeus for a roomful of children ranging in age from two to twelve. Their eyes were glued on me, and in those eyes I read hunger. Not just physical hunger, but a deep-down need for relationships, for someone to hold their hands and tickle them and play.

So throughout the summer I held hands and tickled and played with the children.

I'd open the Bible and point to the words, and then I

would choose children to help me act out the stories. We mimed Jesus calling Andrew and Peter, Peter walking on the water, Jesus healing blind Bartimaeus. But their favorite by far was the story of Jesus healing the deaf man. The children clapped enthusiastically, understanding that suddenly this man could hear.

I mimed how Jesus could heal them too—heal their hearts and give them the love they so desperately needed and hungered for.

A little boy named Vasilica was particularly hungry for attention, most often receiving a rebuke as he ran around the room, unable to sit still, pulling the hair of the girls, who turned on him with silent screams. Vasilica's energy and affection knew no bounds. He didn't care whether he made us mad or caused us to giggle—he just wanted to be noticed.

One day Lidia, one of the full-time staff members, said to me, "He's a handful all right, but he's a bright little fellow. I'm sure he could learn to sign, but no one has time to be with the kids individually."

Right then and there, I decided to make extra time for this six-year-old troublemaker. That first summer I took him on walks with several other kids. We spent our energy climbing the mountains surrounding the village and chasing wild turkeys and climbing trees. By the next summer, I had learned to sign. When I taught Vasilica to sign, he picked it up quickly, and he helped the other children learn. I taught him to read from the same beginning Romanian book I had used years before. We learned together. And I fell in love.

I went back to Romania again the next summer, and when it was time for me to return to Traiskirchen I dared to ask Lidia, "Are these children up for adoption?"

"It's hard enough to find people to adopt healthy babies," she said. "No one wants to adopt a deaf and dumb child."

"But what if they did want to?"

She shrugged. "Yes, I suppose it would be possible."

I knew what I wanted. I decided right then to adopt Vasilica.

But that's not how things turned out.

I turned off the light in our room at Gasthaus Müller and pulled the covers over my head as if I could also pull the covers over my memories and hide them. But it didn't work. As I lay in bed, what I saw were the beautiful dark brown eyes of Vasilica, and his face lighting up in a smile as he signed to me his favorite words. *I love you, Bobbie.*

Stephen

I had come to Vienna to check up on my mom, but my boss was benefitting nicely. I'd sent him one refugee's story, and he'd called me with an enthusiastic, "Good stuff here, Lefort."

So I told him my idea of running stories of Hurricane Katrina survivors—refugees within the United States—side by side with stories of the men I was meeting here, Iranians and Czechs and Iraquis.

Mr. Kimball liked the idea and granted me another week. Pam did not, and had a few choice words to say before clicking off without saying good-bye.

I was glad for a prolonged assignment because, suddenly, I cared. I cared about the refugees and the missionaries and the team of American girls. Something started tugging at my heart as the coffee-house room filled with refugees. The college girls had planned a "musical evening," and I took some photos of the performers and the people listening. When the music was finished, Tracie's aunt entertained the crowd with a story from her Bible-smuggling past. After the refugees left, I helped the workers clean up, and then Julie, an older woman with gray hair but very youthful eyes, said, "Now we need to pray. Our Lord blessed this evening. We will pray for fruit."

Fruit? I thought it was a strange thing to pray for, but no one else blinked.

"And we will pray for Hamid," she continued. "He and his traveling companion have been tortured. But what men mean for evil, God can change into good. Hamid's cousin has appealed to the embassy here. Pray that the paperwork will go miraculously quickly."

Then they all bowed their heads to pray. I sat off to one side and discreetly took photos. I got a little choked up when Mom started praying—I mean, I didn't even think she knew *how* to pray. When Julie asked God to "give fruit," I suddenly understood. She was talking about a type of spiritual transformation.

Their prayers seemed naïve to me. Did they really believe that appealing to some unseen Higher Power was going to break through months of crazy red tape? I didn't know much about refugees, but even I realized that nothing seemed to happen "miraculously quickly" for them.

Still, I admired these people. And I liked this place. It *was* like an oasis. In the midst of the chaos and confusion of the refugees' lives, these people, mostly women, wore smiles on their faces and courage in their hearts and served. That was it—they served these forgotten people as if each one were really an important friend.

Selfless.

That was the word. Interspersed between dozens and dozens of confused-looking misplaced men, women, and children were bright splashes of kindness seen in the lives of the "short-termers" and "full-time missionaries" and "former refugees" and "Austrian volunteers," all serving selflessly because they believed in a God they called their Savior and their Lord.

A few hours later at the Gasthaus Müller, after we'd played

games of Uno and Dutch Blitz, the summer team girls filed
off to bed. But for some reason, I didn't feel sleepy. Snippets
of music from the evening filled my mind. I thought about
Fareed and Tracie, both very far from their different homes,
singing in a third language a prayer to God.

"Not sleepy either?"

I turned to see Tracie herself cradling a cup of coffee in
her hands.

"Nah, kinda wound up. I thought you went upstairs with
the other girls."

"I'm wound up too. And I want to let Aunt Bobbie sleep.
So I thought I'd just . . . keep drinking coffee." When she
smiled, her face brightened and her brown eyes danced. "At
this rate, I'll never get to sleep."

We sat down at a little bistro table where earlier the girls
had played cards. I studied Tracie as she leaned over her cup.
"So you're not a part of this student group, and you're not a
full-time missionary. Why exactly are you here?"

She took a sip of coffee, tilted her head, and said, "I
brought my aunt back to Europe. When my dad keeled over
dead of a heart attack twelve years ago, Bobbie left her work
here and came to Atlanta to help my mom deal with six kids."

"Nice thing to do."

"Bobbie's like that—always serving people. She's like
my second mom. Anyway, a month ago she got really bad
news—inoperable cancer. So I decided we should come to
Europe and she could show me the things she'd always talked
about—while she could still travel."

"Whoa." I cleared my throat. I was never very good at
offering sympathy. "Sorry about your aunt's illness. But I find
it pretty cool that you wanted to bring her back here."

Tracie glanced down at the table, but not before I saw her
eyes tearing up.

"So we started traveling in Venice and then went to Timisoara and Innsbruck, and I asked her why we didn't come here. She'd told me loads of stories about her Bible-smuggling days—stories like the one she told tonight. And I think she was planning to bring me here, but she couldn't quite get up the nerve—not sure why not. Anyway, I just put a little more pressure on her, and voilà."

"Well, she certainly seems at ease with the refugees. I mean, you all do."

"This was Bobbie's life. I guess just being a part of it for a few days is already rubbing off on me."

"I know what you mean. Seems like what's going on here is crazy hopeless, and yet a lot more important than a high school football game or the latest Hollywood gossip."

"I'll grant you that." She fiddled with a loose strand of hair.

"So what do you do in life when you're not following your aunt around Europe?"

Tracie hesitated just a moment before she spoke. "I have no idea. Truly. I thought I had my future planned out. I graduated from college last May. I'd started on a singing career, and I thought I'd be getting married pretty soon. But hey. It didn't work out."

I smiled. "That's . . . vague."

She frowned back, and then looked at me as if trying to decide if I merited hearing more of her story.

"I thought I'd be getting engaged, and instead my boyfriend broke up with me."

"That stinks."

"Yes it does." She gave an exaggerated sigh. "I have a degree in voice. I got a part in an off-Broadway musical, but when Neil broke up with me—on the same day I got the part and the same day I found out about Aunt Bobbie's cancer—well, I freaked. It's stupid, but I blew that chance." She shook her long hair over her shoulders. "But now that I'm away from the situation, I can see how totally wrong he was for me. I mean, I saw it before, but I just didn't have the courage to get out of the relationship. It's a little scary to think I would have agreed to marry him just because I was too big of a chicken to be honest with myself.

"So at the moment I'm jobless and footloose and planning on taking care of my aunt for as long as . . ." She cleared her throat. "For as long as she needs."

"And all this Christian stuff. Do you believe it?"

"I used to, when I was a kid. Then things happened, and I don't know. I got kind of pissed off at God."

I smiled. "You say what you think, don't you?"

She ran her hands over her eyes and nodded. "Way too often."

We sat in silence for a moment. I was remembering the way Tracie's face had transformed—practically glowing—as she sang in front of the refugees. She interrupted my thoughts.

"What about you, Stephen? Are you happy living in Atlanta, or have you thought about coming back to France? Didn't you say the other night that you'd gone to high school in Lyon?"

I shrugged. "I got really worn out with moving all over the place. And I got worn out with being impressed with myself—all the languages I knew, all the travel. I was turning into a big fat jerk, and I wanted something different." I smirked. "According to my girlfriend, I'm still a big fat jerk." I shrugged again. "The trouble is, I haven't ever figured out what it is I want. I like journalism. I really enjoyed covering the craziness in Lyon. But this"—I swept my arm around the room—"what's happening at The Oasis. It seems better. I don't mean just for the story's sake. It just seems better somehow, more meaningful or important."

I looked out to where the moon was beaming through the window. "I'm pretty much in a bad relationship too. I'm not looking forward to going back to my girlfriend. But hey, that's life, isn't it?"

Maybe it was because I was in some remote village outside of Vienna, away from everything I knew, or maybe it was the adrenaline still left from the party, but I felt completely wired. Tracie's numerous cups of coffee seemed to have the same effect on her, and so we talked. We talked by the ping-pong table and drank three more cups of coffee and then we went outside with the moon full, our jackets wrapped around us, and we talked as we walked through dark vineyards, lit up only by the bright white globe above. We talked about our families and our studies and our dreams, and somewhere in the night, Tracie's anger came spilling out, about her father's death and her aunt's control and her responsibility with her brothers and a lot of other pent-up stuff. And then I talked about my anger with my dad and how he had destroyed our family by being absent.

We walked and talked for an hour, maybe two, until we were chilled to the bone, and then we drank one more cup of coffee back in the game room and mumbled an awkward good night to each other at about four a.m.

I didn't sleep. Instead, I remembered all the things I had not dared to say to Tracie . . . how Mom had stopped smiling and Papa had started coming home later and later from the office and then being gone for days and then weeks at a time. And Mom had begun slowly drinking herself to death.

CHAPTER 14

Hamid

*H*amid could not sleep. He lay on his back, holding the document in his trembling hands and whispering "Thank you, Isa," over and over again into the night.

Rasheed lay on the other bed across the room, clutching a similar document in his hand while he snored.

The call had come that afternoon, when Rasheed was playing with the baby and Jim and Hamid were helping the two older children with homework. Hamid's cell had rung, and he'd found Polat on the other line telling him that their papers had come though. In a flurry of excitement, Jim had driven them through town and let them off near the UNHCR building. Hamid and Rasheed again entered a side door, and when they emerged from the main entrance an hour later, they held their official documents high over their heads as they had seen others do. Rasheed, his bruised and battered face breaking into a smile, let out a cry of joy. Hamid felt tears prick his eyes as he kissed the document and silently thanked Isa. The refugees waiting in line cheered and congratulated them. They had their exit visa to go to Austria!

Later, around the dinner table, Jim said, "It is our custom to thank our God for providing us food to eat. I would also like to thank Him for answering our prayers for both of you. It is indeed miraculous."

Hamid bowed his head along with Jim, Anna, and the children. Hamid knew Rasheed would simply sit quietly, eyes staring ahead.

Throughout the meal the two men kept glancing down at the exit visas sitting by their plates. Had this actually happened? Anna and Jim shook their heads in wonder, casting knowing glances and smiles at each other.

Later, lying in bed, Hamid still clasped his exit paper from Turkey in his hands. He thought about Austria, about Jalil, who had perhaps paid all his savings to work this miracle.

Yes, Jim had called it a miracle and an answer to prayer. Hamid agreed.

"Jim and Anna have invited me to go to their church with them this morning," Hamid explained to Rasheed. "These people have been very kind to us. I want to go out of respect for them, for their care."

Inwardly he thought *How I long to attend a Christian church!*

Rasheed frowned, his black eyebrows slanting in two sharp lines. "You're right; they have been good and kind. I like these people. But they are Christians, and remember, it was Christians who got you into trouble in the first place."

"Yes, but here in Turkey, we are free to observe other religions. No one will mind." Hamid searched Rasheed's face to see his friend's reaction.

Rasheed's frown deepened as he said, "Khoda will see. He

sees all and knows all."

"Yes." Hamid felt a pinch of fear. If Rasheed suspected he wanted to go to church for more reasons than simply out of respect for Jim and Anna, he didn't say it out loud. But Hamid read the questions in his friend's eyes.

"But if you wish to go, then go. I'll stay here." Then a smile lit up Rasheed's face. "I'll stay here and dream of Austria and the beautiful women I will meet there."

Hamid sat in the backseat of the Harrises' small car with six-year-old Jacob on his lap and eight-year-old William on his left. Baby Lilly reached out her hand from the car seat on Hamid's right and grabbed hold of his finger. Hamid imagined the day when his baby son would do the same, when little Omid would sit beside him in a car in a village in Austria.

Someday . . .

But not yet.

"I am glad to go to your church," he said to Jim and Anna, "but perhaps I was not wise. Rasheed is a very devout Muslim, and he says Khoda will see and know that I am going to this church with infidels."

"Isa is looking out for you, Hamid," Jim assured him. "Many, many people all around the world have been praying for you. Getting the exit visa from Turkey in this short amount of time is truly a miracle."

"You've been most kind, and I see that Isa is helping me, but still I feel fear."

"You're right to be careful—you should only read the Ingil when you're alone; keep it hidden the rest of the time."

"I have so many questions about this book, about Isa, but I will be leaving you soon."

"Isa will go with you," Anna said. "And when you get to the Government Refugee Housing Center in Traiskirchen, listen carefully as other refugees talk. I'm sure you'll hear about a place called The Oasis. That is where you'll meet other Christians who will help you understand more about Jesus. It may take a few days before they will let you leave the camp. But be patient. And invite Rasheed to go with you to The Oasis. All refugees are welcome. Most who go there now are Muslim. But for those who are seeking, truly seeking Isa, there are Christians who will help you find the way."

Jim parked his old car on a side street and everyone got out.

"Here we are," Anna said, indicating a nondescript building. On the storefront window, written in many different languages, was the word *Welcome* with a cross painted in the middle of the words. This certainly did not look like the churches Hamid had seen in history books and movies, the beautiful cathedrals with stained-glass windows or the white-steepled churches nestled among trees.

As he stepped inside the door behind the Harris family, Hamid felt his heart quickening. The foyer was filled with men and women speaking Farsi, and the sound of his native tongue spoken with no trace of accent warmed him all over. These people were Iranians! What's more, they were Iranian *Christians*. The only Christians he knew were his Armenian neighbors, and now Jim and Anna. But here inside this very plain building called a church, men and women greeted him in Farsi with broad smiles.

He followed Jim and Anna into a rectangular room crowded with fifty or sixty plain metal chairs, most of which were occupied. On the front wall, which was painted in bright yellow, hung a large wooden cross. The effect of the yellow background made the cross stand out, as if the sun were rising behind it, proclaiming some kind of victory. He stared at the cross and his heart stirred, recalling how Jim had explained its significance while Hamid had lain exhausted and ill in the Harrises' home the week before.

Jesus died on the cross willingly, in our place. But then He rose from the dead. The cross is empty. An empty cross is the proclamation of Christ's victory over death . . .

This instrument of torture was the channel God used to overcome death. Hamid liked paradoxes; he continued to stare at the cross. A beautiful paradox indeed.

As they took their seats, Jim whispered to Hamid, "The first part of the church service is called worship time. Later the pastor will preach a sermon from the Bible."

The people worshiped standing up, singing songs accompanied by a guitar and a piano, the joy evident on their faces. Muslims considered music to be worldly and disrespectful to Khoda, but here, Hamid could tell that the people were truly praising a God they loved. They laughed and sang and clapped and even danced! They worshiped out of love, not fear. An inexplicable joy welled up inside of Hamid as he sang the words that were projected onto a screen at the front of the room. The words in Farsi proclaimed things he had never heard before:

Thank you, Lord, for being my Savior
Thank you for your grace
I can never earn your favor
But in humility and joy I seek your face.
Oh, thank you, Jesus . . .

Song after song spoke of a God of love, a God who came to live among sinful people, and who died so that the sinful deeds of mankind could be forgiven. Hamid found himself soaking in the peacefulness of words like *grace* and *forgiveness* and *truth* and *love.*

Later, when the pastor asked if anyone was visiting the church for the first time, Jim stood with Hamid and said, "Many of you have been praying for our friend Hamid this week. He is with us this morning." Hamid felt his face go red as people clapped. "Hamid has agreed for me to share his news." Jim's arm came around Hamid's shoulder, almost protectively. "He was taken and beaten by the secret service, but then an amazing thing happened. He was released, and just yesterday he was granted an exit visa to go to Austria."

There were murmurs of "Praise God!" "Bless you, Lord, thank you!" throughout the room.

"Now pray that Hamid will be kept safe in Austria, that he will meet up with other Christians and be able to find an Iranian church. Pray that he will give his life fully to Isa. And pray that his traveling companion will also have a desire to know Isa al Masi. For the time, he is very much against Christianity."

Then, remarkably, people began praying out loud in Farsi to this God; prayers, one after another, some brief, some long and colorful, were raised to Isa on Hamid's behalf; for protection, for guidance, for his family to be able to join him soon. As he listened to the prayers, Hamid let the tears fall freely. Never had he felt such love, such a holy presence with him.

"Thank you," he murmured to Jim and Anna as they drove home. "God has used you and so many others to save my life. I will never forget you."

Rasa

Rasa twisted and turned in her bed. She couldn't sleep. Under her pillow she had hidden the beautiful Ingil that these kind people, Mr. and Mrs. Garabadian, had given her. They were old, like Maamaan-Bozorg, and Armenian Christians like Noyemi's family. Their Bibles were written with different letters, but Mrs. Garabadian had smiled at Rasa yesterday evening as they ate dinner. "I have a surprise for you, Rasa. It's the New Testament. We will help you read the stories of Jesus." Mrs. Garabadian handed Rasa a copy of the Ingil in Farsi.

"May I keep it?" Rasa asked, wide-eyed.

"Of course, it is for you."

Now for the past two nights, after dinner, she and Mrs. Garabadian took the Ingil, and the old woman read to her in Farsi and then helped Rasa decipher the words, too. Even Maamaan smiled when Rasa pronounced the words in the Ingil. Maamaan seemed to smile a little bit more now. Baba had called, and something very good had happened.

She closed her eyes, holding the little New Testament close and said, "Thank you, Isa, thank you very much."

Alaleh

Alaleh studied the map that Astrid Garabadian showed her. She traced with her finger the route from Van to Vienna, and her face broke into a smile. Tomorrow morning, Hamid and his friend Rasheed would board a plane—a plane!—and fly from Van to Vienna.

He had called her yesterday and said such strange words. "God has answered the prayers of many, my love! It has never happened like this. Tell my Rasa that she was right. Isa hears our prayers."

"Shh, Hamid!" she had warned him. "You must be careful what you say!"

She looked again at the map. Ah, her professor, her dreamer! He had managed to keep his political ideas to himself for all their years in Tehran, but now perhaps he would say something even worse, something religious, about this Jesus. Devout Muslims would not want to hear him talk about Isa, whether Hamid was in Iran or Turkey or Austria.

"If you say these things, your Muslim friends will hate you! Please, please be careful," she had begged him.

But little Rasa seemed to understand Hamid's strange words. When Alaleh explained the miracle of Hamid leaving Van so quickly, Rasa beamed. "Maamaan, it's just like in the Ingil. Mrs. Garabadian told me the story. A man named Peter was put in prison because he loved Isa, and at night, an earthquake came and the prison doors opened and Peter was free. See, Isa is looking after Baba just like he looked after Peter. Isa can open any door. Miss Beverly always said that nothing was impossible for Isa."

As baby Omid nursed at her breast, Alaleh wondered: from where did her daughter's strange and innocent faith spring? Whom could Alaleh thank for taking care of Hamid? Christians! Noyemi's family and now the Garabadians and then this couple named Jim and Anna in Van. Hamid had talked of many other Christians, Iranian Christians in Van and in Austria, who were praying for him. People in churches!

Alaleh trembled. Dear, dear Hamid. Rasa and Hamid, and now even Maamaan-Bozorg, back in Tehran, praised this Isa God. Did they not remember that He was the reason they were in this predicament in the first place? Hamid was an intellectual and a dreamer, and dear little Rasa a mystic, but she, Alaleh, was practical. She understood that no matter how many miracles they saw, they must keep their mouths shut about the Christian god.

She thought of a proverb Hamid used to quote with a wink: *Trust in God but tie your camel tight.*

That was wisdom, Hamid! Keep your mouth shut!

She touched the soft fuzz on Omid's head and wondered how long she and her children could stay with the Garabadians. Any Christian who housed Muslims was risking his life. She did not want harm to come to these good people.

Omid drew back from her breast and gave her his infant smile, a satisfied, sweet expression. Overcome with emotion, Alaleh whispered, "I do not know whom to pray to. But I can say thank you. Thank you to whoever is protecting us thus far."

CHAPTER 15

Tracie

I could barely pull myself out of bed at eight on Sunday morning. I had not slept a wink.

Aunt Bobbie came into the room with a towel draped over her shoulder. "Ah, a hot shower does a world of good." She flashed me a smile, but she looked exhausted too. "What time did you get in?"

I shrugged, "Not sure. But it was really late. I ended up telling Stephen my life story."

Aunt Bobbie raised her eyebrows.

"That's all we did. Talk and walk and drink coffee."

"He seems like an interesting young man."

I grinned at my aunt. Whenever she used the word *interesting* to describe a guy, it meant she had severe reservations about him. She had once called Neil *very interesting indeed.*

"You don't like him?"

"No, actually, I do like him. He's very kind to his mother—that always gets points in my book—and he seems to have his head on fairly straight. A little lost, though, wouldn't you say?"

I made a face. "Lost as in not 'saved'—not included in Jesus's fold—or lost as in not sure what to do next in life?"

"Both and."

"Well, you're probably right on both counts. At least, he says he's a bit confused about what to do next. And he certainly doesn't call himself a Christian." I thought back to my conversation with Stephen. "Anyway, he seems like a really nice guy. Different, you know? Not very American. He's got culture. That's the word. He's lived all over the world, and he knows all kinds of things. And he's a self-proclaimed recovering jerk."

"Is that a good thing?"

"Yeah, I think so. Neil is just a complete jerk. At least Stephen has recognized that being brilliant and cute and accomplished and cultured doesn't necessarily make you a very fun person to be around. He has potential."

"Potential, huh? Does that mean with you?"

I laughed. "No, Aunt Bobs. Don't get ideas. He's leaving in a few days."

"True. And long distance relationships aren't easy."

I seized my chance, a perfect segue into my next question. "Okay, Aunt Bobbie. I've waited and waited. Won't you please tell me a little more about your refugee? What was his name? Do you still think of him? What happened? Is he married now—do you know anything about him?"

"Hold on, Trace. One question at a time." She had gotten dressed in a bright green T-shirt and a jean skirt and was brushing her hair. Now she sat down on the edge of her bed and said, "His name is Amir. And yes, I cared for him. Quite a lot."

"Did you love him?" I started pacing the room.

"Yes."

"And he loved you?"

"Yes."

"Did you consider marrying him?"

Bobbie nodded, took a breath, and said, "Yes, we were planning to get married."

"And then what?"

"And then it didn't work out."

"But *why* didn't it work out, Bobs? Won't you tell me a little bit more?" I sighed dramatically, then sat down on my bed. "No, never mind. Don't say anything; this is just me and my big mouth again asking inappropriate questions. I'm sorry for what I said last night, and it's none of my business if you don't want to tell me about Amir."

Aunt Bobbie leaned forward and met my eyes. "What you said last night was perfectly appropriate, Trace. I think the Lord is pushing me to deal with my relationship with Amir—how it ended." Then, "But to back up and answer your other questions—Amir still lives in Austria and is the pastor of an Iranian church in a little village a few hours west of here. I don't know if he's married; I rather assume not. Carol has kept me informed, in her quiet and unobtrusive way, and she's never mentioned anything about him having a wife or kids."

"Do you think you might see him on this trip, then?"

"Maybe." She turned her bright blue eyes on me. "Maybe, Tracie. I would like to think I'm ready to see him again."

I wanted to know what this man had done to Aunt Bobbie to wound her so deeply. But I could not bring myself to ask that question, so I used her tactic of sharing something about my life in hopes she would relate it to hers. "When I was talking with Stephen last night, I realized something. I could start liking another guy. I wasn't condemned to miss Neil for the rest of my life. I could move on. And I admitted what I'd known for so long. He wasn't the right guy for me anyway."

"Good for you, Trace. If you can move forward, well, that's simply marvelous." She sounded truly thankful. But then she added, "For me, it's a bit different. It wasn't that getting married to Amir seemed wrong to me. It was just that, just that . . ." She cleared her throat twice and tears sprang to her eyes. I had rarely seen my aunt cry. "Some hard things happened that made it impossible," she whispered. "And then your father died, and I knew I should go back to Atlanta. And I wanted to, Tracie. I knew it was the right thing to do."

As I had done the night before, I sat beside my aunt and hugged her tightly, as if I was ten again, and she was listening to my sad story. "Yes, I'm sure it was right for you to be with us, Aunt Bobbie. And now, I hope you'll have a chance to see this man again and make that right, too."

Stephen

Mom and I sat at a table in the corner of a little heuriger down the street from The Oasis, each sipping Riesling that came from the vineyards the restaurant owners tended. We had chosen an assortment of meats and vegetables from the display counter, and I took a bite of a thick sausage.

"Thanks so much for bringing me here, darling," she said. "These little restaurants are completely charming. What a treat to have a little time alone with you."

"It is indeed. I still can't quite believe that we're both here." I furrowed my brow. "Have you heard from Papa?"

Mom shook her head. "No." She reached for her wine glass and took a long drink. "Stephen . . ." Tears sprang in her eyes. "You've seen our marriage failing over the years. And now. . ." She set down the glass and looked at me. "I'm afraid it's over."

My heart fell with a hollow thud of disappointment. No,

I wasn't surprised, but hearing Mom admit it knocked the breath out of me.

We sat in silence for a long moment. Mom wiped a finger over her eyes and forced a smile. "Your dad got another assignment, this time in Hong Kong. I told him he can go if he wants, but I'm not going along. I cannot bear to move again." Her hands trembled slightly.

I reached and covered them with mine. "I'm so sorry, Mom."

"I feel like I lost your father a long time ago, but still . . ." She let out a long sigh, then she concentrated hard on spearing a cherry tomato with her fork and bringing it to her mouth. I searched for something else to say, but nothing came to mind, so I took a bite of a spicy curry chicken salad. Now it tasted bland.

"But being here has given me a new lease on life, Stephen. It's the strangest thing. Like a coincidence that isn't really a coincidence."

I was relieved to change the subject. My initial fears had calmed after being with the short-term team for a week, but I still had questions. "Tell me exactly how you met these girls?"

"It was a month ago, at a church in Lyon. I was at my lowest. I'd just had that conversation with your father—about Hong Kong. A friend of mine who volunteers with me at the soup kitchen invited me to her church. You remember Brigitte? Wonderful woman; she has always been very open about her . . . spirituality. And she knew I wasn't doing well.

"Anyway, I went with her to this church, and it was such a lively place, at least ten different nationalities represented, all worshiping together in French. The American girls were there that morning, and they presented a slide show about their upcoming trip, asking for people to pray for them. And I don't know, Stephen, it was all so strange and new and yet, it was so strong, the feeling that I *had* to go with them. Like I said, it seemed like such a coincidence that I should be there on that day when they were talking about coming to Vienna. You know how I love Vienna."

She sat for a moment, lost in thought, pushing a fat *knodel* around on her plate.

"I imagine that Carol moved heaven and hell," she said, blushing, "to convince those girls I could come with them. I don't actually know why they accepted me on their team, as they call it. I don't share their religious convictions—at least I didn't then—and well, I was a mess. I probably looked like death warmed over."

"Mom." Nothing about that expression described my petite, attractive mother.

"But I suppose Brigitte and Carol and the others somehow felt sorry enough for me that they decided I could come. Or maybe it was because I speak German and I'd been a nurse. Anyway, I'm babbling. But I am thankful to be here. I don't know what's next when I get back to Lyon, but this has been . . ." She searched for a word. "It's been like a lovely parenthesis in my life." She reached out and squeezed my hand. "What about you, Stephen? How are you? How is Pam?"

A parenthesis in my life. Mom had that right.

"I don't know. Right now I feel completely removed from Atlanta. Like another part of my personality is coming alive again now that I'm back in Europe."

"Yes, it's been quite a while since you've been here. Have you missed it?"

"I didn't think so, but now that I'm here, well, yes. I miss Europe, I miss the mentality here, the way people live life. And of course I miss you and Papa." I patted her hand. "And then, I don't know, it's been pretty heady to be covering all the riots going on in Paris and Lyon. But nothing is quite like being here at The Oasis and hearing these stories. I've really enjoyed this week, Mom. And I can't tell you how great it is to see you happy." I grinned and admitted, "I really thought you'd gone off the deep end and were involved in a horrible cult. I'm greatly relieved to be here and see what these people are actually like."

Mom took a sip of wine, but only a sip, and winked at me. "Not a cult, I assure you. And Pam? Are you looking forward to getting back to her?"

"I guess. Pam is not very thrilled about this 'vacation,' as she calls it." I fiddled with my napkin, took a bite of sausage and potato, chewed for a moment. "I thought we were on the same page about life, but I think, well, maybe I'm changing. What I'm doing here seems so much more important than what I was doing."

"I'm sure Pam can't begin to imagine what it's like. You don't have to make a quick decision about a girl, Stephen. If you're not sure about Pam . . ." She looked off, and when she met my eyes again, hers were sad, nostalgic. "Be sure you find a girl who believes in you, Stephen, who supports you. I didn't do that for your father. I drove him away with my nagging. He loved his work." She made a face. "No, he was *in love* with his work. You know, I think I could have fought for him if it were another woman. But I just didn't know how to win with his work. So I nagged and became so depressed, and I don't blame him for leaving."

"He hasn't really left, Mom. He's just traveling. "

"Yes, but with my ultimatum, I don't think he'll come back." Her smile wavered, then she recovered. "Anyway, find a girl who supports what you believe in, and make sure you can support what she believes in too."

I sat with that thought for a few seconds. *But what do I believe in? How can I find a girl who will support me in my beliefs if I don't even know what they are?*

Out loud I said, "And what do you think about the way these people practice their faith?"

Mom smiled, and her eyes twinkled. "I think and I hope and I *pray* that whatever it is they have is contagious and that it will rub off on me! Maybe I've already caught the virus."

I had not enjoyed time with my mother so much since I was a kid. I watched her and realized that Tracie was right. My mom was amazingly gifted. She just needed someone to believe in her. And I noticed with a sigh of relief that she had nursed the same glass of wine for the two and a half hours we'd been sitting in the heuriger. For the time being, something besides alcohol seemed to be filling up the gaping holes in Mom's heart.

"Movie starts in fifteen minutes," Dee announced to us when Mom and I came back to Gasthaus Müller.

"What are you watching?" Mom asked.

"*The Sound of Music*, what else?" Dee laughed.

"Oh, I just love that musical!" Mom enthused. "I'll be right down." And she hurried up to her room with Dee beside her.

I was alone with the ping-pong table. I picked up a paddle and a ping-pong ball and started bouncing the ball on the paddle, counting. Lost in concentration, I didn't notice that Tracie had come into the game room until she said, "Hey."

I slapped down the paddle on the table, and the little white ball flipped off to the side. "Oh, hey," I said, embarrassed.

She blushed and gave a weak smile. "You're pretty handy with that paddle, Stephen." She took a deep breath and said, "I, I wanted to apologize for keeping you up till the wee hours with my melodrama. I'm really sorry for going on and on."

"No need to apologize. I enjoyed talking. I don't think either of us was going to get much sleep."

"True." She grinned, then nodded to the stairway. "I think it is really awesome that you took your mother out to dinner.

I mean, that is about the sweetest thing I can think of, and she was glowing when she came back."

"Yeah, it was pretty great to hang out with her. After all that stuff I told you about my parents last night, she said some things that were . . . helpful. She told me to find someone who believes in me and supports my dreams, and vice versa."

Tracie bent down and retrieved the ping-pong ball. "Sounds like good advice. Advice I should follow too. Neil didn't believe in me. He was always jealous or preoccupied with himself. I wish I'd seen it sooner."

I motioned to the large TV screen. "Are you going to watch the movie? Dee said it'll be starting in a few minutes."

"Maybe. I've seen it before." She winked at me.

I squinted. "What? I don't get it."

"Oh, it's just that I've played every girl part in *The Sound of Music* and know the movie by heart. I've seen it about fifty times. I mean, it's awesome, but I don't know that I really need to see it yet again."

"Then can I invite you to have a glass of wine with me? I know a great little heuriger right around the block."

Tracie's face broke into a lovely smile and she laughed. "Sure. I'd like that a lot."

Ten minutes later we stopped in front of a pale yellow stuccoed building with a lantern hanging above the doorway. The lantern was lit up and wrought-iron ivy encircled it, with another wrought-iron sign with the name *Schafler* dangling on wire underneath.

When we entered the heuriger, the same one I'd been in with my mother, the staff smiled and patted me on the back. The waitress who had served Mom and me said with a wink, "This girl looks more your age."

CHAPTER 16

Hamid

*H*amid waited in line with Rasheed at the security check at the Ferit Melen airport in Van, watching as people removed cell phones and laptops from their carry-on luggage. Hamid's small backpack held only the radio, the Ingil, carefully hidden inside a history book, the cell phone, and his exit papers that said, yes, he could leave Turkey legally and travel to Vienna. He removed the radio and cell phone from the backpack and placed them in a gray plastic tray. He handed the guard his plane ticket and passport. The guard eyed the paper, then Hamid, then the paper again. Did seconds or long minutes pass? Finally, with only a nod of the head, the security guard sent Hamid through.

Rasheed followed behind shortly, and Hamid let out a grateful sigh. They had cleared the passport and security checks. Could it be that they were truly heading to Austria?

Hamid had never been in a plane before, but until this

very moment he had not even thought of this adventure. His other adventures had been enough to crowd his head.

"Are you afraid to fly?" he asked Rasheed.

Rasheed nodded. "A little. But I tell myself we are flying to freedom, and so I am happy."

When Hamid and Rasheed were at last seated on the plane, they looked at each other and began to giggle, giggle as if they were schoolboys, mere children who did not yet know the harsh realities of life. It felt so incredibly good to laugh.

Finally Rasheed's face grew serious. "We are drawing attention to ourselves. We mustn't do that yet. Later, in Vienna, I will draw attention to myself for these beautiful girls, but not yet."

Hamid punched Rasheed playfully and forced a frown. "Yes," he whispered. "Later."

The clouds looked like pastel-tinted cotton balls floating below him as Hamid watched out the window of the plane. Was God up here in the sky? Did He sit on the clouds somewhere in the distance, advising them when to send rain?

Hamid squinted as the sun's light seeped through the window. He closed his eyes and thought of something Rumi, the great Persian poet, had written hundreds of years earlier:

I said, "What about my eyes?"
God said, "Keep them on the road."
I said, "What about my passion?"
God said, "Keep it burning."
I said, "What about my heart?"
God said, "Tell me what you hold inside it?"
I said, "Pain and sorrow."
God said, "Stay with it. The wound is the place where the light enters you."

Yes, light was entering. He stared out the window again as the sun pierced through the clouds. He had been wounded, yes, but oh, how he was ready for the light to enter. And as the plane hovered in the sky, he knew what word the light represented: hope.

Hamid watched as passengers from his flight began retrieving their luggage from the conveyor belt at the baggage claim of the Vienna International Airport. He and Rasheed walked past with their small backpacks, through the sliding glass doors marked *Ausgang* and into a crowd of people. Some waited for loved ones while others held hand-printed signs indicating a person's name. So many people and yet everything—from the black tile floors to the bright signs and the high shining ceilings—seemed clean and modern. Could this truly be Austria?

From the corner of his eye Hamid saw Jalil waving enthusiastically. Ten years had passed since he had seen his cousin in person, but Jalil looked the same—stocky, abundant black hair (now with tinges of gray around the temples), a large hook nose, and a smile that stretched wide and showed several gold teeth.

"Hamid! Hamid, you made it!" Jalil engulfed him in a long hug.

"Jalil! Thank you, Jalil."

Hamid introduced Rasheed, who grasped Jalil's hand with both of his and said, "Thank you. I can never thank you enough. I will always be indebted to you. I will find work and pay you back. I promise."

Jalil nodded. "We are simply thankful that you are both here." Then he frowned, motioning to the bandage around Hamid's head and the scrapes on Rasheed's face.

"Yes, we are extremely thankful," Hamid murmured.

Jalil inspected Hamid's bandage. "This does not look good. You must have a physician check it out."

"Of course, once we are settled. Of course."

Then Jalil introduced them to a tall, lean man with intense eyes. "This is Amir. He is the one to thank. He helped me push your case through to the embassy."

"We're very glad you're here," Amir said. And when he turned his eyes toward Hamid, they were warm and friendly, almost as if he knew him.

"Come, let us get you something to eat. Then we'll drive you to Traiskirchen and the Government Refugee Housing Center. You will have to stay there until the Austrian government decides where to send you in Austria. It may take quite some time," Jalil explained. "For the first few days you won't be allowed to leave the Center. But later you will be given permission to travel, and then my wife and children and I will celebrate your arrival at our home in Linz."

"Thank you. Thank you," Hamid repeated again and again. No other words came to mind.

Hamid's eyes never left the road on the thirty-minute drive from the airport. Austria! Indeed it was a beautiful country, clean, pristine, majestic. The sky seemed larger, the clouds whiter. In the distance were rolling hills that would surely turn into mountains further on. All around him, the trees and vineyards were lit up in glowing yellows and reds. He imagined that he smelled freedom in the air.

They drove beside the wide Danube River, and to his right windmills spun. He studied the blue highway signs on the autobahn with strange long names of cities and villages like Eisenstadt and Guntramsdorf.

When they turned off the autobahn and drove into a small village, a colorful sign proclaimed *Wilkommen in Traiskirchen.* They drove past pastel-colored stuccoed houses with red tiled roofs and a white church trimmed in red brick, with a green onion dome that tapered smoothly to a point. The church looked like a picture he'd seen in a child's book of fairy tales. The houses had flowers even in November, the yards were neat and the grass green. Even the stores were painted in bright and welcoming colors.

They wound around a small road surrounded by vineyards and wooded hills in the distance. "Here's your new home," Jalil said, motioning from the driver's seat.

The Government Refugee Housing Center in the town of Traiskirchen rose like a formidable giant in the midst of acres of vineyards. The autumn vines held out colorfully leafed arms as if directing the way to an imposing assortment of wide three-storied cement buildings with dark red roofs.

Home at last.

No, Hamid corrected himself, this was not home. This was not "at last." Here he had only a short while before being transferred somewhere else in Austria. Still his face broke into a smile. He was free, and once he had gained asylum, then he could send for Alaleh, for Rasa, for baby Omid.

The car went through security gates into a huge compound of buildings. "You must register first—take fingerprints. I have asked that you be interviewed immediately," Jalil explained. "Sometimes the wait is long for an interview, but if you can do it quickly there is a chance you will be issued a white card right away. The card is your proof that you are an asylum seeker. It guarantees you housing and a small monthly stipend while you are waiting to hear if your asylum is granted. We cannot go with you any further. But you are safe here. You'll be assigned a room in the building for single men and families. Over there is the cafeteria where you will have your meals. And a doctor comes by each day," Amir said, motioning to Hamid's head wound. "The medical help is free."

Hamid clasped Jalil's hands. "Thank you, my cousin. Thank you, Amir."

"I come to Traiskirchen fairly often," Amir said before leaving. "I'll look you up next week. Good luck to you both."

When the police came to take their fingerprints, Jalil and Amir bid them good-bye.

Hamid's interview lasted all of ten minutes. The questions were simple. "Where are you from? Why are you seeking asylum? What papers do you have?" With every question, Hamid answered as Jalil had instructed him—brief answers, to the point. The policeman who questioned him seemed almost bored, as if Hamid were just another number, not a human being. And yet, Hamid was thankful he was not mistreated.

After the interview he was taken in a van to a hospital where his head wound was cleaned and treated. The nurse shook her head and mumbled something in German, and Hamid understood her sign language. He should have had stitches, and now it was too late. But at least he had a fresh bandage and medication to guard against infection and for the pain.

Back at the Refugee Center, a guard led Hamid upstairs. "You are on a floor for single men. The rules are strict. No women allowed. Ever," he growled as he opened the door to the room. "Dinner is at seven."

"Hamid! Khoda be praised!" Rasheed was already in the room and in the process of making up the top bunk. "You've changed your bandage."

"Yes, they took me to the hospital after the interview."

"And how did the interview go?"

"I believe it went well. And for you?"

"No interview yet. I must wait."

Although no one else was in the room, Rasheed explained that the three other bunks were already occupied. "I guess we'll meet our roommates after dinner."

Hamid nodded, observing the overcrowded room with the peeling paint and the moldy windows and a stale smell.

One window overlooked the vineyards. He closed his eyes and silently thanked Isa for this place.

On the remaining bunk bed was a stack of sheets and blankets; three rickety chairs sat in the corner of the room. "The bathrooms and showers are down the hall," Rasheed said. "It's quite sparse, isn't it?"

"But we are here," said Hamid.

Rasheed gave a halfhearted nod.

Hamid furrowed his brow and said softly, "Surely you will not complain?" Then he closed his eyes and said, "I murmured when I had no shoes until I met a man who had no feet."

Rasheed broke into a smile and grabbed his friend by the shoulders. "Ah, professor! Always quoting proverbs. But you are right. I won't complain. We have shoes; we have a bed; we are free! Khoda be praised!"

After two days at the Government Refugee Housing Center, Hamid was allowed to step outside the red brick walls of the compound. He let out a breath and followed the group of young Iranian men as they walked along a small back road and joked among themselves. He breathed in the crisp autumn air and watched the leaves on the vines in their bright red garment. He remembered something he had read with Jim in the Ingil. *I am the vine, you are the branches.* Chills ran up his spine. Tonight he had hope!

Earlier that day, one of the refugees had spoken about "a place where you can get coffee and tea and play games. Clothes too. Good people. Kind people. They are Christians but they are kind."

Christians! That was what he wanted to hear. This must be the place Jim and Anna had told him about. "Will you come with me, Rasheed?" he had asked. "Free coffee and tea, games, perhaps girls, too?"

Rasheed shook his head. "I do not wish to associate with infidels. I will find girls elsewhere."

Hamid followed the group of men as they walked past train tracks, a school, and a small restaurant selling kabobs. The smell was enticing. A car drove by, and a young teen leaned out the window and yelled something in German at the refugees.

"What is he saying?" Hamid asked. "He sounds mad."

A young Iranian laughed and said, "He *is* mad. He's Austrian, and he doesn't want us here in his village. He was yelling, 'Scum, go home!'"

"Ah." Hamid wished he hadn't asked.

"Don't pay any attention. You'll get used to it."

Around another corner, Hamid stopped, his face breaking into a smile. In front of him stood a cream-colored building with a glass front; a Plexiglas sign above read *The Oasis*.

A dozen youth were hanging around the door, smoking and talking. One of his companions went to the door, tried it, and shrugged. "Locked."

Hamid's heart fell. How he had hoped to meet people tonight. How he needed to ask questions! They burned in his heart!

Why do Christians worship three gods? How can a god be married to a mortal woman? What does it mean to "please God"? What is this word "grace" that Jim Harris spoke of? And the most important one of all: *How can I, a Muslim, be sure that Isa loves me and accepts me?*

One of the youth pointed to his watch and said in Farsi, "It opens at seven thirty. Ten minutes to wait."

By seven thirty the sidewalk in front of the building was overflowing with refugees of all ages, men and women and children, some of whom Hamid recognized after spending two days at the Center. A jovial middle-aged white man with thick blond hair and a mustache unlocked the door from the inside, smiling, calling out in several languages, "Easy does it. One at a time. No pushing."

Surprisingly, everyone obeyed. They filed in patiently, then spread out across the room—as big as one of Hamid's classrooms at the university—where a dozen or more tables were set up with board games and cards and chess boards. To the left was a long counter, and several women were filling cups with coffee and tea. He headed in that direction with his companions.

An attractive woman with black hair and bright blue eyes greeted him from behind the counter. "Hello," she said in English. "I don't believe I've seen you before. I'm Bobbie."

Hamid hesitated, looked around. Had this woman really spoken to him? With a smile? Her friendly voice reminded him of Anna's.

"My name is Hamid," he replied in English.

"Welcome, Hamid! We're glad you're here. Have you just arrived in Austria?"

Hamid nodded. "A few days ago." Her eyes traveled to his bandage and he said, "Problems with police."

"I'm so sorry. Where have you come from?"

"From Iran."

Her eyes lit up with recognition, as Amir's had done, as if she too knew him. "Can I get you some tea or coffee?"

Hamid nodded again, drawn to this kind woman. Maybe she knew someone who could answer his questions. But the room was overflowing with people, and as the woman handed him a cup of coffee, another man came up to her. "Bobbie! Hello, Bobbie!"

She came from behind the counter and warmly shook the young man's hand, and pain filled Hamid's heart. How he longed for a warm embrace. The touch of human kindness. He stood in the room, looking around, and felt the tears in his eyes. Dare he hope for more kindness?

So far, the only people he had encountered outside the Refugee Center had sneered at him, leaning out a window and calling for him to go back to his own country.

Keith

On Wednesday after work, Keith rode the train from Amersfoort to Amsterdam and walked by the canal, glancing down at his cell phone, opening a text message from Jim Harris. *H and R arrived safely in V two days ago. Thanx for talking to Papy.*

Whoa. That was quick.

Smiling, he waved at Lindsey, who was waiting on a bench beside a wide open field where kids were throwing Frisbees in the chilly November afternoon. He enjoyed watching his wife from a distance, the way her long blond hair fell over her shoulders and onto her bright red coat, the way her blue eyes lit up when she noticed him. The way she ran to greet him and stood on her tiptoes to place a kiss on his cheek.

"Hey there, handsome," she cooed, taking his hand. He especially liked the way her small hand fit so well in his large one.

They walked to the left of the field towards a modern-looking building made of glass and gray stones. It was one of Lindsey's favorite places in Amsterdam: the Van Gogh Museum.

"Just received a very fun text," Keith said as he related the details of Hamid's journey to Lindsey. "I always like my job, but on some days it's as if the Lord is giving me a thumbs-up from heaven."

Hand in hand, they made their way to the museum entrance and joined the line that had formed. "Wouldn't it be great to actually meet some of the refugees who've heard our broadcasts someday? To actually talk with someone like this man, Hamid?"

Lindsey gave his hand a squeeze and grinned up at him. "My behind-the-scenes engineer is getting sentimental on me."

"Maybe . . ." Then turning to her, he asked, "Lindsey, what would you say about a trip to Vienna?"

Her eyes lit up. "Aww, let me think about it for a while," she teased.

"Jim says that The Oasis puts on a big Christmas party celebration for the refugees every year in early December. What if we were to go and help out, and meet some refugees face-to-face? And do a little sightseeing too, of course."

"Maybe go to the Opera House and hear Mozart, or see the Lipizzaner Stallions," Lindsey enthused. "That's one of the best ideas you've had in years!" Then she pecked him on the cheek. "But Amsterdam is pretty amazing too. Let's go inside and visit Vincent."

CHAPTER 17

Tracie

I loved watching my aunt greet the refugees at The Oasis. She welcomed the men and women with her beautiful smile, offering coffee and tea, hugging the boys she had met only last week, telling them she was glad they had returned. I thought of what she'd said to me earlier: "They arrive shell-shocked and confused. Sometimes all it takes is a kind word and smile to give them hope."

After a week at The Oasis, the refugees' stories I had heard were enough to convince me that Aunt Bobbie was telling the truth. I watched the men finding seats, challenging one another to a game of chess as Tom, all smiles, went from table to table, shaking hands, encouraging, offering a little human kindness.

A man I'd never seen before came in and cautiously approached the counter where Bobbie was serving coffee and tea. He seemed surprised but at the same time pleased at her warm greeting, and accepted the cup of coffee gratefully. She came around the counter to speak to another refugee whom she knew, but I could tell that she could barely restrain herself from giving the first man a welcoming hug, too.

Julie hurried over to speak to her. "Bobbie, a woman downstairs who has been watching the Jesus film has asked to speak to someone. She's Romanian, and I don't think anyone else here speaks the language. Will you go down?" She looked at me. "Tracie can take your place at the coffee counter with Connie and Dee."

Bobbie replied with a bright "Sure thing!" but to me her smile looked forced. Julie hurried off, and Bobbie caught my eye. "You okay here?"

I wanted to ask her *Why would a Romanian be here? Refugees aren't coming from Romania.* But she was clearly in a hurry, so I just nodded and went around the counter. I got busy behind the bar area, refilling the coffeepot and pouring cups for the men. I kept an eye on the new arrival. There was something about him that broke my heart. He was a handsome man in his midthirties, tall, broad-shouldered, his skin the color of café au lait. I realized that what I had thought was a turban on his head was actually a bandage. He stood in the middle of the crowded room looking lost, sipping his cup of coffee and staring around him at the different groups of people.

I don't know what pushed me out from around the bar, but suddenly I found myself standing beside him and saying, "Welcome to The Oasis. My name is Tracie. Is this your first time here?"

He nodded. "Yes. First time."

"You speak English?"

"A little. My name is Hamid."

Hamid! Was this the man that we had prayed for a few days ago?

"Where are you from, Hamid?" The Oasis workers had explained to us that this was a safe question. Never *How did you get here?* or *Why did you leave your country?*

"I come from Iran."

Now what do I ask? I thought of the conversations I'd heard Bobbie initiate. "Is your family in Iran?"

He nodded again, then produced a photo of a beautiful young woman and an equally striking little girl. "Alaleh and Rasa," he said, pointing to each in turn. "And baby." He pointed to his stomach, then to the photo of his wife, and smiled.

"She is pregnant, your wife?"

"The baby is already born."

"A boy or a girl?"

His smile grew broader. "A boy. Omid. His name means hope."

I sensed someone approaching us from behind me, and turned to see another man, maybe fortyish, smiling at Hamid. He was clearly Middle Eastern, but he didn't look like a refugee. He reached out to shake Hamid's hand. "Welcome, dear friend. It is so good to see you here."

To my surprise, Hamid hugged the man warmly. "It's good to see you again, Amir," he said. "I thank you again for all you have done for me."

Amir! I stifled a gasp. "Amir?" I repeated, trying to stop blinking and feeling myself blushing. Could this be Aunt Bobbie's Amir? The Iranian refugee?

"Yes. My name is Amir. And your name is?"

"I'm Tracie," I said, recovering and offering my hand.

He was tall, lean, and quite handsome, with jet-black hair and warm friendly eyes. He looked kind.

What did you do to my aunt? I wanted to blurt. Fortunately, I held my tongue and listened as the two men spoke in English about Hamid's first days at the Refugee Center, about Hamid receiving a "white card" and applying for asylum. After a few minutes I politely excused myself and left the main room, hurrying down the stairs and into a small room where Bobbie was in deep discussion with a middle-aged lady and her young daughter.

Bobbie glanced up at me, and I mouthed, "Come upstairs, quick!"

She mouthed back, "Not now," lowered her head, and kept talking with the woman.

I reluctantly climbed the stairs back to the coffee house and resumed talking to different refugees. At one point I saw Hamid walk outside with Amir. A few minutes later, Hamid came back inside alone. On a whim I went out the door and looked down the street. Amir was crossing the railroad tracks and stepping onto the quay. I could see a train approaching in the distance. My heart fell. Aunt Bobbie would not get to see her refugee tonight.

The train came to a halt and Amir stepped on. I trudged back to The Oasis alone.

Stephen

There was a buzz of excitement among the short-termers and the full-time workers. I got close enough to hear the news they were whispering: *Hamid is here! Right here at The Oasis. We prayed, and now he is here.*

There it was again. The innocent faith of these people. *We prayed, and Jesus answered. Hamid made it here.*

"Which one is he?" I asked Dee. I'd heard his story, and the reporter in me salivated at the thought of interviewing him—a refugee fresh off the plane, who had been tortured, who had left behind a wife, child, and baby he had never seen.

Dee nodded toward a man with a thick bandage encircling his head. From his appearance, he had "made it" by the skin of his teeth. He looked battered, and for some reason a protective edge suddenly welled up in me. I had already interviewed six refugees and sent three of the stories to Mr. Kimball, always changing the refugee's name. But two days ago, Bobbie took me aside during one of the "team times."

"Look," she said, "if you think these are good stories, record them. But remember that you are interviewing human beings who have suffered greatly. If your intent is just to have a larger-than-life story for your constituency, I beg you to reconsider. Don't use these men's pain for your pleasure."

I didn't take offense. Bobbie could be as blunt as her niece, and I liked that.

Tracie and I had spent a lot of time together the past four days—or nights, I should say, staying up talking long after the others had gone to bed. I suppose talking with her felt safe—I'd be leaving in three days and we'd probably never see each other again. What I knew for sure was that she had depth, so much more depth than Pam.

I knew I shouldn't be comparing them. That wasn't fair. But in any case, I enjoyed our conversations. She felt as unsure of her future as I did of mine, but she seemed to be opening up to something new and unexpected.

And she lived in Atlanta. Could that be a "coincidence that wasn't a coincidence," as Mom had said? She wouldn't be going home yet, but maybe at some point . . . I pushed the thought away.

Fareed came up to me with a friend in tow, and introduced us. "This is Youcef," he said in Arabic. "He's looking for someone to play chess with."

The chess game kept my thoughts away from Tracie, until I saw her leave the building a while later. I lost my concentration, and Youcef seized the opportunity to make a clever move. A few moves later he called out happily, "Check and mate!" I laughed, shook his hand, and stood.

And found myself face-to-face with Hamid.

In perfect English, he said, "Hello, my name is Hamid."

His eyes darted back and forth.

"Hi, Hamid. I'm Stephen."

"Yes, Stephen." He lowered his voice. "Julie says you are a journalist."

I grinned. "Well, yes, I work for a small newspaper in a big city in America."

"And you interview refugees?"

My eyebrows shot up. "Yes. Indeed. I've interviewed several this week."

"May I tell you my story?" He must have interpreted the shock on my face as a lack of interest, because he continued, "It's for my family. Perhaps it will help my family."

"I'd be delighted to hear your story, Hamid."

"My English is not so good."

I raised my eyebrows again. "It sounds nearly perfect to me. I don't speak much Farsi, but I do speak French and Arabic and German."

The worried look left Hamid's tired face. In Arabic he said, "Then we will speak in Arabic and English and see how it goes."

I looked at him, his exhaustion, the bandage, the way he squinted as if he were in pain. "Hamid, could I take you somewhere and get you something to eat? We could perhaps talk more easily without so much noise."

The look of gratitude on his face pierced me.

I took Hamid to the Schafler family heuriger. By now I had become well acquainted with this farming family, and they laughed happily when we entered.

"Where's the pretty American?" one of the teenage sons asked in heavily accented English.

"She's busy. Tonight I'm bringing a new friend."

We found a booth at the back of the tavern and sat down. A young waitress, one of the owner's daughters, came to take our drink orders. Hamid refused a glass of wine but gratefully agreed to a glass of white grape juice with mineral water.

"It's a specialty of the region," I explained. As the waitress wrote down the order, I added, "I'll have one of those too."

"One of what?" the waitress teased, so I made an attempt at the name in German. *"Traubensaft gespritzt."*

She laughed and said, "Very *goot!*" and left us.

"We have to order the food from the counter," I told Hamid.

He shrugged and followed me to the front of the heuriger. We chose food from the assortment of traditional fare, potato salad, tomato and cucumber salad, vegetable soup, and pumpkin seed bread.

Back at the table, Hamid eyed me for a moment. I smiled back and started to take a sip of my soup.

"Do you wish to pray, Stephen?"

I held the spoon in midair. "Pray?"

"Yes, I know you Christians like to thank God for your food."

Ah, yes. I cleared my throat and set down the spoon. "I'm not a Christian, Hamid. Well, I'm not a Christian like some of the people at The Oasis."

He looked confused. "You do not believe in Isa?"

"Isa?"

"Jesus."

"Oh." I chuckled a bit awkwardly. "Um, well, I've never thought much about it."

His eyes grew wide.

"Until I came here," I added.

"Who do you worship, then?"

Who did I worship? "No one," I said, knowing full well that was a lie.

"Then perhaps you are not so interested in my story. You see, I have come to believe in Isa, as my young daughter has, and that is why I am a refugee."

This was not starting off as I had expected. "Hamid, I'm

very interested in your story, and if there is anything I can do to help you, I will. Anything I can write, any contact I can make. I promise you . . ." I swallowed. "I promise I will be very careful with what you share. I will tell your story just as you wish."

I listened dumbstruck as Hamid shared about Rasa receiving a copy of the Ingil, of the religious police seeing it, and of Hamid's escape, leaving his very pregnant wife, his mother, and his daughter as he fled in the middle of the night. He described the message he had heard by chance over the transistor radio in the Iranian mountains. I watched his face as he spoke of the horrible journey, of the cold, of being awakened by a dream and of his traveling companions being murdered. He told of shivering on the side of a mountain with his new companion and how the smuggler left them there for hours and hours, until they thought they would die. His description of sneaking around the checkpoints, of the dogs chasing them, of his companion giving up and Hamid dragging him along burned its way into my memory. With each detail he shared, something inside me warmed. Something said, *This is what I should be doing. Telling these people's stories. This is important. This is a way I can help.*

I felt a prick in my eyes when Hamid told of reaching his wife by phone and learning he had a baby son. As he shared his journey, he wore pain, fear, hope, apprehension, and relief on his face. And he truly believed that it was God, *Isa*, who had been guiding and protecting him.

When he finished, I knew I wanted to help him bring his family to Austria. I also wanted to learn more about the radio broadcast he had heard, and to contact the family in Van who had sheltered him. More than anything, I felt the flood of inspiration coursing through me, that familiar and welcome feeling I always got when I was onto a story that really mattered.

Hamid looked utterly worn out by the time he reached the end of his tale, so I asked, "May I walk you home? Or get you a taxi?"

"Thank you," he said, shaking his head. "I will manage well now."

"I'm leaving to go back to the States in a few days. I hope I can see you again before I go."

He nodded.

"There's a party at The Oasis Friday night," I told him. "The American girls are going to do some singing and then everyone will be invited to share songs in their languages. There will be games and food, too. The girls are baking cookies and cakes. I hope you can come."

His face softened as he held out his hand and I shook it. "Thank you, Stephen. I will see you on Friday."

I watched him leave and thought of how this had been another strange evening. An Iranian refugee who was discovering the Christian faith shared his journey, having no idea how it had affected me, a French-American, who up until this point had believed in nothing but myself.

Hamid

Hamid's head was pounding but his heart was soaring as he made his way back through the vineyards and down narrow passages until at last the Refugee Center came into view, rising like a cement mountain in the moonlit night. He found Rasheed bundled in his coat, sitting outside in a little courtyard, smoking a cigarette.

Rasheed jumped to his feet and his face washed with relief. "Hamid! I was worried. It's late, and all the other people who went to that place came back hours ago."

Hamid patted his friend on the back. "I'm sorry to worry you. Ah, so much to tell!" Yes, he could talk about many things without mentioning the name of Isa—though Isa had been with him all night, Hamid was convinced. "You must come to The Oasis with me on Friday night. The American girls are putting on a party for the refugees, and there will be music and games and cakes and cookies, not just coffee and tea."

Rasheed threw his head back and laughed. "American girls! Ah, tell me about them."

"There are many of them there. I only talked to one. She seemed nice enough. I am a married man, so I try not to look too closely."

Rasheed punched Hamid playfully. "Yes, yes! I'm sure you didn't notice a thing."

"Amir was there. He asked about you and your injuries. He was glad I had gone to the hospital, but when I told him that I have continual pounding in my head, he insisted that I go back to the pharmacy tomorrow." Indeed the wound had caused him great pain during most of the day. "Anyway, he sends greetings."

He didn't tell Rasheed the best news of the evening: Amir was a Christian, and the pastor of a church! And he had given Hamid his phone number. *Thank you, Isa.*

"Everyone was very friendly, Rasheed," he continued. "And there were many Iranians there."

"Iranians who worship Khoda?"

"Yes, I believe so. People from many different countries with many different beliefs. But people were not discussing beliefs. They played chess and other games. And I met a young journalist." Hamid thought back to his conversation with Stephen. "He is an American, but not a Christian. I do not think he has any beliefs, which I find hard to understand. But he was a good man. He took me to a restaurant and bought me food. Then I told him my whole story, and he recorded it."

"Is that not dangerous?"

"I don't think so. He promised to be careful, and not to use my real name. He said he would like to help me find a way to get Alaleh and Rasa and Omid here!"

"But what can he do? An American?" Rasheed's face was dark with concern.

"I don't know, but he gave me more hope." Hamid looked at his friend. "Don't worry. I didn't tell him your name or the reasons you left Iran. But he will be at the party on Friday. I could introduce you and, if you wish, you could tell him your story there. He is leaving on Sunday."

"Such an evening you had, my friend."

"And you?"

Rasheed shrugged. "I spent time with the men in our room. We did discuss beliefs. We vowed to stay true to our faith, even in this godless country."

Hamid nodded. "Yes, of course." But a trickle of fear passed through him, hearing the intensity and conviction in Rasheed's voice.

As they climbed the stairs to their room on the third floor, Rasheed said, "I'm glad you're safe, Hamid. Tomorrow we'll change the bandage again and find more medicine. And Friday, we'll go to a party!"

Bobbie

The Romanian woman, Elvira, had been so hungry for truth. She had freedom in Romania, but she was seeking a better life for herself and her child in the West. She was not a refugee, but had heard about The Oasis as a place where she could ask about Jesus—and ask she did. Question after question. I was happy to talk with her, even though I hadn't spoken in Romanian in twelve years.

No. That wasn't true. I was not exactly happy to talk with her.

My stomach plummeted as I admitted to myself the

truth: it had broken my heart to speak that language again. Because all throughout my time with Elvira, images of Vasilica's bright eyes haunted me.

Long after Elvira had left with her young daughter, I sat alone in the little closet-turned-movie-room. Tremors took over my body, and then not simply tremors, but pain. Sharp, knife-cutting pain. When at last it subsided and my arms and legs quit shaking so violently, I took my cane and managed to climb the stairs and go to the kitchen, where Julie was helping to wash up.

She took one look at me and said, "We need to get you back to the guest house." She told the others we were leaving, and discreetly ushered me out to the car.

She prayed aloud as we drove through the darkness. "Dear Jesus, comfort Bobbie tonight. You see she is in pain; You know her fatigue. Comfort her; give her Your peace, Lord, as You have promised us in the midst of suffering."

Dear Julie was so quick to pray, so filled with the Holy Spirit, so at home with grieving people. Her whole life was listening to the heart-wrenching stories of refugees and then figuring out a way to meet their needs. She finished praying and then glanced at me. "I'm so sorry, Bobbie. It was a long day for you."

"Not so long, but still it's worn me out," I admitted.

"Yes, in this season, it was long."

She was right. In this season of my life. And when would this season end? And how?

"Julie? You said Amir would come back to The Oasis soon. Do you know when?" I hurried on. "It's just that we are only here for another week, and I believe I must see him."

"Why, he was here tonight, Bobbie! He stayed for quite awhile. He was talking to Hamid. And to Tracie."

Amir was there! I gripped the door handle to steady my hand, which was suddenly shaking uncontrollably again. My heart pounded, and I felt such incredible disappointment that I didn't trust myself to say a word. Finally I recovered enough to say, "I suppose I missed him when I was downstairs with the Romanian woman."

Julie frowned. "Dear me, you're right." Then she brightened. "Jesus! Bring Amir back soon, very soon. I thank You again for answering our prayers for Hamid so quickly. Now, You know that Bobbie desperately needs to see Amir before she leaves. Bring him back soon."

Amen, I thought to myself. *Please, Lord. Please.*

"Shall I help you up to your room?" Julie offered when she'd parked in front of Gasthaus Müller.

"No, I'm feeling a bit better now. Bless you, dear Julie. Thank you."

"Rest tomorrow, and you'll be good as new on Friday. For the party." She winked.

Thank you, Lord, for Julie, I thought as I wearily climbed the stairs to our room. *She knows how bad I feel, but she will not let me dwell on it. She will see the cup half full. And by the sheer power of her prayers, I imagine that I will feel better by Friday.*

I washed my face, brushed my teeth, undressed, and climbed into bed. I didn't expect to see Tracie this evening. She had been staying out quite late each night with Stephen, tiptoeing into the room in the early morning hours, trying her best not to wake me. My niece was coming back to life. I saw it in her eyes and heard it in the way she hummed a tune unconsciously as she went about. Even as I was fading away.

The grass withers, the flowers fade, but the Word of God shall last forever.

I couldn't believe Amir had been so close. I was leaving in a week, and then, perhaps, I was leaving this life forever. I needed to make this right.

As I drifted off to sleep, I let myself remember his warm

smile, his hand in mine, his sparkling eyes, the way he never let me get away with anything. In our four years together, he had forced my hand at every turn. Except . . .

Did I feel a longing or relief that our paths had not crossed tonight?

CHAPTER 18

Amir

You are acting like a schoolboy, Amir admonished himself. *You have been in many dangerous situations, and yet the thought of seeing Jill again has left you terrified.*

He could not deny his disappointment at not having seen her the night before at The Oasis. Or was it relief? It had been so long; had time healed anything for her? Would she want to see him? She had left so quickly in 1994 and begged him to stay away. Maybe she had known he would be there last night, and had deliberately avoided him.

In his small apartment in Mauthausen, he paced. He had a sermon to prepare for Sunday, several families to visit, a young man to lead in a Bible study, but all he could think about was seeing Jill. Carol had said she was only staying two weeks, and that was a week ago.

He dialed Carol's number, his hands shaking.

"Amir, she was there last night! But when you came she

must have been downstairs talking to a Romanian woman who was very interested in the Lord. Such a coincidence. We haven't had a Romanian come to The Oasis in years!"

Romania. The place of Jill's greatest hurts.

"I would very much like to see her before she leaves."

"Of course you would. I'm sure she is eager to see you too. You do remember that her name is Bobbie, don't you, Amir?" Carol teased. "We're having a party with the short-term team Friday evening. Why don't you stop by? I know it means another three-hour drive, but I think it will be worth it."

Worth it, Amir thought. *Much more than worth it. I believe that meeting Jill again is the most important thing in my life to do now.*

Hamid

How quickly the world could shift from a place of hope and goodness to one of sorrow and pain. That next morning when Hamid saw the doctor who served the Government Refugee Housing Center, the doctor warned him that his wound had become infected. He gave Hamid a prescription for antibiotics and for pain medication, which he took to the pharmacist.

He was back in the room, where Rasheed was reading lazily on the bed, when Alaleh called him on his mobile phone. Before he could say a thing to her, Alaleh's shrill cry stopped him cold.

"Hamid! They have killed Maamaan-Bozorg! Murdered her in front of her home."

Hamid could not catch his breath. The hysterical voice of his wife continued.

"They found her with a Bible, Hamid! You must stop your talk of Isa!"

Hamid drew his hand over his mouth to keep from crying out. Rasheed must not know! He left the room in a blur, wobbled down the stairs, out of the building and into the vineyards as Alaleh continued to shriek. "They knew all about her, about us, that we had escaped. They knew everything, Hamid! They took her from Noyemi's. But she said, 'I will not go to prison with you. You may kill my body, but not my soul. I am not afraid.' And so they shot her. Right there in front of Noyemi and all the family."

Hamid fell to the ground, grasping his head, crying out. His mother, his lovely, opinionated, stubborn mother. Shot dead. He gagged and trembled. In a small voice he asked, "And what has happened to Noyemi's family?"

"Taken for questioning! I don't know what else. They will surely tell where we are. The police will come for us and kill us and the Garabadians!"

His practical wife was beyond all reason. Hysterical. He had never heard her like this before.

"My dear Alaleh." What could he say? He could not promise that the authorities would not find his wife and children. And if the police questioned Rasa, she would reply as Maamaan-Bozorg had.

Alaleh and Rasa and Omid must leave Iran, at once.

"We will figure out something, my love. I am so sorry. My heart is so very sad. But good people are here. We will figure out something."

But what? Nothing would bring Maamaan-Bozorg back.

Is it my fault, Isa?

When he hung up, Alaleh was still sobbing.

In his grief, Hamid cried out, "Isa, this is too hard! What you ask is too hard."

Hamid walked about the vineyard for an hour. The pain medication had calmed the pounding in his head, but it did nothing for his heart. He replayed his last conversation with his mother, only two days earlier. "My dear son," she had said. "I am well with Noyemi's family. Don't worry for me. I am learning so much. I have never known such peace."

There was comfort in the memory of those words and comfort that the police had not taken her and beaten her or worse. Maamaan-Bozorg had died quickly. She had chosen to die. But this seemed like cruel comfort. His mother was dead, and he could not go to mourn and bury her. He was stuck in Austria with new fear lodged in his heart.

When he at last walked back into his room, Rasheed met him with a worried expression. He told his friend only half the truth. "My mother has died."

"I am sorry."

"Yes, she was very old. Unwell." He could say no more, but Rasheed did not seem to blame him for his tears. "You go to the party tonight, Rasheed. I don't feel like it."

"Of course not. But I won't leave you alone."

"It doesn't matter. Go on."

"Perhaps Amir will be there and he could help you." Rasheed seemed worried for his friend's frenzied grief.

Hamid nodded. "Perhaps. Yes, then. I'll come along."

"You don't have to go inside—I'll see if he's there, and I will ask him to come be with you."

That evening they walked in silence to The Oasis, following behind a crowd of other refugees. Hamid sat on a bench outside The Oasis. "You go on, Rasheed. Enjoy the music and food."

"And girls!"

A few minutes later, Amir stepped outside and greeted Hamid. "Let's walk a little," he suggested.

Amir listened silently to Hamid's stricken voice as he explained about his mother's murder; he placed a hand on Hamid's shoulder when he cried out in grief.

"My wife and children are hiding with an Armenian family in another city, but they are terrified. How can I protect them? I called Jalil and told him the truth about my mother's death. He is sympathetic, of course, to our loss, but he cannot understand why she would convert. And what can he do? He spent all his money to bring me here."

They took a seat on a bench in a little park. Staring straight ahead, Amir whispered, "We'll find a way, Hamid. Many people prayed and you are here. Tonight we will pray for protection on your family and a strategy to help them leave Iran soon."

Hamid listened to Amir's strong, confident voice as he lifted it in prayer for Hamid and his family. "I'll contact people. Have faith, Hamid. Isa is with you."

Hamid nodded, but he didn't feel reassured. He felt doubt and fear. He wondered if this Isa was worth all the trouble he and his family had seen.

Doubt makes the mountain which faith can move.

Oh, why did this ancient proverb slip into his mind as if Isa Himself had placed it there? Yes, he doubted! Yes! But did he have faith? That was the question that gnawed in his gut as he followed Amir back to The Oasis.

They stood in the back of the crowded room. A young man was playing a beautiful melody on a rusty guitar. A young American woman offered Hamid a cookie, and he took it. It tasted sweet but his thoughts were bitter. *How I long for you to be here with me, Alaleh. Oh, Isa, give her strength. She doubts, and now I doubt. But Rasa, Rasa has the faith of a child. May I have faith like that.*

He saw Rasheed standing in the middle of a group of American girls. Hamid made his way over to them. "I'm going home, but you stay as long as you want."

Rasheed nodded and flashed him a smile. He seemed to be enjoying himself.

As Hamid headed for the door, Stephen caught up to him. "It's good to see you again, Hamid." He held out his hand, and

Hamid shook it with difficulty.

"I'm sorry. I must go now," he managed.

"Your head, your wound is hurting you?"

Hamid shook his head. "Not my head. My heart." His eyes welled with tears. This young man had listened to his story. He might as well tell him the latest news. "The Iranian secret police have murdered my mother. She was living with Armenian Christians and had become a believer. They killed her."

Stephen looked shocked. He offered his hand again, placing his other on top of Hamid's. "I am so sorry, Hamid. I will do my best to find help."

Hamid nodded. "Yes. I am most afraid for my wife and children. Most afraid."

As Hamid left the party, an older woman, the one named Julie, hurried over and tucked a slip of paper into his hand. "For later," she whispered. "Keep it hidden."

Hamid quickly stuffed the paper into his pocket without looking at it. He walked slowly back to the Refugee Center.

It is such a big mountain, Isa, he said in his mind. *I cannot move it. Can you? Oh, please, Isa, give me faith to move the mountain. Or better yet, dear Isa, move the mountain yourself.*

Stephen

Hamid looked like a completely different man from the one I had interviewed two days ago. Then, his body had seemed battered, but his eyes had shone with hope. Tonight he was slumped over, eyes dull, resigned, afraid, listless.

I admonished myself for having told him I would help him. What in the world could I do? *You don't know anything about rescuing refugees. You have nothing to offer.*

But that wasn't completely true. I knew the power of the written word. Surely I could do something.

I sought out Julie and told her what Hamid had shared

with me. She twisted her hands together and whispered, "Dear Lord! Be with this poor man and his family." I think she was actually praying out loud.

"Julie, I want to help Hamid. Is there a way to get in touch with the people in Van who helped him? And to find out about the radio broadcasts? Radio could be an effective way to get the word out."

Her eyes lit up. "That's a good idea." Then clouded. "I'm afraid I can't give out that information, but if you like, I can get in touch with these people and ask them to call you."

"That would be great."

I gave her my cell phone number, and as she scribbled it down on a napkin, she said, "Jim and Anna are the couple in Van. They used to work here at The Oasis. And Keith is the man in the Netherlands. He works for World Wide Radio. They can all give you a wealth of information."

"Then I hope they'll choose to get in touch with me."

"I'm sure they will." She rested her hand on my arm and met my eyes. "Thank you, Stephen. It is not a coincidence that our God has brought you here for such a time as this."

Julie's words haunted me for the rest of the evening, even as I turned my attention back to Tracie, who was singing her heart out with Fareed. I knew then that I did not want to go home. I wanted to stay here and help.

But I had no choice.

My mom was making the rounds yet again with a platter of cookies, and I reached for an oatmeal one, my favorite . . . but at that moment it only tasted bland, as if the sweetness had been replaced by a cupful of despair.

I didn't know Christian lingo, I didn't know much about the Bible, and I certainly didn't know anything about prayer. But I understood Muslim and Christian tensions. The fires in France were all about a persecuted minority acting out and demanding rights. I had close friends in France who were

Arabs, a couple of them devout Muslims. I understood the burning cars as a way of drawing attention to their situation, where the majority of Arabs made less money than the French and often lived in slum dwellings.

But my friends were not murderers. I could not wrap my mind around someone murdering an old woman simply because she'd changed religions.

After the party, the short-term team gathered upstairs in the office to pray. These people had seen one miracle: Hamid had walked into The Oasis only days after their fervent pleading with their God. They needed another miracle. Quickly.

I didn't know how to pray, but I suddenly felt extremely thankful that these people did. And they were doing it. In the middle of the night.

And Julie had wasted no time in getting in touch with the people she'd told me about. Jim Harris called me at midnight from Van. He introduced himself and said, "Hamid called and told us the bad news. I've called Keith in Amersfoort. Julie said you wanted to speak with both of us?"

"Yes, exactly. Thank you for getting in touch. I'm a journalist, and I wanted to know what you would suggest as a way to help this family."

I had never thought of myself as naïve, but I think that's how Jim saw me. He said, "Stephen, this happens often in Muslim countries. Barring a miracle, there is not much to be done."

I wanted to tell him that we'd already seen one miracle. Why not two? But of course, he knew this—far better than I.

"If we could get the wife and children here in Van, then there are possibilities. But from Iran? We'd need an Iranian smuggler and some type of vehicle. We'll be praying and brainstorming."

We agreed to touch base in the morning, and said good night. I had just hung up with Jim when Keith called.

"Thanks for wanting to help, Stephen. I hope I'm not calling too late. Julie said it was urgent." He gave a halfhearted chuckle. "It's always urgent. We've heard similar stories too many times to count. But hey, the Lord is a lot bigger than our problems, right?"

I had nothing to say to that. I told him, "I'm heading back to Atlanta on Sunday, but I'm sure there is something I can do from there."

"It's great you want to help. The good thing about technology is that we can keep up even if you're in America."

"What about the radio, Keith? Is there anything you could communicate over the airwaves?" I was talking off the top of my head. "I'm going to write an article for our paper in the States, but I thought maybe you could . . ." Could what?

"Actually, there is something I can do. Why didn't I think of that earlier? Tomorrow night I'll announce a special prayer request during the live update I give after the eight-thirty program. Coded language. Let me talk to my boss about it in the morning."

"Sounds like a plan."

"Yes, thanks for brainstorming with me, Stephen. Good stuff going on—keep it up."

When I hung up the phone, I felt a sliver of hope.

Tracie was sitting up reading in the game room at Gasthaus Müller when I came inside—waiting to see me, maybe? Though neither of us would say so. I sat down next to her and told her about Hamid's mother.

Her face went white. "It's too awful!" she cried. "Just awful. This is why I don't have faith anymore."

I winced at the anger that had resurfaced . . . but I couldn't argue.

Bobbie

I watched Tracie singing with Fareed, her face fairly

glowing with love and enthusiasm. Once again, the refugees sang their songs; again Armagan played a beautiful sonata on the old keyboard. The girls on the short-term team had spent hours baking hundreds of cookies, which they now passed around, and the smell permeated the room. Nearly a hundred people from all over the globe crowded together, listening, singing, laughing, eating. I think everyone in the room was on a sugar high.

But I felt low. I forced myself not to glance over my shoulder at every turn. Surely Julie or Carol would let me know if Amir came back. Or Tracie. "I tried to tell you, Bobs!" she'd lamented on Wednesday night.

Would he come back?

When the party ended I was helping to clean up when I heard someone call out "Jill!" I didn't even look around, but could not recall any of the short-termers named Jill. "Jill!" the voice said again and then I froze, a teacup in one hand, suds falling into the sink. Slowly I turned around and there he was, coming toward me, warm eyes focused on mine.

"Amir," I mouthed, although no sound came out. His hair was still jet black, his skin that perpetual tan of the Middle East, his charcoal eyes filled with compassion.

I felt my cheeks on fire and set down the cup, wiping my hands on my jeans. I moved toward him, then stopped and took a step back. He was laughing, his eyes dancing. He picked me up in a warm embrace.

"Jill! It's true. You're here! I never thought I'd see you again!" He swung me around, then set me down, holding me at arm's length and studying me with a mixture of awe and concern. "Jill."

I felt dizzy with the smell of him so close—that vague scent of Middle Eastern spices—and I struggled out of his hold, concentrating hard so that I wouldn't completely break down. "Amir. It's great to see you." My voice broke, and I cleared my throat and tried again. "I thought you weren't coming tonight."

"I ran a bit late. We had an emergency with one of the refugees." His eyes were locked on mine.

The rush of adrenaline that I'd felt at the sound of his voice calling my name was abruptly replaced by dread. What could I say to him?

"How are you, Jill?" His eyes clouded. "Carol told me you were ill. I'm very sorry." Again his stare. "But you look marvelous. You look the same."

So did he. As if we'd been apart for twelve months instead of twelve years. My heart ached with the beauty of him—the way he towered over me, lean, powerful, with eyes so dark and deep I had wondered at our first meeting what was hidden in there. Yes, they held depth, but also kindness. I had often been amazed that a man who had suffered so much could display such kindness.

And love. I saw it shining there for me. For me only.

I shook my head to regain my composure and turned to see Julie and Carol watching us. My knees went weak, and I reached for the counter to steady myself.

Carol rushed to my side. "Bobbie, why don't you go outside to talk? It's too stuffy in here." She nodded to Amir.

"Could I persuade you to come with me to our little heuriger?" Amir asked. "It's still open. Do you remember it?"

I swallowed hard and nodded. "Okay," I said to him, not sure what I was agreeing to. "Okay."

The Schafler family heuriger had been a favorite haunt of Amir's and mine. We'd finish up our work with the refugees and head down the street to the little restaurant, where we'd sit and talk for hours. As Amir opened the beautifully carved wooden door, memories bombarded me. The tavern had been enlarged, but the spirit was still the same. The paint on the outside walls was fresh and bright, and a large patio decorated with vines and pumpkins stood ready to welcome customers in the warmer months.

We walked across the patio and stepped inside. A glass-fronted counter held cheeses and cold vegetable dishes; another counter was lined with wine glasses; and a half dozen small chalkboards sat above the counter, displaying the day's specials. I turned to my right and saw the wooden booth, carved with Tyrolean figures, where we used to sit. Our booth.

Frau Schafler, the sturdy and smiling patroness, her face tanned by years of harvesting grapes in the sun, recognized Amir and greeted him with a smile. Then she turned to me, and her eyes held a pleasantly surprised look. "Welcome," she said in German. She nodded discreetly to our booth as if it had been waiting for us for all these years.

We ordered vegetable soup and fresh bread from the counter, and then a waitress came and took our drink orders. It was still the same. The same laws, the same wine, the same food, the same family waiting on us.

The same Amir.

But I had changed. An incredible weariness washed over me.

We made small talk—something neither of us had ever been good at—and sipped our soup. The warmth filled up my belly, but I felt chilled, exhausted.

"You look tired," Amir said as our conversation lagged. "Perhaps it is better for you to rest tonight."

I could never hide anything from him. "Yes, I'm afraid I haven't much strength for conversation tonight, Amir." *But how I long to talk to you! How can it be that I am so very weak at this moment when I need to be strong?*

"Can you tell me about the cancer, Jill?"

"Inoperable. I'm on an oral treatment right now. It makes

me so tired. And gives me tremors."

"I'm so sorry."

"Yes. Strange isn't it, what life holds for us? But my niece was determined we'd come to Europe for a month. Tracie is a great girl."

"I met her the other night. She seems like a fine young lady."

"She's taking good care of me. And coerced me into coming back here to The Oasis."

"Are you sorry you came?"

I smiled easily. "Oh, no. Not one bit sorry. I've wanted to come back for so long." I swallowed. "I'm sorry it took cancer to finally convince me."

With each phrase I pronounced, Amir's shoulders slumped a little more, as if my story were weighing him down. We sat in an awkward silence.

Then the tremors began again, and I silently cursed them. Amir reached over and covered my trembling hands with his. "I'm taking you home now. But tomorrow, if you are well enough, I would like to spend some time with you."

"I know you have so much work, Amir," I said lamely. "And it's the last day for the short-term team. I'll need to be helping Carol out."

Amir sat back in the booth, but his hands still covered mine, forcefully, protectively. He stared at me for several seconds. Then he said, "I'm not one bit worried about those girls—they can handle themselves. And I am perfectly capable of getting my work done at another time. I am spending tomorrow with you."

I blinked hard, but I could not keep the tears from welling up.

CHAPTER 19

Amir

*A*mir closed his eyes and relived the moment that Jill had heard his voice and turned towards him. *Bobbie*, he corrected himself. She looked the same—her blinding blue eyes lit up with faith and surprise, her lovely mouth curved in anticipation and then breaking into that smile that warmed him deep inside. The feel of her in his arms—so strong and yet almost delicate as he held her for that brief moment and breathed in the slightly exotic fragrance that was hers alone.

She was the same, and yet she had changed. Cancer was eating her away, and proud, strong, beautiful Bobbie Blake could not hide it. He had imagined many times what seeing her again would be like, but he had never imagined sitting in their old familiar heuriger with her too tired to talk.

Now he sped through the night to his house. Tomorrow, Lord willing, he would spend with Bobbie, but tonight he had to contact Jalil to see if he could help him think through the tragedy of Hamid's mother's death. He wondered what had happened to the Armenian family who had sheltered her. Armenians were allowed to practice their faith in Iran, but the punishment for proselytizing was severe—even death. It would not help Hamid to know that these kind people had most likely been tortured and perhaps killed.

He arrived in Linz at midnight and rapped on Jalil's door. "I'm so sorry to wake you," he said when Jalil opened the door, his eyes heavy with sleep. "But the situation is urgent."

"Yes. I've spoken to Hamid. I'm glad you came." Jalil's typically jovial demeanor had disappeared, replaced by worry lines scribbled across his face like Farsi print.

Soon Jalil's wife, Darya, joined the men in the little sitting room, her robe drawn closed, her head covered, her eyes fearful. "I never had the pleasure of meeting Jalil's aunt, but I have talked with her on the phone. She was a woman of great strength of character."

"She was a fine woman, my aunt," Jalil concurred. "But I cannot understand why she would do such a thing. Why would she convert to Christianity after she saw the danger simply holding the Ingil had brought to Hamid?"

He sat with his head in his hands, then turned weary eyes to Amir. "I have tried to comfort Hamid. I am afraid for him. Afraid his spirit is broken. And what can we say to him? You know as well as I do that there is not much we can do if his wife and children are still in Iran. Even if he gets asylum soon, even if they have exit visas, I seriously doubt they would be allowed on a plane.

"And I cannot imagine that Alaleh and her little daughter and newborn son could possibly travel the Refugee Highway on foot. It almost killed Hamid. They would never make it."

Amir nodded sadly. "Perhaps we can return to the Austrian embassy and urge them to submit the asylum papers for Alaleh and Rasa and Omid immediately," he suggested.

"Yes, but what good will that do? The Iranian government will not honor such a request. I have used much of my family's savings to get Hamid and Rasheed here. I cannot bribe anyone else." Jalil shook his head. "They must find a way to sneak out of Iran. What part of the country are they in now?"

"A small village in the northwest." Even as Amir pronounced this, he thought of the Harrises in Van. "This village is close to the border. Perhaps we could get someone from Turkey to go in and get them."

Jalil frowned. "It would cost a great amount of money to find a smuggler who would do such a thing."

"Yes, you're right," Amir said, but to himself he thought, *but it would cost only courage for a believer with a great amount of faith.*

Tracie

I suppose it was a good thing—providential, Bobbie would say—that the activity scheduled for the short-termers' last day was to clean The Oasis. The hard physical labor allowed everyone to get out their frustrations. We also unloaded several minivans that were crammed full of nonperishable items like canned goods and bags of pasta and cartons of juices. Later in the afternoon, a dozen veiled women refugees came by to pick up the food that had been delivered that morning.

After all the other refugees had left, Amir brought Hamid by. All of us gathered around him, some of the girls in tears, to offer support. This man's pain had grabbed at our hearts. Stephen promised to write a story. The full-time workers and some of the girls placed their hands on Hamid's shoulders and back and arms, and they prayed, but to me the words seemed a meager offering.

Hamid listened and nodded, obviously in a fog and maybe overwhelmed by all the attention. Yet he stayed, as if hungry for it too.

Bobbie wasn't there. She said she was too weak to go with us to The Oasis. Too weak to spend time with Amir. I felt angry with her, and then I felt guilty for feeling angry. I'm sure some of my emotional distress had to do with the fact that I'd hardly slept in days. Stephen's fault.

His mom and the short-term team were driving back to Lyon in the morning, and planned to leave at nine. But Stephen's plane was leaving at eight, meaning he'd have to be at the airport by five.

It was a miserable way for our last evening to end, with everyone in a state of shock. Once again, when the others had gone to bed, Stephen and I sat in the game room, after all our hours of conversation suddenly at a loss for words.

Finally he said, "I've really enjoyed getting to know you, Tracie. I don't know what else to say . . . about us. I've got to deal with my girlfriend first, and that is not going to be easy."

"I know," I said. "Listen, it's been really good for me too. I wasn't planning on having any strings attached. It was just really, I don't know, helpful . . . hopeful . . . to spend time with you. You're so different from Neil, and that was a relief." I felt myself blushing.

"Maybe we can get together for a glass of wine when you're back in Atlanta," he offered.

I laughed. "At your favorite little heuriger?"

"I'm sure we could find something comparably quaint."

"It'd be great to see you in Atlanta. But I don't know how long I'll be staying here."

"No rush, Tracie." He took my hand. "What you're doing for your aunt is awesome. No one can ever take that away from you."

"Thanks."

We'd already exchanged cell phone numbers and e-mail addresses. I couldn't think of anything else to say.

He leaned over and gave me a kiss on the cheek. I wanted more. I know he did too. But it was the wrong time.

I was on the rebound, and he had a girlfriend. Sort of.

At four thirty, after an hour or two of restless sleep, I watched Stephen drive off in a taxi for the airport. He'd given me an awkward hug, then grabbed me in a wonderful embrace. I wanted to kiss him. I wanted to hold on to him. But we'd both been rational about our relationship. No future. Not now at least.

I stood off to the side as he hugged his mother good-bye. Connie Lefort had come back to life in these two weeks. She stood on her tiptoes and kissed her son's cheek, mussing his hair. "I love you, Stephen. Call me when you get home. I'm still your mother, you know. I need to know you got there safely."

He gave her a great smile, his dimples spreading across his pale, freckled face. He picked her up and hugged her tight. "Love you too, Mom. It's been really great."

Then he got into the taxi. As it drove off, he rolled the window down, waved to me, and blew me a kiss. I was thankful it was still pitch black outside so that Connie couldn't see the flush on my face. She simply looped her arm through mine and said, "I for one am going to try to get a little more sleep. I agreed to drive the first leg of our journey back to Lyon."

A few hours later I was up again, hugging Connie and the short-term team good-bye and watching the van drive away. I couldn't help but smile to think how I had berated them two weeks ago. Had it just been two weeks? It seemed like years.

"Come visit us in Lyon!" Dee called out.

I was considering it.

After the exhilaration of the last days, I suddenly felt complete exhaustion and disappointment as I climbed the stairs to our room. It was inevitable, wasn't it, that I'd come crashing down from the mountain high I'd been on for the past week. Mostly, I was just so sad for Hamid and his family and for Aunt Bobbie, who was lying in bed praying for strength to return to her body.

God was so completely unfair.

I hate you, God!

It felt good to whisper that into the hallway with no one around to disapprove. Then I reprimanded myself. I was terribly sleep deprived. I needed a nap before I tried to settle up with the Master of the Universe.

I tiptoed into the room where my brave and beautiful aunt looked completely flattened out as she slept. Her face sagged to the side and her black curls looked wilted. I flopped onto my bed too, and fell into a much needed sleep.

I awoke hours later with the afternoon sun streaming through the window. Bobbie was sitting up in her bed, reading. "Hey there, sleepyhead," she said with a smile.

I stretched and yawned. "Oh, man, that's just what I needed. Did you get to see Amir?"

She shook her head, but then gave a grin. "Not yet, but he's coming over in a little while. We're going to dinner. I rested all day yesterday and today, and I feel stronger. Praise God, I feel stronger."

"I'm so glad." I got out of bed, plopped beside her, and grabbed her hands in mine. "Are you nervous about spending time with him again?"

She gave me her beautiful smile and said, "Terrified. Excited. Like I'm in high school and this is my first date."

She *was* getting her strength back!

"Ready for a shock, Aunt Bobs?"

"Go ahead and try."

"I want to come back here, to work at The Oasis. I feel like this is the life I was meant to be living, even though I never knew it existed. It was never part of my dream, but now, I don't know. I could see doing music therapy with the refugees and putting on more musical evenings and working with the kids. It's been awesome to be helping the refugees in some little way, being in the middle of the action."

Bobbie didn't answer immediately. Then she said, "That's quite interesting."

Uh-oh—*interesting* again.

"But Tracie, you realize this is not a humanitarian effort. It's different. It's God's work."

"You mean I'm not good enough for this job, right?"

"Oh, Trace, no. Of course that's not what I meant. There are a hundred ways you could use your music therapy skills and gifts with kids to help. I just meant that working at The Oasis is a vocation, not just a job, not just helping. The people working at The Oasis feel called to this work."

"I know that." I said it defensively.

"They feel called by God."

"And I'm not called by Him, is that what you're telling me?"

Bobbie frowned. "No, I have no idea if He's calling you." She peered at me. "Is He? You can generally tell if God is talking to you."

How could God be talking to me when we weren't even on speaking terms? "How would I hear him?" I grumbled.

"Through the Bible. Through others."

I deflated. I knew beyond a shadow of a doubt that God wasn't saying a thing to me. Not yet, at least. Or maybe it was simply I had not learned how to hear His voice.

I missed Stephen already. I felt true fear for Hamid. And I could not bear to watch Bobbie trembling as she stood in front of the little mirror in our room, applying makeup. She had showered, and she wore a bright blue tunic over her designer jeans. She looked beautiful for her date with Amir.

While she was getting ready, I stewed, rehearsing all the reasons God would never "call" me into any type of ministry. I let the anger build until at last it spilled out, right there in our room in the guest house as Bobbie put on mascara.

"Do you know why I'm pissed off at God, Bobbie? Do you have any idea?"

Her back toward me, she slowly shook her head, then turned to face me, the mascara wand in midair.

We had talked of faith and belief so many times, but I had always argued on an intellectual level. I had never confided to her what had happened to me on that last day of camp—the day God appeared to me, the day I learned of my father's death, the day I chose to never, ever trust God again.

So I told her, in a voice filled with the rage that had been building in my heart for so many years. I told my story in minute detail, for I remembered it all. I watched Bobbie's face soften, saw the tears in her eyes, knew she wanted to reach out and draw me into her arms as she had done so often when I was a child.

But she didn't. She just listened while I ranted, pacing back and forth, back and forth from the door to the window and back again. She let me vent that anger, vomit the petrifying truth all over our little room even as she prepared for something oh-so-important to her. She never interrupted my monologue, didn't check her watch to hint to me that Amir would be coming soon. She just listened, first standing and then sitting on the bed with her knees drawn up against her. I didn't even realize how hard I was shaking or how many tears I'd shed until I collapsed in Bobbie's arms, all spent.

Exactly five minutes after I dried my tears, someone knocked on the door. Bobbie glanced at me and I suddenly remembered her date with Amir. I nodded, and she opened the door.

Carol stood there, her brow wrinkled. "Um, are you okay,

Bobbie? Amir is downstairs waiting on you."

"Yes. I was just getting ready to head down. Can you tell him I'll be there in a sec?" Carol nodded and left, and Bobbie turned back to me. "You going to be okay?"

"Yeah, I'll be fine. I'm sorry for spilling my guts like that. And sorry I've made you late for your date."

Bobbie smiled. "I'm glad you told me, Trace. I am so thankful for that." She hugged me tightly. "And don't worry about me being late. We've been waiting to see each other again for twelve years. I doubt a few more minutes will make a difference."

From the little window in our room, I peered down as Amir and Aunt Bobbie walked out the front of the guest house. I couldn't see their faces, but I read their body language—loose and relaxed. I breathed in a feeling of thanks as they got into a little black car and drove off.

I couldn't stand to be alone in the room now; I needed to get out, clear my head, which was pounding horribly. I fled the building, walked rapidly down the street and into the foothills that turned into vineyards. Almost all of the grapes had been harvested, except for the sweetest ones, the rosé, that were only harvested after the first freeze. I stood before the rows of vines, panting, and in my head I was screaming: *I hate you, God! Can't you understand it! This is way too painful, watching Bobbie and hearing the refugees' stories. And now Hamid, so new on his faith journey, and I cannot begin to understand how they can trust when You are not a God who provides. You're a God who takes away!*

I ran further into the woods, drawing my coat closed as the shadows of evening broke around me.

You give and take away.

I stopped beside a stream that gurgled to my right. The wood was quiet, and I tried to calm the rushing of my heart. I sat on a log and closed my eyes and listened for the wind.

When I opened them, there was a deer standing so near that I jumped. She didn't move, didn't seem in any way afraid. She stood still, staring at me.

I sat by the stream with the deer standing with braced legs on the other side. Then I stood up and started towards the stream, as if challenging her to leave. She didn't. She walked over, head held high, then lowered her graceful neck and began to drink.

For one moment I was that little girl again, sitting on a log in the woods of the camp feeling God so near I could have touched Him. And then came a crushing realization.

He *had* come to me; it *was* the Christ, just as much as He had appeared to Hamid in the dream.

Christ had appeared to me that day, not to punish and taunt, but to prepare me for the terrible road ahead. I had refused His love, proud and furious and so confused. But He had come in the form of the deer, in the whistle of the wind, and then He had come in a very human presence. My Aunt Bobbie.

All those years when I felt God had left me alone, He had been there, had provided through Aunt Bobbie and others, had reached out to me, and I would not have Him.

As the deer loped off, I felt the hatred and anger ebbing away, as if they were following the deer into the woods. I sank to the ground, hearing Bobbie's words again: *Do you think it's fair to only accept the good and not the bad in life?*

In a whisper I admitted to the Lord, "I've been so mad at You, and I've blamed You, and I've been afraid to trust You again. I don't know why Daddy died, but now I realize that You never abandoned me." I sat with that realization for a long time, thinking of the tender care my mother and my aunt had unflaggingly provided, never holding back.

"You have always been here, as near as the doe, always providing and holding me, giving me Aunt Bobbie and so many others. And I have screamed at You and cursed You and refused You. Please forgive me." My throat constricted. So many different emotions were colliding in my heart— grief and pain and, somehow, hope.

I felt the wind again, just as I had all those years ago, the gentle touch of God's presence on my face, and I felt a stab of joy in the midst of the other emotions. I stood up and held out one hand, imagining Jesus—Isa—right there beside me. Together we walked out of the woods and back through the vineyards.

When the guest house came into view, a tiny sliver of doubt inched its way in amidst the joy. Had God let me repeat this odd occurrence because I was walking back to tragedy? Was He going to rip away my aunt as He had my father? Was that how God worked?

But when I entered Gasthaus Müller, no one was there. All was silent. I imagined Bobbie was still out with Amir. I thought of how much of her belonged in this place, with the refugees, with Carol and Julie and Tom and JoAnn. With Amir. Ah, my aunt might not die for a while yet, maybe. But I was losing her all the same.

CHAPTER 20

Stephen

I merged onto I-75 North, leaving Hartsfield International Airport behind me. The bright globe of sun was setting directly in front of me as I headed home after over three weeks away. I let out a contented sigh. I loved coming back to Atlanta, seeing the impressive skyline in front of me, those fancy manmade mountains, architectural treasures, highlighted against the pink sky, the sun glinting off them as traffic slowly moved forward.

People in the routine of their daily lives. The interstate veered left and the sun reappeared, big and round, from behind the trees. The gold dome of the Capitol blinked back at me in the distance. Everything was familiar and inviting. Soon I'd step into the apartment, and Pam would greet me with a kiss, and it would be life as usual. Back to normal.

I felt a sinking sensation in my heart. Life as usual. Pam hugging me too hard, laughing too loudly, demanding to hear every last detail of the trip. But there was so much I couldn't explain, so much she really wouldn't want to hear and could never understand.

Tracie. Hamid. Mom.

I had a fleeting image of Hamid, grasping my hands as if he might not let go, thanking me for the article I had promised to write about his family. I saw thin, intense Carol staring at me from over the coffee counter and nodding amidst the crowd of refugee men. "Of course it's worth it," she'd said to me. "Lots of work, hard work. But worth it."

I saw Tracie, lively, pretty Tracie, hair pulled off her neck in a disheveled ponytail-bun, perspiration on her forehead, determination in her eyes as she lifted crate after crate of almost-past-date provisions from the old truck and later distributed them to those veiled women with the worn-out faces who took the cartons as if Tracie were placing gold in their wrinkled hands.

And I saw Bobbie, eyes always so bright and intense no matter her circumstances, sitting in the corner, grasping a Chechen woman's hands and whispering in her rusty Russian, "Yes, yes, of course we will help you find your family. Of course."

And my mom's face, all lit up with some newfound hope as she handed out clothes to the women and children. My mother had found a place amidst the refugees outside Vienna.

I suddenly felt sick to my stomach. I was coming back to what was familiar, what I had worked so hard to make my home. I was moving up in the journalism world. What I did mattered. Surely it mattered.

But somehow those images from Traiskirchen seemed to matter more.

I sighed, watched the sun turn burnt orange and then red, and then disappear once more behind a shining building as I made my way back home.

Hamid

Alone in his room on Sunday evening, Hamid unfolded the wadded piece of paper that Julie had handed to him as he left the party Friday night, when his world was caving in. Now he read the handwritten note.

If you are interested in finding out more about Isa, come to The Oasis at 7:30 pm on Tuesday evening. Come alone. Make sure no one follows you . . .

Hamid closed his eyes and remembered the way Christians had gathered around him the day before, hugging, praying, crying. He had felt supported, with a new confidence and a sort of peace. Many, many people were interested in helping him find a way to get Alaleh and Rasa and Omid into Austria. Jalil had influence, as did Amir and the people at The Oasis. He thought of Stephen, who had flown back to America but had promised he would do something to get the word out.

Hamid wanted to go to this secret meeting on Tuesday. Amir had explained to him how those who had a true desire to believe in Isa and grow in their faith could attend different types of "Bible studies," as Amir called them. However, it was dangerous. Other Muslims did not take favorably to their brothers studying the Bible.

Hamid knew this was true. Rasheed spent more and more time with the young Iranian roommates who embraced fundamentalist Islam but disagreed with the government they had fled. They had escaped for political reasons, like Rasheed, but Hamid knew they were devout Muslims and held Christianity in contempt.

He lit a match and burned the little paper with the instructions. He could take no chances, now that not only Rasheed but also the others were watching him with suspicion. When Hamid had returned to their room the day before, after spending such a holy time with the Christians, Rasheed had glared at him.

"Where have you been?"

"At The Oasis," Hamid replied truthfully.

"Why?"

"Because they want to help me bring Alaleh and my children here. They have connections."

"I am sorry for your loss, Hamid. I grieve your mother's death. I understand your fear for your family's safety. I am afraid for my family too. But I am more afraid for you, spending time with infidels. That is the most dangerous thing of all. You must understand that."

Now Hamid turned on the radio, thankful that his roommates were out for the evening. He listened to the "Life in Christ" program. Then he closed his eyes as the strong, deep voice from The Netherlands came across the airwaves.

"We have an urgent prayer need for a brother in Europe whose family is in danger in a closed country. One family member has already been killed. The others are fleeing, but young children are involved and the way is filled with danger. Let's lift up this family to Papy, for surely He sees all and knows the path they must take."

Hamid swallowed hard. It sounded like this voice was talking about his family! He felt chills run up his spine as he imagined listeners from all over the Middle East praying for him and his wife and children. He brought his hand to his heart and wept as the compassionate voice read Scripture.

"I will lead the blind by a way they do not know. In paths they do not know, I will guide them. I will make darkness into light before them and rugged places into plains . . . "

Bobbie

It was the perfect evening. We talked and talked at the heuriger. I felt strong and alive. I laughed often, watching

Amir's eyes twinkle.

Then he said those beautiful words that first caught my heart years ago, his eyes smiling straight at me. "A friend is like a poem."

"Yes. Yes, it's true. I've often thought of your words."

"Not exactly my words, Bobbie."

"My poet is quoting another poet," I whispered, then felt my face go red. Had I really called Amir *my* poet? He seemed not to notice. "Do you still write?"

He sat back and looked off into the distance. Then he leaned across the table and said with an urgency in his voice, "Now I write my poetry into sermons, always with the prayer that my words will fall away and His Word will stay, implanted in the listeners' hearts, to take root and grow. This is what I write now, Bobbie."

"It's what you were made for."

"Yes, I believe it with all my heart. God made me to speak His Word to those who are hungry for such bread as He offers."

And He made you for me.

The thought startled me and I blushed again, searching for a new subject to turn to.

"Do you remember the first time we met?" he asked, as if he had read my mind.

We spoke in German and English and Farsi; we remembered our first years and Amir's new faith. And for that evening, Amir let me skip over the tragedy of 1994, as if it had not happened. As if I had simply gone from Austria to America because my sister needed me.

We talked of our lives of the past twelve years too, and it felt comfortable and warm and so, so good to be together. I was thankful he did not make me go back. Not yet. For this night we were caught in time before horror and after horror. I felt held up by Amir's friendship—yes, a poem, a lovely poem—as we shared our hearts, and for that one evening the physical tremors and the emotional terrors were kept at bay.

The heuriger emptied of customers, and Frau Schafler finally told us politely it was time to leave. We laughed.

Just like old times.

"May I see you on Tuesday?" Amir asked, as he pulled his car to a stop outside Gasthaus Müller.

"I'd like that very much."

No questions about our love lives, about our feelings for each other. For this one night, I felt safe.

When he dropped me off, all was dark at the guest house. I walked inside to the reception area and then into the game room. To my surprise, Tracie looked up from reading a Bible. Her eyes had a strange type of light in them.

"How was your evening?" she asked, but there was an urgency in her voice that told me what she really wanted was for me to ask about hers.

"It was perfect," I said. "Lovely to be back with an old friend."

My poet.

"You had fun, then?"

"Yes. It was just like it used to be."

Tracie gave me an impromptu hug and held me tight. The angry, brooding child of a few hours earlier had disappeared.

"Oh, Aunt Bobbie, I've had the most amazing encounter. And right after I got up the courage to tell you about the deer at the camp. Oh, you'll never believe what has happened!"

So she told me, in living color, with her face alight with joy and faith, her voice filled with wonder, her eyes sparkling.

"How beautiful," I said again and again as she spoke. I felt tremors, not from the medication, but from the depth of emotion with which Tracie shared her story of Jesus coming to her.

As I listened something happened in my heart, and I knew that the cancer, the trip to Europe with Tracie, the time with Amir, and this very moment listening to her story were all instruments in God's hands to prod me to do what I had refused to do for almost twelve years. To go back, to face the pain and yes, the horror. To look it square in the face and forgive myself, forgive him. I suppose it was an epiphany, as if I stood back from the scene and saw what God was doing—He had orchestrated it all to bring me to this moment of realization so that I could push forward with Him.

He had done this for Tracie, and now He was doing it for me too. She had no idea that her epiphany, her twilight with the deer, would engender an epiphany for me. But God knew. He was so like that, using one circumstance to influence a dozen others, to infuse them with meaning, pushing His children along toward grace and health.

As Tracie finished speaking, her voice still filled with awe, I knew what had to be done. I would truly go back. Not simply to Amir and that unfinished story, but to the one that happened on the side of the Romanian mountain at the little camp for orphans all those years ago.

"The Lord has spoken to me through your story, Tracie. Amir asked to see me again on Tuesday . . . and I will let him know what the Lord has begun in my heart."

"I hope you can forgive him, Aunt Bobbie. I'm so sorry he's hurt you so badly."

"Oh, Tracie. Is that what you think? That he hurt me? Broke my heart—or did something worse?"

She nodded.

"Oh no. I'm the one who was wrong. I'm the one who hurt him, and . . . it is excruciatingly hard to realize the extent of the pain I caused him. I apologized in a letter a long time ago. But to see him face-to-face . . ."

Tracie looked unconvinced. Not ready to believe that her aunt the "super rescuer" could be the one in the wrong.

"Tracie," I said, "will you take a walk with me? I know

it won't be quite as exciting as walking with Stephen"—I ducked as she pretended to swat me—"but I want to tell you a story. A long story."

We headed out into the night and walked towards the vineyards, and I began.

"As you know, when the wall of Eastern Europe tumbled down in 1989, my 'career' as a Bible smuggler was instantly a thing of the past. We had to find new roles as missionaries. And since I had fallen in love with refugees, and with one in particular, I stayed and worked in Traiskirchen."

"Aunt Bobs, was Amir the first guy you ever fell for?"

"Oh, I suppose I had dreamed about being in love. I'd noticed cute boys, but I was more inclined to arm-wrestle them or tackle them in football than to hold their hands and gaze into their eyes. Until I met Amir."

"What made him so special?"

"Well, for starters, he seemed very unimpressed with women, and that impressed me. He didn't give a second glance at girls in their short, short cut-offs or low-cut blouses that revealed way too much. Oh, he must have noticed, but what he liked about me was so far from just physical. He told me I was the most passionate woman he'd ever met. He could see that I loved teaching the children. I still remember what he said. 'It's like as soon as you get around them, you are the most of Jill that I have ever seen.'

"I thought that was an apt description. 'The most of myself.' Some people had trouble figuring out what their spiritual gifts were. I never tried to figure out anything. My gift, for I was pretty sure I only had one, was with children. They seemed drawn to me, as I was to them."

I told her about working at the orphanage in Romania, about losing my heart to little Vasilica and my decision to adopt him.

Tracie looked distressed. "But—what happened? Bobbie,

did you have to give him up to take care of us instead?"

"Oh, Tracie, no. Nothing to do with that."

"Then what?"

I took a deep breath. "Tracie, not even your mother knows what happened next. I've never told the whole story to anyone besides Peggy."

Tracie paused to face me, and looked as serious as I've ever seen her. "You don't have to tell me, Aunt Bobs. Not if you don't want to."

"But I do want to, Tracie. It's way past time for me to face these memories." We resumed walking. "The next summer, the summer of 1994, we planned a camping adventure for the orphans at a rustic resort in the mountains. Amir came along to help. We saw it as a chance for him to get to know Vasilica in a non-threatening atmosphere.

"And just as I had, Amir fell head over heels for Vasilica. 'He's going to be our son, Jill!' He was so excited about our future as a family. Though I didn't have a ring on my finger yet, it was understood between us, and among all the team members, that Amir and I would soon be engaged. We were young, and adventurous, and ready for whatever God had next.

"A few days before the end of camp, Amir and I took twelve of the children on a fairly challenging hike. Amir led the group, then each child walked with a partner, and I brought up the rear. Their ears didn't work well, but my, could they climb! Up and up and up we went on this winding road that tourists from all over the world came to hike. We perched on the walls of a ruined castle, which I had pointed out to them from below, rising out of the mist like a fairy tale. Romania always seemed dark and mysterious to me, even magical. Oppressive, yes, but beautiful.

"As we rested on the wall, I signed to them the story of how the castle was protected in centuries past because it was built right into the mountain. On the other side of the castle, off limits to the tourists, the walls fell away into a ravine far below. The children listened to my story and nodded, enthralled.

"When we arrived at a wider part of the path, the children ran, heads back, mouths opened with laughter that no one heard. Silent laughter. Amir and I felt the magic, the joy, the freedom of these orphans. We came to a particularly steep point, and I signed for the children to stop, to hold their partners' hands and wait. Amir motioned for me to go first; he'd help me up and then he'd lift each of the children up to me. He held out his hand, and I took it."

Here I faltered with my story, and Tracie took my arm and led me to a log—her log, where she'd seen the deer. We sat down on it, drawing our coats tight, and watched the little creek gurgle past. At last I found my voice.

"I remember everything about that scene so sharply, Tracie. The electricity in his touch. The love in his eyes. The flutter of joy in my heart as I thought about the love we shared and the little family we were about to become. And then the scream.

"Amir and I jerked around. The children just stood, staring at us, because of course, they had heard nothing. Somehow I knew it was Vasilica. I jumped back down and raced past the others, around the bend to the end of the line. Vasilica's partner was there, alone. He was examining a flower, stooped down, touching its petals. I signed to him, 'Where's Vasilica?' but it took him a moment to realize how urgent this was.

"He pointed down the hill and shrugged. Amir had gathered all the other children in a circle. He told me to let him go, but of course I paid no attention. Of course I took off down the path without him. I came to the castle wall where we had perched and looked across to the forbidden ledge, praying the whole time for it not to be true, but as I lifted myself onto the ledge and looked over, I saw Vasilica's crumpled body a hundred feet below.

"It was horrible irony that Vasilica's first word was his last. His high-pitched scream, the first sound I'd ever heard from him, was what had warned us of his death. I wanted to go down into the ravine, but Amir was much more calm. He said that we had to take the other children back to the camp and then get help. And even though I knew he was right, I hated him for that. I knew Vasicila had died the moment he touched the rocks so far below. But what if he hadn't? What if he lay there, bleeding and in excruciating pain as his life ebbed away?

"We told the children that Vasilica was lost. It took us two hours to get back to the camp. It took a day for them to locate Vasilica's body. The policeman assured us he had died immediately, and then said, 'He was an orphan. At least he has no family to mourn him, no one who's waiting for him to come home.'

"He couldn't know how his words pierced me, but I blamed him anyway. I hated that policeman and wanted him dead instead of Vasilica. I think I would have strangled the man if Amir had not been there beside me, holding my hands, gripping them so tightly I couldn't move.

"Ever after, I remembered that viselike grip of Amir's, not the tender, firm one of our climb. I remembered the way he had to force me to stay on the trail. Of course I also remembered how he held me that first night as I sobbed. And how he wept too.

"The last two days of camp were a daze. We tried to care for the children. The other staff played with them and smiled. There were papers to sign, a nightmare of papers. I thought we might even be sued by the orphanage, but we weren't. But in my own heart I'd been tried and found guilty. And my punishment was to live with the image of Vasilica's body twisted on the rocks below.

"The mission sent in professionals to do grief counseling for the whole team, even for the children. Over and over people said to me, 'Bobbie, it was an accident. Accidents happen.'"

I stopped my monologue, out of breath, out of energy, and glanced at my niece. Tracie, with a wisdom beyond her years, had not interrupted my story once. Tears were streaming down her face, and she was shivering in the cold. She still didn't say a word, she just grabbed my hands and squeezed them in hers, almost as if she were trying to squeeze out all the pain. Then she reached up and softly wiped her hand across my cheek. I had not noticed that I was crying too.

"I need to take you back to the guest house and warm you up," she said, as if I were a young child or a wayward teen.

I stood, letting her hold me around my waist. As we walked back through the vineyards, I told her the rest of the story.

"I kept going for three months. But I could not speak to Amir of it. All I could think was that it was in the moment he took my hand and smiled at me, the moment I realized how much he loved me and I loved him, that I took my eyes off the children, and Vasilica went tumbling to his death. I, Bobbie Blake, was always completely in control. But the one brief moment that I had allowed my emotions to take over, tragedy struck. Vasilica died, I died, and my hope of love died.

"So it came as a strange relief, a pathway out of my despair, when your father died. I'm sorry to say it like that, Trace. But I had to leave Austria, Romania, and Amir. I did it all wrong. I didn't even tell Amir good-bye. I just ran. And after it was done, I could never imagine going back to make things right.

"Your mom knew there had been a tragic accident, knew

an orphan had died, but she never knew that this was *my* orphan, the child I was going to adopt. She never knew how I blamed myself—and Amir—for the accident.

"I talked about it with Peggy a hundred times. I prayed for forgiveness, and I wrote to Amir, telling him I was sorry. But Peggy insisted that real healing would only come when I went back and faced the memories . . . and faced Amir."

As we left the icy night air and stepped into the lobby of the guest house, I sank into a chair, covered my face with my hands, and cried again. For Vasilica, for Amir. For lost love. For cancer.

And I cried for hope. *Oh, Lord, give me hope.*

When I was silent again, spent, Tracie hugged me tight and whispered, "Thank you for telling me, Aunt Bobbie. I can tell how much it cost you. But you're the bravest woman I have ever known."

She kissed me on the top of my head, then fixed me a cup of herbal tea and placed it in my chilled hands.

"Drink it and try to relax," she whispered. "I'm going up to the room. Don't stay down here too long, please." She headed for the stairs and then turned to me, "And I will be praying that the Lord will bless the time you have with Amir on Tuesday."

I sat in the darkness a little longer. *Give me hope.* No Bible verse comforted me, but I heard a verse nonetheless, and I smiled at its soothing meaning.

A friend is like a poem.

CHAPTER 21

Stephen

*T*he e-mail from Keith McDaniel in Amersfoort was brief: *J and A at embassy today. Talk to Papy. Urgent.*

I knew it was coded language for prayer. Unfortunately, I had no idea how to "talk to Papy." Of course, I had seen the short-term team in prayer. But I would not pray. Instead, I continued to work on Hamid's story, which was set to run in the *Peachtree Press* the next morning. I recalled the crowded room at The Oasis, the men, many so young, with that lost look in their eyes. They had left everything. Fled with the clothes on their back. For what? And Hamid describing with such love and longing his wife and daughter and newborn son. Hamid weeping, telling me that his mother had been shot and killed.

"There you are! Didn't you hear me call you from the kitchen?" Pam stood in front of my desk. "I asked if you'd looked at the swatches. That old sofa has to be recovered. I can't put up with it another month."

I glanced up at her. She was wearing a tight-fitting sweater that flattered her lovely figure, and tight designer jeans. Her blond hair had a new stylish cut, her makeup was perfect. And she wore a perfect pout on her face.

"Would you listen to me, please? Ever since you came back from your holiday in Europe, you've had this faraway look in your eyes."

My "holiday." How to explain it to Pam, whose life revolved around making things look beautiful—herself included—going to parties, being seen in all the right places.

"Did you see the invitation to the Charity Ball on the kitchen counter? We need to RSVP by tomorrow. It will be good for your career, and I found the most gorgeous gown to wear. Cost a fortune, but I figured we have lots to celebrate . . ." She sidled up to me and put her arms around my waist.

I rubbed my hands over my face. "Sorry, Pam, you're right. I'm not myself."

"Let me get you a glass of wine. You take a shower. Dinner can wait. Maybe you'd like dessert first?" She lifted her eyebrows and gave me her best seductive smile.

I gave a weak grin. "Yeah, a glass of wine, maybe." I sighed and headed to the shower.

The gnawing in my stomach, though familiar, was the truth. What was I doing with Pam? I felt worn out by her endless stream of talk—words, yes, words that meant nothing. They bounced back at me as if she were speaking a foreign language. What had happened to me in Europe? Was I losing my mind?

I'd tried to follow the progress on Hamid's family. Two phone calls to Jim Harris and Keith McDaniel had revealed that Hamid had heard nothing from Alaleh. I knew I was living in a hazy, distracted manner, but I couldn't make Pam understand. I felt trapped, pressed down to nothing. She was right, we needed to talk, but not about swatches of material.

I wanted out.

I dressed and went into the living room, where Pam was lying on the sofa, reading a decorating magazine. "Look, Pam, we've got to talk."

"Really? You'll grant me a little of your precious time?" She smiled, pretending she was kidding, but there was an edge in her voice.

"Yes, but not about decorating. We have to talk about us."

"Us? What do you mean, about us?" Her eyes narrowed.

"This isn't working for me, Pam. Us, you and me. I think we need to step back and reevaluate."

Her face went pale. "What are you saying, Stephen? You invited me to move in with you. You encouraged me to re-decorate this place, which suggested to me that we were in something of a relationship!"

"I know, Pam. I know. Something changed," I offered feebly.

"Oh, that's great. You gallivant around Europe, hardly bothering to communicate while you're away, and come back 'changed.' Meanwhile I'm here trying to make our life what I thought we both wanted it to be."

My head pounded, my stomach roiled again. "I'm sorry. It's just not working."

"Not working! Are you scared of commitment, is that it? I haven't asked you for a ring, Stephen. I haven't asked for anything."

I tried to look at her and feel something besides repulsion. "Pam, that's just it. I don't feel like we have a relationship. It seems so. . ." I searched desperately for the right word. "So superficial. It doesn't seem like we have anything in common."

"What's really going on here, Stephen? Did you meet someone in Europe?"

"No, it's not like that." *Yes, I met someone, a lot of people, needy people and people with a purpose.* "I'm just . . . I'm not right for you, Pam. I don't think we're heading in the same direction."

I saw fear flicker in her eyes. The hostility vanished, and she began to cry. She came to me and threw her arms around me. "Stephen, you're just jet-lagged. Why don't you take a few days off and get some rest? I'll make the decisions about the apartment, and you won't have to worry about a thing."

I unwound her arms from around my waist. Holding her hands down by her sides, I looked her in the eyes. "Pam, listen to me. I'm sorry to end it this way. You can keep the apartment, the furniture. Everything. I need time to think about what I saw in Austria. To process."

I longed to see a flit of understanding in her eyes, a softening, a spark of interest in what I'd seen. But her expression was ice cold.

"Leave then," she said. "Go 'process.' But don't expect me to be waiting around when you come back!"

I went into our bedroom and pulled the suitcase out from under the bed. It still had the tags on it from the flight home from Vienna. In a daze I took out clothes and put them in the suitcase, removed my files, packed the briefcase, looked around for anything else I might want. Toiletries, my suits.

Pam stood in the doorway, arms crossed tightly across her chest.

"I can't take my filing cabinet now. Give me a few days and we'll talk again, okay?"

She didn't say a word; she just held the door open, eyes blazing.

"I'll call you in a couple days," I said. And I walked out.

Alaleh

"We must go, Hamid," Alaleh whispered into the cell phone. "The Garabadians have been so good to us, but it is too dangerous for them, for all of us, if we stay any longer." She sniffed. "We don't know what has happened to Noyemi and her family. We're leaving very early on Thursday morning, and going on horseback. It's the safest way."

"You cannot do this! Omid is too young. Rasa too. The cold! Alaleh, I have traveled that route. It is not one for children."

"We have no choice. We cannot stay here in this village. When the police come—and they will—there can be no trace of us, Hamid. Or they will kill us all."

"You have paid a smuggler, then?"

"The Garabadians know of a man. He cannot get us into Turkey, but he will get us to another village that is very close to the border."

"Then we will send someone for you from Turkey. I have friends there now," Hamid said quietly.

"People you trust?"

"Yes. Tomorrow I will go to the embassy here again with Amir and Jalil. If my papers for asylum have gone through, then we can apply for the reunification. It will not be long now, my love."

She heard his breaking voice and knew he longed to comfort her. But he knew, as she did, that riding by horseback in the mountains in December could mean death for their children. She would not scream her terror and anger to him. What could he do?

"We'll find a way, my love," Hamid reassured her wearily. Then in a halting voice, he asked, "Was there a funeral for Maamaan-Bozorg?"

"We think your uncle came and got her body. We know nothing else." Alaleh paused. "The Garabadians had a memorial service for her here in their home. They believe she is in heaven with this god, Isa." She wiped her fist over her eyes angrily.

"I love you, Alaleh. Just hearing your voice, I have hope. We'll be together again soon. I believe it."

Soon, thought Alaleh bitterly as she snuggled Omid to her breast. Her dreaming husband and their dreaming daughter; let them believe what they wanted. She did not believe at all.

Alaleh had tearfully confided to Rasa that Maamaan-Bozorg had died—but to the little girl's repeated *How?* Alaleh would not reply. She couldn't talk about it. But the night before, she had come out of the room where Omid was sleeping and heard her daughter talking to Astrid Garbadian—asking her the same question, "Do you know what happened to my grandmother?"

She could have slipped into the room right then, and their kind host would have taken her cue from her. She was Rasa's mother, after all. But she wanted to hear what the other woman would say, so she stayed around the corner and listened.

"You know that it is dangerous for Muslims to read the Ingil, Rasa. The police in our country do not allow this."

"Yes," Rasa replied. "And I know that Maamaan-Bozorg believed the words of the Ingil and trusted in Isa."

"Well, the police found this out. They came to Maamaan-Bozorg's house and were going to take her away, but she refused to go with them." The old lady cleared her throat and lowered her voice. "And so they shot her. I am so sorry to tell you this, little child. You are perhaps too young to know such hard truth."

Alaleh strained to hear how her daughter would reply.

"Miss Beverly said that when people who love Isa die, they go to be with Him in paradise, and there is no more crying or pain or death. They live again forever with Him. Is that true?"

"Yes, my child."

"So that must mean that Maamaan-Bozorg is happy now.

Because she is with Isa."

"Yes, I believe this is the truth."

"Then I will try not to cry too much. I will not tell Maamaan why. She does not love Isa yet. But I know in my heart that Isa is taking care of Maamaan-Bozorg and Noyemi and all of her family. Even if they are dead, somewhere they are alive with Isa."

Where did the child get such a faith? It frightened Alaleh—but at the same time, it gave her some little sliver of hope. Rasa's strong spirit would make what they had to do the next day a little bit easier.

The horses looked sturdy, surefooted, calm. The bay threw its head in the air and then snorted; the dappled gray swatted its tail at an invisible fly. Surely no flies were out in this freezing weather! Alaleh lifted Rasa to sit on the bay mare in front of Davood, the man in his early thirties to whom Alaleh was entrusting her life and the lives of her children. He gave Rasa a smile and tweaked her cheek as he settled her in the saddle in front of him.

Rasa was bundled in so many layers of clothes she could hardly move. Two scarves encircled her neck, and Astrid Garabadian pulled an extra woolen hat over the one that already covered her thick black hair.

"Be sure to wear both sets of mittens, you hear?" the old woman said to Rasa, twisting her hands together with a worried expression on her face. Astrid's husband, Agop, brought out one last blanket and wrapped it around the child so that Rasa was all but hidden beneath the clothing.

Rasa's eyes twinkled from under her layers and she said, "Maamaan, don't frown so! We are going toward freedom!"

Ah, Rasa! At least she saw this as an adventure instead of a death trip. Omid was strapped securely to Alaleh's chest, he too wrapped in so many layers that only his little mouth and nose were visible. Her son's warmth spread to her, and she stifled a sob. Would life ever again be simple? Waking up and fixing her husband breakfast, reading books to Rasa? Fear lodged and sprouted in every part of her body.

Isa! It is your fault! If indeed you are real.

And yet, Isa's followers were the ones who had cared for all of them, offering shelter and hope. Alaleh reached down and grasped Astrid's hand tightly in her own gloved hand.

"God be with you," the older woman said through tears. "God protect you all."

"And you too."

Alaleh wondered if the religious police would come for the Garabadians. Why would they be willing to die for their faith? Even Maamaan-Bozorg had been willing! Such a strange faith.

The sun was rising behind the snowcapped mountains, radiating pinks and soft oranges and deep purples. Astrid handed up one last blanket that Alaleh wrapped around herself. She took the reins of the gray gelding and followed the bay mare in front, into the mountains, toward freedom, toward life. Toward Hamid.

Please, God. I do not know whom to pray to, but please grant us courage and safe passage.

Rasa turned and looked back at her mother, her eyes lit up with childish joy. "Maamaan, Mrs. Garabadian taught me a new song last night. It comes from the Bible. She said it is for our journey." In her sweet voice, Rasa sang out a hopeful melody. "I will lift up my eyes to the mountains. Where does my hope come from? My hope comes from the Lord who made heaven and earth. He will not allow your foot to stumble . . ."

Rasa continued to sing the song of God's protection from the heat of the sun and the cold of the night. His protection from evil. His protection for their very souls.

Oh, how Alaleh desired protection for her soul. As the horses walked slowly over the rocky terrain, gradually weaving their way into the foothills and then onto a steeper path, she repeated in her mind the last line of Rasa's song: "The Lord will guard your going out and your coming in from this time forth and forevermore."

Bobbie

I arranged to see Amir in one of the upstairs rooms at The Oasis Tuesday evening, knowing we'd need more privacy than a heuriger provided. We sat facing each other on the worn couches. The light blue walls around us were covered with photos of smiling refugees, the bookshelves filled with Bibles in various languages, DVDs for learning German, Bible commentaries in English, and an assortment of old novels.

Amir gave me a brief update on Hamid, and I told him of Tracie's revelation.

Then we plunged into silence.

Amir wore jeans and a sweatshirt and a look of intensity on his face. *What a beautiful man you are*, I thought to myself. He had aged well; he wore his thick black hair carefully combed back from his broad forehead. Long, black eyelashes surrounded his deep charcoal eyes, which were staring straight at me. I felt so vulnerable in front of him. My stomach kept flip-flopping. There was so much I needed to say.

At last he spoke. "May I ask you the hard questions now, Jill?" Then he smiled. "I mean, Bobbie? It is hard for me to make that change."

I nodded. *Yes, yes, you ask me, because I am having such a hard time speaking.*

"Why did you never come back?"

I cleared my throat twice, then said quickly, "Too painful. Too many memories. It was my fault. If I had only been paying more attention, Vasilica would not have died."

"It was an accident."

I shook my head vehemently, feeling the rage well up. "No. It wasn't. I was infatuated with you, Amir. I let myself fall in love, and this is what happened. Death."

Amir's gaze was almost angry. "That is what you believe? You were *infatuated* with me? A silly crush? We were in *love*, Jill. We were getting married." His voice broke a little. "We were adopting a child together. This was not infatuation."

My heart slammed in my chest. "You're right," I whispered. I stared down at my hands.

"Look at me, Jill! I want you to hear this."

I raised my head, felt cold sweat break on my brow, felt something much more terrifying than tremors. Again his eyes pierced through me with a holy intensity.

"We planned that hike," Amir stated, as if he had been rehearsing these lines for years. Indeed, he had probably gone over them thousands of times. "We knew it by heart. There was nothing of inattention in our actions. I was helping you climb to the next level." He sounded incredulous. "I will not let you continue to punish yourself for something that is untrue. I've never understood why you took the accident out on us."

"I was responsible for his death," I said again.

"Even if you were, you have to forgive yourself. Why did you choose to punish *us*?"

The hurt in his eyes melted me. Why? Why? "I didn't deserve you, Amir. And I think . . ." I couldn't get the words past the thick dryness in my mouth.

Amir waited.

"I think I blamed you, too. I blamed you for causing me to lose control. If I had been thinking clearly, I would have realized that Vasilica should not have been at the end of the line."

Amir's eyes bore into me. "Yes, you blamed me—you explained that in the letter you wrote me. But you were wrong.

It wasn't my fault or yours. Or Vasilica's. It was an accident. And now you must stop living with a lie. You must let yourself live again."

He leaned back on the couch, his face intense, broken.

"I've lived. I rebuilt my life, and I regained control," I said a bit defensively. "At least I had, until this bit with cancer." I had my hands clasped so tightly that my knuckles were white. "And now I see that by my desperate clinging to control I've lost the opportunity for love. I can't have another orphan. There are hundreds of thousands to choose from, but they don't need a mother who will die before the papers are even finished."

I glanced up at him. Oh, how admitting this hurt! Didn't he see that I had wanted a child so badly? That I had loved Vasilica with everything within me?

"And I don't need a husband to watch me die either," I said, before Amir could speak.

Amir frowned and sat forward. In a voice much harsher than usual, he said, "I'm not asking you to be my wife, Bobbie."

What was *wrong* with me? That was not what I had wanted to say! Here I was again, almost blaming him when what I needed to say was simply how sorry I was. Why could I not pronounce the words that I had rehearsed back at the guest house?

I could tell Amir was not happy with the conversation either. This kind, good man looked deflated, and there was a smoldering anger in his eyes. Anger at me. Perfectly deserved. We sat in silence for long minutes. I could not meet his eyes, but I prayed for strength, for courage to do what I needed to do.

At last I got off the couch, walked the few feet between us, sat down beside him. I took his hand and held it tightly. "I cannot look at you," I said, "but this is what I need to say. I'm sorry, Amir. I am sorry I let one tragedy become two. I am sorry I was too hurt and fearful and proud to let you help me and then to find help for us."

I looked up, and his eyes were awash in pain and compassion.

"I did it all wrong. I ran away selfishly to protect my heart. I would not let myself see what I had done to you. I'm so sorry." My voice broke. "I did love you, Amir. And I knew you loved me. I threw away the relationship that was the most important to me." I cleared my throat and whispered, looking straight at him. "I don't deserve forgiveness, Amir. But I ask for it. I want so much for you to forgive me."

His arm came around my shoulders and he held me, not in the intimate way of lovers, but as a brother, a friend.

"Thank you, Bobbie," he said at last. "I forgave you long ago, but today I forgive you for you. It is an important step."

We sat in a comfortable silence then until my heart stopped racing, and I felt my jaw and my arms and shoulders relax. I let Amir's forgiveness wash over me, and I knew I was letting the Lord's forgiveness descend on my very weak shoulders as well.

After a while Amir asked, "When are you and Tracie heading back to America?"

"Our ticket is for this Saturday."

"Could you change it?

"Why?"

"To stay longer, of course."

I would not let my heart hear the love in his voice. "I'm on an oral treatment for cancer. I finish my pills next Monday. I have to check in with the doctor."

"You can have a blood test done here. Medical care is much cheaper in Austria than in the States."

The temptation zipped past me. "I'm afraid it would be impossible."

Why would it be impossible, Bobbie? You know your heart

is here.

"Call and ask your doctor."

From Amir's grave expression, I could tell he was fully aware of all that implied.

"Anyway, you must stay at least a week longer. To give me time to take you back to Romania. We're going to his grave."

At first I was too shocked to speak. Then, my heart pounding in my chest, I whispered, "No."

But Amir was the one person who had never accepted my "No."

"Yes. We are. And we are going to sit beside it and mourn."

CHAPTER 22

Hamid

*P*raise God, they were all alive. No matter that Alaleh sounded so distraught—after four days of silence, he had heard her voice! Even the hearty cry of Omid brought relief. His heart sank at the thought of them heading into the mountains on horseback, but what else could they do?

We will send someone for you from Turkey. I have friends there now. Was it an empty promise? Could he even get in touch with Jim and Anna in Van? These thoughts raced in his mind as he prepared to attend the meeting tonight at The Oasis.

Like a shadow cast over him, Rasheed watched Hamid's every step. His presence no longer seemed friendly, but hostile. How he wished Rasheed would not spend time with their roommates.

"Are you heading to that oasis place again?" Rasheed asked.

Hamid shrugged. "I thought I might go get some coffee, play a game of Uno or chess."

Rasheed hopped off his cot, came and stood beside him. "Be careful of that place. They are blasphemers. Christians! They are the enemy."

Hamid did not respond, so Rasheed came up very close to him. "I know what you're doing. I know you have a Bible, and when I find it, I will burn it! And then we'll come after you."

Hamid's heart fell as fear zipped through him. "Why do you talk to me this way, my brother? After all we have been through together?"

For a moment, the look on Rasheed's face softened. "Yes, it's true. You have been good to me. I would never be here without you. But I am afraid for you. And my friends—they tell me terrible things about the Christians. Please, I don't know what they will do to you if you continue associating with those infidels."

Hamid did not doubt Rasheed for a minute. He had seen the anger in these young men's eyes, their pent-up hatred, their need for some sort of revenge. He felt the fear twist in his gut. Nowhere was safe, even inside the pristine fields and mountains of Austria. Was there no protection for him? No hope?

But he had not come this far to give up the journey. Hope burned in his soul, and tonight The Oasis was offering a Bible study for true seekers. That was how they put it. A Bible study in Farsi. He recalled Julie's instructions *Come alone. Make sure no one follows you. Come to the back door. Knock three times. Wait and knock again.*

Would he be able to get away from Rasheed's scrutiny?

At five o'clock he headed to the little corner store, bought a pack of cigarettes, and put his cell phone to his ear. He spoke loudly to no one, "Yes, sure we can eat together. I'll meet you in town. Seven thirty."

He prayed Rasheed had overheard and would believe that he was meeting another Iranian for a bite to eat. On their small stipend, the refugees occasionally left the bland cafeteria food and splurged on a kebob.

At seven o'clock Hamid walked for thirty minutes to lose Rasheed and his friends. He got on a bus, got off, walked back toward The Oasis.

Back door . . . Knock three times. Wait and knock again.

He counted the seconds that seemed like hours, looking over his shoulder. Waiting. Then out of the shadows he saw a figure emerge, walking up the street toward him. He trembled with fear. Rasheed? No, it was another young Iranian who had arrived at the Refugee Center only three days earlier.

Hamid stamped his boots and ran his hands up and down his arms to warm up. "Cold out here tonight," he mumbled.

The young boy nodded, suspicion in his eyes. Hamid started to turn away when the door swung open and there was Julie, welcoming them.

"Come in! Hurry, yes, that's good." She stepped outside, glanced to the right and the left, then closed the doors. "No one was following?"

The men eyed each other. Julie laughed. "No worries. Both of you got invitations. Hamid, do you know Samwel?"

The two men nodded civilly to one another.

"So welcome to our Nicodemus Gathering. Don't worry. It's safe." She led them up the back stairs, and they passed Amir and Bobbie headed down the same stairway. Amir met Hamid's eyes, then Amir and Bobbie reached out and clasped Hamid's hands.

Julie led Samwel and Hamid into a small room Hamid had not seen before. The windows were covered and the light low. Four other men were huddled in the room, glancing around suspiciously when Hamid and Samwel entered.

"Everyone is present now," Julie said. "Please have a seat." She motioned to the circle of metal chairs. "Thank you for coming. I want to introduce you to Mark, our guest speaker. He is from Iran." The men nodded as Mark came in and Julie left the room.

"Tonight I will be glad to answer any questions you might have about the Ingil, about Isa, the Christ. But first, I want to tell you my story . . ."

The stocky man, perhaps fifty, had black hair streaked with silver and piercing dark eyes. When he began to talk in Farsi, the six men sitting around him listened intently. Mark told of escaping Iran, of his flight through the mountains and into Turkey, of the way Isa had come to him in a dream, and of meeting Christians at The Oasis. Hamid felt he was listening to his own life!

Then Mark answered question after question about the differences between Islam and Christianity, about sin and forgiveness. Time seemed to stand still as the questions continued. The men spoke, argued, wondered, but reverently. And throughout that evening, the burning sensation, the quickening never left Hamid's body. Truth! He was sure.

As Mark spoke of the blood of Christ, about salvation and how to advance as a follower of Isa, Hamid felt a presence in the room. He had felt it before on that night in the mountains when the voice had spoken in the dream. Something almost tangible, but not quite. He wanted to reach out and touch it, but he kept his hands in his lap, folded together tightly, even as his heart burned.

Then Mark asked the question, the one question, that Hamid had been waiting to hear. "Would any of you like to follow Christ? To give Him your life? Here and now?"

No one spoke. The men looked around and turned their heads down. Did they all feel the tug-of-war, the conflict that he felt, Hamid wondered. For it was a conflict. As surely as if someone were clutching his throat, he felt the constriction, the fear. He pushed through it and forced himself to a standing position. "I believe. I want Isa!"

The five other men stared at him and then, one by one, they stood. As Mark prayed, their heads bowed, a smile came onto Hamid's face. Soon they were all crowded into a tight circle, their shoulders touching; two men were weeping, crying out to God for forgiveness, asking for help. They prayed and wept and somewhere the Spirit of God wrapped Himself around Hamid's heart and comforted him. There was no doubt. He was changed.

As they prepared to leave, Mark said, "Some of you may be transferred from this camp, even tomorrow. But you leave with the Bible in your hands, and we will tell you how to move forward in this new faith. Remember, you have been sealed by God's Spirit and you have a protection over your heart that no one can take away."

Protection.

"You will never be alone again. Isa is with you." He handed each one a Bible in Farsi.

When the others had gone, Hamid approached Mark. "You were persecuted for your faith. You survived. I'm afraid. Already my wife and children are in hiding in Iran. They are trying to escape. Now I have Iranian brothers threatening me here. What do I do?"

Mark put his hands on Hamid's shoulders and began to pray, a long powerful prayer. Over and over he implored God for protection on Hamid, on Alaleh and Rasa and the baby.

"You have put your faith in Isa al Masi, is this not true?"

Hamid nodded slowly. "Yes, I have. In spite of my fears."

"Then trust, my brother. Trust."

When Hamid returned to his room, Rasheed was there with three of their roommates. "So where were you tonight?"

demanded one of the young men, Asad.

"I met a friend in town, and we had supper together."

"I don't believe you," said Nader.

Hamid remained quiet. He caught a look of fright in Rasheed's eyes.

"And what is in your backpack?" asked the third man. Taher was a little older, a little bigger.

Hamid shrugged. "My important papers. Things like that."

"Show us!" Taher demanded.

Hamid opened the backpack, feeling incredible relief that Mark and Julie had insisted he leave the Farsi Bible at The Oasis. "Another time you'll come here, and we'll give you a Bible. But it's not safe yet, not if what you have said about Rasheed and his friends is true."

Finding nothing of interest, Taher threw down his backpack in disgust. "Come on, Rasheed. Maybe next time."

They left the room, but Rasheed looked back. On his face was a mixture of fear, compassion, and warning.

I'm a Christian, Hamid thought, as Rasheed walked out of the room and closed the door. *I stood up in front of the others and declared my love for Christ.* How long, he wondered, until he would declare the same thing to Rasheed? Would it mean a beating, or worse? But Rasheed needed to know. Would Hamid ever have the courage to tell him the truth?

Hamid sat on his bed and took out from under his pillow the little book that Jim Harris had given him in Van. It was carefully camouflaged as a history book; if anyone picked it up and thumbed through the first pages, they would find stories of ancient Rome. In the middle of the book was hidden the Ingil. Hamid opened to a passage that Mark had shared earlier in the evening.

He read the verses over and over again. Brand new words. Words of life, of hope. *If any man is in Christ, he is a new creature. Old things have passed away. Behold all things have become new.*

Could it be true? He felt something fresh and good and hopeful welling inside, stronger than his fear for his family or his grief for his mother.

"The Spirit of God lives in you now," Mark had assured him. "He will never leave you alone. You can move away from Him, but He will always be with you."

The Spirit of God. Muslims accused the Christians of worshiping three gods. But tonight for the first time, some things had made sense. And this power of the Spirit, he believed it was there. Yes, a God who loved enough to die for His people and then who rose again and left His Spirit to guide them. Over and over Hamid read the verse. A new creature.

At last he closed his eyes and dreamed of Alaleh. Tomorrow he would talk to Carol and Jalil and Amir and Jim Harris. Tomorrow they would find a way to bring his family here, guided by this Spirit.

Bobbie

The little town of Baden, Austria sat exactly three miles from Traiskirchen. Well known for its thermal baths, Baden welcomed wealthy Austrians from all over the country to come for treatments. The town was posh, clean, overflowing with flowers, even in early December. Carol and I sat in the waiting room of the oncologist who had successfully treated Carol's cancer years earlier. He'd agreed to see me on the spur of the moment, following a cancellation.

A nurse led us to a sterile room, and Dr. Schobesberger came in a few minutes later. He was tall and slim with a shock of white hair, white eyebrows, and a thick white mustache. After greeting Carol and me warmly in English, he studied the records my oncologist had faxed him the day before.

When he spoke, his voice was filled with kindness.

"I am familiar with this treatment. However, we have a different approach here. It is rather experimental and not approved in the US, but it has been effective at times in your type of cancer."

I cleared my throat and tried to ask a question, but no sound came out. Was this man offering me hope? At last I said, "I don't have a visa, so I'm only allowed to stay for two more months. Would it be worth starting a treatment for such a short time?"

"Our medical care is free for citizens; but for others it is still very inexpensive. If I were you, I would attempt it."

I took a deep breath and nodded.

He added rather seriously, "And I would also apply for a visa."

Carol gave my hand a squeeze and smiled. Visas were not so easy to come by anymore.

"When would I start?"

"We will do a blood test, and the results take five days." He looked at his calendar. "Come back in a week. If all is in order, we'll start the treatments immediately."

I couldn't wait to call Peggy and tell her all my news. She gave a cry of delight when she heard my voice. "Bobbie! I was just talking to the Lord about you and that refugee!"

"Amir?"

"No, the other one. I'm reading an article about him in the *Peachtree Press!*"

"About Hamid?"

"He changed the name, but it's clearly the man you asked us to pray for. Did you know that Stephen is trying to raise funds for Hamid's family?"

"That's wonderful news. Stephen promised when he left that he'd write an article. I like him, Peggy."

"I think I do, too. But what news do you have for me?"

I told Peggy about my conversation with Amir. "The Lord opened my eyes to let me see the truth and to share it with Amir. He has forgiven me, and I feel so light!" Then I told her that Amir wanted me to stay longer and go with him to Romania, to Vasilica's grave.

Peggy didn't hesitate a second. "I hope you said yes."

"Yes . . . yes, I did. I think . . . I think . . ."

"You think the timing is right and this is a necessary next step, and so do I."

"I have something else to tell you too," I said. "I've just seen an Austrian oncologist, and he's suggesting an experimental treatment here. Something not available in the US." I tried to act calm. "I'm afraid to get my hopes up, Peggy, but then again, I feel so hopeful. I can't even describe it."

"I can hear it in your voice, my child. I am beyond delighted. I can't wait to tell the Prayer Band."

"Oh, Peggy, thank you. Thank you for everything."

Peggy gave a contented sigh. "It's such a privilege, Bobbie. So much of the time, the story God is writing goes on behind the earthly scene, somewhere in the heavenlies. But every now and then the Lord pulls back a curtain-slice of the sky and we get to see the bringing together of all the plot lines in real time! And I must say, I like the way this plot is playing out. I'm ninety-two years old, dear Bobbie, but I hope the Lord lets me stay around just a little bit longer to read the next few chapters!"

Tracie

The joyful feeling had not left in the past few days. Suddenly the Bible verses and songs I had learned as a child came flooding back as if I had become reacquainted with old friends. I leafed through the English Bible I'd found on the shelf in the game room until at last I found the verse I'd memorized at that camp when I was ten. *If anyone is in Christ, he is a new creature . . .*

Yes, I felt new. Hopeful, trusting. Maybe God would speak to me! How could I doubt? He had spoken to me, twice, almost audibly. I'd heard plenty of "testimonies" throughout the years, the before-and-after stories of people who had converted to Christianity. But I'd never heard a story like mine—my two encounters with God through the visit of a deer. *It's completely supernatural*, I thought to myself.

Aunt Bobbie came into our little room, her face radiating hope. "My oncologist in Atlanta has agreed that I can follow the treatment here, Trace! I'm thinking we could change our tickets for another two months. But you certainly don't have to stay. I'm sorry you and I haven't traveled as much as I'd planned. And if you wish to return on Saturday, I'll completely understand—"

I interrupted her. "Are you kidding? I'd love to stay. Right here. I may not have a call from God yet, but at least we're talking." I winked at my aunt. "And who knows? He may tell me something soon." Then I added, "And if there's one thing I am sure of, it's that I'm not leaving without you, Aunt Bobbie."

When I called Mom with the news, she balked a little at first. "I hate for Bobbie to get her hopes up for something very experimental." Then she sighed and said, "Of course, stay, sweetie. Take good care of her. I'm so glad she's gotten to see her refugee."

It felt like my life had suddenly become a wide open field, and I could run in any number of directions. No constraints. At the same time, I had not forgotten all the verses in the Bible about trusting God to be the light to my path, about the way of Jesus being narrow.

Amidst all the uncertainty and the concern for Bobbie, I nonetheless felt lighthearted. I found too, that I no longer thought of Neil throughout the day. It was as if that relationship had been swept away like a bad memory. But I did think about another young man. I missed him. He should be here to live the continuing story of Hamid and Aunt Bobbie. And me. My story. I found that I wanted desperately for him to be on this path with me.

We'd agreed not to call or e-mail for two weeks. A mere five days had gone by since he'd left, but it felt like years. New birth and new longing and new heartache. I tried to pray for Stephen and his girlfriend and failed miserably. I decided that was much too lofty of an ambition. So I simply prayed that somehow Stephen's desire to keep helping the refugees, and especially Hamid, would be realized.

CHAPTER 23

Amir

*D*iscernment, that was what Amir needed. He sat at his desk in his little apartment in Mauthausen, Bible opened, eyes closed, heart so very confused. He had thought he would be planning a flight to Romania with Bobbie, but an hour ago, Jim Harris had called with a plea for his help on a very different type of trip—smuggling Hamid's family out of Iran.

Alaleh and the children had already set out. A worker in Iran picked up the family and was taking them by horseback to another village. A three-day journey, maybe four. From there, someone would have to take them by car out of Iran. Jim described the person they'd need: someone who could speak Farsi and Turkish without an accent and who wasn't afraid to drive through checkpoints with hidden cargo.

Amir had gone on such rescue missions before, twice, after his own escape. In both instances he had known deep down that God was calling him into that life-or-death situation. Three other times he had said no, equally convinced that he should not participate. But in all of these decisions he had had one thing that was sorely lacking now.

Time.

The young Franco-American, Stephen, was doing his part. Amir had read the articles online, human interest stories, with the names changed but a convincing tale of Hamid's flight and journey, of his mother's murder, and of the danger Alaleh and the children were now in. And he was raising money to help their cause.

And Keith and Jim had come up with a plan: they would purchase a minivan and transform it into a vehicle to smuggle people. They'd also need false papers.

Jim said the situation was urgent.

Amir glanced down at the Bible and read the familiar words from Isaiah: "And if you give yourself to the hungry and satisfy the desire of the afflicted, then your light will rise in the darkness and your gloom will become like midday, and the Lord will continually guide you and satisfy your desire in scorched places . . ."

"Show me, Lord," he prayed.

Tomorrow in the early morning, he and Jalil would accompany Hamid to the embassy in hopes of procuring Hamid's asylum. Should he then leave the following day for Turkey? Was this what God was asking, another mission, another defying of death threats? And giving up on Romania with Bobbie?

He thought about the other missions, the frenzied screams and gunshots. Picking up young Emad, slinging the boy across his shoulder, the shoulder that had also received a gunshot, and crawling, crawling to safety. Emad had lived, but a bullet had pierced the chest of his mother, and she had perished.

Some made it, some didn't. Sometimes God granted their

prayers for safe passage and sometimes, for reasons only the Almighty knew, He allowed the worst to happen.

Discernment. Amir's heart told him to stay in safety, to be with Bobbie, for whatever time they had left. But then he thought of Hamid, with his bandaged head and grieving eyes.

What to do, Lord?

From his hifi system a voice came across the sound waves on the World Wide Radio station. Amir recognized Keith's deep bass.

"Once again we are asking for special intercession tonight for a new believer from a closed country who is seeking asylum in the European Union. His family, including young children, are fleeing their country. Pray for safety. Pray for protection. And pray for Papy to raise up someone to help them get out safely."

Then the voice began quoting Scripture: "If you give yourself to the hungry and satisfy the desire of the afflicted, then your light will rise in darkness and your gloom will become like midday and the Lord will continually guide you . . ."

Tears came to Amir's eyes, and peace settled in his heart.

He would go.

Hamid

Hope! Hope! Hamid held the papers in his hand. Asylum granted.

Jalil and Amir congratulated him as they left the embassy.

"Now you will see, my cousin," Jalil said. "Alaleh and the children will be here soon."

Amir met his eyes and nodded.

Thank you, Isa. After a six-hour wait, he had received papers declaring that he was a legal alien. The papers for family reunification were issued too. At the Tuesday night meeting Mark had predicted that some of the refugees would be transferred quickly to another part of Austria. Now that

Hamid had asylum he could choose where to live, but the government worker had informed him that there was a room available for him at a pension for refugees wishing to learn German.

Hamid looked at the address of this pension—it was in Linz, Austria. Where Jalil lived! And Amir's church was in a neighboring village! The three of them laughed again out loud when they read this information.

"I'll see you again soon, my friends," he called out as he left them at the train station and turned toward the Refugee Center.

"Yes! In Linz!" Jalil called after him.

Fifteen minutes later, euphoric, Hamid entered his room. He had barely stepped inside when someone slammed into him and knocked him to the ground.

"Infidel!" Taher screamed, holding up the old history book. "You are hiding the Ingil and reading it!" Taher ripped out the New Testament, spat on it, and threw it on the floor beside Hamid.

The first kick was to the gut, then to his groin. Then the fury and strength of his roommates rained down on him until Hamid felt the blood seeping from his nose, his head wound, his mouth, his eyes. Again and again the men assaulted him, and as Hamid struggled to protect himself, he thought, *The irony. The terrible irony. I have my papers, I am free, I can legally bring Alaleh and the children here. But I will die now, my blood soaking the paper that granted me freedom and the book that gave me life.*

From somewhere far away he heard Rasheed's frantic cries. "Stop! Stop or you will kill him!" And then everything went black.

Bobbie

Amir was late getting to our little heuriger, but his eyes were shining and his smile reached all the way across his face.

"Hamid is legal! Jalil and I just left him at the Refugee Center. He got his asylum papers and applied for reunification."

I stood to greet him, and he grasped my hands in his. "Oh, Jill . . . Bobbie, it's so good to have you here to share this with me."

We laughed a little awkwardly before taking our seats at our booth. The other booths were empty, and I wondered if Frau Schafler had shooed all the other customers away so that Amir and I could be alone. Probably not the Frau, but perhaps the Lord.

"I was thinking we could go to Romania tomorrow, since you've got five days before you get your test results." Then he frowned. "But there is a little hitch. Keith and Jim have asked me to fly to Van and then drive into Iran to find Alaleh and the children."

"Whoa! That's a 'little hitch'? Are you serious?"

"Very serious."

"When?"

"Tomorrow."

"Tomorrow!" *You're leaving when I've only begun to get you back.* "Why you, Amir? Have you done this before?"

"A couple times, yes. They need a native Iranian."

"Wait. Are you even allowed back in your country?" I asked.

"No. So I'll need a fake passport, fake license, and most difficult, a visa for Iran."

I did not like his answers. "How do you plan to get these people out?"

"Jim Harris has a convoluted idea that we can smuggle them out in a van."

"A van?"

"Yes, he's rounding up a few engineers to convert an old minivan."

Then it hit me. "Just like the old days!" I said, suddenly inspired. "Yes, of course. We'll drive into Iran as if we're delivering innocuous supplies, pick up the woman and children, and hide them."

Amir almost laughed out loud. "Bobbie, you're not invited. They just want me."

"Oh, please let me go. I've done it before. Dozens of times, more than dozens of times. I can be a big help, Amir. Trust me."

"Trust you! Bobbie, this has nothing to do with trust." Amir had slipped into Farsi, something he used to do when he felt very intently about an issue.

"Amir! I was a smuggler! For five years! That was my profession, remember?"

"Of course I remember. You were a smuggler of *Bibles*, not people! It's completely different!"

I ignored his remark. "I know what to do, Amir. We need a van, and we need chickens! Lots and lots of chickens!"

"Are you completely insane?"

"Only partially. Listen, Amir. Let me go with you tomorrow into Turkey! I've watched the guys work on the vans. I know what they did. Please. We'll go together. And if all of you decide I can't make the trip into Iran, well then, I'll wait for you to come back into Turkey."

Amir just stared at me.

"What? What is it?"

"You're acting like the Jill I knew all those years ago," he said with a catch in his throat. "It's in your eyes, your voice."

I touched his hand. "I feel like Jill did all those years ago. Give me this chance, one last chance to make a difference. Then I'll come back here next week, and start the treatments. Whatever that means."

Amir stared off in the distance for a moment, then back at me. "And your deep fatigue and the tremors?"

"You just said it—I'm coming alive again. I feel fine."

"I am not convinced, and yet for some reason, I cannot forbid you to come. Maybe it's because this has all been planned out in advance by our Heavenly Father." He rubbed his eyes, as if trying to see more clearly. "I learned from Jim that Stephen has wired money from the States to help with the purchase of a van and the false papers. And plane tickets."

"Wow. Leave it to Stephen."

"Yes, but Bobbie . . . please spend some time seeking God about this, okay?"

I sat back in the booth and nodded slowly. My wise and gentle poet. "You're right. I promise I'll do that tonight."

Our conversation turned to other subjects then, but later I gathered my courage and asked him a question I'd had for a long time. "Why didn't you ever marry, Amir?"

He looked surprised. "You really want to know?"

"Of course."

"Once you turned me down, I got what you Americans call 'cold feet.' I was afraid to pursue another American, or an Austrian for that matter, and there were so few Iranian Christian women. And then I reasoned that my lack of having a family made me more available for the ministry God was giving me. I didn't have any distractions, and I could throw myself completely into the work."

I nodded. How well I understood that reasoning.

"I threw myself into it so completely that I forgot how very lonely my heart was. That's what I did, Bobbie. I guess I never really got over losing you."

One look at his face, and I knew it was the truth. "I never got over losing you either."

Stephen

From the bathroom in the hotel room, I heard my cell ringing. I stepped out, towel around my waist, and picked up the phone. Who would call at such an hour? I looked at the number, didn't recognize it.

"Hello?"

"Stephen?" The voice broke into a series of sniffs and sobs.

"Pam?" I said. "Where are you calling from?"

More sobs. Finally, "Stephen, it's Tracie. I'm sorry to call so early. But I thought you should know right away."

"Has something happened to Bobbie?"

A deep breath. Silence. Hard breathing. "Sorry." Now I recognized Tracie's voice. "Sorry—I lost it. Oh, Stephen. No, Bobbie's okay—I mean, she's going to start an experimental treatment with an Austrian doctor . . ." Her voice trailed off, and I thought we'd lost the connection. Then, "No, it's Hamid."

Now cold fear stabbed me.

"Did something happen to Alaleh?" I'd been so busy writing my article that I hadn't even tried to contact Keith or Jim in the past twenty-four hours.

"Alaleh and the children left with a smuggler on horseback through the Iranian mountains . . ."

"Dear God!"

"It's not that, Stephen. It's Hamid. He was attacked last night. Right after he had received his papers for asylum, a group of young Iranians beat him up. He's not good. Oh, Stephen. It's so unfair! He's been through so much!"

I sank onto the bed, my face in my hands.

"I thought you'd want to know," she repeated. "Bobbie just called; she and Amir went to the hospital to see him last night. He's in a coma." She sniffed again. "I, I think I'm going to stay here for a while. With Bobbie."

This revelation was no surprise to me. Still, I asked, "At

The Oasis?"

"Yeah. I know it sounds nuts, but some things happened to me after you left—good things—and Bobbie's going to need me for this new kind of treatment and"—another sniff—"I just need to be here. I know there's not much I can do for Hamid or Alaleh, but I can help Carol and Julie and the others with the regular refugee programs and free them up to work on Hamid's case."

"But you can't just stay, can you? Aren't there forms, visas? You're not on a trip now."

"We still have two more months before we need a visa." She paused, crying again. "I'm crazy, aren't I? You're not thinking of leaving everything and rushing over here."

If she only knew.

"I'm sorry. I probably shouldn't have called. I just needed to talk to someone who has been here. Who understands." Then she admitted, "I needed to hear your voice."

"I'm glad you did." I looked around me in the bare hotel room and felt a crushing loneliness.

"I read the two articles you wrote about Hamid. That's amazing, Stephen. And you're trying to get money to help Alaleh and the kids."

"We got money, Tracie. And we can potentially get a lot more."

I heard her sniffing over the line.

"Tracie, let me talk to Kimball. See if there's anything else I can do."

"Like what?"

"Like come back over."

"Why would he let you do that?"

"You never know."

"And . . . and what about Pam?"

"Let's just say that Pam isn't in the picture anymore."

"What?"

"I left. I'm at a hotel. Have been for three days."

"I– I'm sorry."

"No you're not," I teased. How could I be teasing? But I was so relieved to hear her voice.

She didn't reply.

"I'll call you back in a day or two," I said. "Let me know if anything changes with Hamid."

"Okay."

"And Tracie?"

"Yes?"

"Thanks for calling. I mean it. I'm so glad you did."

CHAPTER 24

Tracie

I stood outside the little hospital in Baden. Like everything else in Austria, the hospital was perfectly clean, the stuccoed walls a soft pastel blue, the window boxes holding bright yellow and orange mums. Fresh air and a light scent of lavender greeted me when I stepped inside the lobby. In spite of the welcoming atmosphere, I did not relish this visit.

I walked to Hamid's room, thinking that in a few more days I'd be coming back here for Aunt Bobbie's treatment. But not yet. At the moment, Aunt Bobbie was in Turkey.

First she told me the heart-wrenching story of Vasilica and Amir. Then we changed our plane tickets so she could stay for the new treatment. Then, only hours later, she informed me that she and Amir were getting on a plane to Van, Turkey.

"You can't fly off like this, Bobbie! What about the tremors?"

"I took my last pill yesterday. The side effects should lessen dramatically. Maybe even disappear altogether."

Her nonchalance worried me, yet I couldn't deny that in some strange way my aunt was coming back to life.

I sat beside Hamid's bed. He was no longer in a coma, but he went in and out of consciousness. What a story for this gentle professor who had fled to save his daughter's life. The horrific journey, the torture in Van, the miracle of exit papers, the joy of seeing him show up at The Oasis. And now he'd been beaten beyond recognition.

I whispered out loud, "Lord, I know You've shown Yourself to me, dramatically. But I must say that I still think life is so unfair. Please, please, do something for Hamid. Please heal him and bring his family here safely. Life is unfair, but You are bigger than life."

As I prayed, the tune from a song I'd learned years before played through my mind, a Scripture verse put to music. Very softly I hummed the melody. Hamid reached for my hand, and I took his. His eyes fluttered open and with the greatest of efforts, he turned his head toward me. "Sing?" he mouthed.

"You want me to sing, Hamid?"

He nodded. And so I sang in English the words to the song. I sang the truth of Jesus to both of us. "These things I have spoken unto you that in me you may have peace. In the world you will have tribulation. But be of good cheer. For I have overcome the world."

Bobbie

It was not completely true that the tremors were gone. But I suppressed them as Amir and I rode from the airport in Van towards Jim Harris's home.

Amir took my trembling hand and said, "I should have refused to let you come. I'm sorry."

"It doesn't hurt, and I really think this is important. It

feels like . . . it feels like the Lord is giving me a second chance to redeem some of the lost years."

"I hope so."

The taxi twisted through the streets of Van. The city proclaimed to me that I was no longer in Europe as we drove past buildings with flat roofs. Instead of church steeples, minarets and mosque domes rose on the horizon.

We arrived at the Harrises' home and Amir paid the taxi driver. Anna Harris met us in the road. I recognized her from photos I'd seen in prayer letters that Carol had sent years ago, when the Harrises worked at The Oasis. She was small-boned, thin, with a soft yet determined look in her pale blue eyes. She wore a loose-fitting top and long skirt and a scarf over her hair.

"It's good to finally meet you," I said, and she gave me a genuine American hug and led us into the house.

Amir had met Jim before, and now he made introductions for me. "Tell us, how is Hamid?" The frown on Jim's face was a mixture of anger and incomprehension.

"We were at the hospital late Thursday night," I replied. "He's in bad shape."

"He was in bad shape when he stayed with us," Jim said.

"Well, now the head wound is reopened, ribs broken, nose broken, some internal hemorrhaging."

"Does his wife know?" This from Anna.

"Jalil talked to Alaleh a few days ago. Now I've got Hamid's phone," Amir said. "If and when we can get in touch with her, I'll just say Hamid's been ill. I'm afraid if she knew how precarious his condition was, she'd turn around and go back home."

"After what happened to Hamid's mother? It'd be a death sentence," Jim said soberly.

Two young men joined us for a lunch that Anna had prepared. Jim introduced them to us. "Ali and Emad are both Iranian. They have chosen to stay in Van. They have also both chosen Isa." Jim smiled at the men. "And both are very good with cars."

Amir leapt to his feet and embraced the young man named Emad. "It is so good to see you again!"

"Amir," Emad said. He shook his head, while holding tightly to Amir's shoulders. "Why am I not surprised that you are the one who will risk your life to bring this family out?"

As we ate, we listened to Ali and Emad's stories. We learned that Amir had in fact been the one to help Emad escape Iran four years ago—a harrowing escape in which Emad's mother was killed. The bond the two men shared was palpable.

After lunch, Jim led us out to the parking lot, where a dilapidated gray minivan sat. "Stephen's money arrived yesterday, and we bought the van this morning," he said. "And Keith faxed some ideas for transforming it into a smuggling vehicle." He patted the van almost affectionately, then looked at me. "I've heard you have some ideas too, based on your smuggling days."

I nodded.

"So let's look over everything and make some decisions."

While Amir and Anna discussed the false papers, Jim, Ali, Emad, and I talked in a mixture of English and Farsi. Jim and I explained the way the vans had been rigged in the past.

"Once we had to smuggle an important political figure out of Romania," I told them. "We built a fake floor in the van so that he could lie flat underneath it. Then we loaded the van with chickens in pens. The noise was deafening and the smell overpowering, but it worked! If the baby cries, we'll make sure the chickens cluck even louder."

Emad elbowed Ali, both smiling brightly.

They think I'm nuts.

"And where will we get these chickens? Is it possible to come up with a truckload of chickens when Amir gets to this remote Iranian village?" Jim sounded doubtful.

I actually had not thought that far, but before I could answer, Emad was gesturing excitedly, then speaking in rapid-fire Farsi that I couldn't understand.

"Well, if you don't say!" Jim turned to me. "Emad says Iran is a huge exporter of chickens, and he knows several people in the business. He will try to arrange for one of them to bring the chickens to the checkpoint where Amir will be picking up Alelah and the children."

Chills went up my spine. Our convoluted plan just might work.

Emad waited for Jim to translate his idea and watched my reaction. Then the two young men looked at each other and shrugged. "Anything is possible," Emad asserted. "God has saved us through very strange occurrences before."

I smiled back at them. "I agree with you, Emad. We have the Lord on our side, and He often tells His people to do crazy things. What do you think, Jim?"

Jim had been squatting by the van, examining something. Now all six-plus feet of him stood up, and his dark brown eyes twinkled. "It sounds like a plan to me!"

For the rest of the afternoon, as Jim and Emad and Ali worked on the van, Ali would from time to time come over to me and say in his halting English, "Chickens!" and then he'd make a squawking sound, and they'd all laugh. I laughed too, but in my mind I prayed. *Dear Lord, we are once again headed out on an impossible mission. We need You now more than ever.*

One of my favorite verses from Isaiah, which I had memorized during my Bible smuggling days, came to mind, and I held it there for the rest of the afternoon: *I will lead the blind by a way they do not know, in paths they do not know I will guide them. I will make darkness into light before them and rugged places into plains. These are the things I will do and I will not leave them undone.*

I prayed fervently. *Yes, Lord, for us, but especially for Alaleh and Rasa and Omid. Please, dear Lord.*

Hamid

From somewhere far away a light shone as Hamid struggled to open his eyes. Perhaps he was in paradise with seventy virgins waiting for him. No, perhaps it was the Christian paradise, and Isa was smiling.

Isa was light.

What *was* that light? His head was spinning, spinning around him; he tried to open his eyes and turn toward it. It was only a blur, a hazy, gray form, then it took the shape of a person and, terrified, Hamid tried to recoil. But he couldn't move. Now he remembered the attack, the beating, blow after blow.

"Hamid!" It was the whispered voice of Rasheed drifting to him. Rasheed! The traitor, the one who had betrayed him. Perhaps Rasheed had even delivered the blows. Perhaps even now he was coming to beat the last breath out.

Hamid felt a touch on his shoulder. He could not turn his head, could not make a sound. He winced, although the touch did not hurt.

"You're awake! Thanks be to Khoda, you are awake!"

Awake perhaps, but awake where? He stared at a white ceiling, then was aware of various tubes protruding from his body.

Rasheed leaned over, and now Hamid could see the haggard face of his friend. Friend? Betrayer.

"I'm so sorry, Hamid! They wanted to teach you a lesson. I could not say no; I was afraid. They found the Bible. I could not protect you."

Hamid tried again to formulate a word, finally managing a raspy, "Where?"

"You're at the hospital in Baden. This is the third day. You were injured badly. The head wound reopened, and your nose is broken. Ribs broken. You must stay here." Then Rasheed leaned closer, "But I have your asylum papers. When you are well enough, Jalil and Amir will come and take you to Linz to the pension that has a room waiting for you."

"You too?"

Rasheed shook his head. "No, I don't have my papers yet. I must stay at the Refugee Center. But when the staff at the Center found out about your beating, our roommates were forced to leave for a few days . . ."

He'd been in the hospital for three days! Alaleh and Rasa and Omid were already two days into their journey through the Iranian mountains on horseback. Rasheed faded in and out of focus until he was not there anymore at all. Just black.

The next time Hamid awoke, he heard several voices whispering around him. Jalil leaned close and said his name. Hamid tried to nod and felt his head move. But the pain! He tried to focus on the form of Jalil. Then he distinguished Julie's voice.

". . . and if the healing continues, you will be going to Linz in a few days . . ."

In and out, in and out, Hamid received information as if through a walkie-talkie that sputtered static half the time.

"Alaleh?" he managed.

"Rasheed brought us your phone," Jalil said. "I talked to Alaleh when she and the children were on their second day of travel. I told her you were a bit sick, unable to talk, and wanted me to communicate with her."

Alaleh would be so worried not to hear his voice. She would know something was terribly wrong.

"And now?"

Julie leaned down and whispered, "Now Amir has your phone. He and Bobbie are with Jim Harris in Turkey, fixing up a van to rescue your family. You must rest and get well, and then they will come to you."

I have friends in Turkey who will come and get you, he had told Alaleh. And it was true.

Thank you, Isa, Hamid thought to himself. *If only they get there in time.*

All went black again.

CHAPTER 25

Rasa

*T*he weather had turned bleak. Huddled around the small fire with the others, Rasa felt her fingers and toes began to sting as they thawed. Omid cried and wouldn't be comforted, and their guide, Davood, paced and paced around the fire. Maamaan just looked numb.

Rasa reached out and took Omid from her mother, bringing all the blankets around her little brother, and looked down into his scrunched-up face. She knew the culprit. Diaper rash! She washed the dirty cloth diapers out whenever they passed a stream, but in the rain and humidity, they did not dry. Now she applied a thick ointment to the bright red rash on his bottom, trying at the same time to guard him from the bitter cold. He howled in protest.

The journey on this third day had been horrendous. It stormed, pouring rain with lightning and thunder, until they were trembling and soaked through all their many layers.

Maamaan coughed repeatedly and looked hollow and scared, almost as if she had given up on something. On what?

Rasa snuggled her baby brother close, feeling the fuzz of his dark hair against her cheek. Then she felt the fire in his forehead and gasped. Little Omid was not merely screaming from the rash. He had a high fever. She knelt down beside her mother and said, "Maamaan, Omid is too hot! I think he's sick."

She handed her brother back to Maamaan, who looked up at Rasa with tears in her eyes, took Omid and brought him close. She whispered, "I know Mrs. Garabadian has packed medicine in the saddle bags. Try to find it, Rasa. It will help with the fever."

In the shadows Davood continued to pace, occasionally throwing wood on the fire, but always looking around, as if someone might come out of the shadows. Perhaps a bad man was after them. Rasa didn't know. She felt fear zip through her.

Even though I walk through the valley of the shadow of death, I will fear no evil, for you are with me.

That was from Mrs. Garabadian's favorite psalm. Rasa repeated it again and again in her mind as she searched for the medicine. She brought it to her mother, who fed the medicine to the baby through a small plastic dropper. Omid continued to scream so loudly that surely everyone within many miles could hear him.

Davood glanced at Rasa and shook his head. His eyes spoke loudly and clearly: Make that baby be quiet!

Please, Jesus! Please, Isa. We are cold and afraid, and now Omid is sick and Maamaan is very sad.

Rasa tried not to think of the pain in her fingers and toes as she held Omid close and gently patted his back. "Shhh, dear little brother," she whispered. "Shhhh. Everything is all right now."

She walked over to where the horses stood, asleep on their feet. She wondered how these beasts could sleep with Omid's noise, but surely they were even more exhausted than the humans. The trek over the mountains had been so long and hard. Rasa stood beside the bay mare, bracing her head against the warmth of the animal. With one arm cradling Omid, she took her other hand and touched his burning forehead. "Take away the fever, dear Isa. Please save us. You are all we have."

Was it minutes or hours later that Omid stopped crying and began to breathe slowly, steadily? Rasa did not know; she only could whisper a thankful prayer as she cuddled on the ground beside her mother and brother and the dying fire whose embers glowed in the dark.

The next morning Rasa could not make herself stand up; the pain in all her body was too fierce. She tried to force her eyes open, but they were caked shut. Her hands did not respond at first when she tried to move her fingers over her eyes to remove the crust. When at last she managed to open her eyes, she saw that her mother was sitting atop the gray gelding, with Omid strapped in tightly to her chest. Maamaan was mouthing something to her.

". . . get up and Davood will help . . ." Her voice faded in and out. Why did Maamaan not speak clearly?

A freezing, biting rain fell steadily, stinging Rasa's cheeks as she lay faceup on the ground, unable to move. At last Davood bent down over her, giving her a pitiful smile. "Dear little Rasa, be brave now." He lifted her in his arms onto the bay mare. "I know you're sick, but you must try, dear child, to sit up."

Rasa winced and cried out as she straddled the saddle. She would have tumbled back to the ground if it weren't for Davood holding onto her tightly as he pulled himself up behind her. Her teeth chattered, and she had no strength to grip the horn on the front of the saddle. Davood took a blanket and tied it around himself and Rasa, again and again.

"How much longer?" her mother asked Davood as the horses began to trudge along the path. In Maamaan's eyes was a wildness that Rasa had never seen before, something strange and uncontrolled.

"Two days if we make good time."

They had not made good time so far, this Rasa knew, and the path seemed even more treacherous this morning. The horses' hooves slipped in the mud, Omid cried out, and freezing rain pelted them as they trudged up the steep mountain, winding in and out of the forest. This trip no longer felt like an adventure, and Rasa batted her eyes so that tears would not fall.

The journey went on forever, and Rasa slipped in and out of sleep. She dreamed of Baba and Maamaan-Bozorg and of a friendly white mountain. When at last they stopped for the night, Davood lifted her from the mare and set her on the damp ground. Every part of Rasa's body ached.

The peacefulness she had felt for the past three nights had disappeared. Each night as they huddled by the fire, Davood brought out a radio and tuned it to a station that spoke of Isa. Just as Baba had said, the radio had brought wise words about Isa and the Ingil. Rasa had listened to the messages with hope.

But tonight as Davood produced the radio, Maamaan said bitterly, "I do not wish to listen to talk of this god! I hate this god!"

Omid's fever had broken last night after Rasa had given him medicine and prayed. His little bottom was still raw, but he did not protest as loudly. If only Rasa could give her mother some sort of medicine to help with her sickness . . . but she did not have anything that worked against fear and anger.

I only have you, Isa. Help me be brave for Maamaan. And please, whatever you need to do, do it so that Maamaan will learn to trust you too. She needs you, Isa.

Rasa lay awake that night with a throbbing in her head, a wheezing in her chest, and numbness in her hands and feet. *Please, Isa.*

Alaleh

Omid sucked at Alaleh's breast listlessly. Rasa had frostbite and perhaps worse. Her daughter's eyes no longer danced with adventure. They were blurry with fever and pain. Alaleh gave Rasa the last of the medicine and bitterly cursed the weather.

She wondered if she was losing her mind. She had no more tears to cry. She had no more strength to continue. Hope had fallen as if from the bay mare and lay forgotten somewhere along this treacherous path. Again and again the thought bombarded her: *We are all going to die!* She was going to watch her children die and then she would be next. And there was nothing to be done. Even Davood, this silent and wise guide, looked frozen with fear.

What was the use of continuing? Something had happened to Hamid, of that Alaleh was sure. On the second morning of their journey she had found a signal for the cell phone and called his number. But it was his cousin Jalil who answered, saying that Hamid was sick.

Now she wondered if he were dead. Nothing would keep Hamid from talking to her, no matter how sick he was. He knew of the dangers of the journey and would have kept the phone by his side, desperate for her news.

Now there was no signal and no news, just a steady drenching rain soaking through her clothes and into her spirit.

"We are nearing the village—a day's journey now. But we

must make no fires, no noise either," Davood warned as the night descended around them.

No fire! They would surely freeze to death.

"The police sometimes patrol this far away from the borders to the village," he continued. "But the rain will wash the hoofprints away. They won't find us."

Police! Would they have to outrun the police as Hamid had done? At least they had the horses.

Numbly, Alaleh gathered Omid and Rasa beside her. Davood too came and offered his body warmth on the other side of the baby. The children made no sounds at all. She watched the slow up-and-down movement of Omid's chest and then Rasa's. For now at least, they were still alive.

If only she could make her mind work. If only she did not feel such a heaviness pressing down so hard on her chest. She was hot; she was cold; then she felt nothing at all.

She must have drifted to sleep, because suddenly Davood was shaking her awake, begging with his eyes for her to take the baby, to get on the horse. Hurry, hurry! She heard the faint sound of a man's voice and then the tramping of feet in the distance. She saw far away the beam of a flashlight. Davood helped her mount the gelding and handed Omid up to her.

Rasa! Where was Rasa? She mouthed her daughter's name and Davood shook his head. She started to scream and his hand came over her mouth. He begged again with his eyes, then mounted the bay mare.

Her daughter! Where was her daughter? They were leaving Rasa? No! No! The police would find her! And did the police have dogs?

Davood grabbed the gelding's bridle and pulled the horse alongside the mare, and then the horses were galloping through the dark, Alaleh clutching the reins and the saddle with one hand and holding Omid tightly against her, laying her body low over the horse's neck and mane, ducking the branches that slapped in her face. She did not know how long they galloped. She only knew that when they slowed down, there was no flashlight following them, and there was no Rasa.

Her wail started deep in her throat and came spilling out in silence as Davood took Omid from her. Tears and rage spilled down her face. How could he have left Rasa! Had he seen that she was already dead?

Davood helped her off the horse and led her into a very shallow cave. Bats flew out in their faces as they ducked to enter. Alaleh trembled uncontrollably and Omid cried weakly.

Davood knelt beside them. "I know this land," he said. "I know every meter of it. I have traveled it hundreds of times. You're safe here. I'll take the bay and get Rasa. Trust me."

Alaleh could not make her mouth work, but her eyes said clearly *I do not trust you!*

"I have hidden her well. She was too ill to sit on the horse, and we had to leave quickly. I'll bring her back now. Trust me," he said again.

Alaleh trusted no one. Was her daughter still alive? Dare she hope?

Davood wrapped extra blankets around Alaleh and Omid before he left. "I'm pulling a stone over the cave. No one will find you. I'll be back in a few hours."

Alaleh drank the water and forced herself to eat the stale bread. Omid was still alive. She must live for Omid. She sobbed in the silence of the cave as Omid nursed hungrily at her breast.

Rasa

The flashlight came over her body; she saw it reflected on the dried leaves and bark on a nearby tree. Rasa lay perfectly still just as Davood had instructed.

"You are too sick to ride the horse right now. I've hidden you among the sticks and leaves," he had whispered as he first wrapped the blankets around her and then piled on the damp leaves. "These police do not have dogs. They'll come and search, but if you are still they won't find you. They will follow us. And little Rasa, I will come back for you. I promise."

She did not panic when she heard men's voices speaking in Farsi only a few feet away.

"They've been here. See the horse droppings," one voice said.

"Radio ahead," said the other. "They're heading to the village. We'll have men waiting there for them."

Even though I walk through the valley of the shadow of death, I will fear no evil . . . Rasa repeated the verse over and over in her mind until fatigue overtook her and she slept among the leaves.

She woke hours later, when Davood lifted her from her hiding place.

"Oh child, you're alive. Praise God!" There were tears shining on his face. Gently he lifted her onto the mare's back, pulling himself up behind her and again wrapping blankets around both of them so that she was secured in a sitting position. She had not one ounce of strength in her body.

Davood urged the bay forward at a slow pace and said, "If you can sleep, that is best, dear Rasa."

She tried to whisper but no sound came out of her mouth. She tried again. "Men told village."

"You heard the men searching for us?"

She nodded.

"They are warning others to wait for us in the village?"

She nodded again and was surprised by Davood's answer.

"Good. Good. Let them wait for us for as long as they wish. We will go another way."

The last thought Rasa had was, *I am like the horses, I am so tired I will sleep while I am sitting straight up.*

Alaleh

Alaleh was rocking Omid back and forth in her arms when Davood brought her daughter into the cave. Rasa was alive! Alaleh handed the sleeping baby to Davood and took Rasa in her arms, snuggling her close, but she could not get her child to wake up. For an hour she held Rasa, begging her to open her eyes. At last Rasa blinked and stared at her mother through glassy eyes, as if she were in a trance.

Davood lit a fire and gradually the cave warmed up. How thankful she was for the shelter it provided from the incessant rain. Their clothes began to dry out. Alaleh made a hot broth, which she spoon-fed to Rasa as she hummed the song Mrs. Garabadian had taught her daughter.

Live, sweet child, live!

"We must stay here another day," Davood said, as he encouraged Alaleh to eat bread and fruit. "While the police search. They've notified the village, so we'll go another way. I'm going to find a signal and call our contacts. They will meet us outside the village."

Alaleh nodded. What else could she do? All that day she watched her daughter. There was no more medicine. She placed cool compresses on Rasa's head and slowly warmed her frostbitten fingers and toes with her hands. Then she pressed Rasa's body to her chest, wishing her warmth to bring Rasa back even as fever raged there.

She watched the sleeping child, her thick black hair, now wet with perspiration, her fine little nose, her face so soft and sculpted. Her child. Her mystic child. Her dying child. Alaleh let the tears fall as she spoke in a trembling voice. "Isa, I don't know you. I cannot pray. But you listened to my daughter. You saved my life during the birth of Omid and the life of my son when Rasa prayed. So now, won't you save her too? I have nowhere else to turn but to you, Isa."

She kept her eyes closed and laid her hand across the burning forehead of her daughter and continued to talk to this strange God Isa throughout the long endless day.

CHAPTER 26

Amir

*A*ll throughout the day Amir worked beside Jim, Emad, and Ali, transforming the van into a smuggling vehicle. He did every task that was asked of him, but his mind strayed again and again to one simple thought. *She called me her poet.* Oh yes! Her poet. *Jill . . . Bobbie, how I long to be your poet again.* Oh dear Lord, could this happen?

For so many years he had lost hope of being Bobbie's poet. Truthfully, he had lost hope of being a poet at all. Yes, he used his gift with words to make his sermons appealing, to honor the Lord. But he no longer wrote poetry.

It hurt to think of how his creativity had dried up so quickly. With Bobbie gone, his inspiration left. He filled in the gap with God, with church, with caring for so many others. But his poems had gone away, and how he had grieved this. Now, somewhere in the back of his heart or mind, he felt them coming again. In swirls and curves. In Farsi. A hope, a new beginning. A poem.

And if in your heart I have stayed all these years
Like a warm memory, like a burst of sun,
Like hope,
Then come back to the now with me,
Come back and let us make the future
Together . . .

"Your papers will be ready tomorrow morning, Amir," Anna said, interrupting his thoughts and patting him on the back.

"Let the fireworks begin!" said Jim, erupting in a deep belly laugh. Amazing how he could joke when Amir was embarking on a life-threatening mission.

"I guess I am ready," Amir replied. He forced a smile, but his throat went dry. He had gone back into Iran twice in the past sixteen years, each time with a fake passport, a fake identity, each time to help another refugee escape. He had never told anyone how hard it had been on him, or what happened the last time, after Emad's mother was killed and Emad had reached freedom. Amir had escaped the police by the skin of his teeth, and a warning had come through his supposedly-secure e-mail once he arrived back in Mauthausen: *If you ever try to reenter Iran, you will be caught and executed!*

That e-mail had shaken him to the core.

And now he was returning. Now he believed he *should* return.

"Hey, guys!" Anna motioned to them, and they all hurried over. "We've gotten word from Davood. Alaleh and her children are hidden in a cave several miles outside the village. The little girl is barely conscious. He sounded pretty worried. You'll need to leave tomorrow morning, Amir." She turned to Jim. "Is that possible, honey?"

"If we don't sleep, it's possible." Jim grinned. "I like a challenge!"

Amir felt the fear creep up his spine. He knew Davood well. This man who had traveled the mountains, who smuggled not for money but for God, never showed worry or fear. If he was afraid for this woman and her children, things did not bode well.

He whispered to Jim, out of the hearing of the young Iranians, "You are an American. I know how you think. You believe in miracles and you love happy endings and you think you can do anything if you have enough support and money and willpower. But I must remind you that in most of the world, there is not enough money or support, and no matter the willpower, it doesn't always work out.

"I traveled the Refugee Highway in 1989. I was on horseback and foot. I came in winter. I cannot imagine a young mother with two small children surviving this trip. I am warning you all, you have worked hard and I will go with God's protection and with prayers on my lips. But this is not a Hollywood action film, and I cannot promise a happy ending."

Jim met his eyes and gave a long sigh, no longer smiling. "You're right, Amir," he admitted. "We're doing the exciting part, but the news is not good. And you are the one now who must carry out the mission. Now more than ever, we must pray."

Bobbie

"May I get Lilly up?" I asked Anna as the baby woke from her nap. In my two days in Van, I had spent every moment possible playing with the Harris children.

"Sure. She shouldn't scream for long since she knows you now," Anna said with a wink.

"No worries." I headed into Lilly's room, grinning.

I'd been surprised and then not surprised at all at how quickly my heart and Anna's were knit together, even though we had never met before Saturday. I had felt the same immediate kinship with Peggy. As missionaries, we shared a common bond. We had left everything, we had raised support, we had lived in a foreign land and learned a foreign language and had felt that horrible spiritual oppression. So much of where we were now was familiar. So as the men worked on the van and we prepared meals, I had told Anna my story.

With Lilly in my arms I came back into the living room and continued our conversation. "I know it sounds as if I have come a long way in admitting the truth, but in reality, I only just admitted it to myself and a few others a couple days ago. It is as fresh as the meat in the market."

"Your story is safe with me, Bobbie. I'm so glad we've met. I heard about you, of course, when we came to work at The Oasis in the nineties, a few years after you left. Those on the team talked about you."

"Yes, I imagine they did—my sudden departure, my doing it all wrong."

Anna's voice was soft. "No, there was no gossip. There was only genuine love. And you were missed. I gathered that you had lived through something heartbreaking."

"And now you know."

"Yes." Then she smiled. "And now you are back with your refugee."

"For the time, I am."

Anna gave Lilly a kiss on the cheek and squeezed my hand softly. "And we are praying that the Lord will give you more time with him."

I felt the lump in my throat and swallowed. *More time, dear Lord. With Amir. Time to grieve, time to love again, time to live. Time.*

Anna's voice trickled into my thoughts. "You're the one who came up with the idea of chickens, right?"

I grinned. "Yes. But only because we did this once before and it worked perfectly."

"Well, that's good to hear, dear Bobbie Blake, because now you must explain it exactly to Emad so that he knows how many chickens and how many cages to order."

Stephen

"You've done a good job, son. There's a lot of buzz about your stories, and our readership has grown by leaps and bounds. Keep those stories coming!" Andy Kimball slapped me on the back, his large belly moving up and down as he chuckled.

"It's good to hear, sir. And yes, I will."

"What's the latest news with our refugee?"

That was what he called Hamid: "our refugee."

"I've just learned that Hamid was beaten up for his faith and his wife and kids are on the run, riding horses in the Iranian mountains. Very dangerous."

"Excellent!" Kimball enthused.

Excellent? Had he even heard what I said?

"I want you to be there for the reunion. You hear?"

"Excuse me?"

"Get going, boy. I want you in that hospital room when Hamid sees his wife and daughter and meets his son for the first time. Lots of photos too."

Suddenly I thought of Bobbie's words to me: *If your intent is just to have a larger-than-life story for your constituency, I beg you to reconsider.*

"You're sending me back to Austria. Now?"

"That's what I said."

"There's no telling if the wife and kids will actually arrive, sir. This could end poorly. And Hamid is in very bad shape."

"Doesn't matter. You cover it. People are eating this story up! I want all the details of the refugees and those missionary people too."

Kimball wanted a story, but I wanted to help. I really, really did.

"Yes, sir. Um, do you want me to talk about prayer?"

"Prayer?"

"Yes. The missionaries are a little bit . . . strange. They pray. A lot. Together. They believe God is the one who is answering their prayers for the refugees."

"Aha. Well, I suppose it's worked pretty well so far."

"Yes. Kind of miraculous, actually, all that's happened."

Kimball had been pacing the room excitedly. Now he braced his thick hands on his desk, his large gut hanging over it, and looked up at me. "Are these people 'strange' in a good way or a bad way?"

"Oh, a good way sir."

"Fine. Then get your tail back over there and keep writing the story. Every day till it's done."

"And my interviews with the Katrina victims?"

"Don't worry about that. We've got plenty of people who can deal with that angle."

I left Kimball's office in a daze and with a very strange question of my own. Had this God heard my unspoken wish—maybe even a sort of prayer—that I could go back to The Oasis and somehow keep helping?

Back in my hotel room, I answered my cell. "Hello?"

"Stephen, dear! So great to hear your voice."

"Hey, Mom! It's great to hear your voice too. How are you? How are things in Lyon?"

"I'm well. I'm more than well. Your father came back from Hong Kong on the same day I got back to Lyon, and he's decided not to move. We're going to try to work things out." She paused. "Nothing's for sure, but I have a smidgen of hope."

Way to go, Dad. "Wow! That's . . .that's amazing."

"He said he wished I'd given him an ultimatum long ago." Her voice turned soft, reflective. "We talked, Stephen. And we listened to each other. And I believe we heard each other. Maybe for the first time in years."

"I, I don't know what to say except that is fantastic."

"Brigitte had been telling me we had to learn how to communicate. Carol and Julie helped me see that too. And they were right." She paused. "They helped me understand how to keep my mouth shut at times."

Mom's voice sounded so light, so hopeful. As she talked I was seeing her, laughing and playful, as she had been when I was a boy, before all the strain.

"I went back to Brigitte's church yesterday. It was so wonderful to be with all the American gals from the trip again. They gave a report about our time at The Oasis. Oh, Stephen, they've become like daughters to me. Like daughters." She hesitated, her voice breaking. "And teachers. I'm learning so much about this faith."

I felt myself reeling, in a good way.

"And how about you, Stephen? Things any better with Pam?"

"I'm afraid not, Mom. I'm still staying at the hotel. But my third refugee article just appeared yesterday, and money keeps coming in for Hamid's family."

"I'm so proud of you, dear."

Then I admitted what I had hardly had time to digest myself. "And Mom, get this—Mr. Kimball is sending me back to Austria."

I heard Mom gasp. "When?"

"I'm flying out tonight. He said our readership has increased so much in the past few days that he wants me over there covering the story."

Mom actually squealed through the phone line. "Stephen! That's marvelous!" She hesitated just briefly, then asked, "Have you heard from Tracie and Bobbie?"

"I've talked to Tracie. Unfortunately the news about Hamid isn't good." I briefly related the last report I'd heard.

"Yes, Carol sent an e-mail to all of us here in Lyon yesterday, asking us to pray."

"That'd probably be a good idea, Mom."

Then Mom's voice lightened again. "I really like Tracie, Stephen. She's a sharp girl. Talented, thoughtful, feisty. Just the kind of girl you need."

"Mom!" And in spite of the way my head was spinning, I hung up the phone with a big grin on my face.

Tracie

I had visited Hamid twice, once on Saturday and again on Sunday. I'd gone to an English-speaking church with Julie on Sunday morning. I'd called home three times. Now it was Monday afternoon, and I didn't know what to do with myself. I found myself pacing around the guest house and then driving the little Peugeot to The Oasis, where I found Carol and Tom in the upstairs office, each busily engaged in computer work.

I was too nervous to sit still, so I blurted out, "Carol, please give me something to do. Anything."

Both of them looked up at me, surprised. Tom grinned. "You look completely undone."

"It's horrible waiting to hear from Bobbie and Amir and waiting on Hamid to get better and wondering about Alaleh and the kids. I need to work."

"Well, there is plenty of that to go around," Carol said, laughing. "About 150 men will be descending on us in two hours for Clothing Day. It's not the most glamorous work, but we could certainly use the help."

"Aunt Bobbie always said that one of the things that surprised her most about missions was how every task was important," I said. "When she first arrived, she thought she knew what kind of 'ministries' she'd be involved in, but she learned that serving means doing whatever is asked."

"Bobbie is right," Carol said. "And she was always one of the most willing to jump in and help with any task. It's such a joy to have her back. And having you here too is an added bonus."

I could see that Carol was sincere.

"We could also use help planning the Christmas party that's coming up on Saturday," Tom said. "Would you like to be in charge of the music for the evening . . ." He hesitated, "Or do you plan to still be here on Saturday?"

"I plan to be here as long as the Lord allows."

Tom and Carol looked at me, then at each other. Carol lifted an eyebrow and said, "It sounds like The Oasis is rubbing off on you in a good way."

"In a very good way."

"And of course," she continued, "we've got the coffee house evening tomorrow night. We can always use help setting up and serving there."

By now I had a big smile on my face. "Okay, okay! I can see that I won't be bored. And I'll go back and see Hamid after I work in the clothing room. Show me where to start."

Carol's computer dinged and she studied her screen a moment. Then "Oh, my!" she said. She looked at me and her eyes were filled with mischief.

"What?" I said, baffled.

"An e-mail just this second came into my inbox. It's from Stephen."

I felt the heat spread across my face.

"Listen to this: *Carol, I have a bit of surprising news. My boss wants me to return to Traiskirchen to continue reporting on Hamid's story. I'll be arriving tomorrow afternoon. If it is all right, I'll plan to stay at Gasthaus Müller. I can take care of myself, but I just thought I should warn you that I'm coming.*"

My whole body was tingling, and there was no way I

could hide my surprise or excitement. I stammered, "Um, that is really . . . it's really . . ."

"It's great news all around." Tom laughed and gave me a fatherly squeeze.

Hamid

Tracie came into his hospital room, her face flushed. "You look so much better this afternoon, Hamid!"

Yes, he felt better, if better meant that he no longer drifted in and out of consciousness and the pounding in his head subsided occasionally. His vision was not as blurry now.

"It's true. I feel better." Then he dared ask, "Do you have any more news?"

"Yes! Yes, we do. Amir is driving into Iran tomorrow morning to get Alaleh and the children. He and others are working hard to finish rigging up the van. You see—it's good news."

"And do you know how my family is doing? Are they well?"

Tracie's face clouded for just an instant. "I don't really know about that. Only that the smuggler has contacted your friends in Van—the Harrises—and given a location where Amir is to meet him with your family."

Thank you, Isa.

"And I have a surprise for you, Hamid." Tracie handed him a Bible and an iPod. "Gifts from Julie. She knew you would want a Bible, and she said there are at least twenty of Amir's sermons on the iPod, all in Farsi. You know Julie—she said she hoped that would keep you occupied and encouraged as you wait on your family."

"Tell her thank you. It is a very good gift."

The visit with Tracie lasted only a few minutes. This young woman seemed to know instinctively that he was too tired for conversation. But before she left he asked, "Could you sing me those songs that you sang last time?"

He closed his eyes while her lovely voice filled the hospital room. She sang of faith and hope and love, and Hamid dreamed that soon, very soon, Alaleh and Rasa and Omid would be listening to these same words with him.

A little later, with the headphones in place and the Farsi Bible opened on his lap, Hamid listened to the first sermon. Amir was preaching from the book of Isaiah. Hamid remembered such beautiful words from this book, words that Jim Harris had read to him. *The grass withers and the flowers fade, but the Word of God stands forever.* And a verse about youths growing tired and weary and fainting, but anyone who waited on the Lord would gain new strength.

Now Hamid focused on the words in Farsi in his Bible, following along as Amir's strong and confident voice came through the headphones: "'The desert and the parched land will be glad. The wilderness will rejoice and blossom . . . Say to those with fearful hearts, be strong do not fear, your God will come, he will come with vengeance and divine retribution; he will come to save you.'"

Hamid thought of the months of running, the torture, the latest beating. "'Then the eyes of the blind will be opened and the ears of the deaf unstopped. Then will the lame leap like a deer and the mute tongue shout for joy. Water will gush forth in the wilderness and streams in the desert.'"

Streams in the desert. He closed his eyes and pictured this description. Streams in the desert. An oasis. And hadn't he found just that? An oasis.

Amir was still reading the Scriptures, his voice clear in the iPod. "A highway will be there. It will be called the Way of Holiness." A highway! A highway of holiness. So different from the Refugee Highway that Alaleh and Rasa and Omid were journeying on. "The unclean will not journey on it. It will be for those who walk in that Way."

Hamid felt tears prick his eyes. A promise of something in the future. A safe place to travel, not the terror of the Refugee Highway.

"'No lion will be there, nor will any ferocious beast get up on it. They will not be found there.'"

And he heard again the crazed barking of the dogs, felt for just an instant the incredible fatigue in his legs, Rasheed leaning on him and then forcing themselves to run, to run! What were Alaleh and the children experiencing even now?

"'But only the redeemed will walk there.'"

Redeemed. He was redeemed!

"'And the ransomed of the Lord will return. They will enter Zion with singing; everlasting joy will crown their heads. Gladness and joy will overtake them and sorrow and sighing will flee away . . .'"

Hamid felt his head spinning. Yes, the painful throbbing was still there, but there was something else too. How he wanted to travel on this highway! A safe highway with God as the leader, God giving hope and joy. An oasis—that he had found. Perhaps, perhaps the highway was only another step away, after all.

CHAPTER 27

Bobbie

Late Monday night I found Amir huddled over a map. "Did you want to see me?" I asked.

He nodded without looking up. "It's decided. You'll come with me."

"What?" Much as I longed to be with Amir, I had not begged to go with him after that first day. I'd assumed it couldn't work. "But how?"

He looked up at me, and his face was awash in fatigue. He ran his hands over his eyes. "We got false papers for you, too." He patted a thick envelope lying on the table beside him. "Everyone agrees it will be better if I do not travel alone."

"Everyone?"

"Jim. Keith. Those at The Oasis. Jalil. We've been discussing it."

I swallowed. "Okay."

"You've done this before, Bobbie. You know what it's like

to smuggle someone. And you are fearless . . ."

I used to be fearless, Amir. Now I am plagued with doubts.

". . . so if anything happens to me, you can continue. You can bring them safely out of Iran."

"If anything happens to you! What are you saying, Amir?"

He reached his hand out and softly held my arm. "What we are attempting is very dangerous. If anything goes wrong, you will continue with Alaleh and the children. You understand?"

"What could go wrong?"

He didn't answer, but by his look I knew what he was thinking. *Many, many things could go wrong, my dear Jill.*

"I'm not afraid, Amir. Or perhaps I am, but remember what I used to say to you? 'Courage is fear that has said its prayers.' I'll go."

I felt the tremors in my hands and tried to conceal them, but Amir looked over at me. "Bobbie. It's no use trying to hide what is going on. You are not well, and I have a death threat on me if I ever return to Iran. We are doing something very foolish." He gave a faint smile. "But we are fools for Christ's sake, and if He wills for us to accomplish our mission, then I suppose we will. No matter what."

I squeezed his hand. "Yes, you're right."

"Now come sit with me and study this map. We must know the route by heart . . ."

At four a.m. in Turkey, using Anna's computer, I sent an e-mail to Peggy explaining what was happening and begging for prayer. I used coded language which I prayed she'd understand.

I had barely pressed send, perhaps three minutes had passed, when a ping sounded and a reply landed in my inbox.

It simply said, *Got it. Will send word to Band and beyond. Now go to sleep!*

Alaleh

Alaleh heard the words Davood was pronouncing: he had found a signal and had talked to Hamid's friends in Van. Now he assured her that a car was on the way—someone was coming to get them tomorrow. But her heart remained as cold as her daughter's hands. The fever that raged in Rasa now left her chilled. How could a body that had been so very hot plummet to this cold in such a short time? Alaleh knew the reason: Rasa's body was shutting down.

Baby Omid was swaddled in layers of blankets, and he slept peacefully on top of other blankets beside Alaleh. Rasa also slept, but not peacefully. She gasped for breath every once in a while, and when she did, the gasp was shallow, pitiful. Alaleh wondered if she would go crazy with the grief of watching her child die. Panic twisted itself around her, choking her with fear as she cradled Rasa in her arms and held her tightly, protectively.

Help me, Isa! she thought unconsciously. *Show me what to say to Rasa, to sing to her, so she will listen, and hope and live.* She wished she had paid more attention to the words of the song that Astrid Garabadian had taught Rasa. She hummed the tune as best as she could.

From out of the darkness in the cave, Davood began to hum along with her. Then he began singing the words, yes, the words that Rasa had sung that first day—was it just five days ago or was it in another life? Rasa's little face had been bright with excitement as they began the adventure.

Adventure?

Death trap.

Davood's voice continued, soothing away Alaleh's fear and anger. "I will lift up my eyes to the mountains. Where does my hope come from? My hope comes from the Lord who made heaven and earth. He will not allow your foot to stumble . . ."

The tune was haunting and simple, the words repeated again and again. Alaleh felt warm tears on her cheeks, felt a wrenching pain in her heart, heard the rasping of Rasa as the child fought to breathe. Throughout the night, she and Davood sang the song. She supposed that Davood sang it with hope. Alaleh sang it as a dare to this God to keep his promises. Rasa believed he would. Keep them, Isa!

The Lord will guard your going out and your coming in from this time forth and forevermore.

Tracie

When Stephen stepped through the sliding glass doors at the Vienna International Airport, I was actually surprised at how quickly my heart started beating. His short strawberry-blond hair looked a bit disheveled and his green eyes were tired, but when he smiled at me, my stomach did a little flip-flop. I waved and moved forward among the dozens of people. And then suddenly he was in front of me.

He set down his suitcase, picked me up in his arms, and swung me around. "It's so good to see you again, Tracie! So good."

Stunned, I half expected him to kiss me on the lips, but he didn't. But just being held in his arms, my insides continued dancing precariously.

"Welcome back!" I managed.

"Thanks for coming to get me." He set me down and his pale face reddened, accentuating his freckles. "Sorry for that overly enthusiastic greeting. I think I got a little carried away."

I looked him straight in the eyes. "I admit I was a little startled—but in a good way."

Then we both started talking at once, asking each other questions, stopping, waiting and talking again, until we ended up in a fit of laughter. "You go first," Stephen said at last.

"I just wanted to say it is pretty amazing that your boss

sent you back over."

"Sure is." Then he scrunched up his nose and, eyes twinkling, said, "Almost like an answer to prayer."

That caught me off guard again. *Yes. Exactly. I had prayed that the Lord would allow Stephen to keep helping Hamid.*

Stephen laughed at my expression. "I'm actually quite serious."

"You prayed to come back?"

"No. But it was like I wanted to and then, before I dared ask for it—to pray—well, it happened."

Before long we were once again seated in the game room of the guest house, once again sipping on cups of strong coffee. This time, no one else was around. At all.

"Any news on the rescue mission?" Stephen asked, suppressing a yawn.

"We heard last night that Amir *and* Bobbie are driving a van into Iran today. Then they're going to fill the van with chickens."

"Chickens!"

"Evidently that tactic worked before in smuggling someone out of a closed country."

"Have you talked to your aunt?"

"Yes, I did. At five o'clock this morning." Now I yawned. "And she sounded a combination of excited and nervous and scared to death."

"I'll bet."

"She said the money you wired bought the van, the repairs, the plane tickets, and the fake papers."

Stephen chuckled, "Glad I can be of help on the black market."

"Stephen?"

"Yes?"

"I'm really scared for all of them. Evidently Hamid's daughter is horribly ill, and I don't know about the baby.

What if . . . what if they don't make it?"

He took my hand in his, and it felt comfortable and completely natural there. "Somehow, I don't think that's the right question to ask at this time."

Stephen

I had showered and shaved and changed into a pair of jeans and a fleece. Tracie was waiting for me in the game room. Beautiful Tracie. *Slow down, Short Stuff,* I warned myself. I was falling head over heels, but perhaps that was only a crazy rebound from Pam. Still, being with Tracie felt natural, good, and amazingly peaceful. Right. I let myself admire her down-to-earth beauty as she flashed me a smile, her thick blond hair falling to her shoulders.

Wow.

"You're glowing, Tracie," I teased, as she drove us to The Oasis. "I mean, you always look great, but today, I don't know. You look radiant."

She turned, and a red stain spread across her cheeks. She flashed another smile. "I can't hide that I'm glad you're here." She concentrated on the road, but after a minute she added, "And I wanted to tell you about something really amazing that happened to me."

And so she did. For an hour we sat in the Peugeot outside The Oasis, and she told me about her two encounters with a deer and how they seemed to be encounters with God.

"Am I freaking you out?" she asked, stopping at one point in midsentence.

"No, not at all. You know a journalist always loves a good story. And this is good. Really good."

And a bit strange, in the way I had mentioned to Andy Kimball.

I listened intently, not only because I was interested in Tracie, but because I couldn't shake the pinching in my gut, the way I experienced her story as something almost visceral, and, if the truth be told, a little bit scary.

My mother and Tracie had both recently made new spiritual discoveries. That was how I described it. Almost in spite of themselves, this Jesus had intervened in their lives, and in Hamid's, not to mention the lives of all the long-term missionaries and the short-termers who already proclaimed a sincere and active belief.

Maybe it was jet lag, but my brain felt foggy, as if I were trying to get something to come into focus, something I could begin to make out, but not distinctly. I literally shook my head to clear it as Tracie got out of the car, and I followed her into the building.

When she turned and said, "So we can set up the room for the coffee house and then go visit Hamid," she flashed me another smile, and then the fog cleared. And what I saw was faith.

Hamid

Hamid wanted to stay in Traiskirchen to welcome his family, but he had no choice. Tomorrow he was going to the pension in Linz. Private citizens were paid by the Austrian government to rent rooms to the refugees, thirteen euros a day per refugee.

"Some of the owners are very kindhearted people and help the refugees. But others tend to put way too many refugees in each pension. To them it is a money-making business, and the accommodations they offer are often in deplorable condition. It is difficult, living in such close quarters with many others," Jalil had warned. "But you will be near my family. We will take care of you."

Rasheed came to say good-bye; he was still waiting for his asylum papers to come. Once again he told Hamid how sorry he was about the beating.

"I did not think they would do this to you! I'm sorry!" Rasheed paced back and forth in the hospital room. "But you are getting stronger. I see it." Then, "When are you heading to Linz?"

"Jalil is coming for me tomorrow."

Rasheed sat down in the chair beside Hamid's bed. "Hamid, I promise, I will watch for your family when they first arrive at the Refugee Center. I'll help them. I will let no harm come to them."

Hamid nodded, but in his heart he thought, *Isa will make sure no harm comes to them, not you, Rasheed. I do not trust you.*

Before leaving the hospital room, Rasheed asked, almost timidly, "And you will continue to follow this god who causes you so much trouble?" He nodded to the Farsi Bible that sat in plain sight on the table beside the bed. "Why do you not throw away this book and forget this god? I don't understand you at all, my friend."

Of course not. How could you understand? But I will try to explain it to you.

"Even if I tried, I cannot make this God leave, Rasheed. He is inside me, as a Spirit, living in my heart. It says this in the Ingil, and I believe it is true. No matter what man does to me, Isa will stay with me. In here." Hamid slowly covered his heart with his hand. "The Ingil says my heart is sealed with this Spirit. I cannot get rid of Him now, Rasheed."

He would continue to pray that Rasheed too would come to understand and believe in Isa. Tomorrow, another journey. And even now, were Bobbie and Amir venturing into Iran? *Please, Isa. Grant them courage and safety.*

He thought of Bobbie's enthusiasm, and the wise and gentle manner of Amir. Together, could they accomplish this huge mission? It seemed impossible.

A gentle hand can lead even an elephant by a single hair.

Hamid smiled to think of this proverb, one he had often quoted to his students in times of great difficulty.

So give them a gentle hand to lead the elephant of the secret police. May they lead them far, far away from Alaleh and Rasa and Omid.

He dared let his mind drift to Alaleh, to the thought of holding her in his arms again, of lying close together in a bed. It didn't matter which bed. Together, that was what mattered.

CHAPTER 28

Bobbie

*I*n the predawn light Amir and I set out from Van, driving almost due north toward the border town of Bazargan, Iran, less than four hours away. The immense Lake Van Golu glittered in never-ending blue to the west, accompanying us for half of the 200-kilometer journey.

At two a.m. the men had finished concealing the hidden compartment in the van. Jim, Anna, and I tested it out, wiggling our way through the trapdoor behind the front seat and lying shoulder to shoulder in the hideaway, underneath where the chickens would be kept in cages.

"It's brilliant!" Jim enthused when we reemerged from the secret compartment.

Anna turned up her nose. "It's horribly claustrophobic."

I agreed with Anna, and yet I felt such hope, such adventure!

"All we need is for it to work for an hour or two," Amir

reminded us all.

Anna and I had also purchased food and medicine for Alaleh and her children, and we hid these supplies underneath the fake floor. The packet of false passports with the mandatory Iranian visa sat between Amir and me, along with three different maps detailing our drive.

I watched as Mt. Ararat rose before us, a hundred miles in the distance, its 5000-meter peak blindingly white with snow. I tried to imagine this dormant volcano as the landing spot for Noah and his ark thousands and thousands of years ago. "Isn't it so beautiful, Amir? The scenery takes my breath away!"

But Amir said nothing. His eyes were glued on the road, his mind somewhere a million miles away. At last he said, "I'm sorry, Bobbie. I'm very distracted right now. I'm thinking through every possible complication and how to react."

"Then I will let you think."

I watched the intensity on his face, his rugged features every bit as heartbreakingly beautiful to me as Mt. Ararat. I silently prayed for the Lord to send His peace into this old van, to renew our courage and trust.

Eventually, Amir took his right hand off the steering wheel and placed it on top of mine. We sat like that for a while, both of us staring at the flat expanse before us and the jagged white mountain in the distance.

At last Amir said, "Talk to me, Bobbie. Tell me stories. I need to be distracted from my distractions."

So I told him stories about taking care of Tracie and the T-tribe, and I told him how Peggy had been telling me to return to The Oasis for years. I talked on and on to quiet his fears. To quiet mine.

Mt. Ararat proclaimed its splendor for miles on end, and finally Amir broke into prayer, quoting the psalms, announcing God's glory. In this way we traveled for the last hour, and as we approached the town of Dogubayazit and turned due east, Amir breathed out the entirety of Psalm 121, one of my favorites.

He whispered the final verse with a catch in his throat, "'The Lord will guard your going out and your coming in from this time forth and forevermore.'"

In some ways I felt like I was back in the 1980s, smuggling literature into Eastern Europe. Then I'd been young, and naïve and invincible. Today I felt older, tired, and I wondered for the hundredth time how this would turn out. But one thing remained the same as years ago—we were stuck unless God showed up.

Before reaching the border town, we stopped by the side of the road at a gas station and I changed into a long black dress and black scarf that Anna had given me to wear. Immediately I felt a new type of heaviness and oppression, as if this black garment had sunk through my skin and into my spirit. Did Iranian women feel this way, I wondered, as I tucked my abundant hair under the scarf.

We arrived at a big iron gate with a Turkish flag on it and then drove through to the area of Turkish emigration. The military were everywhere with their tanks and jeeps. The line of cars in front of our van stretched for a kilometer, but eventually we reached the first checkpoint, where an officer took a cursory glance at our passports, handed them back to Amir, and nodded for us to continue.

As we drove up a road bordered by wire fences, all around us were black market money changers offering to change our Turkish lira for Iranian rials. Before us were the gates out of Turkey. Once again the guards checked our passports for our Iranian visa and then stamped us out.

It had worked!

As Amir inched the van up another incline towards the

Iranian border, an enormous mural of the Ayatollah greeted us, and beside it, a huge sign that said in English, WELL COME IN IRAN." Amir and I gave each other a fleeting grin.

When several Iranian soldiers came up to the van to inspect our passports for our Iranian visa, Amir stiffened, spoke to the men in Farsi, and waited. And waited. I sat perfectly still, eyes wide open, but praying feverishly in my mind a prayer I had prayed so often before at border crossings. *Blind their eyes, Lord. Let them accept these documents.*

At last the foreboding iron gate opened for us to enter onto Iranian soil. Amir drove through the gate, parked the van, and we were directed to the immigration desk. Amir filled out the forms and I watched, breathing a sigh of relief when, after another long wait, accompanied by my silent prayers, our passports were stamped again.

Only as Amir got back into the van and headed away from the Ayatollah and the gates did he relax a little.

"We made it!" I said.

"Yes," Amir agreed, "but this was the easy part."

As we headed toward the nearby village of Bazargan, he motioned to the hundreds of trucks waiting in long lines to cross the border back into Turkey. "That is what we face on the way back."

This time I took his hand and squeezed it. "Amir?"

"What, Bobbie?"

"Remember, you're my poet."

He said nothing.

I leaned over and gave him a soft kiss on the cheek. "Thank you for letting me come. It's going to be okay."

Somewhere beyond the village of Bazargan, Amir pulled the van behind a modest home and into a barn. One by one, Amir and a man named Aref loaded cages filled with chickens into the van, until it was crammed from floor to ceiling.

Our calculations had been precise, and the last cage slid in. The first row of cages behind the driver's seat was stacked from the original floor to the ceiling. Then the empty space under the false floor was hidden by these cages, and behind that first row, the other cages were piled on top of the fake floor so that it was completely covered.

Sixty-three chickens squawked continuously from their wire cages. I had forgotten just how overpowering was their smell, and if I hadn't been so nervous, I would have laughed. Instead, I climbed back into the van and took Amir's hands in mine. "We go in God's strength. I believe this, Amir. Do you?"

"Yes, my Bobbie. Always in His strength."

Amir

Davood's voice sounded on the verge of panic. "There are roadblocks everywhere! The police suspect we are still on this side of the border."

"Don't worry, Davood. I'll figure out a way."

Amir shut off the cell phone and tried to think clearly. He and Bobbie were waiting, hidden off the road, for Davood to bring the little family to them.

A very simple sacrifice would save the operation.

He was confident that Bobbie could get them back across the border. It would be a challenge, but she would make it and it would further her healing. Even now her eyes shone with the glorious adventure, the danger, and the love of God. She would get this family safely out of Iran and then she would return to Austria for this new treatment. Amir did not know if the treatment could prolong her life, but he knew that all that had blocked Bobbie from peace was gone. She had done what she needed to do to be whole before the Lord and before herself.

Then he thought of the grave in Romania. Yes, one thing

remained undone, but he had planted the idea in her mind, and surely she could act upon it alone. Or perhaps Tracie would go along with her.

He loved her fiercely. *Her poet.* She had admitted it again! It hurt to realize it now at the same moment that he also realized he would never see her again. The days they had shared were all that were to be allotted them.

But he still had *this* day, these few more minutes.

"Bobbie, if anything happens to me, I've put all of your documents here." He pointed to the glove compartment. "And Hamid's cell phone, too. You drive, you forget about me. It isn't important. You take the family away. I'll catch up with you later."

"But why would we be separated?"

"This is simply a backup plan—I want us to have at least discussed the possibility, even though it won't happen."

She flinched. "And if it does, how will I find the way?"

"I have complete confidence that you'll find it. You've studied the map."

"And what will happen to you?"

He forced a laugh. "Me? If they question me, it will all be very routine. They will argue and be mad and then they'll let me go. But it may take a few hours, and that time is most valuable." He glanced over at her and forced his jaw to relax, forced his voice to sound light. "Perhaps I will bribe them with chickens!"

She smiled, but worry still wrinkled her brow. "So I should drive a little ways and then pull off the road and wait for you there?"

"No. No, you needn't wait. Bobbie, you know me. I can get out. I've done it before. Three times. No fears, okay?"

Heavenly Father! How terrified I am!

"Okay." She did not look convinced. "But surely it won't happen."

Yes. Yes, Davood has told me. They are waiting. But if all works well, they will take only me.

Dare he say the rest? But if this was his last chance to tell her, how could it hurt to confess what she already knew?

"These last days have been sunbursts for me, my dear Bobbie." He drew her close beside him on the front seat, and now he dared to hold her in his arms. "Thank you for coming back. Thank you for telling me the truth of your heart. And I tell you my truth." He turned so that he was looking directly into her lovely blue eyes. "I love you. I love you, *Jill*. I have never stopped loving you." He inched forward on the seat of the van, hesitated, saw in her eyes that she was ready, and kissed her gently on the lips. Sweetness, the taste of ripe raspberries sprinkled with sugar. The taste of paradise.

She purred beside him, and he kissed her again.

Then she whispered, "May this be the first kiss in a very long future of kisses."

This is the last even as it has barely begun again.

Now she kissed him forcefully, then closed her arms around him, her head resting on his shoulder. "Surely the Lord will give us more time, Amir."

No more time!

"Of course He will, my love. But no matter what, remember always, you are loved by me. I give you again my love. Forever." Another kiss. How he wanted to stay here with her!

But Davood would arrive soon with the family.

"Rest for a few minutes, Bobbie. Close your eyes until they come."

The chickens squawked, the engine hummed, and Bobbie slept in Amir's arms.

Bobbie

I was happily dreaming of Amir's kisses when the horses

arrived, winded and snorting their disapproval. At the sight of the little family I couldn't stop the tears from rising.

The woman's face was so pale underneath layers of blankets and scarves. Her baby was fastened to her chest, so I couldn't see him yet. But the little girl, Rasa, looked like a limp rag doll draped across the bay mare's withers.

I felt a pinprick of fear and remembered the stillness in another child's body.

Gently, the smuggler lifted Rasa off the horse and held her out to Amir. I opened the van door, and Amir laid her on the front seat. She was alive, but her breathing was so shallow I strained to hear it. I climbed into the driver's seat and hurriedly removed one cage and opened the trapdoor, reaching inside to get the medicine from the hidden compartment. Then I filled the dropper with the liquid and coaxed it through the child's pale, cracked lips.

The woman, the delicately beautiful Alaleh, let out a sharp cry when Amir explained where she was to hide. I saw her eyes brim with tears and new fear. Amir explained that we would give the baby something to make him drowsy so he would sleep, so they all would sleep.

Yes, the baby needed to sleep, but little Rasa, oh, dear God, she needed to wake up and live. By the time we had them secured in the compartment and swaddled in blankets, I was chilled to the bone—from the weather, but also from fear.

Alaleh

These people were kind. They were risking their lives for her, but maybe they were wrong. How could this work?

She and her children would suffocate in this van, lying flat on their backs underneath dozens of chickens. The clucking was incessant and the smell overpowering. As the van began its journey, Alaleh felt Omid stir beside her and she whispered to her baby, "If you must cry, dear little one, do it now, before the authorities get here."

She tried to calm her breathing; she must not panic, she must remain strong for the children. For little Rasa, who lay so very still beside her. She wondered where Hamid was at this very moment. *We are coming, Hamid, my love. Please be there. Be okay.*

"Maamaan?" Rasa's feeble voice pulled Alaleh from her thoughts.

She reached for her daughter's hand under the layers of blankets. "Rasa?" she whispered.

"Maamaan?"

Rasa was awake! The fear that had gripped Alaleh's soul only moments before vanished as she listened to her daughter's tiny voice.

"Maamaan, it smells bad."

It smells bad!

Alaleh laughed out loud. Her daughter could smell; she could talk. *Thank you, Isa*, she said in her mind.

Rasa was awake.

Amir

"The guards are everywhere. You must take the smallest of back roads. I will show you on the map." Davood traced the lines, and Bobbie nodded as she strained with Amir to follow along. Amir was thankful she did not understand the rest of what Davood confirmed in Farsi.

"They suspect that people are being smuggled out, and they are checking every car and van long before you get to the border. The chickens are a good cover, but the American woman must hide with the others. You must be alone, Amir."

Davood mounted the bay mare, leading the gray beside him. Amir watched with his heart in his throat as the smuggler rode away. Now it was up to them.

They had driven no more than a few kilometers when Amir again pulled off the road.

"Are we already at the border?" Bobbie asked.

"No, it's just a checkpoint along the way," he said. *A new checkpoint, looking for us.* "Listen to me. Go below with Alaleh and the children. They mustn't see you. If they take me, they'll think the car is empty except for the birds. If I'm forced to get out of the van, wait ten minutes. No longer. If I don't return, then take the back roads to the border, the way Davood showed us. Do you understand?"

She didn't question him; she simply nodded and then removed the closest chicken pen and crawled under, unlatching the hatch to the trapdoor. She had even practiced how she could get back out of the hiding spot in case no one was there to help.

They moved forward, and minutes later the first roadblock came into sight. Amir slowed the van to a crawl and finally stopped. The police came around it, three men armed with rifles. "Papers!" Then, "What have you got in here?"

"Chickens, sir. Exporting chickens to Turkey."

The guard stared at Amir long and hard, then opened the back of the van and clucked his tongue, like a chicken himself. "How are you bringing these chickens out of Iran? Do you have the necessary papers?"

"Of course," Amir said in Farsi. Calmly he retrieved the papers.

"I will need to see the passport too, sir."

The three men huddled together, studying the papers. A few minutes later, one came back to the driver's side of the van and said, "Come with me, sir."

"My chickens! Are you worried about the chickens? You see I have the papers. All is in order."

"These papers for the chickens do not interest us." One of the guards tossed them back into the van, holding Amir's papers in his other hand and motioning. "Come with us."

As Amir climbed out of the van and shut the door, he prayed for Bobbie. *Lord, give her the courage to leave me. Grant them safety.*

Then he thought of his favorite proverb, so lovely it should have been in the Bible: *Every man goes down to his death bearing in his hands only that which he has given away.*

I am giving it away, Lord, all of it away for You.

Bobbie

Ten minutes, eleven, twelve. I lay squeezed in tightly beside Alaleh and little Rasa. I counted the seconds and still Amir had not returned. *O Lord! Please.*

Go! Go!

Alaleh grasped my arm as I pushed my way out of the hidden compartment. I stumbled through my Farsi, "Don't worry," with my heart in my throat. I replaced the hidden door and pushed the chicken cage back in front of it, scrambled into the driver's seat, and turned on the engine, feeling completely out of control.

O Lord, take control. I am so scared.

I squinted up ahead, a mere twenty yards away, and saw the makeshift hut where the guards had most likely taken Amir. Surely they would notice the van moving!

O Lord, blind their eyes!

I backed around until the van was headed in the direction we'd come from. Frantically, I reached for the maps, concealed under the driver's seat. In my mind, I rehearsed what Davood had said, "Drive back toward Maku; at the entrance to the town, take the side road to the left . . ."

They will come after us, Lord. I am afraid for us. For Amir.

An image from my years of Bible smuggling flashed into my mind: the van packed with Bibles, our contact compromised, the police on our tail, and my partners and I singing through our fear, singing praises to God and then, amazingly, losing the police.

I began to sing, loudly, over the squawking of the chickens, the songs we had learned at The Oasis for the musical evening. I sang those words with all the conviction I could muster. Singing the truth of Scripture in English and German and Farsi and Arabic, a peace settled on me as I drove through the gray afternoon.

Somewhere on the backroads en route to Maku, I suddenly recognized the truth. Amir would not be coming. He had known this would happen, known he would be detained. Perhaps he had even chosen to be detained so that we could escape. His embrace, his long, luxurious kisses, his declaration of love, they were real—but they were all I would have. He had told me good-bye.

He had hinted at the truth for days. *It's very dangerous for me to return. If I'm fingerprinted, all will be lost. There is a death threat on me.*

Tears fell freely down my cheeks. I had gotten my second chance, and God had made it right. Amir knew that I loved him, would always love him. I was forgiven and loved by him. I could leave Austria in peace. I could leave this world in peace.

But how I longed for a different ending.

Rasa

Rasa heard the sound, so familiar, from far, far away. She tried to move, but she could not; she was swaddled in blankets and trapped in a very narrow space. Above her, Maamaan had explained, were chickens! Many, many chickens. Rasa had no trouble believing that she was hiding in a van carrying poultry.

But floating over the stench was a song! She strained to hear the beautiful words in Farsi. A song Mrs. Garabadian had taught her.

"Maamaan! Listen to the words! Listen!"

Maamaan was crying, her hand gripping Rasa's so tightly. "Yes, my child, listen to the words and pray to your Isa. We are on our way to the border. Pray."

Rasa's mind was too foggy to pray. She felt as if she had awakened from a month-long nap. Her mouth was swollen and her arms and legs throbbed with a deep-down aching. She could not imagine exactly where they were, but she knew Maamaan and Omid were beside her, and chickens were protesting above her, and further away, someone was singing.

Rasa closed her eyes. Someone was *trying* to sing. There was really no tune at all, but the voice was practically shouting the words from the psalm. *Though I pass through the valley of the shadow of death, I will fear no evil.*

Rasa breathed in the comforting words, and as her senses burned with the stench of chickens, her heart burned with one thought: They were almost there. Mountains, freedom, Baba, life. *Isa!*

Bobbie

The border in Bazargan was open twenty-four hours a day. This late in the afternoon the line to reenter Turkey was much shorter than what Amir and I had observed earlier. As I waited behind dozens of trucks, I prepared the papers and my story.

When it was my turn, the Iranian guard leaned in the window and yelled at me. "Chickens! You cannot take so many chickens!"

In English I explained, "It is all legal. I have all the necessary papers." I held out the documents and begged the Lord to calm the frantic beating of my heart.

The guard left with my papers, calling to another policeman, and together they pored over them, glancing back and forth, back and forth at me and the van.

"You are an American and you live in Turkey?"

"Yes, that's right."

"And why are you wearing the veil?"

"Out of respect for your country, sir."

He frowned, seeking to intimidate me. I didn't flinch. "So many chickens. Valuable! Very valuable." He shook his head and pointed for me to leave the line of vehicles and follow him in the van somewhere.

Then I saw it in his eyes. He wanted a bribe.

I parked where he indicated and stepped out into the afternoon chill. I went to the back of the van and opened the doors. "I will give you a fourth of my chickens, but that is all. I must make money. You may have the top ten cages."

He looked angry for just one moment, then he gave a smile. "I am glad we have reached an agreement, Madame."

And just as I had witnessed in days long gone, I watched God's mind-boggling plan unfold as the policeman unloaded ten cages of chickens, stacking them one on top of the other on the pavement beside the van. The chickens squawked their displeasure, and the guard held his nose. Then he smiled, a satisfied, almost wicked, smile. He motioned for me to follow him into a little glass-fronted hut.

I watched, tears brimming in my eyes, as he stamped my passport.

"You may leave Iran, Madame. Safe travels to you and the chickens."

CHAPTER 29

Hamid

*H*amid passed the time in the hospital by reading from the Gospels as Jim Harris had counseled him. No one disturbed him here. Would he be free to read the Bible in Linz? He wondered what other refugees would occupy the pension. Surely in his room alone, a room where eventually Alaleh and Rasa and Omid would join him, surely there he could read in safety.

When he reached the fourteenth chapter of John, there it was again—something about a Helper, God's Spirit, given to those people who believed in Isa. Yes, this Spirit would not leave, and even more, this Spirit would guide and help and direct and teach. How could Rasheed understand such a thing when Hamid could barely get his mind around this concept?

God with him. God in him. Now he saw the meaning of this word trinity. As a Muslim, he had been taught that the

Christian trinity comprised God, Mary, and Jesus. But now Hamid understood it was God the Father, Isa, and this Spirit Helper. They were three but they were one. It was a mystery.

Hamid loved the beauty of mystery. His heart soared with the thought—God in him forever! He felt warm tears on his face as he whispered his thanks. "I never would have chosen this path, this highway, but You, God, have brought me here. And if this is the path that was necessary, then I say thank you. Thank you. I am free now, Isa."

Hamid wondered what Isa thought of the great Persian poet, Rumi. Surely He would agree with this wise man: *You have to keep breaking your heart until it opens.*

My heart has been broken, Isa. And now, this heart is opened wide to You.

Tracie

Stephen and I entered Hamid's room at the hospital hand in hand. Hamid was sitting up in his hospital bed, headphones in his ears, eyes closed. The sight of his bruised face still caused me to wince, but overall, he seemed to have regained a bit of color. When he saw Stephen coming toward him, his face broke into a wide smile. He removed the headphones and reached a feeble hand out to grasp Stephen's outstretched one.

"My friend," Hamid said. "Tracie told me you were coming back. It is good to see you again, so soon."

"Yes, yes it is." Stephen cleared his throat, and his eyes filled with emotion.

"And my friend Tracie." Hamid now held out his hand to me.

I came over and squeezed it softly. "It's so good to see you sitting up and listening to the iPod!"

"Sermons. Amir's sermons. Very good for my soul." Indeed, his bloodshot eyes nevertheless held a sparkle of life.

I felt my own eyes pooling with tears as well and wiped a finger under them as I backed away. "I'll let you and Stephen talk."

Stephen scooted the lone chair next to Hamid's bed and took a seat. "My boss has sent me back, Hamid, to have this story. But I won't betray you. I will not write anything that you do not wish."

Standing off to the side, observing the two men, my heart flooded with something soft and good.

"I trust you, Stephen," Hamid replied. "And Tracie has told me that your newspaper articles raised the money for papers and the van and much more. I am grateful that your boss has sent you back. I will answer all your questions." Then Hamid smiled. "And if they want a photo of me for your paper, take my picture!" He actually chuckled. "One look at this scarred and beaten face and they will never doubt your story, this is for sure!"

Stephen gave a sad smile and once again took Hamid's hand in his, and in that gesture he stole my heart. This Stephen was a good man. And just as he was perhaps getting a glimpse of the new and improved Tracie, the Tracie who let go of stubborn control and bitter disappointment and stood, arms wide open to the unknown future before her, I felt I was peeking into Stephen's soul, seeing his heart soften, his ambitions changing. I liked what I saw.

I left him there, promising to return later when we would take Hamid to his new home in Linz. Then I drove to The Oasis, and with Tom's help picked out clothes for Hamid as well as sheets and towels and a blanket.

"And don't forget cleaning supplies," Carol added, seeing my arms loaded with the clothes and sheets. "Those places are often rancid. You sure you and Stephen don't mind cleaning?"

"Nothing could make me happier than to help Hamid, Carol," I said.

"Wonderful!" she enthused. "I'm sure Jalil and his wife will pitch in too. And we've contacted some of the members of the church in Linz."

After I'd packed up everything in bags and put them in the Peugeot, I concentrated on preparations for the Christmas party. Julie and I sat in the little upstairs den beside the office.

"Typically we have over two hundred people," Julie said. "Three nearby churches send volunteers and get gifts ready for each family. We take family photographs and have them printed for the refugees. That's always a big hit."

"Tom is the official photographer," Carol called out to us from her desk.

"I love that job," Tom admitted. "And Carol is the official elf!"

"Elf?" I asked.

Carol chuckled, and I saw mischief in her eyes. "Official elf, huh? We'll see about that, Tom. I may just have another idea!"

Julie had arranged with Fareed to meet me at The Oasis that afternoon to plan out the songs for the party. I felt filled up and overflowing with ideas and energy. As Fareed and I rehearsed, the heartache and horror he had endured now escaped through the words of the songs and reached down to begin healing his young soul. I witnessed yet again how music was indeed a therapy for dealing with deep trauma.

Fareed had just left and I was heading back to the Peugeot to pick up Stephen when my cell rang.

"Hello from Lyon, Tracie!" cried Connie.

"Hi!" I answered, surprised.

"Guess what? I got the invitation to the Christmas party, and I'm coming!" Then she sobered., "I'm so sorry about Hamid. And I've heard that Amir and Bobbie have gone into Iran to get his family?"

"Yes, it's all a bit overwhelming. Frankly, I'm really worried."

"Completely understandable." Then her voice lightened again and she asked, "Have you seen Stephen yet?"

"Yes, we've talked. We're driving Hamid to Linz this afternoon."

"That's wonderful, Tracie. But I hope you find time to go back to that little heuriger and talk about other things than refugees, too."

I was laughing as I clicked off the cell. Connie Lefort was no more subtle than my dear Aunt Bobbie.

Bobbie

As I drove across the border into Turkey it started raining, but I would have been squinting through the windshield anyway, as tears blinded my eyes. We had made it! I had felt this thrill before, many times, when we crossed a border into freedom after a challenging smuggling trip. But now two opposite emotions fairly exploded in my chest. Joy: the sense of God's presence, His care, His goodness. Dread: Amir was not with me. He was trapped by the police in Iran.

I'm not in control, Lord. I give You the control. Help me concentrate on finishing this mission even as my heart mourns.

Only when I had driven for fifteen or twenty minutes longer did I remember Hamid's cell phone, the one Amir had left in the glove compartment. I pulled off to the side of the road and dialed Anna's cell.

"Anna, we made it! We made it across the border."

"Praise God! Oh, Bobbie! What wonderful news!"

I broke into tears, recovered, and in a trembling voice asked, "How long must I wait before I can let Alaleh and the children come out of hiding?"

"Amir will know best. Just trust him."

I paused before whispering, as if the secret police could still hear me, "Amir isn't here, Anna. He was detained. I brought them out alone."

I heard a deep intake of breath, and Anna whispered, "I'm so sorry."

She quickly informed Jim, and he came on the line. "Bobbie, once you're an hour into Turkey, it will be safe. Pull over in a secluded spot and get them out. Is the child well enough to travel here tonight?"

"I don't know. She was barely conscious when we put them in the hidden compartment. That was three hours ago."

"Well, if she is strong enough, the best thing is that they get to Van as quickly as possible. I'll talk to Polat, the man at the UNHCR. We can take them there tomorrow and get their exit papers. The money continues to come in from the US, and of course Hamid has his asylum papers, so all is good on this end. We'll fly them to Vienna on Thursday."

I could hardly take in the flurry of information. "Yes, okay. I'll hope to get there tonight."

Then Jim said, "What happened with Amir?"

As I explained the whole afternoon, everything except the kisses, my voice came out in little hiccups. I finished by saying, "He told me not to wait. He said the police would be angry and question him, but then release him and he would get out."

"Ah. Yes. I'm sure he will." But Jim's hesitation and then his gravelly voice betrayed his real thoughts.

"How will Amir get out of Iran, Jim?" I dared to ask.

"Don't worry about Amir, Bobbie. He's faced these problems before and has proven himself extremely resourceful. You just concentrate on driving here."

An hour later I did as Jim said, and found a secluded place to park the van. I hurriedly removed the chicken pens and opened the trapdoor.

"We made it! We're safe!" I fairly shouted in Farsi into the compartment.

I helped Alaleh and Rasa and Omid out of their little prison. They were shivering, and the baby's face was wrinkled and red as he wailed his displeasure. Alaleh brought him close and rocked him in her arms, and he calmed. She looked at me, this young mother, so fragile and lovely, trembling and crying and then saying over and over in English, "Thank you. Thank you. Thank you." I believe those were the only English words she knew.

I rejoiced to see that little Rasa was awake. She lay across the front seat of the van, and I carefully spoon-fed her yogurt and fruit juice and more medicine. Her eyes were glassy, but open, and she gave me the faintest smile and said, "Thank you," also in English.

We left the van doors open for a moment, letting the cold air rush through to blow away some of the stench. Alaleh stood in the drizzling rain, taking in deep breaths, little Omid huddled into her chest, hidden again under layers of blankets.

Rasa couldn't stand, but I picked her up in my arms and let her breathe in the fresh air too. Before we got back into the car, she gasped and whispered in a Farsi even I could understand, "Maamaan! Look at the mountain! It is so beautiful!" She lifted a feeble arm and pointed to Mt. Ararat and pronounced a word I did not know. But then I saw what she was pointing to. The rain had stopped, and in the fading light a rainbow arched over Mt. Ararat as if daring the mountain to match its beauty.

I stood silently and stared at the rainbow, sent, I was sure, especially for us to remind us that God was in charge.

Rasa whispered again in a raspy breath, "These are good mountains."

"Yes, but better ones will come," said Alaleh. Then she looked at me, as if for the first time noticing that Amir was not here. "The man?"

"He stayed," I said, motioning with my hand to the direction we'd come from.

Alaleh's brow furrowed. "In Iran? No!"

"Yes," I said.

Her eyes filled with tears. "Why?"

"For you, for the children, for Hamid. For God."

"It is impossible," Alaleh said. "He has traded his life for ours."

My throat went dry and tears sprang to my eyes. All I could do was nod in agreement.

Amir

Amir watched a rainbow crest over Mt. Ararat, far away from where he stood, in the misting rain of Iran. Could Bobbie see this rainbow? Had she made it across the border? What about the child? He squinted to see the deep purple, the hazy pink, the fading yellow in the rainbow, his heart working furiously. It was God's promise never to leave His people.

"Oh, God, don't leave them. Protect them," he prayed.

As soon as he'd left the van and gone with the police, he realized that they knew something wasn't legitimate. The guard spat out the words to his colleague. "Illegal. False papers. Fingerprints."

Amir had prayed they wouldn't take his fingerprints. If they did . . . all was lost. He was glad they were yelling, though, and he began yelling back, as loudly as he dared, so that they would not hear the van start up and drive away.

Amir wondered if they would execute him in the woods. Surely not. They would drag him back to Tehran and torture him for hours, and then they would stand him before a firing squad. He knew the stories.

As one guard leaned over the table studying the papers, another came toward Amir, his rifle held high, as if he would bring it down on Amir's head. Instinctively Amir backed away, and at that precise second a shot sounded and the guard collapsed in front of him. Before the other guard could react, a second shot was fired and he too fell across the desk with a crash. When the third guard rushed into the hut, the third shot rang out and he fell too.

"Amir! Hurry!" Davood's voice was calling to him from outside.

In a daze, Amir stumbled out of the hut. The smuggler was still mounted on the bay mare, a rifle in his arms. "It's only a tranquilizer bullet. We must tie them up. They'll awake in an hour."

Davood dismounted, hitched the horses, and brought out several long ropes from the bay's saddle bag. Quickly the two men tied up the guards, attaching them securely to the chairs and then stuffing a rag in each mouth. "That should keep your Bobbie safe for an hour, maybe two. We must pray she'll get through the border before word gets out about these men."

"Yes indeed."

"Now we must go."

Davood mounted the mare and motioned with his eyes to the gray gelding, who reared and danced beside him. Amir pulled himself into the saddle and followed Davood, who leaned low on the mare's withers and urged her into a gallop. While tree limbs clawed at his face and scratched his arms, Amir galloped behind.

They rode for miles through the forest until they arrived at the foot of more mountains. Only now did Davood stop, dismount, and lead the horses to a tiny clearing in the woods.

"Thank you for sticking around, Davood. I thought it was over for me."

"You did the right thing, distracting the guards. The van got away without notice."

Amir felt immense relief. "Do you think they'll make it across?"

"If this Bobbie is as clever as you say, surely she'll get them out." He glanced at his watch. "It's seven. Hopefully the guards have not yet been found." He shook his head. "You were crazy to risk coming back, Amir."

Amir could only agree.

Then Davood's face broke into a smile. "But you've done this before. You remember these mountains, yes? They will be your friends, your very good friends, until you arrive in Turkey." He gestured to Mt. Ararat and the fading rainbow. "Isa will be with you."

Amir felt heavy fatigue wash over him. Yes, he had crossed those mountains before, and now it looked as if he would do it again—on horseback and then on foot. Just as he had done in 1989. Then his goal had been freedom and safety for his parents and himself.

Now he had one goal. One very precise goal: Bobbie Blake.

CHAPTER 30

Stephen

We walked into the room at the pension in Linz: Hamid, Jalil, Tracie, and I. There were no other people there, but the spacious room was occupied—filled with roaches. Somehow I had not expected to find roaches in pristine Austria.

We unloaded Hamid's few belongings, most of which Tracie had gathered together at The Oasis, and Hamid looked about with a wide, bright smile. "Isa be praised. We will have a room to ourselves! It is a gift. A slice of heaven."

True thankfulness for this roach-infested squalor!

Jalil said in English, "Evidently, the previous occupants moved out yesterday. A family of six in this one room."

"They certainly weren't Girl Scouts," Tracie declared. When Jalil stared at her blankly, she said, "Scouts always leave a place cleaner than they found it."

"Well, then again, who knows what shape it was in before they arrived?" I quipped, and Tracie stuck out her tongue at me.

"I'm taking you home for a day or two, at least until you're stronger, Hamid," Jalil said. "Darya has everything ready. She is most anxious to meet you."

Limping, Hamid followed Jalil out to his car. "Thank you, cousin. You have been so kind." He looked back at us. "You have all been so very kind."

"I'll send the story out to my boss tonight," I promised Hamid. "With the photos." We both smiled at that. "It'll make the *Peachtree Press* tomorrow morning."

"I cannot say anything but thank you," he whispered.

"We'll come back to Linz and get you as soon as we have word that your family is arriving at the Vienna airport," Tracie promised.

"And when they arrive," I teased, "you know what my boss said. I have to be there for the reunion."

Hamid smiled. "You may be there for the reunion, Stephen, when I first see them. This is fine. Take all the photos you want." Then his eyes twinkled with deep desire. "But then I will bring them back here, and we will be alone."

Jalil laughed. "Yes, I promise, we will give you some time alone."

Tracie couldn't seem to tear herself away from Hamid, and she added one last thought. "Remember that there is the Christmas party on Saturday afternoon. You must be there for the party, Hamid."

"I will not miss this party. You come and get me, and I pray Isa will be pleased to let me attend this party with my family."

For half an hour Tracie and I worked in silence, cleaning Hamid's new residence. I think the enormity of the refugee life overwhelmed both of us.

"Did you see how happy Hamid was to have this one room?" I asked finally. "He called it a slice of heaven."

"Maybe it is heaven, Stephen," Tracie said, throwing open the window. "It's a new start and nothing like his other world."

I frowned and leaned on my broom. "Is that what faith does? Gives you a new set of eyes? Do you see everything in life differently now, Tracie?"

She stood in thought, her back against a little corner sink, and I studied her delicate features.

"Good question. And I think the answer is yes. Faith has changed my perspective on things. On my wants and needs and desires." She picked up a sponge. "Aunt Bobbie says that eyes of faith see potential, and when they look at the past, they see that it was just a stepping-stone to the future."

Bobbie

Alaleh cradled Omid with one arm and rested the other on Rasa, who lay on the seat between us. At first Alaleh tried to stay awake, tried to talk to me in a mixture of Farsi and the few English words she knew.

"Sleep, please. Rest. You can rest peacefully now," I encouraged her.

She gave me a look of gratitude and exhaustion, leaned up against the window, and closed her eyes.

The only sounds were of chickens clucking and Rasa's raspy, shallow breathing.

I spent the first hour thanking God for the miracle that these people were sharing the van with me and the chickens. Then I began praying for Amir. With a sliver of moon as my companion, I relived every moment I had spent with him in the past ten days, and let the tears run down my face.

He traded his life for ours, Alaleh had said.

Oh, Amir, is this what you've done? Can it be true?

New questions bombarded me: *Why should I stay in Austria for a new treatment if Amir is gone? Why this plummeting heart?* Then a stab of guilt. *Didn't I want to stay for*

The Oasis ministry? Wasn't that my motive? Or was it only for Amir?

The questions threatened to spiral me into doubt, so I forced myself to do what I had done for two decades. I recited Scripture out loud to combat the fears, the doubts, and the lies that were coming and twisting themselves around me again.

"Be strong and courageous!" I whispered into the night. "Do not tremble or be dismayed," I said, as if daring my tremors to start up, "for the Lord your God is with you wherever you go." How I loved that verse from the book of Joshua.

"Be with me, Lord," I prayed out loud. "Be with Amir wherever he is. Help me trust You again, Lord, just for today. I cannot see past this moment, so be with me now."

I had barely pronounced the last word when Alaleh struggled awake. She blinked, and then the hand that was resting on Rasa's back went to her daughter's head and then her mouth.

"She is not breathing!" Alaleh screeched in Farsi.

Alarmed, I pulled over off the road, parked, and put my head down to Rasa's. Indeed her breathing had all but stopped, and the child seemed not asleep, but unconscious. I shook her gently. "Rasa. Rasa, dear!"

To my great relief, the little girl stirred and coughed with difficulty. Alaleh began to weep softly.

"She's okay," I reassured Alaleh even as I prayed for the Lord to quiet the fear in my heart. "And we're only an hour away now. We'll soon be where we can get her to a doctor."

Rasa's eyes flickered open. "Sing?" she murmured.

Alaleh, eyes wide, said, "I do not know the words."

"What words?" I asked.

"The ones you sang to us when we were hidden," Alaleh explained.

I almost laughed. "I don't sing well," I apologized, "but I

will do my best."

So I sang again the words of Scripture in English and Farsi, and somewhere along the road, Alaleh joined in. We sang to God, for Rasa. We begged with our hearts for our God to hear.

At last we pulled up in front of the apartment, and Jim and Anna rushed out to us so quickly that I knew they must have been waiting by the window. Jim carried little Rasa inside and Anna cradled Omid. I helped Alaleh, who limped along stiffly.

"We must get Rasa to the hospital," I told them. "She's terribly weak and at times losing consciousness."

Anna frowned. "It's not wise to take her to the hospital. Let me call our doctor. I've already warned him we might need him tonight."

The doctor arrived at midnight and examined all three of the refugees.

"I believe the child can travel on Thursday if she rests all day tomorrow," he told us. "I'll leave you something to boost her system."

"But she must be present to receive the exit papers at the UNHCR tomorrow morning," Jim said.

The doctor frowned, laid his hand across Rasa's forehead, and said, "Then she must eat and sleep. It sounds like she has a big day awaiting her."

So through the night Anna, Alaleh, and I sat beside Rasa's bed, spooning warm soup into her mouth, bathing her in warm water, dressing her frostbitten feet and hands. Finally Anna insisted that Alaleh herself take a bath and then sleep.

"You are safe now, Alaleh, and we will make sure your children are fine. Sleep." Then she placed her cell phone in the young mother's hands. "But first, you must call Hamid and tell him the good news. You are free."

Alaleh began to weep and whispered in Farsi, "Thank you, thank you. I didn't dare ask you. But now I will call."

After a joyfully tearful phone call to Hamid, she slept. But Jim and Anna and I sat in their den and prayed, voicing our fears to the Lord. Where was Amir? How would dear little Rasa travel in her condition?

Then in the middle of the prayer, I gasped.

"What is it?" Anna asked wearily.

"The chickens! I've left the chickens in the van. What in the world are we to do with the chickens?"

For some reason, our fatigue and tension and worry all came tumbling out in a fit of uncontrollable laughter. Anna and I giggled hysterically until tears ran down our cheeks.

Jim regarded us a bit helplessly, thinking perhaps that we'd completely cracked up. "Chickens, ladies, are the least of our worries! I guarantee I can get rid of every last one at the market tomorrow."

Hamid

Hamid had begged Jalil to leave him at the pension for just these few hours. He did not wish to insult his cousins by reading the Bible at their apartment. But here, he was alone. Alone and not alone at all. The Helper was here. The Helper would invade this small space and keep him, keep his family.

The wallpaper was stained and peeling and a roach scurried across the floor, but a clean fresh smell permeated the room. Some people from a local church had come this morning with furniture, and Hamid sat in wonder on a faded couch. Everything in the room was used or borrowed, but he felt like a king. They had an armoire, a desk, a coffee table, three chairs, this couch and a bed. A double bed for him to share with Alaleh.

The church people had shaken their heads in embarrassment at the state of the room. "We are sorry that you must live here."

Hamid was not sorry. Was it not written in the Persian proverb: *Some people look for a beautiful place; others make a place beautiful?* He would make this place beautiful.

He sighed contentedly, remembering how he had heard his wife's voice in the night! The voice of an angel!

And then this morning she had called again to say they had their exit papers in hand and were flying tomorrow! Stephen and Tracie would come tomorrow morning to pick him up and drive him to the Vienna International Airport. Only one day more to wait.

But Amir would not be coming with them.

Yet even as Hamid considered the news again, he thought of something that Amir had said in one of the sermons Hamid had listened to on the iPod. It came from somewhere in the Ingil. *To me, to live is Christ and to die is gain.* Amir had been willing to sacrifice his life for the life of Hamid's family.

Once again, Hamid thought of how costly it was to follow Isa. Costly, yes, but worth it.

CHAPTER 31

Bobbie

When we returned from the UNHCR with the exit papers, Anna insisted that Alaleh, Rasa, and Omid eat lunch and then go immediately back to bed. She scurried about like a nurse, administering Rasa's medicine, checking on Omid, tucking Alaleh into bed, determined that her patients rest well.

In about twenty hours we would board the plane for Austria. But for now, I had time to think.

Amir caught, held by the police, tortured . . . I could not bear to let my mind go in this direction. What had he said to me? *"I can get out. I've done it before. No fears, Okay?"*

Oh, but how I was afraid.

"Surely the Lord will give us more time, Amir."

"Of course He will, my love. But no matter what, remember always, you are loved by me. I give you again my love. Forever."

He would love me forever. Then I would wait. After all, I'd

been waiting for twelve years. What could any longer matter?

When I talked to Tracie on the cell phone, her voice was lined with concern. "Aunt Bobbie, are you all right?"

"A little tired is all." In truth, I had rarely felt quite so exhausted.

"I'm so proud of you, Bobs. You got them out!" Then her voice dropped. "I'm so sorry about Amir."

"Yes. It was quite a shock." I tried to make my voice sound hopeful even as that dread sat in the pit of my stomach. "But Amir is resourceful. I'm sure he will find a way out."

"Of course he will, Bobs. I'm sure of it too!"

I was thankful for her fresh faith.

"Stephen and I took Hamid to Linz and we cleaned the apartment—"

"Hold on a minute—Stephen? He's there with you?"

Tracie laughed, and in a jumble of excitement explained how Stephen's boss had sent him back over to cover Hamid's story. And I heard it in her voice—she was a young woman in awe of God's timing and a young woman in love.

"So I'll see you tomorrow, Bobs. Love you so much."

I clicked off Anna's cell and sat in thought. I acknowledged my deep, deep fatigue, the emotional, physical, and spiritual exhaustion. How many times before had I felt myself slipping towards despair after a difficult smuggling mission was completed? I always thought of the prophet Elijah, who wanted to lie down and die after he had won the amazing confrontation against the prophets of Baal.

Wait on the Lord. Wait on Amir. Wait on a treatment.

Then my subconscious argued back. *The tremors are stronger than ever. No treatment is going to help. And how do you know that Amir will return?*

I felt a hand on my shoulder. "You must rest too, Bobbie." Anna spoke softly, and her warm eyes communicated what we both knew.

After a great victory, I needed to allow myself time to recuperate or I might simply fall apart. She led me to Baby Lilly's room, turned down the covers on the single bed, and tucked me in.

I slept.

Late that evening, after Jim and Anna's children were in bed, sharing their room with Rasa and Omid, the adults sat in the den. Anna had given Alaleh a beautiful blue blouse and colorful skirt, and now this young mother fairly glowed.

She came to me and spoke in Farsi, and Jim translated the parts I could not understand. "Jim says that this man Amir was very dear to you. This is true?"

I nodded.

"I am so sorry for what has happened. But Jim also says he has escaped before, yes?"

Again I nodded.

She had tears in her eyes, and she reached out a tentative hand to touch mine. "Surely if your God would save me and my family"—she waited for Jim to translate—"He will save this good man who has risked his life for us."

"That is my prayer," I stammered.

Alaleh continued. "I believe your God listens when His people talk to him. And if you will permit, I will talk to Him with all of you. I will ask Him to bring this man out of Iran safely."

I could not find any words but "Thank you."

Rasa

Rasa rested her head on her mother's shoulder, coming in and out of sleep. She and Maamaan and Omid were on a real airplane with the pretty lady, Bobbie! She hardly had the strength to feel excited and yet something fluttered in her heart. Maamaan said she would see Baba in just a little while.

"Rasa, dear Rasa, look!" Maamaan said.

She lifted her head with difficulty and squinted to look out the window of the airplane. Huge billowy clouds passed by and, far below them, jagged white peaks spread out in a long range.

"These are the good mountains, Rasa," Maamaan cooed softly. "You were right all along, my angel. We have made it to the good mountains."

Rasa slipped her hand into her skirt pocket and fingered the wooden cross that was concealed there. Good mountains! And a country where she would not have to hide the cross in her pocket. Soon they would really be free. She was too tired to do anything but smile.

Hamid

Hamid paced back and forth, back and forth in the shiny open corridor of the Vienna International Airport. Could it be that he had arrived a mere two and a half weeks ago through those very same sliding doors? And soon, any minute, would Alaleh truly walk through those doors with his daughter and infant son?

Jalil and Darya stood beside him, silently watching. Tracie held onto Stephen, who had his camera poised and ready. Hamid continued pacing, actually limping, a sharp pain jabbing him in the ribs with each step. But the waiting was much harder to bear than the pain.

Isa! Please bring them.

As people began exiting, he held his breath. For ten minutes people came out, but not his people. He remembered the customs, the papers, everything.

Oh, hurry! Or did they miss the plane? Were they detained in Turkey?

He remembered Amir's exhortation coming straight through the iPod: *When you are afraid, repeat Scripture in your mind. Repeat the promises of God. This will calm you.* Hamid only knew a very few verses by heart, but he repeated them now. If only his heart would quit jolting so in his rib cage! It hurt!

And then Alaleh appeared, dressed in a bright blue blouse and a long floral skirt, her thick black hair tumbling over her shoulders, her whole posture proclaiming her freedom. He knew she was beyond exhausted, and yet she had never looked more stunning. Her lovely black eyes with the thick lashes were flashing love. And his son! She held his son close to her breast. Then Bobbie stepped through the glass doors with little Rasa in her arms.

Hamid rushed to them and threw his arms around Alaleh and Omid and held them tightly, almost fiercely. He breathed in the fragrance of his wife and then met her lips with his. Oh, how sweet! It tasted like his very first kiss, and he tingled with the simple joy of it.

When he turned toward Rasa, she tried to smile and whispered, "Baba, we made it."

Dear little Rasa! He felt a chill run down his spine to see his daughter looking so frail. Carefully, he took her out of Bobbie's arms. Her face was ghostly pale, and she coughed weakly. She reached with difficulty to touch his swollen face and began to cry, pitiful little sobs. "Oh, Baba, you are hurt, and I am sick, but Isa has saved us. He has saved us."

"Yes, Rasa. You're right. And now you and I, we will both get well. I believe this, do you?"

She sniffed and nodded and then buried her head in his chest. For a few minutes he stood there, little Rasa in his arms and Alaleh holding onto him. He was vaguely aware of a camera's repeated flash, and then Jalil took Rasa, and Alaleh held out Omid to him. "Hamid," she said, "meet your son."

He took his tiny son in his arms, and then he turned and faced Stephen, who clicked the camera and the flash lit up the air.

Bobbie

I watched with a pinching in my heart as Hamid held little Omid in his arms. I had no words, only an overwhelming feeling of gratitude and something akin to disbelief. I knew what I was witnessing—a miracle, a God-ordained, humanly-orchestrated miracle.

Suddenly I was tackled, and Tracie wrapped me in a bear hug. "I'm so happy to have you back, Aunt Bobs! How are you holding up?"

I hugged her back. "I'd say I'm being held up by love."

"Held up by love. I like that." Her eyes teared up. "Thank you for being so brave, so willing, in spite of everything."

In spite of everything. Oh, Amir . . .

Stephen came over and gave me a warm hug too. "Sounds like you're the hero of this mission, Bobbie. Pretty amazing stuff. Would you mind if I snapped a few photos of you with Hamid, Alaleh, and the kids?"

"I wouldn't mind at all."

Hamid handed Omid back to Alaleh and took both of my hands in his. "Thank you, Bobbie," he said, weeping. "I can only say thank you. And because Amir is not here, I tell you thank you to him too. I read in the Bible this verse: 'And this is love, that a man lay down his life for his friends.'"

I sat in the waiting room as Rasa was admitted to the Baden Hospital. We'd had to wait until Alaleh and the children had been checked in at the Government Refugee Housing Center and only then, four hours later, were we allowed to take Rasa to the hospital. I read the worry lines on the doctor's face as he examined her and then motioned for her to be whisked away. Alaleh had not been allowed to leave the Center, but Hamid was with us, and followed the gurney as it disappeared down the hall. I had spent the past two days reassuring Alaleh that her daughter would be fine, but in truth I felt nervous.

Then Tracie walked with me to the elevator, and we took it to a different floor where my appointment was scheduled with Dr. Schobesberger. After a short wait we were ushered into a small room, and a few minutes later the white-haired doctor greeted me with a kind smile. "How was your week off of the treatments, Miss Blake?"

I had no idea what to say. "I suppose it was as good as could be expected considering the circumstances."

He accepted that without question and looked down at his clipboard. "Your blood test results show that there is little or no change, either for the good or bad, from your oral treatment."

Tracie grabbed my hand and held it tight. I felt my stomach falling.

"So I suggest we start this new treatment immediately." He proceeded to explain it. Words like *natural, strengthening the body to fight the cancer,* and *experimental program that lasts at least six months* floated past. With every word he pronounced, I heard a different voice in my head. *Why would you stay here if there is no Amir? You can't ask Tracie to stay for months on end. And if she doesn't stay, who can help take care of you if the cancer worsens?*

I shook Dr. Schobesberger's hand and left the room with Tracie, feeling completely in a daze. One sentence the doctor had pronounced was clear to me: "Well, then, the treatment will start on Monday morning."

We walked back to little Rasa's room and found her awake, with Hamid sitting beside her.

"Hello, Miss Bobbie," Rasa said softly in English, looking up at me timidly.

"Hello, Miss Rasa," I returned. "My! I think seeing your

father has helped you. You already look stronger."

Hamid translated my words, and then Rasa continued speaking in Farsi, with her father translating back and forth between us. "The doctor says I must stay here for a whole week. He says if I do everything he tells me, then I will soon be very strong." But then she frowned. "But Baba says you are very sick."

I smiled at the child. "I am not well, it is true."

"But Isa heals His people, doesn't He?"

"He always heals His people fully in their souls. But sometimes He chooses not to heal their bodies. Not until they get new bodies in heaven."

She screwed up her forehead as she tried to understand. "Miss Beverly told me about new bodies in heaven. I guess that is what happened to my grandmother. Isa did not keep her from dying." Tears came to her eyes. "But sometimes, Isa heals. He healed Maamaan and Omid. We will pray, and maybe He will decide to heal your body and your soul."

Tracie drove me to Gasthaus Müller, and I climbed the steps wearily to our little yellow room. I tried to remember what the doctor had said, but it was no use. I felt as if I were walking through a fog. I needed to sleep again. But first I took the cell phone and punched in Peggy's number.

"It's me. I'm back."

"God be praised."

"Yes," and then I told her the whole long story. Peggy knew how to listen. When at last I paused, she said, "I am so sorry about Amir."

"I think I'm still in shock over it all."

"And now you are wondering what to do next?"

"Yes. I can't ask Tracie to stay here with me. She has a life to live—and if what I'm seeing is right, she's in love."

"And have you conveyed to Tracie the decision you have

made for her?"

Dear Peggy! She didn't mince words. "Are you saying I'm grabbing at control again?"

"I am. Please give that child a choice in the matter. And what is your heart telling you, Bobbie?"

"I'm afraid. I have no guarantee about a new treatment, and I'm not sure about the visa, and why in the world would I add extra worry and concern for the missionaries here?"

"And Amir?"

"How can I know if he is coming back?"

"You cannot. You must decide without knowing. I urge you to spend some time seeking the Lord. You have barely had time to think in these last days. God is not in a hurry, dear Bobbie. No matter how we feel."

"Yes, you're right."

"And Bobbie. Have I told you how proud I am of you?"

"Thank you, Peggy. And please thank the Prayer Band. You know I didn't do this on my own strength or will." I got a little bit choked up. "On that trip, at least, I knew beyond a shadow of a doubt that I was not in control. And the Lord proved faithful, as always."

"Yes, He's like that."

"Please convey my love to the Prayer Band and remind them that there is still a refugee stuck in Iran."

CHAPTER 32

Stephen

For the second time that day, I drove to the Vienna International Airport. When Mom stepped through the sliding glass doors, I hugged her tight, practically lifting her off the ground.

"Oh, sweetie! It's so good to be with you again so soon," she said. "Your father sends his greetings and said that you'd better come to Lyon before you fly back over to Atlanta or he'll have words for you!"

"So he's there now?"

"Yes." She took my hand the way she had when I was a young boy. "We're making our way, tiny step by tiny step. I'm guardedly hopeful."

"Then maybe you and I should fly back to Lyon together in a few days."

"Nothing could make me happier. And you know what your father will say?"

In unison we quipped, *"Vaut mieux tard que jamais."* Better late than never.

And suddenly I was back in my childhood, with Mom and Papa holding hands and happily talking back and forth, she in English and he in French.

And I knew then, *this* was home. Home was not a place for me. Home was family. For many years I had fled my family because of its tensions. But now I knew. Someday I would settle down and make a home for myself. Perhaps I'd have a pretty blond wife and several kids. But for now, walking beside my mother, I was home.

I dropped Mom off at The Oasis, where Carol immediately put her to work. Then I headed to Gasthaus Müller with her luggage and tucked myself away in my room to write the fifth and sixth stories for the *Peachtree Press*. I had some great digital photos of Hamid's reunion with his wife and kids to include. Mr. Kimball was so excited about the way the story had turned out that he planned to run it for three more days.

"And see if you can get that other guy back too," he'd said on the phone, as if I had the slightest bit of control over Amir's situation.

If only I could, I thought to myself. *If only I could.*

Tracie

I knew Aunt Bobbie was deeply disappointed with the blood test results, but she hid it well. The oral treatment had not helped, and now she was entering into something completely experimental. In her fatigue, I don't even think she'd really grasped the breadth of the treatment. No chemo. A much more natural approach.

I knew she was thinking every moment about Amir as well, and I couldn't imagine anything I could say to help her feel better, so I kept my mouth shut.

We were back at the guest house and I was putting on

makeup, getting ready to go out for dinner with Stephen and his mother.

"Nervous?" Bobbie asked.

"A little, yes. I don't know—it just seems like this is a real date, even with Connie present. Like maybe we're beginning to define our relationship."

"I'm sure it will go well, Trace. Connie has already practically adopted you." Bobbie hesitated and then said, "I wanted to mention something to you. About this new treatment. I realize it's no guarantee, and it sounds like it will last at least six months. From all appearances, you may be starting up a very serious relationship, and I certainly don't want to hinder—"

I stopped her midsentence. "Wait a minute, Bobs! Remember, you're not allowed to plan out my life any more. I'm a big girl." I gave her a warm hug. "And anyway, you've spent your life sacrificing for me."

She started to protest, so I hurried along. "I know you'll say it was not a sacrifice, that you did it out of love. Well, that's exactly how I feel. I love you, Aunt Bobbie, and I am happy to stay right here and help you through this treatment—whatever happens. You will *not* tell me what to do. I'm staying."

Bobbie sighed and gave a slight nod. "Just as Peggy predicted." Then she added, "What about Stephen?"

"Stephen has a lot of things to figure out about his life. And I have no doubt that he'll finagle a way to get back over here regularly if he wants to see me. You don't need to worry about Stephen."

Bobbie

I stayed in bed all day Friday while Tracie, Stephen, Connie, the full-time missionaries, and countless volunteers worked to prepare for the Christmas party the next day. I wanted to have enough strength to attend.

When I'd gotten back to our little room the day before, I'd found a bright green-and-red elf costume lying across the bed—a costume I had worn twelve years ago at one of the very first Christmas parties given at The Oasis. Carol must have dug it up from somewhere.

But in truth, I did not feel like celebrating. I felt like Elijah. I wanted to lie down and die.

Amir.

But surely God was feeding my soul to renew my strength, just as He had done for the prophet. I would do as Peggy instructed. I would wait and pay attention to what He said to me in the silence of this day.

I thought of Sally and the T-tribe, of Vasilica, of Amir. I let the thoughts go past, just waiting on the Lord. I remembered snuggling Anna's baby Lilly so close, and then holding little Rasa in my arms, and I felt that long-repressed but still familiar ache. Empty arms.

The Lord would fill them up again, right here in Traiskirchen. Not today. Today I would rest. But it still burned in my soul, the fierce love for the refugees, for the children. In the silence I heard it, I felt it, I sensed it somewhere deep in my being. I had come home.

Rasa

Rasa could hardly sit still through the morning—this afternoon she was going to a Christmas party! A real party celebrating this holiday that was so important for Christians. The doctor told her she could leave the hospital just long enough to attend the party *if* she promised not to get too excited. How in the world could she not be excited?

Baba and Maamaan were coming too, with little Omid. At first Maamaan had refused, saying that Omid would only cause noise, but Rasa had begged and begged. "There will be babies too! I know it. Miss Bobbie told me that the *whole* family is invited."

The small wooden cross was sitting by her hospital bed, and Rasa reached for it and held it. She thought of the first time she had heard of this cross when Miss Beverly had held up a larger wooden cross and explained the story of Isa, a God who loved people so much that He became like them and then died for them. A God who loved her and wanted to know her.

Help me know You more, dear Isa. Help Baba and Maamaan and Omid and me to know You more every day.

Bobbie

By Saturday morning I had regained enough strength to head to The Oasis with Tracie, Stephen and Connie. Carol, Julie, Tom, and JoAnn met us there to set up a puppet stage and prepare the tables for the party. We were also joined by Keith and Lindsey McDaniel, who had come from Holland at Carol's invitation.

By three in the afternoon, two dozen volunteers had shown up to help us pack Christmas bags for the refugees. The three Austrian churches sponsoring the party had provided an abundance of small personal items, and together we packed over three hundred gift bags for people of all ages. They created a splash of green and red color on tables at the front of the room, and someone had put on an old CD of Christmas carols.

The mood was bright and cheerful, but I still felt such a hollowness in my heart. How I longed to look up and find Amir walking in the door. I swallowed again and again, but my throat remained dry and tears threatened at any moment to spill out of my eyes.

At five o'clock we opened the doors to the refugees, and by five thirty the room was filled with men, women, and children. As they entered, they were directed to a side room for family portraits, which they would receive the next week. I could hear Tom's good-natured chuckling as he greeted each family.

When Hamid arrived with Alaleh, Rasa, and Omid, I walked into the photo room with them, and tears did spill out of my eyes as Tom took their family portrait.

Then I led them over to where Keith and Lindsey were serving up punch. "This is the man who helped design the van to sneak you out," I explained to Alaleh, and she smiled the most beautiful smile.

Then she blushed and whispered something to Hamid in Farsi. He translated, "She says she was not very happy about the van and the chickens at first, but now she thinks it was a brilliant idea and she thanks you."

Keith let out a deep belly laugh and said, "I actually had nothing to do with the chickens. That was all Bobbie's idea." Then his face sobered and he seemed a bit choked up. "It is a very great pleasure for Lindsey and me to meet you, Hamid"—he clasped his hand—"and Alaleh." Then big Keith knelt down, looked into Rasa's eyes, and said in Farsi, "We've been praying a whole lot for all of you. It's so good to see you here."

As Keith spoke, Hamid's expression changed from a smile to a perplexed look, then startled, and then utterly joy filled. He reached for Keith's hand again and said, "It was you! You are the voice on the radio after 'Life in Christ.'"

Now Keith was the one who looked startled. "Yes," he admitted. "How did you know?"

"I would recognize your voice anywhere," Hamid replied. "It conveys kindness and strength and compassion. I cannot tell you how many times I felt hope when I heard your voice."

Keith's eyes misted over as he said, "Thank you for telling me, Hamid. You'll never know how much that means to me." Then he switched again to Farsi and began teasing Rasa as

Lindsey held out her arms to hold baby Omid.

Connie kept busy filling and refilling coffee and tea-cups. Stephen was taking photo after photo, and I heard him speaking to refugees in French and Arabic at different times throughout the evening.

Tracie sang her heart out, a medley of American Christ-mas carols in which the refugees joined along, as Fareed taught them the words in English. The Austrian volunteers worked nonstop in the kitchen, loading and reloading tray after tray of homemade Austrian pastries. Midway through the party I changed into the elf costume, as I had done twelve years ago. I forced a smile on my face as I passed out candy, played with the kids, and had my picture taken with them.

And then it was time for the puppet show.

Alaleh

Alaleh had gained permission to leave the Refugee Cen-ter that morning, and now she sat with Rasa in her lap and Hamid beside her, with Omid asleep on his shoulder. She smiled with a lump in her throat. They were all here, together.

This place called The Oasis was packed to the brim with families and there was a happy banter of voices, in many dif-ferent languages—Farsi, Arabic, German, and English. Rasa could hardly sit still in her lap. She wiggled back and forth, turned to smile at her father, threw her arms around his neck. Dear Rasa! Her child was coming back to life.

"Maamaan, Baba, look! It's starting."

Alaleh turned her attention to the front of the room where a puppet stage had been erected.

Alaleh thought she would watch the puppet show for Rasa, but almost instantly she felt a certain flip-flop in her stomach. The play was called "Jesus, the Refugee." Alaleh lis-tened as the narrator, speaking in English and being translat-ed into Farsi, Arabic, and German, told of Mary and Joseph going on a long journey. Mary rode on the back of a donkey, and she was heavy with child. The narrator, a man named Tom, explained how tired they were, how long the trip took, and how once they reached the desired village, there was no room for them!

Ah, yes, she understood that. No room! She found herself nodding silently, and, to her surprise, many other heads were nodding too. Yes, they could all understand this story.

She nodded again when the narrator told of Mary giving birth to Baby Jesus in a barn. She thought of Omid's birth in that crawl space and bit her lip to keep from crying. This story was so very hard and so very familiar!

Then the narrator explained how Mary and Joseph had to take the baby Jesus and flee into another country for safety because of an evil king. Alaleh felt a tear trickle down her cheek. She looked over at Hamid and took his hand. He too was crying. Why had she never heard this story before? Jesus had been a refugee just as surely as baby Omid was one now.

Astrid Garabadian had told her about Isa as the Savior born of a Virgin. She had heard that He was God and perfect and could forgive sins, that He was magnificent and powerful, that He had chosen to give these things up to become like her—a human. But Alaleh had never heard that Jesus had been a refugee.

Suddenly, Isa seemed all the more interested in her life, in her family's life. Alaleh could not stop the tears as she watched the makeshift stage and the felt puppets tell a story that broke her heart and brought it alive with hope. This Isa, this Jesus, did understand, just as she had heard. Isa could identify with all of her pain.

Isa, the refugee.

Alaleh brushed the tears away with the back of her sleeve. Then she held Rasa's little hands tightly and whispered to her mystic daughter, "I like this Isa. I like Him a lot."

Hamid

Hamid watched the puppet show with a catch in his throat. In so many ways, Jesus's story was similar to his family's. He was so enthralled with the puppets and the narration that at first he did not notice Rasheed as he sank into the chair on his other side. He reached over to shake Hamid's hand. Hamid hesitated for only a second, then he met Rasheed's eyes and shook hands.

Rasheed watched the puppet show, leaning further and further forward in his seat as the story progressed.

When the show ended, Hamid said, "I am surprised to see you here, Rasheed."

"Yes, I know. I came in case there were some beautiful women to meet." He smiled, then sobered. "And I came because I hoped to see you and your family."

"Let me introduce you then," Hamid said, and he presented Alaleh, Rasa, and Omid to his former traveling companion and roommate.

"I am so happy to meet you all!" Rasheed said. "It is a miracle that you are here!" Then he explained to Alaleh all that Hamid had done for him. "I will never be able to repay your husband or buy back forgiveness. I will always owe him a huge debt."

Hamid watched Alaleh's face cloud, then she furrowed her brow and looked straight at Rasheed. "You have traveled many miles and many weeks with my husband. You have surely heard him quote his favorite proverbs, yes?"

Rasheed nodded. "Yes, I have."

"Then you will not be surprised if I tell you what he has said to me for all these years when a friend or a colleague has disappointed us: 'The best of men are men at best.' Only God is perfect, and we do not expect you to be God, Rasheed. Men make mistakes. We will forgive you."

Hamid wondered at his wife's words. They had not yet been alone for him to hear all that was in her heart, but soon he would have time to listen and share with her. On Monday, Rasa would leave the hospital and Alaleh and Omid would be released from the Refugee Center, and they would travel to Linz on the highway. It was a long highway, a very long highway, but they were going home.

Bobbie

The Christmas party was over, and I had slipped away to change back into my jeans and sweatshirt. When I came back into the main room, Tracie grabbed my hands, her face glowing. "Aunt Bobbie! Will you join Stephen and Connie and me at the Schafler heuriger?"

I shook my head. "You don't need me, Trace. Y'all go and enjoy. Julie's going to take me back to the guest house."

"No, you *have* to come. I really, really want you to be there."

I narrowed my eyes and furrowed my brow. "Tracie Hopkins, are you going to announce something tonight?"

She just blushed.

Had Stephen asked Tracie to marry him? Wasn't that a bit sudden?

"Are you sure it's that important?" I pressed.

"Positive."

I acquiesced. "Okay. But I won't stay long."

"Oh, thank you, Aunt Bobbie! It means so much to me."

Stephen, who was carrying one of the folding tables back to the storage room, walked by and said, "Trace, Mom and I are going to finish cleaning up. We'll join you in about ten minutes."

"Sounds good to me." Tracie was beaming.

She took my arm and fairly sailed out of The Oasis and toward the little heuriger. I had rarely seen her this excited. I hobbled along beside her with my cane.

When we got to the heuriger, she said, "Oh, shoot! I forgot my purse. You go on in and I'll run back to The Oasis and get it."

I felt a mild irritation as she took off at a run back down the street. She wasn't usually so scatterbrained. Frau Schafler greeted me immediately with a big smile, and then she motioned for me to go over to the booth where Amir and I used to sit. I hesitated, wondering if I could possibly feign joy for Tracie if I were sitting in *that* booth.

As we walked to the table, I whispered to Frau Schafler, "Oh, it looks like it's already taken." I felt relieved. A man was sitting there, his back to us.

Then he stood and turned around, and I gasped.

Amir.

He looked as if he had literally just stepped out of the mountains; he had a three-day-old beard, his jeans were filthy, his shirt stained, and his black hair, which he always wore carefully combed, fell in his face.

But to me he looked like the closest thing to heaven I had ever seen.

We stood for a moment, frozen in time, then he reached for me, and I went quickly, delightedly into his arms.

"Hello, Bobbie Blake," he said, and the love in his voice warmed every inch of me. "Your niece thought perhaps this was the best place for me to meet you. You see, I've just arrived home."

EPILOGUE

January, 2006
Hamid

*H*amid walked into the little church in Linz for the morning service, hand in hand with Alaleh, cradling his infant son in his other arm. Today, the Austrians and the Iranians were having a combined service with a meal afterwards.

Rasa ran ahead of her parents. "Gustav! Gustav! We're here!" she said in German and gave the elderly Austrian a big hug. Little Rasa was already picking up the language, and in two days she would start first grade in a nearby Austrian elementary school.

Dear old Gustav came to their pension every day and read from the Bible in German as Hamid and Alaleh and Rasa followed along in their Farsi version. On Sunday afternoons and Wednesday evenings, Hamid and Alaleh joined the Iranian church members for worship and for Bible study. And every Thursday morning Amir drove from his little town an hour away to have breakfast and Bible study with him.

Hamid sighed deeply. His wounds continued to heal, he slept at night in a bed with his lovely wife, and he watched his children adapt to life in Austria. Sometimes they talked of Maamaan-Bozorg, remembering his strong and stubborn mother with such fondness. Sometimes they cried with the grief of missing her. Not everyone had made it safely out of Iran.

But everyone has made it safely home.

With Omid still in his arms, Hamid went to the front of the church and knelt before the simple stone altar while the ancient stained-glass windows cast color all about him. Once again he thought of a favorite Persian proverb: *The branch that bears the most fruit bends itself thankfully toward the ground.*

Let me bear much fruit for You, dear Isa, he prayed. *I am Yours.*

Tracie

On a Sunday morning in early January, with Stephen at my side, I spied her. She stood up with difficulty at the end of the church service. As she took hold of the walker, Stephen and I made our way to where she stood. We were holding hands and we felt, quite frankly, a little lost in the crowded sanctuary of New Dawn Church.

Stephen gave Peggy his charming smile; her brow wrinkled as she clearly was trying to place him. I came up quickly, took her old, wrinkled hands in mine, and squeezed them gently.

"Mrs. Milner! You're the person I'm looking for! I'm Bobbie's niece—Tracie Hopkins." It had been years since I had been to Aunt Bobbie's church, and I wasn't sure she'd recognize me.

She gave a little gasp and then a chuckle. "I know very well who you are, young lady. How wonderful to see you again."

"And this is Stephen Lefort."

"And now I know very well who you are too, young man." She reached for his hand. "I have read every one of your articles. Excellent! I feel like I know Hamid and his family personally."

"Glad to hear it, Mrs. Milner," Stephen said, his cheeks red.

"Peggy! Please call me Peggy." Then to me, "So Bobbie finally convinced you to come back to Atlanta, Tracie?"

"Oh no. She didn't convince me. I decided for myself. That was our deal since she and Amir—"

A chuckle escaped Peggy Milner's lips, and she said, "Yes, I was just kidding with you. Bobbie called yesterday and told me her news."

I beamed. "So you know!"

"Yes, I know."

Then Stephen asked, "We were wondering, Mrs. Milner—I mean, Peggy. Well, um, we think God is doing something in our lives."

Stephen searched for his words and as he struggled, I think he grabbed a place in Peggy's heart.

"Would you be able to suggest to us how we should, um, proceed now that we're back in Atlanta? I mean, Tracie has a better idea than I do. Maybe there would be a man who would meet with me and help me investigate my spirituality?" Now his face was bright red.

"I'm sure we can work that out," Peggy said, and I saw a twinkle in her eyes.

"And if it wouldn't be too much of an imposition, Peggy," I added, "I would love to come visit you at your apartment. Perhaps I could fix you a cup of tea and I could ask you my questions?"

"Nothing would delight me more."

With Stephen on one side and me on the other, Peggy

shuffled behind her walker out into the foyer, saying, "I guess the good Lord wants me to stick around awhile longer."

Bobbie

Dread sat like piles of rocks in my stomach as we approached the little cemetery in Criscior, Romania. Why had I let Amir bring me back? To see what? They had dumped Vasilica in the ground; not even a true grave. My heart twisted inside.

I balked, but Amir reached and took my hand. and squeezed it until I met his eyes. *It will be okay,* they said. A sad, kind smile.

We wound in and out of the gravestones until Amir stopped in front of one. The figure of a young boy cradling a lamb was carved into the small stone, along with these words: *Then the eyes of the blind will be opened and the ears of the deaf will be unstopped. Isaiah 35:5 Vasilica Leittit, 1986-1994.*

The graveyard was small and cared for. A pot of bright yellow mums sat by his grave. I fell to my knees and wept.

Oh, Vasilica. How I loved you!

I remembered how I'd spent such long months learning to sign, late into the night, when the refugees had left the building. How I had flown three times to Romania each year to visit him. He would cling to me and cry when I left.

I thought of the months and months I'd spent on the paperwork, mounds of paperwork, and the four different times I was told no, I could not adopt, before the miraculous yes. Not until I held that paper in my hand did I dare tell Vasilica that at the end of the summer he was coming home with me!

For two weeks we lived in a reverie, Amir and Vasilica and I. We were together, and someday soon this little boy who had stolen my heart would be my own child. And soon after, in the not-too-distant future, this good, kind, handsome godly man would be my husband.

Bliss.

And then the nightmare.

When Vasilica died, I left all the paperwork in Romania, left it crumpled on Lidia's desk. And then I left forever.

But now, as I sat beside his grave, and the tears fell so freely, I knew it was right for me to be back. I didn't realize how fiercely I was grasping Amir's hands until he gently unpried them. Then he took me in his arms and held me as I wept.

Much later, as the sun began to set over the frosted Romanian hills, we walked back to the little orphanage, deep in thought. Amir was the first to break the silence. "And now, Bobbie Blake, it's time to go home."

"Yep. Home to start more treatments."

"Home to plan a wedding."

"Yes. That too," I whispered.

I stared down at the simple gold ring that now adorned my left hand, then looked up into Amir's eyes, so full of love. He bent down gently to kiss me on the lips, and I tasted bliss again.

We did not know the future, but we had the now, we had each other, and we had the Lord.

"Soon I will promise to love you for as long as we both shall live," Amir whispered, his voice so tender and soft in my ear.

"Yes. It might be a month, it might be a year."

"No, my dear, Bobbie. It will be for eternity."

ACKNOWLEDGMENTS

As brand-new short-term missionaries heading to France, Paul and I trained with others who were going to smuggle Bibles behind the Iron Curtain. At conferences during the 1980s we routinely heard the mind-boggling stories of God's provision during those smuggling trips. Then in the '90s, after the fall of the Iron Curtain, we heard about the ministry to refugees in Traiskirchen, Austria and a new welcome center called The Oasis.

In 2010 Paul and I received a new calling from the Lord, and we became Member Care Providers for all of the ITUSA missionaries in Europe. In our new job, we have the privilege of visiting the places we had heard about for so many years.

On one of our visits to The Oasis, as I watched our colleagues serving coffee, tea, and Jesus to refugees from the Middle East, the Lord sparked my writer's imagination and my heart. *The Long Highway Home* is the result.

A special thank-you to:
Julie Soltis, Carol Halm, Tom and JoAnn Richards, Dan and Marie Lincoln, Werner and Lisa Schobesberger, Hamid and Debbie Fallahian—for sharing many Oasis stories with me and for serving so well for so many years.

Also Scott and Vicki McCracken, Kenn and Lisa Dirrim, Kent and Myrna Morley, Tim and Donna Sirinides, Ilir and Kate Cami, Christy Taylor, Tasha Hayes—I also gained much information and inspiration from your ministries to refugees in Athens, Greece. I am grateful to your team, to author Helena Smrcek, and to many former refugees for recording their stories in the book *Kingdom Beyond Borders*.

All the unnamed refugees who have shared their stories of flight and freedom—I only pray that my words will give my readers a hint of your suffering, your courage, and your faith.

Harry and Eileen Bettig—the very first idea for this story came as I sat across from Harry in a restaurant in Ermelo, Holland and watched his eyes glisten as he told stories of how the radio programs on Trans World Radio were changing lives in closed countries around the world.

Marieke Michelsen—my smart, savvy, and beautiful Dutch publisher. Thank you for believing in this story (and all my other ones throughout the years!) and for making it available to my Dutch readers.

Sandra van Tongeren—I met you first as my translator in Holland. What a delight to have you as my editor for *The Long Highway Home*. Thank you for your enthusiasm for this story. Your exuberant faith blesses me.

My dear friend and fabulous editor, LB Norton, who helped me get the English version just right! Thank you, thank you, *merci*.

My amazing agent, Chip MacGregor—supplying me with wise counsel, a listening ear, timely information on the business side of writing, and lots of encouragement along the way. Thanks for not giving up on me, no matter the state of publishing!

Jere and Barbara Goldsmith, my over-the-top generous parents, and Doris Ann Musser, my energetic and lovely mother-in-law, and all the others in the Goldsmith and Musser families for their support throughout all our years on the mission field: Jere and Mary Goldsmith, Glenn and Kim Goldsmith, H.A. and Rhonda Musser, Janet Granski, Scot and Carol Musser, Bill and Beth Wren, and all my nieces and nephews.

Friends on both sides of the Atlantic who cheer me on: Valerie Andrews, Odette Beauregard, Cathy Carmeni, Dominique Cottet, Margaret DeBorde, Marlyse Français, Kim Huhman, Letha Kerl, Laura McDaniel, Heather Myers, Trudy Owens, Michele Philit, Marie-Hélène Rodet, Thom Shelton, Marcia Smartt, Cheryl Stauffer, Lori Varak.

My dear readers—stories are meant to be shared, and I am so thankful that once again you have taken the time to let me share this one with you.

My husband, Paul—I'm so thankful we get to serve together in our Member Care ministry. Your love and support and wonderful good humor and joy keep me going. I am filled up to overflowing with your love. You are the best gift I have ever received.

Andrew and Lacy, and Chris—no mother or mother-in-law could be prouder of the young adults you have become. And remember, we're on a journey. One day at a time. Thank you for so much love and encouragement from across the pond.

And for Jesse, Nadja'Lyn, and Quinn—what everyone says is true: grandchildren are a pure and simple delight. I am over-the-top thankful to have babies and toddlers in my life.
And finally, all praise and adoration to You, my Lord, who inspires and guides me daily. I love the journey we are on together and rejoice in knowing that this long highway will ultimately lead me "home."

A final note to my readers:

'The Oasis' really exists in Traiskirchen, Austria. The workers there recently celebrated its 25th birthday. The harvest is indeed great among the refugees and the need for full-time workers is also great.

International Teams is committed to refugee work around the world and has been working with refugees for decades in strategically located places along the refugee highway. Presently, International Teams serves in about 60 countries, but specifically works with refugees in: Austria, Bulgaria, Greece, Italy, Ukraine, Malawi, the Middle East, and Central Asia, as well as in several cities in the US.

If you are interested in more information about this ministry, please visit International Teams at www.iteams.us. If you want to explore service opportunities at The Oasis (whether as a volunteer, a short-termer or a career missionary), visit go.iteams.us (in the US) or write to highway@iteams.at (in Austria).

World Wide Radio, the radio ministry featured in The Long Highway Home, is fictional but inspired by the work of Trans World Radio. With a global radio network complemented by new technologies such as the internet and smartphones, TWR delivers God's Word to 160 countries in more than 230 languages and dialects. The ministry is particularly effective at engaging people in areas isolated by geography, crisis or hostility to the gospel, including a growing number of refugees like the novel's character, Hamid. For more on TWR's ministry, please visit twr.org, and access multilingual Gospel content at twr360.org.

ELIZABETH MUSSER writes 'entertainment with a soul' from her writing chalet—tool shed—outside Lyon, France. Elizabeth's highly acclaimed, best-selling novel, The Swan House, was named one of Amazon's Top Christian Books of the Year and one of Georgia's Top Ten Novels of the Past 100 Years (Georgia Backroads, 2009). All of Elizabeth's novels have been translated into multiple languages. *Two Destinies*, the final novel in *The Secrets of the Cross* trilogy, was a finalist for the 2013 Christy Award. *The Long Highway Home* has been a bestseller in Europe.

For over twenty-five years, Elizabeth and her husband, Paul, have been involved in missions' work in Europe with International Teams. The Mussers have two sons, a daughter-in-law and three grandchildren who all live way too far away in America. Find more about Elizabeth's novels at www.elizabethmusser.com and on Facebook.